TERRA

IKSIR

DEVDAN

EAST ZENITH

ARI

SALBATA

N
NW
NE
W
E
SW
SE

PRAISE FOR

RUNE of the APPRENTICE

"Within just a few moments of reading *Rune*, I was drawn into the adventurous, magical world Jamison Stone has created—my heartbeat pulsed, my breath grew shallow, my fingers trembled as I leapt from page to page—and this was all in merely the first chapter! Stone has hit it out of the ballpark with this book, and you will not want to put it down. An epic read." —Ben Greenfield, *New York Times* bestselling author of *Beyond Training*

"*Rune* is an epic journey about transforming the darkness within so that we can achieve true peace in the world around us." —Chade-Meng Tan, *New York Times* bestselling author of *Joy on Demand* and *Search Inside Yourself*

"Stone presents us with a fresh, superbly crafted fantasy epic that conquers both world and character building. *Rune* is tantalizing to the imagination, and invigorating for the soul." —Tal M. Klein, author of *The Punch Escrow*

"An engaging story filled with magic, swordplay, and even pirates! The world that Stone has imagined is vast, the political webs complex, and the interaction between the gods, magic, and men is well thought out and well described. Easy five stars." —Dave Barrett, author of *It's All Fun and Games*

"Through Stone's eloquent prose, readers can feel Aleksi's heart-pulsing race against time as we're drawn into a world of rich history and magic. I was on the edge of my seat, across oceans and over land, until the last page." —Zachary Tyler Linville, author of *Welcome to Deadland*

"Stone has crafted an exciting fantasy epic set in a mysterious world of intrigue and adventure. Intricately written and populated with characters we not only root for but also deeply identify with, *Rune* is constructed with tangible enthusiasm that pours from every page. The flowing prose is experienced rather than read—and done with vivid clarity. I'm highly anticipating the next in the series!" —J-F. Dubeau, author of *The Life Engineered* and *A God in the Shed*

"Stone writes beautifully. The characters of *Rune* are alive and vibrant, the world in which they dwell is both exciting and rich, and the story which propels it all is not only engaging, but profoundly deep." —Stuart C. Lord, editor of *Common Good—Common Ground*

"An epic blend of anticipation, magic, and adrenaline. Lovers of huge worlds and heroic characters will feel right at home. With a solid foundation of deep characters and mythic storytelling, Stone's breakout debut novel is one you won't want to miss. *Rune of the Apprentice* is fantasy at its finest!" —Chris Cole, author of *The Body of Chris*

"Stone has created a world of fantasy that can be matched by few others. His characters vibrate with life, and the tension he creates is palpable. The story weaves its way through land and over sea, focusing on an ultimate adventure that is sure to be cataclysmic. I barnstormed through *Rune of the Apprentice* in a matter of hours, and I'm desperately wanting to read the next in the series. Put this book on your must-read list!" —Peter Ryan, author of *Sync City*

"Stone has created a vivid world filled with rich detail unlike any I've ever seen. His diverse cast of engaging characters brings his vision to life so brightly that I cannot wait for the next installment." —Terry Mixon, author of The Empire of Bones Saga and The Humanity Unlimited Saga

"Through beautiful prose, Stone inspires the minds of our youth to choose a path which restores peace. *Rune* reminds us that we are not strangers, but instead, friends, peacemakers, and most importantly, need to dedicate our lives to protecting those who have lost so much due to cruelty and injustice." —Ahm Mainuddin Ahmed, founder of Fatema Matin Women's College and Char Fasson Orphanage and advocate lawyer at the Supreme Court of Bangladesh

"Stone conjures a seafaring pursuit with the fate of nations under the sails of the Illusive Diamond that instantly pulls you in. It's absolutely the perfect universe to geek out over, built to satiate the desires of any epic fantasy fan." —Rick Heinz, author of *The Seventh Age: Dawn*

"Stone's writing style is clear, engaging, and highly recommended! In just the first chapter alone, *Rune of the Apprentice* will provide immediate immersion into a mystical and mysterious world that will keep you coming back for more." —Erik A. Lenderman, author of *Principles of Practical Psychology: A Brief Review of Philosophy, Psychology, and Neuroscience for Self-Inquiry and Self-Regulation*

"Stone is a masterful world-builder, and I felt like I was truly stepping onto Terra from the moment I started reading. There is a depth and complexity to the world and characters that breathes life into the narrative itself. Reading *Rune of the Apprentice* is a fun and magical adventure that left me thinking about the world and its characters long after I put the book down." —D. L. Wainright, author of *The Hollow Sun* and *Fractured Masks*

"Stunning, engaging and epic . . . *Rune* takes larger-than-life immersive world spaces to the next level." —Rob McNamara, author of *The Elegant Self*

"As with all good fantasy, *Rune of the Apprentice* draws one into a world filled with compelling characters and ever-deepening mystery . . . Stone's debut leaves the reader eagerly awaiting the next installment." —Nataraja Kallio, author of *Hatha Yoga: A Manual for Teachers*

"I was immediately captivated by the world created by Stone—the world of a teenage boy, Aleksi, cast out of innocence into the machinations of adult politics and manipulation. Aleksi is forced into a life of danger and uncertainty and into the possibility for a hopeful, better future. He has the skills and the magic—does he have the courage?" —David Atekpatzin Young, Native American storyteller and healer, author of *Chicansimo* and *A Magic Feather*

"Stone creates a striking, realistic world in *Rune* with alluring characters and exciting stakes, steeped with an original mythology that leaves you wanting more." —Paul Inman, author of *Ageless* and cohost of the *WriteBrain* podcast

"A detailed and beautifully crafted new world. The descriptions of Terra's geography and its inhabitants are so vivid that I could easily imagine myself walking through the avenues, squares, and marketplaces of Mindra's Haven. Probably one of Stone's biggest achievements is his capacity to portrait his hero's internal struggle. Aleksi is young, powerful, and good at heart but lost. Having the reader rooting for Aleksi from beginning to end requires the work of a skillful storyteller; Stone is definitely that person." —Ricardo Henriquez, author of *The Catcher's Trap*

"An enthralling read. . . . This is high fantasy at its finest, and Stone follows in a tradition of storytellers who have taken fantasy to the high seas. Somewhere I imagine Abraham Merritt is smiling." —Matthew Isaac Sobin, author of *The Last Machine in the Solar System*

"A big, sweeping fantasy with a super-cool and unique mythology. Eagerly awaiting book two . . ." —Christopher Leone, author of *Champions of the Third Planet*

"An intricate tale set in an even more intricate world that begs you to sip deeper on the hearty ale this story is. Stone weaves this tale like a master artist crafting the finest tapestry. Take your time, let the world and characters waft around you, drawing you in. You'll be very glad you did." —Brian Guthrie, author of *Rise*

RUNE

OF THE

APPRENTICE

BOOK I OF THE RUNE CHRONICLES

RUNE

OF THE

APPRENTICE

BOOK I OF THE RUNE CHRONICLES

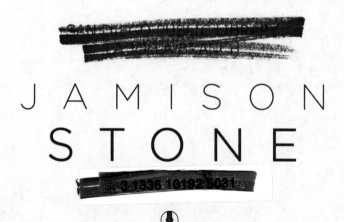

INKSHARES

Published by Inkshares, Inc., San Francisco, California
www.inkshares.com

Edited and designed by Girl Friday Productions
www.girlfridayproductions.com

Cover design by M.S. Corley
Map illustrated by M.S. Corley
Cover photographs © Sergey Nivens/Shutterstock; © oriontrail/Shutterstock

ISBN: 9781941758915
e-ISBN: 9781941758922

Library of Congress Control Number: 2016930436

First edition

Printed in the United States of America

This work is dedicated to the Hero and Heroine within us all.

PROLOGUE

There are moments in the history of people and planets when myth, legend, and inescapable destiny rule. Such times are bound by prophecy and, once begun, are impossible to halt—for the fates of all, unknowingly intertwined, move toward a numinous end that will not be denied.

It was on such a night that destiny stirred, once again, on the planet of Terra. Hanging in the starry sky like great watching eyes, Terra's two moons shone with a silvery-blue light which radiated from deep within their cores. Far below, on Terra's surface, the orbs cast a soft glow into a small clearing in the woods nestled onto the side of the impossibly tall mountain of Devdan's Zenith.

The glade's thick pines swayed gently in the wind. Whispering through the branches and soft grasses, a breeze circled a solitary man, ruffling the dark robes that hung from his shoulders. Growing stronger, the gust pushed back his long hair, causing it to shine like black gossamer in the shafts of silver moonlight that fell through the shadowed canopy around him.

Behind the man, the monolithic citadel of the Masters' Academy rose proudly from the side of the colossal mountain. Like always, the Academy's sanctified crystal towers were ablaze, tirelessly casting back the darkness of the night. Looming above the spires, the mountain's

Zenith reflected the light of the moons, caressing the heavens much as a lover would.

With his back to the Academy and his hair strewn about him, the man sat nobly in the grass. His legs were crossed, feet resting on opposite knees. As the breeze blew across his face, he closed his eyes and cupped his hands as if clutching an invisible sphere. The man silently mouthed an ancient invocation, and his hands shook in the shadows. He intoned the Runic language of Numen—an occult burden that few in Terra knew the weight of.

A translucent light appeared. Pulsing in time with his heartbeat, it slowly grew within the space between his palms. Forming itself into a small ball, the glow shone through his fingers, casting long shadows against the grass. As the light grew stronger, intricately flowing Runes coalesced on the ball's surface. The cryptic glyphs danced across the sphere in a scrolling line, detailing the orb's power and purpose. With his Runic casting complete, the man lowered his hands and let out a great sigh.

The Runic ball expanded. Swirling like incandescent water, it cast an eerie glow within the clearing. As the sphere grew to a diameter of nearly two meters, the man felt its edges flow over his robed body like shimmering quicksilver. After it fully enclosed him, the Runes on the orb's outer surface shone with a new, multicolored ferocity. The man felt himself grow buoyant as he was lifted several centimeters off the grass. As the sphere's exterior took solid form, the outside world was completely blocked from view. The man was gently lowered onto the orb's smooth inner surface.

The man's long hair shone dimly in the faint light of the sphere's inner walls. He bowed his head and took a long apprehensive inhalation. Upon his face was a look of uneasiness, and his shoulders were tensed in anticipation of the conversation to come. Exhaling slowly, he forced his body to relax.

Raising his palms to the curved walls, the man focused his mind and once again mouthed a silent command. With a sudden flash, the interior of the sphere sprang to life, revealing a full 360-degree panorama of a small stone room with a low-burning fire.

Many kilometers away on Terra's Northern Continent of Simn, a large, muscular man of dark presence sat alone in a stone room. Lit by a tepid fire, the room had a thin rug and only a single wooden door, bolted shut.

The man wore a long cloak accented with deep greens that matched the bright emeralds of his eyes. Tailored in the style of the North, his clothes were intricately embroidered with the designs of the noble aristocracy. Upon both hands and forearms, however, he wore ornately crafted gauntlets of a much more sinister style and origin.

He sat on a low cushion with his eyes half-closed until a glimmer of light arose before him. His eyes perked up as a holographic projection of a robed man with long dark hair slowly took form in the barren room. Imbued with a translucent Runic glow, the visitor's visage cast faint shadows in the dim room.

The long-haired man's projection pressed his hands together before his heart and bowed his head low. The light of the fire seemed to pass through his luminescent body and eerily dance across the stone walls.

The muscular man did not return the bow. "The hour grows late, Nataraja." His voice was a deep rumble, akin to a massive boulder slowly rolling forward, with nothing to stop its inevitable movement.

"I apologize, Lord Asura," Nataraja answered. "Getting away from the Academy was difficult tonight."

"You know that was not my meaning."

"Aleksi has proven . . . challenging to shift, Master. His anger is growing as intended but now threatens to overtake him." Nataraja forced his voice to remain calm. "Lord, I need more time. Please just grant me—"

Asura raised his armored fist, cutting Nataraja's words short. Blue fire raced across Asura's gauntleted arm and flowed into his hand. No one else in known history had dared awaken a Runic tool of such ominous power, passed down from an age long forgotten.

"What difference does a drop of time make?" Asura asked roughly. The smoky-blue light in his fist then fractured, and pristine white sand seeped through his mailed fingers.

"Lord, it does not have to be this way." Nataraja strained to keep his voice controlled as he watched the grains fall to the floor. "Aleksi will turn and join our cause. I am so very close—"

"After Rudra abandoned the boy, you had five years to complete your mission. Yet Aleksi's Rune is now awakening and I refuse to allow his power to go unchecked—lest he seek out Rudra and aid his so-called *Resistance*."

"My Lord, I—"

"You have failed!" Asura boomed, wiping the last of the sand from his palms. "I wanted him, but your charade as Aleksi's Master ends tonight. Go now and collect your things. Your time in the East is done."

A look of confusion passed over Nataraja's face. "Lord, Aleksi is still just a youth and has so much potential. I beg you—"

Before Nataraja could utter another word, Asura clapped his hands. A wave of concussive energy swept through the room, striking Nataraja's holographic projection in the chest and causing it to momentarily blur.

When Nataraja spoke again there was desperation in his tone. "Master, please do not command me to kill the boy."

"No need," Asura answered coldly. "I have sent a shadow to deal with him. I assume you know which one. A fitting end for the youth, don't you agree?"

Anger flashed across Nataraja's face, but he quickly regained his composure.

"Always remember," Asura continued, eyeing Nataraja carefully, "it is *your* failure that has killed Aleksi. Although this boy's blood does not warm your blade, just like the last one it will forever stain your hands."

Fury shone in Nataraja's eyes as his projected image disintegrated into bits of light that sheared off into nothingness.

"I will know you by your actions, Nataraja," Asura said, as he once again tightened his gauntleted fists. "Choose your path *carefully . . .*"

Back in the clearing on the Eastern Zenith, Nataraja's Runic sphere once again returned to flowing light. The light soon disintegrated and dispersed into the shadows, leaving Nataraja alone in the darkness among the wind, trees, and grass.

"No, not like La'vail," Nataraja whispered bitterly as a ripple of anger moved across his face. "Not Aleksi, too . . ."

Nataraja was immediately on his feet and sprinting, long hair flowing behind him. Faster than any normal man should be able to move, his body became a flicker of light as he raced toward the massive citadel that protruded from the great mountainside above.

Soon, Nataraja approached the fore-gates of the Masters' Academy. Two guards stood facing the night. Each held a guttering torch that cast a halo of warmth into the cool evening mist. Nataraja swept past them in a flash. As he did, one of the guards called out.

"Master, is everything . . . ?"

Nataraja flew across the stable yard and up a back stairway that led to the students' sleeping halls. He raced up a winding flight of stone stairs and came within sight of Aleksi's door. Without losing speed, Nataraja raised a hand. The air around his outstretched arm rippled with light. Nataraja's Runic power silently ripped the door off its thick metal hinges and cast it aside.

Bursting into the darkness, Nataraja held out both palms and whispered under his breath. Answering his command, the wall lamps ignited, burning bright in the small room. Now that it was illuminated, Nataraja could see that the chamber was bare. Before him was a writing desk devoid of papers, an empty closet, and a wooden chest at the foot of a neatly made bed. The room's only window stood open. Outside, there was a clear view of the moons shining down on the large island of Adhira just off the coast.

Nataraja's black hair shone in the lamplight. Nataraja was in his midyears, and when they saw him in profile, women still thought him tempting—but after they looked into his hardened green eyes and saw that fierce stare, any thought of seduction evaporated. That very gaze now swept the room with the unmistakable glare of *violence*.

As he scanned the chamber, Nataraja noticed that the only thing out of place in the boy's quarters was its very emptiness. Aleksi was gone, and yet there was no lingering smell of death. A sudden breeze blew through the open window, and Nataraja turned sharply, as if listening to a faraway sound. Dropping into a defensive stance, he extended one hand out in front of his chest, and a luminescent blue barrier emanated from his palm.

Abruptly, a whirl of wind rose up from the night and a throwing knife flew in through the window. It ricocheted off Nataraja's energetic shield, struck the wall, and fell to the wooden floor with a metallic clang. The room's lamps were suddenly extinguished, and the chamber was plunged back into shadow. Nataraja had disappeared.

A thick, smoky darkness silently seeped in through the open window. It spread out across the floor like heavy, shadowy vapor, its color blacker than a starless night. This darkness did not belong to Nataraja, yet he knew it well—it belonged to Nevain, his stepson and former Apprentice. Pooling over the floorboards, the darkness settled into the room's corners and smothered all sound. Shrouding the chamber like black silk, it even drowned out the light of the moons. To most, this depth of gloom brought a terror that seemed to suck the very life out of all it touched. Nataraja, however, was not impressed.

After a moment, a cloaked figure glided in through the window. Enveloped in a wispy mantle of the blackness, Nevain floated toward the center of the room, causing dark tendrils to swirl about his boots with each silent step. In a startling flash, he spun and threw three more daggers into the shadowed depths where Nataraja hid. The daggers, however, pierced the inky dark only to be buried in the wall with a loud thunk.

The lamps suddenly flared, viciously burning away the black, causing Nevain to shield his light-sensitive eyes in anguish. Nataraja loomed behind the young man, seeming to materialize out of the room's thinning darkness. Before Nevain could turn, Nataraja slammed his fist into the young man's lower back, breaking his spine with an audible crack.

Nevain's mouth contorted in a soundless scream as his legs collapsed beneath him. Hitting the ground, the young man struggled to move but found his lower body numb. Flipping Nevain onto his back, Nataraja took two dark daggers from the young man's belt and plunged them, one at a time, into Nevain's hands, pinning him to the floor.

"Is this how you killed your brother, La'vail?" Nataraja asked in a voice that was cold and controlled. "And now you plan to do the same to Aleksi?"

". . . Master Nataraja . . ." But before Nevain could say any more, his mouth slackened and his eyes rolled back into their sockets.

As his stepson slipped out of consciousness, Nataraja placed a hand on the young man's chest. Soft white light emanated from Nataraja's palm, and Nevain's body convulsed as his eyes wildly snapped back open.

"My little shadow," Nataraja continued, "if you wish to ever walk again, you will answer my questions quickly. You do not have much time." Nataraja's tone was tight, but his green eyes were alive with fury. "So I ask you again, is this how you killed your brother, La'vail?"

"Master, please forgive me!" Fear rang in Nevain's voice as he futilely struggled against the daggers pinning him to the floor. "All I have done has been under the direct order of High Master Asura! I swear it!"

"So it *was* you that killed La'vail!" Nataraja bared his teeth and his face filled with rage. Nataraja took another knife from Nevain's leather belt. The blade seemed to carnivorously swallow the light from the lamps. Seeing this, the young man's green eyes grew even wider. "After all I have taught you, you dare to repay my love by murdering not just my son, but now my Apprentice, too? Nevain, I don't care if High Arkai Kaisra commanded you to commit such an act. You are a fool to obey!"

Nataraja plunged the dagger into Nevain's gut. The young man gritted his teeth and grunted as Nataraja slowly twisted the blade. Blood seeped through Nevain's cloak as his torn flesh glistened in the hot lamplight.

"I have one last question for you, my lost Apprentice," Nataraja said calmly as he continued to twist the dagger. "Did you come here alone or are there others? Speak quickly, or I will let you die."

"Father," Nevain cried in anguish as the blade continued to gouge his stomach. "Please have mercy! Please!"

"You are no son of mine," Nataraja yelled, digging the dagger deeper into his stepson's flesh. "Answer my question!"

"I . . . I am alone! I swear it on Mother's grave."

Nataraja lowered his head and let go of the dagger.

"Please," Nevain whispered with a soft desperation in his tone. "I can feel it. I can feel death taking me. Father, I beg you. Don't let me die . . . I was only following our lord's orders . . . both times."

After a long moment, Nataraja let out a great sigh and placed his right hand over the young man's blood-soaked torso.

A look of relief flooded across Nevain's pale face. "Thank you, Father."

"Only following orders," Nataraja whispered. "Oh, Nevain, that was my greatest folly. And for your sake, I am so very sorry . . ."

Confusion crept into Nevain's eyes.

"Sleep well, my little shadow," Nataraja continued sadly, "knowing that you have blindly served your lord's will." Nevain's eyes widened as Nataraja's hand glowed red. "I, however, will never make that mistake again . . ."

A look of horror swept across Nevain's face as his body emitted tremendous heat and light. "No, Master!" Nevain sputtered, as fire and pain flooded through his chest. "Asura will know of your betrayal!"

"And by then," Nataraja whispered, "it will not matter . . ."

A fire raged inside the young man, burning out his lungs as he let out a soundless scream. "I send your soul back to High Arkai Kaisra," Nataraja continued softly, as a tear ran down his cheek. "May he show you the forgiveness I never could . . ."

✦◉✦

Terra's two moons still hung brightly in the starry sky. They had moved a great distance, however, and now shone through the room's open window in a glorious shaft of silver brilliance. The elegant light framed Nevain's lifeless body slumped on the floor. Idly staring up at the ceiling, his dull eyes reflected the moons' soft glow. The cinders that were crusted around the gaping hole in the young man's charred chest cavity were now cold, but despite the open window, the scent of burnt flesh still enveloped the room.

"Kai'la, my love," Nataraja said roughly with emotion thick in his voice. "Please forgive . . ." The Master sat some distance away on the bed. He held his head in callused and tearstained hands. "Please for-give *me*."

After several long moments, Nataraja raised his head and brushed away strands of damp hair. Turning to look out the window with raw eyes, he gazed down at the twinkling island of Adhira and Terra's great ocean beyond.

"Go fast, young Aleksi," Nataraja whispered. "You are not ready for what follows you. Nor for what you will find . . ."

Huddled on the deck of a small sailing ship, Aleksi watched the dawn of a new day break over the Eastern Zenith. The ship quickly surged westward, riding the wide channel's unusually fast current to the island of Adhira. Although his heart still longed for one last glimpse of the majestic towers of his departed home, Aleksi knew he would not be able to see the Masters' Academy at such a distance. So instead, the youth cast his gaze past the sky's highest clouds and up to the moun-tain's lofty crystalline peak as the shimmering Zenith shone its new rays of morning light.

The morning's damp breeze was piercingly cold. Instead of being illuminated by a sun, Terra received its daylight from the Zenith of each continent's sacred spire mountain, a gift of the Arkai. As Aleksi watched the Eastern Zenith's globe give off its first glimmering rays of light in the dark sky, he wrapped his sleeveless cloak tightly around himself.

The one-masted vessel was bound for Mindra's Haven, known by all as the shining star of Adhira and the most renowned city in the Eastern realm of Devdan. Mindra's Haven, however, was not Aleksi's final destination. Ultimately, he needed to find passage halfway across Terra's great ocean to the war-torn Central Continent of Vai'kel. After Aleksi arrived in Vai'kel, the youth knew not where fate would take him—only that if he did not get there quickly, he would soon be dead.

Other than a few low-denomination black pearls of currency, Aleksi had only the clothes on his back, the sword at his hip, and a frayed letter from Master Rudra in his pocket. Aleksi slipped a hand into his cloak and felt the cryptic message's weathered parchment. It was smooth to his touch, worn from many attempts to decipher its occult meaning. Letting out a great sigh, Aleksi slipped the page from his pocket and silently reread the strange message by the growing light of the Zenith's new dawn.

> *Aleksi,*
>
> *I sense your Rune has finally begun to awaken. Others can feel it, too. Dark assassins have been sent to corrupt or kill you—to steal your Rune for their own or to prevent its power from entering this world. If they succeed, you will become the catalyst of the Guardians' destruction, for it will be by your hand, or lack thereof, that Terra's salvation will be plunged into darkness.*
>
> *To flee the grasping shadow, you must go to the city of ruin that the Guardians neglected. At the precipice of eternal ignorance, turn from the edge of darkness, for if at any time upon your journey you take a life in anger, you will fall willingly into the hands of those who hunt you. As the repercussions of your rage burn through your body, drink deeply from the light of Mindra—his power of compassion and healing is freely given if you can but open your heart to his eternal song.*
>
> *Next, find the ancestral place of healing which was once dedicated to the Northern light. As you search, give not into your temptation, but remember the Masters' Vow. Once you arrive, let the wounded blindly run away from his fears. As you bear the token of your father while seated by a cold flame, a soon-to-be-resurrected leader will tell you to forsake your lineage. Save him from both flame and steel, for he will lead you to your safe passage before giving the children of Mindra a new hope against the looming shadow.*
>
> *As you search for your past, your house, and its fateful ruin, you will cross the sea on a ship of many facets. When torment returns, the myth of the moons and their holy birth will temporarily cleanse your wounds. As your*

mettle is tested, please remember: the truth is never as simple as a deceiver would lead you to believe. Contemplating your choices from the loft perched in light, do not unveil the truth of the noble, for the leader must seal the fate of his people untainted, lest he condemn us all to shadow. Finally, when you find Vai'kel's last hope in dire need, give her your strength and trust in your heart, for it will be love that will save you both and awaken your true power.

Most importantly, however, never forget that only I can teach you how to harness your Rune and protect yourself from its devastation. Until you have it mastered, you are a threat to both friend and foe alike. But fear not: your fissured heart will lead you to your answers, and then, finally, to me. I know that you have great faith but also great doubt—remember that both are needed, yet it will be great determination which will allow you to transcend to salvation.

When you are well on the path, I will send word again. But remember to make all haste, my Apprentice, for shadows follow your every step. Never forget that if at any point on your journey you choose to fall prey to its alluring power, then its corruption will reign over Terra, eternal.

~Rudra

Anxiety spread across Aleksi's face and he looked down at his right palm. It was covered in a clean white bandage. The youth focused his mind and felt the nerves in the flesh of his hand pulse and burn with Runic power. It was as if sharp, white-hot tendrils spread out from his palm and extended into his fingers and wrist.

Is the forsaken word of that man really worth abandoning Master Nataraja and my tutelage at the Academy, and defying the Masters' Law? How can I trust him after what he did? Is that broken outcast truly worth dying for?

A familiar soft blue light emanated from the flesh of Aleksi's bandaged palm. Although it showed itself only infrequently, the glow had begun the same night Rudra's letter appeared under his pillow. The light meant only one thing—Rudra was right, Aleksi's Rune had begun to awaken. Rudra had told him many years ago that if left unguided by a trained Master, the Rune would send its metallic tendrils up his central nervous system and into his brain too quickly. Not only would this kill him, but dying in such a way would overload his newly synchronized Rune and cause an explosion of colossal magnitude. Anger welled up within Aleksi and, scowling, he crumpled Rudra's letter in his bandaged fist.

Whether it was right to leave or not, it does not matter now. The choice is made and there is no turning back . . .

Huddling on the ship's damp planks, Aleksi wrapped his hooded cloak around himself even tighter as he squinted and futilely tried one last time to make out the Masters' Academy on the western slope of the towering Eastern Zenith. Despite his Rune, Aleksi knew it no longer mattered if Rudra's ominous letter was true or false. The moment Aleksi had left his Academy, he had sealed his fate. The youth now had no choice but to continue to follow Rudra's cryptic path and do his best to outrun both the Academy's Enforcers and the Shadow Assassins.

Aleksi let out a great sigh. Even worse, if the letter was accurate, then those who followed him would be the least of Aleksi's worries. Born in the South and now known only as Terra's Bane, Rudra was a forsaken Master hunted the world over—yet if he was telling the truth, Rudra was also the youth's only hope of survival. For although much of the letter was cryptic and confusing, one thing was perfectly clear—Aleksi looked down to his glowing palm once again—his Rune was beginning to awaken, and the youth was therefore in unfathomable danger.

CHAPTER I

Majestic clouds glided above the fissured island of Adhira before disappearing into the horizon beyond. At the center of the island lay Mindra's Haven, the former capital of Devdan and home to the greatest trading port on the Eastern Continent.

In an age long past, the island of Adhira was shattered during a fierce battle of ascendancy waged between Terra's deific protectors and the invading Dark Ones. Legends say that the Dark Ones periodically descend from the stars to steal Terra's sacred power—a power that radiates up from Terra's core into her mountains' crystal Zeniths, giving Terra her light and warmth.

In response to each invasion of the East, Mindra, High Arkai and leader of the Eastern Guardians, was said to have flown down from his Zenith with his ethereal legions to fight the attackers. The stories say that in the most recent encounter, the Guardians once again repelled the Dark Ones and secured an age of peace for the planet and her peoples. Despite this, the island of Adhira was scarred deeply by the conflict—for wherever the Dark Ones had touched, only ruin remained.

To bring healing and renewal, the Guardians remained in Mindra's Haven for a generation. While among the people, they taught the secret ways of Numina and ushered in an age of rebuilding, renaissance, and enlightenment. Devdan's capital was rebuilt during this time and prospered greatly. At the heart of the city, a grand and noble temple was constructed so all could receive the Guardians' numinous teachings. Many came and went, until the saying "I have been to Mindra's Haven" came to denote one's faith in the Guardians' great power and divine grace.

Sadly, after the Guardians returned to their home and the ages passed on, the peoples of Terra began to lose their way. In this Modern Age, with the ancient history of the destruction and divine rebirth of Mindra's Haven receding into the mists of time, the former capital no longer ruled over the now politically divided continent of Devdan. However, in spite of many generations of territorial wars, Adhira was still able to maintain a fraction of its former glory, and Mindra's Haven, the jewel of the island, remained a place of pilgrimage. Although no longer seen as a seat of divine power, the city still acted as the Eastern hub of international trade while also providing culture, Runic assistance, and military protection to the peoples whom it had once governed so many years ago.

Even though any factual record of these legends had been lost to all but the Masters in their occult Academies, the Eastern peoples still held on to the hope that High Arkai Mindra's great hall would once again serve as a place of holy revitalization for the Eastern Continent. To fulfill this hope, Mehail Bander, Chair of Adhira's High Council, had proclaimed there was to be a gathering of the three prime leaders of Devdan's Eastern realm on the eve of High Arkai Mindra's annual festival. This meeting was to create Devdan's Covenant of Eastern Amity, a treaty that would shape the destiny of the continent, if not the whole planet of Terra.

Inspired by the prospect of reunification, Devdan's citizens had been locked in hopeful anticipation of the festival for many long months. Their wait, however, had come to an end, for the festival was to commence at dusk.

As the clouds streamed from the shining sea toward Adhira's fertile fields, myriad great ships surged on the currents entering and exiting the mouth of the large island's foremost western channel, known as Honor's Gate. The deep channel, a remnant scar of the Dark Ones' attack, cut through the island, wrapping around the much smaller landmass of Mindra's Haven. As the epicenter of Adhira, Mindra's Haven was the locus of ancient destruction and the Guardians' generous rebirth.

Beyond the fort on the eastern side of Mindra's Haven, the harbor shallowed into a marshy estuary where large docks were used by residents, fishermen, and coastal traders. The domestic merchandise exchanged ranged from rare *hari* pelts, found only on the Eastnorthern windswept steppes of the Pa'laer, to the mysterious *amala* fruit, traded from the Akasha people in the Farden forest to the Eastsouth. As always in such harbors, however, the farther into the marshes one traveled, the more the rough-and-tumble traded in goods less reputable. There was even talk that for the right price, Eastern smugglers sold shards of Runic Power Armor, mysterious weapons, and other outlawed ancient equipment scavenged in the badlands and ruined cities out past the Eastern Zenith. Although only the boldest dared defy the Masters to go all the way to the impenetrable mountain range of Dagger's Veil, many adventurers risked life and limb to search beyond the Modern Age's boundaries of civilization for a chance to find relics of ages past and reap their powerful rewards.

On the western side of Mindra's Haven, facing directly into the outer sea channel, sprawled the mighty port of Azain. Renowned the globe over, this expansive harbor was arguably Terra's greatest international dock and trading center. Day and night, longshoremen and sailors off-loaded and provisioned ships from ports across the world while traders and travelers of every shape and stripe made contact just outside the city walls. Deals were cut in the open under the Zenith, with raucous voices amplified by the ocean air—and other kinds of pacts were made in the dead of night, when shadowed whispers were swallowed by the fog and damp.

On this day, with the city alive with celebration, the pier pulsed with activity. The ruckus culminated along a wharf reserved for multimasted deep-draft merchant ships—the backbone of Terra's international trade economy. These uniquely rigged vessels, many of which hailed from the Thalassocratic Islands of the West, were sailed by men known for their daring exploits and incomparable seamanship.

Domadred Steele, captain of one such vessel, was perhaps the most famous of them all. He was outlawed in the North and wanted for treason in the West, and his ship, the *Illusive Diamond*, had more stories in her wake than half the ships in the harbor combined.

Over a kilometer out, Domadred stood at the wheel of the *Diamond* and felt a change in both the currents below and the winds above. With the bright Zenith light before him, his heart stirred. As the ship carved through the channel toward the headland, Domadred ran a hand over his angular beard and smiled up at the Eastern Guardians atop their mountain-spire home.

Domadred had been at the wheel of the *Diamond* since dawn for the simple pleasure of riding current and wind. As the tall three-masted ship continued forward, the channel opened up, revealing the majestic harbor before him. Domadred drew a black-cowled hood over his braided and bead-laden hair and called his son to the helm.

"Take her in, Son, but keep your head hooded. While aboard ship, let none see your features. We pass for Southerners from Neberu only at a distance."

"Yes, Father," Brayden replied, beaming with pride as he pulled his cloak forward and took Domadred's place at the helm. Although young, Brayden was tall and strong for his age, and more than capable of manning the wheel to bring the *Diamond* into safe harbor.

As the ship pointed just off the westerly wind, Domadred stepped back and climbed into the rigging. As the captain ascended, he gazed down on the *Diamond*'s camouflaged decks. Disguised as she was, the ship looked like a deep-water trader from the South. Domadred's crew even wore the iconic hooded capes of the few Southerners who dared venture out of the safety of their darkly shrouded lands. Most all of the amethyst-eyed people of Neberu had little choice but to hide their pale and sensitive features from the powerful rays of the Zenith, and so remained hidden in their realm of eternal night. Mimicking the Southerners' plight was the perfect disguise for those brave enough to risk it.

The *Illusive Diamond* fell off the wind, and Brayden ordered the topsails down and the jibs and staysails loosed. As the ship sailed wing and wing, she entered the breakwater, and the land brought the breeze around so that it blew against the *Diamond*'s stern. Surfing the great swells of the channel, the ship's glistening hull sliced through the water as dolphins played in the wake of her bow. Eventually, as the ship entered the outer harbor's crowded shipping lanes, wind and wave died down and more sails were furled, causing the *Diamond* to ghost onward toward port.

From the crow's nest, Domadred took in the island of Mindra's Haven. As he was outlawed and unable to safely travel in his own home islands, the hectic harbor before him was a salve to his soul. The very extravagance of the harbor, with its patchwork of culture and custom, stirred his heart. It was a melting pot of crews in garb and style as different as the sailing vessels they manned.

As they coursed past ships at anchor, Domadred scanned the bustling deck of a massive trade vessel from the West. The Thalassocratic capital ship was nearly twice the size of the *Diamond* and had a complement of sailors and marines so great that the local docksmen never needed to go aboard. Domadred watched as the Western men passed cargo down the nets and into waiting lighters. Famous for their stamina and ability to move as one, the sailors worked with confident speed. With bronze flesh, their frames were sculpted by their dedication to the sea. Their bead-laden hair shone like spun gold, and their eyes, like Domadred's, were a deep sapphire identical to the great ocean of Terra herself. The Westerners stacked their cargo in orderly rows, each bale and barrel embedded with the cerulean crest of their Thalassocratic people—Domadred's people.

The *Diamond* slipped past a shallow-keeled coaster from Neberu. Like Domadred's disguised men, the Southern ship's hooded crew were fully covered despite the day's warmth. Hiding their sickly pale faces inside long black cowls, the light-wary Southerners off-loaded their cargo of luminescent cloth, which glowed faintly even in full day. The captain of the coaster saw the *Diamond* and saluted Domadred by extending his palms to the deck of his ship, clearly showing his rank via the intricately embroidered scrolling along his sleeves.

Returning the hail, Domadred smiled as he caught an echo from across the harbor. This deep and insistent rumble could come only from the hypnotic voices of Northerners singing one of their naval work songs. No doubt the men of Simn were winching casks of their renowned red wines from the hold of their ship. The casks would then be deposited into nets where the levy takers inspected and counted them before they would be dispersed to the grog shops and great tables of the city.

Out of nowhere came a shrill cry Domadred had heard only twice before in his life. Cold chills coursed through his body as he swiveled in the rigging to face port side. Several ships away, there was a sporting vessel from the South-Western Isles of Sihtu with a deck covered in cages. In the foremost cage, a night prowler raged against the light, shredding the tarp enclosing its small prison. The creature sent itself into a blind frenzy as the light burned its nocturnally adapted eyes. In response, a tattooed and scantily clad South-Western beast tamer came up on deck. Domadred watched as the dark woman leapt across the cage. Drawing the animal's attention, she fed it morsels of meat infused with a tranquilizing agent. Within a moment, the prowler grew clumsy and sat down. As the creature quieted, the beast tamer dragged a fresh tarp across the bars, and soothing darkness once more reigned inside the beast's cage.

The *Diamond* suddenly heeled over and came about, now pointing directly toward the docks. Domadred had to smile; the ship's movement was fluid and perfectly timed. Brayden was about the same age Domadred had been when he first conned a ship into this harbor. The memory came from long ago and brought with it images of bloodshed and fire, causing Domadred's smile to fade.

"Hold on, old man!"

Domadred looked down and saw Brayden smiling up at him from the quarterdeck. The captain held tight while the *Diamond* rocked back and forth as she docked. Domadred climbed out of the crow's nest and slid rapidly down the ratlines. He landed on the quarterdeck smoothly and winked at his son.

"I'm going belowdecks," Domadred said, resting one hand on the pommel of his sword. "Once we're docked, you know the drill. Be as quick as you can and come find me."

Brayden nodded.

As the *Diamond* moored and her hawser lines were snugged fore and aft, a small complement of dockworkers came aboard to speak with Rihat, Domadred's quartermaster. Dressed in traditional baggy tan pants and brown vests, the men checked the *Diamond*'s false papers thoroughly until Rihat slipped them each a high-denomination black pearl. Pretending to be fooled by the forgery, and finding that there was nothing that needed unloading, the dockworkers turned and left the ship. After they had departed, Domadred swung over the ship's gunwale and shed his black cloak as he landed upon the crowded dock.

Now dressed only as himself, Domadred donned his broad-brimmed captain's hat and entered the mass of humanity on the pier, causing the beaded strands in his long hair to clink softly. Close up, the wharf looked more like a swirling pool of social chaos than a place where business was done. In the midst of this roil of life, however, Domadred noticed a moving force that cut through the swarming masses like a plow. It was a large group of men, and they seemed to be headed in Domadred's direction.

After a moment, Brayden appeared. The boy had far fewer beads in his hair, denoting his rank as an apprenticing mate, but had a lavish dark-blue cloak thrown across his shoulders. A bit extravagant, but it was only natural; Brayden took after his father.

"Something is coming, Son. Take a look." Domadred cupped his hands together, making a stirrup for Brayden. The boy stepped up and rose above the crowd.

"Armed men," Brayden responded. "And they are moving toward us quickly."

Though unable to clearly see the group, Domadred detected its ripples in the crowd. In addition, he now heard the sharp report of boots ringing above the tumult of the port.

"Could we finally have been outlawed in the East and the Harbor Watch tipped off?" Domadred said, still holding his son aloft. "If they come any closer, we will be forced to return to the *Diamond*, cut line, and flee."

"No . . ." Brayden said, squinting. "Not the Harbor Watch. Those men are the Honor Guard from the High Council of Mindra's Haven."

"The Honor Guard? But for whom?"

"I'm not sure."

"Are you certain it's the Honor Guard, Son? They have no business here on the docks."

"Who else wear such breastplates? But wait . . ." The boy raised his hand to block the Zenith's light from his eyes. "There's also a squad from the Eastnorthern plains of Pa'laer." Domadred was about to open his mouth in protest, but Brayden glared down at his father before the captain could say a word. "Yes, it's definitely them. I see their tan leather mail *clearly*."

"Well," Domadred chuckled, releasing Brayden, "then let's go find out why they are here."

Father and son pushed their way toward the fray, coming to a great post that anchored the billowing cloth stalls of the dock's day traders. As gulls cawed overhead, they both climbed atop a series of stacked barrels for a better view.

Across the waterfront, Domadred saw the High Council Honor Guard adorned in their iconic, burnished red-gold breastplates. Their sole purpose was to protect the High Council; therefore, it was a great surprise to see them here, unaccompanied by their council members, who handpicked them. What was even more astounding, however, was that the Honor Guard marched next to two other platoons foreign to Devdan's lands. To their right filed the Farden forest warriors of the Eastsouth, dressed in their light-green leather armor, and to their left was a regiment of Eastnorthern guards from Pa'laer, wearing their traditional grey baggy pants and sleeveless leather plate mail.

Domadred could hardly believe his eyes. Not only did old adversaries march together, but they all guarded the Pa'laer leader, Arva Vatana, a lord loathed and reviled by all but his own countrymen. Arva Vatana was a massive man who rode a massive stallion. His long dark hair framed high cheekbones and he had a tanned complexion accustomed to the plains of the Eastnorth—the expansive grasslands that formed the northernmost portion of the Eastern continent. The long swallowtails of his ornate red leather coat fell to either side of his steed. Matching his eyes, the gold filigree woven into his clothes and saddle flashed in the Zenith's rays.

To Domadred, however, the most surprising thing of all was who led this group of soldiers. At the head of the column was a man renowned in the East and beyond, General Beck Al'Beth of Mindra's Haven. An honored veteran of Vai'kel's Unification War, Beck was a highly decorated general of Adhira and just the man Domadred had sought in coming to this curve of the world.

"Come with me, Son," Domadred said, pulling at Brayden's arm and motioning toward Beck. "The Guardians have smiled down on us this day. Let us make music to please them!"

The dock's mass of humanity gave way to Beck like flowing water. The general had an unmistakably large scar that ran down his right cheek and crossed the corner of his mouth. Upon seeing it, soldier, trader, and mercenary alike knew who he was and showed him the utmost deference. Despite this, Beck felt unease washing over him just as he felt Arva Vatana's eyes on his back.

The night before, in a private audience with Mehail Bander, Chair of Adhira's High Council, Beck had once again tried to dissuade the council from allowing Arva entrance into Mindra's Haven. Beck had said that the Pa'laer lord was a warmonger whose pride would be the undoing of not only his own lands, but the whole continent as well. Mehail's simple reply had been running through Beck's mind ever since. "Peace is worth the risk we take. I am willing. Are you?"

Lost in thought, Beck forced a smile as a laughing boy waved and dashed in front of the brigade. *Peace... What peace could be found with a man like Arva?* Beck took a deep breath as he marched on. Mehail constantly reminded him that he was a general and easily riled by the pandering half lies of politicians. Arva, however, was no politician—he was a warlord.

On one vital point, however, Mehail Bander was right. If the East did not find peace with itself, these endless territorial wars would tear the continent of Devdan apart, making them all easy picking to the imminent aggression of the Northern Empire of Simn. For Eastern treasuries, despite their best efforts, were still drained from their involvement in Vai'kel's Unification War in the Central Continent. Although it had ended not less than ten years ago, that brutal campaign was still felt the world over. Many even whispered that the Bankers Guild of Mindra's Haven was dangerously close to bankruptcy, for the postwar Northern tariffs instituted by High Lord Asura had prevented the Bankers Guild's strongboxes from ever replenishing. Others whispered this was all part of Asura's plan.

To make matters worse, Adhira's standing army was at only half its strength due to the many legions of men still stationed in Vai'kel to aid in the land's occupation. Their orders were to police Mystari and the other cities located on the Central Continent's eastern side. Sadly, instead of putting down revolts or hunting bandits, the majority of Adhira's soldiers actually spent their time preventing Asura's Northern "Peacekeeping Forces" from brutalizing the citizens they were supposed to be protecting.

Suddenly, the same blue-cloaked boy darted in front of Beck before disappearing back into the crowd. Beck unclenched his fists and grew alert. Scanning the throng of citizens and traders, he noticed the boy talking to a man whose face was concealed under a wide-brimmed captain's hat. The boy then circled around toward the convoy again.

Following the sailor with his eye, Beck could not make out any distinguishable features. A gap then appeared, and Beck saw the sharp profile of a tight-cropped beard and familiar face framed by long bead-braided hair. The man turned to look Beck in the eye and smiled.

Domadred Steele! It can't be . . . Not here, not now!

Domadred gave Beck a blue-eyed wink and disappeared. Beck knew that if Arva recognized Domadred, he would have the captain cut down immediately. Domadred had feasted on Arva's meager fleet as it traded with the North, using the plunder to fund the efforts of the Resistance, a fragmented group dedicated to ending the occupation of Vai'kel. Although incredibly selective about whom he plundered, Domadred was the most infamous pirate of the Modern Age. If Arva recognized the captain, it would matter little that Domadred happened to be Beck's oldest friend and ally from the Unification War—the warlord would demand blood.

Suddenly, the boy broke from the crowd and ran toward them. *Is that Brayden? What is Domadred thinking, putting himself and his son in such danger?* At the very same moment, however, Adler Karll, the highest-ranking member of Beck's guard, stepped out of formation and caught the boy by the back of the neck.

"Is it really you, High Lord Arva Vatana?" Brayden called out, not resisting the soldier's grasp. The boy's eyes were not filled with fear but shone with amazement and wonder.

As Brayden's words left his mouth, all motion on the dock stopped, and the absence of the sound of the platoons' boots came as a shock to Beck's ears. Before Beck could intervene, Arva Vatana spoke with a loud chuckle that boomed across the crowd.

"Yes, it is I, High Lord of the Eastnorthern plains of Pa'laer! What of you, boy? What is your name?"

Suddenly, Domadred burst out of the crowd. "Brayden, my son! I told you not to bother this important lord!"

Ignoring his father's words, Brayden projected his voice so that all could hear. "Are the stories true, my Lord? Were you truly born astride a warhorse? Is that why you ride with such confidence and grace?"

Arva threw his head back and laughed aloud, motioning the youth forward. Everyone in the crowd looked on expectantly. As Brayden shook himself free of Adler's grasp, Domadred turned to Beck and bowed profusely. Beck's golden eyes smoldered, but he remained silent.

"Do you know of the Guardian's Flame?" Domadred said in a whisper only they two could hear. "It is a reputable place for outlanders to meet at midnight, or so I have been told." Beck did not answer and turned his eyes back to Arva.

"To answer your question, son," Arva said loudly, still looking at Brayden, "I have spent more time upon a horse than not. Such is the way of the Pa'laer plains riders. But you have the sapphire eyes of the Western isles, so likewise, I am sure you ride your sea ship with more confidence than the ground, do you not?"

"Yes, Lord," Brayden replied as he stepped next to the skittish stallion. "I ride the waves much more assuredly than I tread the dirt, for I am a son of the sea and was born on her swells."

Arva Vatana laughed again. "You, a child of the open ocean, and I, a horse lord roaming the free plains of the Eastnorth. Although from different worlds, we are not so dissimilar, you and I."

Domadred came up behind Brayden and began to pull him away.

"Leave him be, sailor," Arva bellowed, motioning to the crowd and beckoning the boy closer. "There is nothing to fear, for I am here in Mindra's Haven flying under the banner of *peace!*" The crowd then let out a cheer of praise. "Son, would you like a gift to commemorate this great occasion?"

Brayden nodded. Arva reached into his coat pocket and produced a black pearl for all to see. Its dark and multicolored iridescent surface was etched with Runes that glimmered like oil in the Zenith's light. Arva then pressed it into Brayden's palm. The boy's eyes grew wide with awe and Brayden took Arva's hand firmly into his own and kissed it profusely.

Arva smiled and looked at Domadred. "Your son is very polite. You have taught him well, sailor."

"I have done the best I can, Lord," Domadred said, bowing his head low.

Withdrawing from Arva, Brayden grinned up at his father. The youth then palmed something into Domadred's pocket. Domadred's eyes widened as he looked back at Arva. The large man's hand was now adorned by one less ring.

Arva suddenly squinted, examining Domadred with a curious gaze. "Sailor, have we met before?"

Domadred chuckled humbly and averted his gaze. "Never, Lord. I would surely have remembered such a glorious thing, as I will this day for the rest of my life."

Stepping away and bowing deeply, Domadred turned and tipped his hat to Beck. "My noble General, I am so very sorry to have disturbed you. May the Guardians smile upon you and yours."

"And you, too, sailor," Beck said coldly.

As Domadred and Brayden disappeared back into the throng, Beck gave an order and the phalanx of fighting men instantly began marching. The soldiers' boots reverberated on the dock and the crowded onlookers were all quickly set back into motion—all except for one.

Standing like an island among the flowing current of people, a lone youth was concealed by a long sleeveless black cloak. With his sword sheathed at his hip, he had a sharp yet inquisitive look that spoke of strength, power, and the tumultuous curiosity of adolescence.

CHAPTER II

With his hand resting on the pommel of his blade, Aleksi watched as the troop of soldiers marched toward the city gates. Under his hooded black cloak, he wore a sleeveless V-neck shirt that clung to his sculpted chest. Except for the white bandage that covered his right hand and wrist, the youth's arms were bare to the shoulder, and strong. Farther down, he wore faded black pants tucked into sturdy but worn calf-high boots.

Aleksi's hood was up, concealing an attractive face already marked by experience, though not yet by age. He had dark hair that fell to his shoulders, elegantly framing his striking green eyes. The color was eerily piercing, a telltale sign that his genealogy was of Northern descent. Most would call the youth beautiful, yet there was an unusually tense air about him. The people on the dock seemed to unconsciously sense Aleksi's strangeness, and gave the youth a wide berth despite the throng.

Matching the flow of the crowd, Aleksi stalked toward the city gates. The captain of the trade ship on which Aleksi had just traveled had undoubtedly set sail to return to the Academy the instant Aleksi had debarked. Although he would have never acted while Aleksi was aboard, the captain would now make all haste to tell the Masters of Aleksi's presence in hopes of claiming a substantial reward. Sadly, if they were not aware already, the Academy's Enforcers would soon know their runaway student was in Mindra's Haven.

Although leaving the Academy had been the most painful choice Aleksi had ever made, he now felt a measure of excitement, too. The Academies of Terra were secluded places of power reserved for a select few. Once respected and revered by all, their tall towers were now feared but mostly forgotten by the masses, having profoundly little contact with the outside world. Now outside of that sanctuary for the first time, Aleksi was experiencing a land where all austerities, traditions, and former restrictions were removed and rendered meaningless. In essence, for the first time in his young life, Aleksi was free.

As long as the Shadow Assassins and Academy's Enforcers don't find me, that is.

The Masters' Vow was clear: if Aleksi was captured by Enforcers, he wouldn't even have the luxury of being dragged back to the Academy in shackles for a trial—student deserters were immediately put to death when found by a Master. The youth swallowed hard at the thought. Aleksi was unsure which disturbed him more: the actual killing of a student, or the fact that a Master could do such a thing to one of their wards.

Even worse, if Rudra's letter is correct, the Rune on my palm will kill me in a mere matter of days. As a child they told me this Rune was a blessing from the Arkai. Oh, how wrong they were . . .

Aleksi opened his hand and looked at his palm. Almost as if in response, the Rune pulsed painfully under his bandage and once again emitted a soft glowing light. Scowling, Aleksi quickly clenched his fist. As the sharp burning sensation dug its way deeper into his hand, Aleksi looked over his shoulder. Seeing nothing suspicious, he tried to ease his growing anxiety by focusing his mind on the crowd around him. Mindra's Haven was alive with the anticipation of tomorrow's proclamation. Many said that on the festival morn, the new Covenant of Eastern Amity would be signed, thereby solidifying the strength of the East and unifying the continent. All agreed that if that came to pass, it truly would be a thing of celebration, possibly ushering in a new age for Terra.

As he moved with the flow of the crowd past the docks and toward the city entrance, Aleksi's hand reflexively dipped into his pocket, unconsciously fingering the worn parchment of Master Rudra's cryptic letter, the fateful warning on which the youth had wagered all. His anxiety now became anger and Aleksi once again tried to suppress it. Shaking his head, Aleksi removed his hand from his cloak and looked up at the massive gates of the city wall. Before he started searching for Rudra's obscure clues, there was something inside Mindra's Square that he wanted to see first.

As Aleksi passed under the gilded archway of the city gates, Mindra's Square, one of the largest marketplaces in the world, came into view. Like so many before him, Aleksi was utterly astounded by the sheer mass of humanity that was the market. He could hardly take in the immensity of the many divisions of colored stalls, stands, and tents. Winding paths connected by hundreds of tented roundabouts all fed in and out of the swelling chaos of people.

As the crowd filtered into the marketplace, a massive crystalline statue came into view. Aleksi saw the gigantic monument of the High Arkai Mindra standing proud and shining in the light of the Zenith. Said to be true to scale, the statue rose nearly twenty stories tall. Standing with its enormous wings spread wide, the mammoth work covered much of the marketplace in oddly lit shadows that shimmered on the multicolored stalls and tents below.

The monument depicted Mindra, like all Guardians, as humanoid, with the exception of its colossal wings. Due to its shining light, however, the statue's features were obscured. The only things that could be seen clearly were its dazzling eyes of molten gold. Bright as the Zenith, their light was piercing and too powerful to look at directly. Even if the statue was depicted as clothed was a mystery, for although an Arkai or Guardian had not been seen for many ages, it was said that you could never directly look upon one. Their forms were always obscured by their splendor—a numinous light that was both powerful and terrifying.

Aleksi made his way deeper into the throng. At the Academy, he had heard much about the statue, and he was excited to finally see it with his own eyes. His teachers had said it was carved of *nimral,* a crystalline material created by Runes that possessed strange properties. Aleksi had seen nimral before, but this was undoubtedly the largest-known piece in all of Terra. This massive statue was said to have been a gift from the Guardians, bequeathed to remind the people of Devdan of High Arkai Mindra—their protector and savior.

As Aleksi continued walking, he shifted his attention from the statue to scan the ocean of colorful tents and stands. The youth passed hawkers and vendors, buskers and grifters, and thousands and thousands of people hailing from all across the world.

Despite trying his best to keep a low profile, Aleksi couldn't help but notice a beautiful woman who had light-green eyes imbued with icy-blue flecks, clearly signifying her heritage from the North-Western plateaued plains nation of Kaymahn. Her booth was adorned with jewelry and pastel-dyed leather jackets, jerkins, and vests, each stitched with multicolored beads that twinkled in the Zenith light. North-Westerners were famous for their buffalo leather crafts and specially beaded jewelry.

Seeing Aleksi's deep-green eyes, the woman bowed her head, causing her beaded necklace to splay across her ample cleavage. Aleksi felt heat rise into his cheeks as he returned the bow. The youth had been taught that the beads of the Kaymahn peoples were Runic in nature and each color and shape possessed unique properties and effects. Although the beads were weak in isolation, if enough were conjoined in close proximity, their power was said to be cumulative. More importantly, however, their method of creation was a closely guarded secret, with the North-Western capital city of Iraja being the home of the most powerful elder craftspeople.

Blending his pace with the movement of the crowd, Aleksi found his attention drawn to a wagon laden with long spears and round bucklers made of metal the color of flowing sand. Each shield was intricately carved with profoundly detailed desert scenes depicting shifting sands, blowing winds, and scattered stars. The etchings were inlaid with metalwork of slightly different shimmering hues, giving the scenes the illusion of movement and perspective. The Academy was a place of harsh austerity and this was the first time Aleksi had seen such artistic expression applied to the surface of weapons and armor.

Noticing that Aleksi was admiring his craftsmanship, the dark-skinned artisan closed his eyes, crossed his hands palms up in front of his chest, interlocked his thumbs, and then finally bowed his head to Aleksi in a show of deep respect. When the man opened his eyes again, Aleksi saw they were the color of honey and possessed flecks of molten red. Knowing the man hailed from the South-Eastern nation of Salbata, Aleksi returned the intricate bow so as to not offend. Despite this, the youth risked the disrespect of keeping his own eyes open—he could not afford to be reckless and let his guard down. Aleksi had read at the Academy that although the South-Easterners did not dwell in large cities, they were still known for their ferocity in battle, art, philosophy, honor, and love. Judging from the weapons' artistry, Aleksi assumed this man's work and demeanor were born from the same pride made famous in the many stories about these passionate people.

Continuing through the market, Aleksi saw people from every nation of Terra haggling, arguing, laughing, and interacting together as one cohesive sea of humanity. Everyone was busy browsing, buying, selling, or trading under the rippling shadows of Mindra's great wings—seemingly without a care in the world.

Aleksi always thought it was strange that the Masters never let their students see the lands that they would one day be tasked to protect. *How are we supposed to truly care for these people when we have no real knowledge of their lives and struggles? We are given the Runic power to preserve all life, but at the cost of being unable to truly live ourselves . . . Is power worth such a price?*

Although thrilled to finally see these sights with his own eyes instead of reading about them in books, Aleksi knew that he must be vigilant and not get distracted from his mission. Rudra's letter made it very clear that one of these people could be an assassin waiting for him with a silent blade. Pulling his hood farther over his face, Aleksi quickened his step. *Regardless if it's Shadow Assassin or Enforcer, if either finds me, I'll have little hope of resisting them. So if I am to outrun them, I must make all haste to decipher Rudra's letter.*

As Aleksi continued moving, a large man dressed in golden silks with a rounded belly raised his arms wide as he boisterously heralded his wares: a cartload of glass orbs arranged on shelves—each orb was of a different color and filled with swirling, luminescent gas. When the man's arms flung out, however, Aleksi reflexively raised his wrist in a quick block to avoid being struck in the head. Startled by the unintentional attack, Aleksi pushed the man back and grasped the hilt of his sheathed sword.

The fat merchant was surprised by the blow and, losing his balance, stumbled against his cart of baubles. Because of his girth, the man's impact caused several of the glass spheres to fall from their shelf and shatter onto the cobblestones with a crash. When the orbs broke, they released a smoky white gas that instantly evaporated away into nothingness. Regaining his footing, the fat merchant looked down at his broken wares and spun at Aleksi, his large jowls rippling in anger.

"You fool!" the man shouted. "You have broken three Runic Kellrab orbs from Neberu. They are worth black pearls so concentrated they should be darker than your Northern hair!"

"The fault was yours, sir, for you struck me first," Aleksi answered, turning to leave.

"Do not take another step!" the merchant shouted, reaching out and grabbing Aleksi's coat. Aleksi moved reflexively in response—rotating his arm in a wide arc, he dislodged the man's hand and once again pushed him back. What had at first been annoyance turned to anger, but Aleksi once again turned to leave.

"Those were Runic artifacts and I demand compensation immediately," the man sputtered. "If you do not pay, I will call the market's guards!"

"Again, the fault was yours." A strange sensation emanated from Aleksi's bandaged palm, and a dangerous power grew within him. "Despite that, I will give you a single pearl for your trouble. But know that I am being generous, because only a fool would think that those orbs were Runic. They are obvious counterfeits and are hardly worth the colored glass they are made of."

"You insolent whelp! Pay for what you broke or give me something else of equal value!"

Feeling the dark power of his Rune intensify, Aleksi made no response and the fat merchant scowled at Aleksi's sword.

"If that blade at your hip were real, it might come close to paying your debt, but by looking at you I can tell that sword is nothing more than a dull replica worn only for show and boastful bluster!" The man then spit at Aleksi, soiling the youth's face with his phlegm.

Aleksi's anger flared and he used his left thumb to slightly slide his blade from its sheath. "I kindly ask you to take my offered pearl and let me leave in peace. I would hate for anyone to get hurt over such a petty trifle." Under his hood, Aleksi's youthful gaze shone piercingly as the Runic pulsing of his palm grew stronger, causing his temper to flare. The merchant's eyes narrowed and danced between Aleksi's face and his sheathed blade. The man then looked over Aleksi's shoulder and nodded with a smirk.

Aleksi instinctively swiveled and shifted his weight forward as a pair of strong hands grabbed him by the shoulders from behind. Luckily, Aleksi's quick and skillful movement had caused his assailant to be put off balance. The youth felt his anger grow into intoxicating rage as he took a step to the side of his attacker and grasped the man's right wrist. As the man tried to regain both his balance and grip on Aleksi, the youth simultaneously pivoted his hips and upper torso while taking another step. This time, the step was backward, causing the man to be thrown farther off balance and stumble forward onto his knees.

Aleksi, maintaining his double-handed grip on his attacker's arm, slid one of his hands to the man's elbow, wrenching the man's arm behind his back at an unnatural angle. The man let out a hollow grunt of pain as Aleksi slammed his knee into the man's rib cage. Tightening his grip, Aleksi leaned into his assailant's center of gravity, pinning his chest and face to the cobblestones.

The assailant let out a muffled wheeze of pain as Aleksi looked back up at the fat merchant, whose face was now pale and trembling.

"If you or yours lay a hand on me again," Aleksi said harshly, feeling the dark power of his bandaged palm surge within him, "I will claim it as retribution."

"Re-re-release him!" The fat merchant stammered, wringing his hands. "I-I am a very important man and ca-can have you killed with a si-single word!"

"You dare to think you can *kill me*?" Aleksi's eyes had been cold as ice but now grew hot with uncontrolled fury as the pain of his Rune surged up his arm. Still looking at the fat merchant, the youth snarled and once again tightened his grip on his assailant's arm. "Let your vassal's pain teach you how profoundly mistaken you are!"

In one sharp movement, Aleksi pivoted his hips and his attacker's wrist, elbow, and shoulder broke simultaneously with a loud pop. The fallen man let out a muffled cry of agony and the small but quickly growing crowd of onlookers all took a reflexive step backward—several of them gasping.

Releasing the man's broken arm and taking a step toward the fat merchant, Aleksi felt the hot fire of his rage continue to build. Instead of suppressing the dark emotion, the youth reveled in its power and gripped the hilt of his sword even tighter. "All here saw that I offered recompense and was attacked unprovoked. If it happens again, I will spill your blood and see to it that your ignorance is made *eternal.*"

The fat merchant was now speechless—his entire body trembling and his pupils fully dilated in terror. Despite this, Aleksi felt a seductively powerful urge to kill the man where he stood. As the intoxicating feeling grew, Aleksi's left thumb reflexively released his blade from its sheath and the burning Rune on his palm urged him to deadly action. The power was overwhelming and Aleksi's vision narrowed until all he saw was the merchant's quivering body—and all Aleksi felt was the desire to *destroy*. At the brink of action, the cryptic words of Rudra's letter suddenly sprang into Aleksi's mind.

"At the precipice of eternal ignorance, turn from the edge of darkness, for if at any time upon your journey you take a life in anger, you will fall willingly into the hands of those who hunt you."

Aleksi released his grip on his sword with silent shock and felt the rage flood from his body in one quick rush—in its place all that was left was deep sadness and clawing shame. With a flourish of his long black cloak, Aleksi turned and, pushing aside the onlookers, reentered the flowing crowd of the market. Behind him the fat merchant stumbled over himself and rushed over to his wounded and whimpering guardsman as the collection of gawking market members watched in shock.

Wiping the phlegm from his face, Aleksi looked down at his throbbing palm. His Rune had begun glowing once again. Quickly clenching his fist to hide the light, he felt the nerves of his bandaged hand pulse painfully with numinous power.

What have I done?! Am I no better than the fallen Masters of old? Aleksi thought as he continued to make his way toward the shimmering statue of Mindra at the center of the square. *A Master is supposed to preserve life, not take it! Unless that man can afford immediate Runic healing, his arm will be crippled forever. Maybe Nataraja is right about me . . . Maybe he is right about everything . . .*

As he quickly moved on through the mass of people, the burning pain in Aleksi's palm steadily grew stronger and spread up his wrist. *This Rune is too powerful. I could hardly control myself. If anyone reports what happened to the market's guards, it could alert those who search for me. How could I be so reckless? How could the Rune affect my emotions so greatly? What is it doing to me?*

Suddenly, the pain intensified exponentially and Aleksi doubled over in agony. Instead of burning dully as it had for the past several days, the Runic pain in his hand surged up his arm as it dug its sharp metallic tendrils deep into the nerves and bones of his wrist and forearm. Aleksi had known a life of pain—in truth, his life had *been* pain. Nataraja had always said that pain was the ultimate teacher—the ultimate purifier of emotion and thought. But this pain was different. This pain was not a teacher but the signal that without the help of a Master, Aleksi's Rune would soon kill him.

At this rate, the Rune will kill me before anyone else gets the chance!

Aleksi's breath came in ragged gasps as the tendrils of fire moved past his elbow and into the flesh and bone of his upper arm. His vision blurred, causing him to stagger and fall to one knee on the cobblestones. Several people near him glanced over, but when they saw him double over and clutch his arm in agony, each turned away and hurried onward.

As the pain threatened to consume his body and mind, Aleksi looked up and saw the shimmering statue towering above him. Understanding suddenly flooded into Aleksi's mind, and through sheer will he urged himself back to his feet. Stumbling past people in the crowd, he forced his legs to move toward Mindra's luminescent brilliance.

Cradling his throbbing arm and shambling through the masses, Aleksi finally arrived at Mindra's statue. He staggered up the steps to the figure's foundation and collapsed at the base of its shining beauty. Although the Rune was now bright enough to shine out from his bandages, its glow was obfuscated by the far greater light of the statue. Feeling white-hot fire surge through his body, he placed his glowing palm on the statue's smooth, radiant surface. Despite the torrent ripping its way through his arm, somehow Aleksi was comforted.

Not knowing what else to do, Aleksi steeled himself against the anguish, pressed his palm harder against the statue, and *listened*. The sound was extraordinary: behind him, he could hear voices rise up from the market, selling wares, shouting news, and toasting friend and neighbor; yet in front of him, coming from the statue itself, was a sweet, melodic vibration unlike anything he had ever heard. Aleksi gritted his teeth as the Runic inferno raged on, and tried to open himself to the statue's sound. It was almost a hum, or a sympathetic resonance with the Zenith's light. Suddenly, the nerves of his bandaged arm pulsed not in pain, but in harmony with the statue's light. As he pressed his glowing palm even more firmly against its surface, the statue leached the pain first out of his hand and then from his entire body.

Continuing to take ragged breaths, Aleksi felt tears run down his cheeks as the pain was drawn out from his body and consumed by the light of the statue. Flooded with relief, he lowered his hooded head in reverence as the statue's grace silently flowed through him. By the grace of the Arkai, he was not going to die—at least not yet.

How could Master Rudra have known? How could he have predicted this in his letter?

With the pain now reduced to manageable levels, Aleksi wiped the tears from his face. His Rune had stopped glowing. Unable to look directly at the shimmering stone due to its brilliance, Aleksi shakily pressed his palms together and bowed his head deeply.

Thank you, High Arkai Mindra. I vow to somehow be worthy of your blessing.

After the bow was completed, Aleksi swallowed hard and, still averting his eyes, turned away from the statue. No one in the busy marketplace around him even gave him a second glance. They were going about their business as if nothing had happened.

A fitting gift from the Guardians, Aleksi thought as he squinted his eyes and looked back toward the luminescent statue towering above. *All these people just plod along, paying no mind to this shining marvel above them. They give no thought to the mysteries of Terra and the Guardians who protect them from the encroaching darkness. They also give no thought to those who misuse this power . . .*

Although it was yet to be proven, many Masters debated if the statue itself was created as a Runic tool. Those who argued so claimed it must be one of extraordinary power and might. While all logic would suggest that this was highly probable, no actual Runes had been observed on the figure, even by the most powerful of the High Masters. This implied that either the hypothetical Runes did not exist, or they were too potent to be accessed by anyone who walked Terra in the Modern Age.

It was taught at the Academy that Runes, although normally conjured out of thin air, could also be imbued onto, and therefore *in*, physical objects, giving the objects astonishing powers. It was theorized that much like a Rune Blade, the Runes in this statue were hidden and lying dormant until a Master of appropriate synchronization was able to awaken them. Spread across Terra there were many such tools with engraved Runes. Some were great, and some were small. But despite their size, their actual effects varied depending on the Runes themselves. The object's strength also depended on the one who originally cast the Rune, while being further affected by the one immediately using it.

Conversely, some Runes were always active. These Runes—which didn't need to be invoked by a Master—granted passive abilities to objects: an indestructible wall, an ever-fruitful tree, or even personal items, such as a privateer's distance-seeing spyglass. Likewise, other Runes needed only the simplest of cues to work, like a door that opened only at a special word, or a hearth that never went out so long as there were people in the room. The most powerful Runes, however, needed an equally powerful Numina user to activate them. Only those educated at the Academy possessed the level of Runic training required to awaken such objects and unleash their power upon friend and foe alike.

Supposedly, in the Ages of Lore, Masters had much more control over Numina and were able to cast Runes into all manner of things, ranging from weapons and armor to jewelry and personal belongings. It was said that Masters would even imbue humble objects like farming equipment and building materials. They could grant boons such as increased intelligence, fortified strength, and other potent enchantments. Legends even told of abilities such as weightlessness, thermodynamic change, bodily regeneration, and other miraculous feats that many now hardly believed. Sadly, legend also said that some Masters, having fallen to darkness, created Runic tools that possessed much more sinister purposes. Unfortunately, the skill of Rune imbuing had been lost to the Masters, and the remaining Runic items were heralded as priceless artifacts, highly coveted and constantly fought over.

In addition, although they were now only spoken about in the Academies, there were legends of Masters in ages past who had Runes imbued directly into their flesh. In the Modern Age, it was commonly believed that only the High Priests and Priestesses of the Order of the Arkai possessed a physically imbued Rune. The High Order of the Arkai's Runes, however, were a sacred gift personally given by their patron Arkai and passed down through the ages through holy succession. In contrast, with no Arkai to mitigate their Runes' use, the Rune-imbued Masters of ages past were a different matter entirely. Due to their rarity and vast ability, these powerful men and women were referred to in hushed whispers only. For although there were many inspiring stories of imbued Masters who used their power to protect, there were also an equal number of dark legends of Masters who used their vast Runic abilities to corrupt and enslave. Because of this, the knowledge of how to actually perform a biological Rune imbuing was not found in any of the Academies' treatises, and most believed the potent secret was lost to the sands of time.

And then the seemingly impossible happened: Rudra was born—a baby whose body was covered in Runes . . . Aleksi looked down at his bandaged hand, feeling it once again pulse with numinous power. *And even though all the Masters of the Academy say the contrary, if Rudra's past gives any glimpse of my future, then my being born with even a single Rune is infinitely more of a curse than a blessing . . .*

Aleksi let out a sigh and looked back up to the great statue looming above him. After bowing his head, Aleksi stepped away from the luminescent stone and continued onward through the crowd.

But instead of arguing endlessly about what to do with these last Runic tools—or with me—the Masters should be more concerned with why they have lost the ability to imbue in the first place. They should be concerned with why the Guardians have neglected us these past ages— what we have done to deserve being abandoned, and what we need to do to be redeemed.

Still cradling his bandaged hand, Aleksi left the statue and continued on through the market. Although weakened, he kept his gaze alert and scanned his surroundings carefully for any sign of danger. Eventually, the crowd thinned and he saw the entrance to the city's main boulevard. On this side of the square, space was open and free of tents and trade. Aleksi saw that there were even long paved paths and grassy places for people to congregate, recline, and mingle.

In one such space, Aleksi saw a ring of five children holding hands and singing as they danced in a circle. Their song was eerily melodic and foreboding:

> "We rest our heads and sleep us together shall take
> To the land between eternal dreams and wake.
> So long as darkness does not us interrupt
> We shall dance till dawn in the Dreamscape uncorrupt."

The children then all curled up in the grass next to each other and pretended to go to sleep. If what Aleksi had been taught at the Academy was true, he doubted very much that these children knew the true meaning and purpose of their song—or the risk they faced invoking the Dreamscape's power.

Looking past the playing children, Aleksi saw many more paved paths in this part of the square. Most of them led to gardens with fountains and pools of water, clusters of trees, and even several small ponds with benches and tables. As he passed, Aleksi saw a mallard and her line of baby ducklings close in tow headed to a nearby pond. Although they paid Aleksi little mind and continued waddling across the flagstone as he strode by, the sight reopened a deep pain which had been dormant for a very long time.

Training at the Academy was so austere that students were never allowed to see their former families once they began their tutelage. Aleksi pulled his hood farther over his face. *Even though they are separated so young, at least the other students knew their parents. My earliest memory is of Master Rudra leaving the Academy to go on one of his missions. When I asked him, or any of the other Masters, what happened to my parents, all they would say was that they were dead. Rudra was all I had, and then . . .* Aleksi pushed away the memory of Rudra's exile from the Academy. *He, too, was taken from me.*

Farther on beyond the paths, instead of sharing an edge with the city wall and harbor like the market, the eastern half of the square was lined with soaring buildings jutting up to the sky. Crafted exclusively by the Guardians, these structures stood far larger than anything that could be attempted in the Modern Age. This magnificent precinct was known as Guardians' Plaza. There was everything here a wealthy traveler or native could want when coming to the Eastern capital. This made Mindra's Square and its surrounding buildings of Guardians' Plaza the center point of the city's culture and life.

With residential spaces above, the buildings' lower levels were lined with luxury storefronts all eager to tend to those who could afford their services. The shops were filled with respected and well-dressed yellow-eyed maidens and men, all staffing their stations with pride. Looking higher, Aleksi gazed up at the buildings' finely carved upper levels, which housed the wealthy in lofty spires and majestic towers. Since Terra's Zeniths were stationary, each building's most coveted side was the one that directly faced the Zenith's light. These locations were for the most elite of the elite, and Aleksi could not imagine the black pearl cost of a Zenith-side penthouse in Guardians' Plaza. The buildings' gallant points rose high above the other structures in

Mindra's Haven and reflected the Zenith's glimmering light upon their lesser neighbors.

Looming above them all, however, at the front of Guardians' Plaza, was the glorious Mindra's Temple. Heralded as the shining star of the city, the famed temple was a beacon of hope to the Eastern people and abutted the entrance of the city's center boulevard. The temple was the tallest building on the entire Eastern Continent and possessed a large crystal spire atop its massive center dome. This magnificent structure housed both the Eastern Order of the Arkai, led by Mindra's High Priest and Rune holder, Trailen Kaftal, and Adhira's High Council, the ruling body of Mindra's Haven, headed by Mehail Bander.

As Aleksi came closer to the temple, he saw scores of workers setting up massive fairgrounds for the festival. In addition, he noticed droves of people congregating around the temple in anticipation of tomorrow's proclamation. The lower floors even seemed to be open to visitors, but despite Aleksi's profound curiosity, he dared not enter.

Aleksi felt his bandaged palm burn painfully with anticipation. Looking back, the youth saw a hooded figure following him through the crowd. Aleksi quickly ducked behind a pair of workmen carrying a large pallet of wood and doubled back on his stalker. Keeping his head low to avoid detection, Aleksi circled around and watched the man carefully.

Just as Aleksi was about to disappear back into the crowd, he saw the hooded figure quickly scan his surroundings and draw a wickedly curved dagger. Aleksi's heart raced as he firmly gripped the hilt of his sword, preparing to strike. Instead of lunging, however, the hooded man intentionally bumped into a sailor directly in front of him and deftly used his dagger to cut the sailor's purse from his belt.

That's no Shadow Assassin—just a petty thief. The Academy's Vow states that I must enact summary judgement for such obvious crimes. Aleksi clutched the hilt of his sword and gritted his teeth. *However, that same Vow also demands my execution for abandoning the Academy. If Master Rudra's letter is correct, too much hangs in the balance and I must do all in my power to avoid detection. No matter my Vows, justice must wait—on both accounts . . .*

Opening his hand, Aleksi looked down at his bandaged palm. Underneath the cloth wrappings, his Rune was once again emitting a soft glowing light that pulsed in time with his heartbeat. He knew that if he came too close to the temple, the Order's acolytes would be able to sense his growing power, and he would surely be detained for questioning as to why he, a student of the Academy, was alone without a Master. If he lived through the ordeal, he would undoubtedly be held captive until the Enforcers came to deliver their fatal punishment.

Because of this, Aleksi cut a large arc around the temple as he made his way to the city's center boulevard. Aleksi had never imagined that *he* would forsake the vow and disobey the Masters. But Rudra's letter had already predicted much more than what Aleksi thought possible. If anything else of the letter was true, Aleksi's threatened fate was profoundly clear.

CHAPTER III

As Aleksi made his way past the temple and down the long boulevard through the heart of the city, he pulled Rudra's folded letter from his pocket. Opening the parchment for the countless time, he studied the scrawled words on the worn page carefully. Although he had received the letter only several days prior, he had read the prophetic words many hundreds of times, desperately trying to understand their hidden meaning. Whatever Rudra's intent had been by keeping his message so obscure, it made the task of following his beckoned trail nearly impossible. Fear crept into Aleksi's heart as he shoved the paper back into his pocket. If he could not make sense of his Master's riddles, all would be lost.

Trying to take his mind off the pulsing pain underneath the bandage and his desperate situation, Aleksi looked about the crowded street. With the temple now at his back, the wide thoroughfare of Guardians' Plaza was lined with towering buildings of beautifully carved stone. They reached into the sky and stretched on farther than he could see. Instead of looking up at the striking masonry, however, Aleksi found his attention caught by the magical *wae'yrr* trees.

These majestic maples were created by the Guardians and gifted to the inhabitants of the city in their time of need. The arranged rows ran along either side of the central boulevard as it continued westward through the city. Spaced out one by one, each tree's bushy green foliage touched the adjacent trees' canopies in tight succession. Swaying gently in the breeze, they cast a cool shade on the pedestrians who strode on the street's footpath below. But as Aleksi passed under their shadows, he wished he might have time to see them at night.

During the day, the wae'yrr trees simply looked like oversized sugar maples: large, but nothing extraordinary. At night, however, they came alive with light and were truly magnificent. Due to the grace of the Guardians, their leaves glowed brightly, as if their very veins were imbued with the holy light of the moons. Although trees that had glowing leaves were not a rare thing in Terra, only a Master of profound ability could ever transplant such a tree, let alone foster one from a seedling. Because of this, few cities had such trees within their walls, let alone many hundreds of them lining their central boulevard. And so the illuminated boulevard of glowing maples was just another of the famed relics of Mindra's Haven—a gift from divine caretakers long since absent.

Even though the Masters have lost so much of their ability, they still could share what gifts they have with the people here. Is their fear of corruption truly so great it prevents them from doing anything? Aleksi's palm pulsed with power as he remembered the overpowering rage that caused him to break his assailant's arm in the market. *Maybe they are justified in their fear, but a life in solitary meditation is not a life lived. There must be another way . . .*

As Aleksi continued down the road, he tried to keep his mind from dwelling on his dire situation. Even though the trees were not glowing, they still were quite stately, and he forced himself to take a calming breath as he turned his face up to their shaded canopy. The sky was blue, the Zenith was warm, and a cool, salty breeze blew off the ocean. It felt clean and fresh across his face yet was not able to soothe his agitated heart.

Suddenly, Aleksi heard a child crying. Looking to the side, he saw what he presumed to be a father and son standing outside a bakery storefront. An overly plump boy was wailing and banging his hands on the window, pointing to the sweet cakes inside. The boy was dressed in fine clothes, and on the ground next to him was an ornately painted ball. His father was trying to distract the child with the lavish toy but was finding no success. As Aleksi walked on, he saw the father pick up his son and bring him inside the bakery. The ball was left out on the ground, forgotten.

Moving farther down the boulevard, Aleksi noticed that the majority of the people around him were dressed in urbane, well-tailored clothes. The vast majority of them had golden eyes and moved with a deliberate grace that conveyed a sense of both pride and honor. Aleksi saw rich Eastern silks and was surprised to glimpse Northern jewels from Simn adorning many of the men and women. Although some of the people around him wore laborers' garments, they mostly rode in wagons, getting transportation to some unknown location. It was clear that those actually shopping and mingling in Guardians' Plaza were dressed much differently than those in the working class, and both groups knew it.

Aleksi had read of the famous Eastern aristocratic honor, but now walking among them, it truly was unmistakable. Lords and ladies strode the street in sumptuous dress next to expensive carts and coaches pulled by snorting steeds of the finest breed. While some carriages and wagons were laden with goods, most had beautifully painted exteriors with silk veils concealing their inhabitants from not only the Zenith's rays but also the probing eyes of their neighbors. Although far too rich for Aleksi's taste, this part of the city was a place of grace and dignity, and its people were better than the masses, at least in their own minds.

As Aleksi continued walking in the shade, he caught sight of an elegant lady in a long, flowing blue-and-gold-embroidered dress and wide-brimmed blue hat. She was coming toward him along the road's footpath and held a long cylindrical parcel. As they passed, the woman nodded with a respectful smile. Although most of Aleksi's face was concealed under his hood, he did the same. Despite the kindness, Aleksi still had a sinking feeling in his gut. Deep down, he knew that he was not going to find the answers to Rudra's riddles here in Guardians' Plaza. To follow his Master's call, he would have to enter the decrepit boroughs of Old City.

A wave of hopelessness washed over the youth. With each read-through of the letter, his deep and unsettling fear had grown stronger—a fear that he would not be able to understand his Master's hidden meanings and would be left to fend for himself against the Academy's Enforcers and *worse.*

One last time, Aleksi thought, pulling out the worn parchment. *I will read it one last time . . .* Aleksi read the flowing script quickly. Once finished, he shoved the letter back into his pocket and clenched his jaw. Nothing Master Rudra did was ever without careful deliberation and potent purpose, and the letter had already proven itself startlingly accurate. But many parts of his letter were impossible to make any sense of.

As for where to go next, "city of ruin that the Guardians neglected" is easy enough. But the "ancestral place of healing" could mean any number of things. And how am I supposed to find it with no more than an obscure clue of its dedication "to the Northern light?"

Aleksi pulled his hood lower over his face. *And none know of my father or lineage. It was Master Rudra who brought me to the Academy as an orphaned babe, so unless he was lying all along, this is either a test or some kind of deception. But either way, it is wasting time I don't have. If I don't learn to control my Rune quickly, it won't matter how many layers of bandages I wear—not only will the Rune's light shine bright enough for all to see, its power will tear through my body and kill me! Why didn't Rudra just come get me himself?*

As Aleksi kept walking, he swallowed and tried to force down the fear that grew in his chest. Aleksi didn't know which possibility scared him more: the thought that he would actually learn the truth about his parents' deaths, or the realization that Rudra had known all along and had never told him.

Aleksi felt that Old City's name was slightly misleading. Originally abandoned after the Dark Ones' attack, Old City was really just the ruined outskirts of Mindra's Haven that the Guardians never rebuilt. This was because when Guardians' Plaza was completed, none needed to reenter the dilapidated remains of Old City, let alone live in them. However, as the generations passed and the population of Mindra's Haven increased in size, those less fortunate could not afford to live in

Guardians' Plaza. Forced to seek shelter elsewhere, the poor and refugees had begun to repopulate Old City. Sadly, their rebuilding efforts were haphazard at best.

It did not take long for the Eastern High Council to intervene. The councilors knew that if they did not take action, a very dangerous ghetto would soon grow within their city walls. So, under official contract, the city's artisans were ordered to go sector by sector, rebuilding on old foundations. Knowing that they were constructing for the poor, however, most builders were more interested in cutting costs and maximizing profits than constructing anything that would stand the test of time. So as the years passed, the buildings of Old City had required constant repairs and looked like a patchwork blanket stained with filth compared to the splendor and sheen of Guardians' Plaza. In fact, according to what Aleksi had heard, the tattered blanket of Old City did more to smother its inhabitants than provide actual shelter.

Continuing down the boulevard, Aleksi could slowly see the transition as he left Guardians' Plaza. There was no definite threshold except for the wae'yrr trees. They tapered down until finally becoming no more than bushes, then stopping completely. While the wide boulevard did continue on, the size of the buildings, much like the trees, also shrank both in size and dignity. Their masonry became less ornate and was made of normal rock and mortar instead of Guardian Stone. In addition, the tallest among them was only four or five stories high, and soon for every stone building, there were at least five wooden ones. It was a gradual shift, but eventually Aleksi could just tell—he was in Old City.

Although the boulevard was still quite busy, the youth noticed that the peoples' dress and demeanors had also drastically transformed. Instead of graceful ladies and wealthy merchants, he now saw simple traders and manual laborers. Elegantly laced silks and debonair coats were now rough cottons and thick working leathers.

In truth, this place should be called Laborers' City, Aleksi thought, as he looked over a group of dirty workers sitting on a stacked pile of barrels. The rough men were smoking their break's tobacco and talking about the work to come. Those who lived here were the lower class, performing the hard exertion of sweat and blood. And it was here,

Aleksi guessed, that he would find an ancestral place of healing and the next step in Rudra's mysterious letter.

Aleksi had read in *Lulister's Chronicle of Mindra's Haven: The Grand Capital of Devdan* that nearly all of the apothecary shops in Mindra's Haven were in Old City. The author wrote that this was because the higher classes relied on the temple and its Runic tools to heal their ills. Historically, Terra's various temples would provide Runic blessings for free, but now in the Modern Age the temple acolytes needed a black pearl of relatively high concentration to be able to perform such a feat. These black pearls were not given to the acolytes as payment but were a needed ingredient to perform the Runic healing itself. While the wealthy could afford such an expense, the common folk were forced to rely on the less expensive herbs and potions whose medicinal recipes had been passed down through the ages.

As Aleksi walked farther, he found that there were seemingly endless apothecary shops. They came in many shapes and sizes, and catered to the general populace as well as those with special needs. Almost all of the shops sold dried herbs, spices, and general-use drugs while also having their own compound rooms with copper distilleries and brick hearths. And while the alchemists and soothsayers clustered in the dark rooms were always ready to try and make a sale, they were never willing to listen when Aleksi tried to ask for information. Possessing unique ointments and elixirs they claimed could not be found anywhere else in all of Terra, each store owner was much keener on pushing their own wares than promoting another apothecary by giving directions.

After searching for several hours, Aleksi felt anger grow in his chest. What made matters worse was that those few who did have answers gave him different directions. Three men all standing together and referencing one another thought they remembered a shop called the Northern Hand, but they each thought it was in a different place.

Aleksi realized that idle wandering would get him nowhere. Letting out a deep sigh, the youth decided to take a more strategic approach and go to the headquarters of the Apothecary Guild. There, he hoped he might be able to find more accurate information.

While he had known little of current events when he arrived, Aleksi already had become quite aware of the political climate of Mindra's Haven from the gossip he overheard while walking. The youth even recognized Arva Vatana, the Eastnorthern leader of Pa'laer who had been atop the large warhorse on the docks earlier in the day. Other than swordplay, Aleksi's favored artistic pursuit was drawing, and the youth paid special attention to Arva's drawn likeness sold by street hawkers. The many artists shouted the horse lord's name and lineage, heralding tomorrow as the day the East would be reunited under one rule. In addition, Aleksi carefully inspected the many drawings of Beck Al'Beth, the general who had been leading Arva's escort. As the youth paused to inspect the pictures, one artist even said that Beck and Arva had met as enemies on the battlefield just four years prior—and it was from Arva that Beck got his large facial scar. Although it was quite obvious that tensions were high and much rode on these peace talks, people still seemed to be very optimistic regarding their outcome.

As Aleksi continued past the run-down buildings of Old City to the Apothecary Guild center, he was suddenly surprised to see a group of twenty-five men dressed like Pa'laer soldiers in tan leather mail marching down the street. To his eye, however, as he was trained in the various martial arts of Terra, Aleksi could tell that these men were *not* from the Eastnorth. Instead, they walked with the telltale tight hamstrings of the Northern mercenaries trained in the clandestine fighting style of the Hanval. Any Master or Apprentice of the Academy would be able to see past the facade, but the untrained eye would not know what to look for and be easily fooled.

As the group walked past, Aleksi paused to get a glimpse of their eyes. Strangely, they were not Northern green. Instead, they had the flecked-gold eyes of the Eastern peoples. Their real color had undoubtedly been concealed to complete the men's disguise. The captain of the group, seeing Aleksi, nodded to the youth with a smile. Seemingly in response, the Runic sensation within Aleksi's bandaged palm flared, causing sharp tension to cascade through his hand and wrist.

Feeling his anxiety deepen, Aleksi returned the man's nod and hurried on. He knew of several potions one could take to temporarily change the color of one's eyes, but not only were the ingredients expensive and quite rare, but the Runic ability to make such a thing was incredibly occult. What was most disturbing to Aleksi, however, was the common knowledge that the relations between the East and North had been unprecedentedly tense since the Vai'kel Unification War. And as the youth watched the group continue its march down the street, he knew without a doubt these men were from the North. Why they were disguised as Pa'laer soldiers and in the East, however, Aleksi knew not. Sadly, whatever the reason, it could *not* be good.

While a Northerner by blood, Aleksi, being a student of the Academy, held no political alliances. In addition, he had grown up in the Eastern Academy having no memory of anything else. To him, the North was just another place—very far away, in so many ways. Despite this, the men's presence troubled Aleksi in light of the looming peace talks. Yet the youth knew it was not his place to interfere. Masters and their Apprentices were forbidden from intervening in the maneuverings of the outside world. Even worse, Aleksi had to deal with the immediate threat before him and needed to keep as low a profile as possible to avoid detection—especially after what had happened in Mindra's Square. Glancing down at his bandaged hand, Aleksi quickened his pace and continued onward.

When he finally reached the Apothecary Guild, Aleksi entered the large building and let out a sigh. His legs were already tired from a day's worth of walking. As Aleksi's eyes adjusted to the room's muted light, he saw that the building's interior was much nicer than he had expected.

Before him was more of a meeting place than a site of business. Despite several official-looking booths built into the walls, the large space seemed to be much more of a social hall than anything else and was filled with worn tables and sturdy wooden chairs. The decor was not fancy, yet not drab, either. The location's clientele matched its interior. And although this was still Old City, the building was undoubtedly supported by the patronage of its members and very well kept. In addition, large colorful banners hung from the ceiling, displaying the guild's patronage and officials. Each apothecary had its own crest and they were all clearly displayed on the flags above.

Walking farther into the hall, Aleksi heard the shrill cries of two gaunt children holding on to the patchwork dress of their mother. Their clamor was underpinned by men's chuckling and the officious drone of the guild official speaking to the woman. Upon closer inspection, Aleksi saw that her dress was worn and dirty while the official was garbed in a formal jacket inlayed with ornate golden stitching. He eyed the mother and her crying children disdainfully.

"The black pearl fee is nonnegotiable, madam," Aleksi overheard the official say to the woman. "The price has not changed since last year, so you have had more than enough time to prepare. If you cannot pay, however, we will have no choice but to revoke your license and inform the authorities you are selling your wares illegally."

"All I'm asking for is an extension," the woman began, holding her children close. "We do not even have food to eat let alone wares to sell. After my husband died last year, I had to auction everything except the building itself to repay his debts. Sir, we have nothing but the clothes on our back. But given time and a loan I can reopen our store, and through hard work and the grace of the Guardians, I will—"

Aleksi kept walking and approached a group of young men sitting at a nearby table. Each of the men held a metal mug with a different crest stamped on its front. Far too many people today had already taken notice of the deep green of his eyes, so Aleksi kept his hood up to conceal their color as he spoke.

"Excuse me, good sirs, do any of you know of an apothecary specializing in remedies which hail from the Northern Continent?"

"What fool would ever choose Northern tinctures over the far-superior Eastern extracts?" one of the men answered with a laugh.

"Well, that's obvious," another of the men retorted. "The same fool rude enough to address us with his hood raised."

"I mean no disrespect," Aleksi answered, pulling back his hood and clenching his bandaged fist as a wave of frustration flooded through him. "I am but a traveler from Simn, looking for a remembrance of my Northern home." Aleksi knew the men now would be able to see the green of his eyes, which would add legitimacy to his asking. He just hoped it was worth the risk.

The young men looked at Aleksi disdainfully and shook their heads. "Sorry, lad," one of the men said. "Here in Devdan we have no need for anything from the North." Several of the other men grumbled their agreements. "No *green eyes* in this guild. Not now, not ever."

A frown spread across Aleksi's face and he clenched his fist tighter. "Please excuse me, then." Aleksi turned and headed for the magistrate's booth. Before the youth could take more than a step, however, an old man seated at another table cleared his throat and pointed to the ceiling.

"Oh, Katar," the man said gruffly, shaking his raised finger, "if only your knowledge of guild history were as strong as your bigotry." The men at Katar's table looked at the old man over their drinks. The old man then pointed his finger higher and shook his head disapprovingly. The men's gazes rose to the banners above.

"Indeed, we do have an apothecary specializing in Northern wares," the old man continued. "It's that one there. The hand clutching an orb of green light. It was called the Emerald Promise." Many of the young men at the table were now nodding. Katar, however, lowered his head over his mug. "Eamon was the owner's name. He defected from the North a good many years ago."

"Thank you, sir," Aleksi said in a careful tone. "Where can I find Eamon and his shop?"

"Oh, I'm sorry, lad," the old man said, shaking his head. "I was not clear. Yes, *he is* part of the guild; once a member, always a member. Unless you're expelled, that is." The old man shot a scolding glance at Katar. "But Eamon died just a few years after the Vai'kel Unification War, if memory serves."

Aleksi's heart sank.

"His shop is still there, though, somewhere down an alley on Parmenth Street, although I'm not exactly sure which one. The sign still hangs proudly, though, of that I'm sure. Although it is a little dirty now, I'd wager."

"After all this time the shop is still there?"

"'Tis guild law," the old man chuckled. "If there is a death, the guild magistrate waits ten years for a next of kin to claim the shop and repay any debts. The guild pays the land taxes in the meantime, which are meager here in Old City. If it's unclaimed after the ten, it belongs to the guild. It's a pretty good deal they have worked out for themselves."

"How can I find the exact address of the Emerald Promise?"

The old man tapped his nose. "If an old-timer like myself can't remember, your only option is to ask the magistrate tomorrow morning to open the official Runic ledger and look."

". . . Tomorrow?" Once again, Aleksi felt anxiety clutch his heart. "It can't be done sooner?"

"The magistrate has gone home for the day in preparations for tonight's festivities." The old man eyed Aleksi carefully, causing the youth to avert his gaze. "Come to think of it, I think the shop's ten years are just about up. Where did you say you were from again? You wouldn't happen to be next of kin, would you?"

"No," Aleksi said, pausing uneasily. "A . . . teacher of mine told me to speak with Eamon, nothing more. Thank you for your time, sir. Please excuse me." Aleksi made a bow to the old man and quickly replaced his hood before turning on his heel and walking toward the door.

Aleksi soon found that Parmenth Street was one of the longest in the entire city, second only to the main boulevard itself. This street, however, instead of going straight, wound around and merged with other streets in a weaving, patternless mess. Aleksi wished he could have gotten better directions at the Apothecary Guild but also hadn't wanted to draw any more attention than he already had.

Along the way, Aleksi asked others on Parmenth Street if they knew of an apothecary named the Emerald Promise. Sadly, no one seemed to know what he was talking about, and after they realized he was not going to buy anything, they shooed him away.

Aleksi quickened his pace angrily. The jagged cobblestones were another difference from Guardians' Plaza, and despite his sturdy boots, they made walking very uncomfortable. To make matters worse, Aleksi knew he did not have much time before the Zenith's rays would begin to grow dim. With no wae'yrr trees here in Old City, he would have to move quickly if he wanted to search by light.

Dusk descended as the Zenith's light dimmed into a soft ocher glow. Continuing to walk down Parmenth Street, Aleksi saw two gaunt children playing by the side of the road. They were covered in dirt, wore tattered clothes, and had two sticks and a round rock. They hit the rock back and forth with the sticks until a woman, presumably their mother, walked up to them. In the fading light, Aleksi recognized her by her worn patchwork dress. He watched as she removed a crusty loaf of bread from her bag and the children sprang up eagerly.

Seeing its small size, however, one of the children began to cry. The woman tried her best to soothe the child as she broke the bread in half. By the way the young ones devoured it, the bread was likely the only food they had had all day. The suffering of the broken family cut deeply into Aleksi's chest. He was unsure, however, which pained him more: to see the children go hungry, or to see a mother in such a desperate situation still display so much kindness and determination.

Has High Arkai Mindra truly forsaken those who need him most? What divine justice has brought this family to such poverty and ruin— brought this mother to such destitution?

Aleksi reached into his pocket and pulled out a black pearl. Even though the light was quickly fading, he could clearly see the pearl's multicolored Runes shimmer across its surface like oil on water. This pearl was of a low "stack," signifying its low concentration and worth. Despite this, it was more than enough to not only provide food for the mother and her children for months, but also pay her debt to the Apothecary Guild with money left over for supplies. Aleksi twisted the pearl between thumb and forefinger and Runicly split the stacked pearl into ten new pearls of a lesser concentration. Each was of the exact same size as the original but possessed a lighter Runic color and lower one-tenth stack denomination. One of the new pearls could easily feed the family for over a month but would not provide enough for the woman to reopen her store and regain the ability to truly provide for her children.

The Academy teaches that a Master's role is to protect, for the weak fall prey to the powerful. And yet, at the Academy they cull the weak in order to fortify Terra's strength against the encroaching darkness. But is this justice not the same that they teach against—is it not grounded only in the interest of power? What of those who do not fight the darkness by wielding a sword in battle? What truly is strength? Is it not this family whom the Masters should protect and nourish the most? Is not this woman's strength—the power of love and determination—an even greater power against the Dark Ones?

Before he had left the Academy, Aleksi had gone to great lengths to take these pearls from the vast stores sequestered away in the Eastern Academy vaults. They were all he had but more than enough for his journey to Vai'kel. As he weighed the ten new pearls in his hand, he looked over at the mother and children. Their paltry dinner was now gone and the second child had begun to cry as well. Aleksi's heart ached and a tear slid down his cheek. The woman sat down by the side of the road and held her children close to her chest, rocking back and forth as she whispered gentle words. Closing his fist around the cluster of black pearls and causing them to Runicly reform back into their original stacked orb, Aleksi took a deep breath and walked across the cobblestones to her.

All have forsaken this family—their city, their guild, and even their Arkai. The Masters claim to use their power to serve the people, but they are no different than the rest. They clutch at power for power's sake . . . Well, I refuse to live my life at the expense of others. There must be another way, and I will find it!

Bathed in the last of the Zenith's artificial red twilight, Aleksi stopped before the woman and extended his hand and the pearl— offering her all the money he had. "May Mindra's blessing be bestowed upon you and yours."

Startled, the woman bolted up and stood motionless as her children clung to her ragged dress. Although tears still ran from their wide eyes, both children were now quiet and scared. The woman's eyes flashed from the iridescent black pearl in Aleksi's outstretched palm to his sword, and finally settled on Aleksi's hooded green eyes. Holding her children close, the woman took an uneasy step backward.

Aleksi could feel both her desperate desire to take the pearl and also her deep apprehension and fear. He extended his hand farther, saying, "Earlier today you called upon the grace of the Guardians. Please consider this as a gift given freely from the Arkai—nothing more."

Just as the woman was about to take another step backward, the dying light of the Zenith reflected off a nearby window and shone onto Aleksi's freshly tearstained face. As she saw the pain and compassion in Aleksi's watering eyes, the mother's fear evaporated. Releasing her children, she rushed to Aleksi and embraced him. Unsure of what to do, Aleksi stood motionless as she held him tightly.

"Wherever she is now," the woman said, pressing her cheek against Aleksi's chest, "I know your mother is very proud of you. Thank you, son. Thank you . . ."

Something inside of Aleksi crumbled and tears ran down his face. As the woman continued to hold him close, Aleksi gently placed his arms around her. He then felt his chest heave as he silently sobbed. Aleksi could not remember a single thing about his mother, let alone the last time anyone had held him.

After some time, the woman released him, and after giving her the black pearl, Aleksi nodded a silent farewell. As darkness overcame the sky and stars twinkled overhead, Aleksi left the family and continued on for hours as if wandering in a daze.

Aleksi shook his head. The night was dark and he was utterly lost. He was covered in a sheen of anxious sweat despite the cool evening breeze off the water. The youth felt his heartbeat pounding in his skull painfully. His entire body ached and his feet throbbed with every step. Although his bandaged palm hurt most of all, its Runic light had long since grown dark.

Around him only a few of the neighboring buildings were lit, and poorly at that. One of Terra's moons had risen, but it lay low on the horizon. The tall buildings of Guardians' Plaza obscured its soft blue light. By now, Aleksi was so deep into Old City that it felt like a forsaken barrow of the dead. Nearly all of the buildings' windows were broken, and many of the adjacent doors were boarded up. As Aleksi stalked on, the only sounds he heard were his own boots on the cobblestones and the rough breath in his chest.

Angrily, Aleksi threw back his hood. He knew he should stop, calm his mind, and ease his agitation. Or at least, find some food or water—he had hardly eaten all day, and his head hurt terribly from dehydration. But instead of stopping, Aleksi felt his body move of its own volition, searching restlessly for the apothecary. He had nowhere else to go and nothing to return to. He also had little time left if Rudra was to be believed. He *needed* to find the Emerald Promise, and soon. Fueled by pure desperation, he willed his body to continue and he searched on.

What seemed like hours later, Aleksi entered an intersection where half a dozen streets, lanes, and alleys all came together in a jumbled disaster. Aleksi threw up his arms in exasperation. He had been going in circles! The moons had fully risen and now illuminated the dirty streets in an eerie blue light. The youth was beyond tired and his body was fueled by restless delirium.

Looking about, Aleksi saw that there were sporadic trash piles on the side of the road next to slumped bodies huddled in the alleyways. Aleksi hoped they were just sleeping. Other than those sprawled on the ground, he had hardly seen anyone in the past several hours of searching these back alleys. The thought of tripping over a corpse made his empty stomach churn painfully.

In a brief moment of clarity, Aleksi realized everyone must be in Guardians' Plaza enjoying Mindra's Festival. The youth let out a caustic laugh. They all were drinking and celebrating, while he, and those too feeble to walk, haunted the back alleys of what felt more like a crypt than a city!

Taking a deep breath to calm his mind, Aleksi turned his face up to the sky. Closing his eyes, he said a desperate prayer to the moons, Rahu and Ketu. He felt their blue light shine softly upon his face. Sadly, he felt no divine inspiration or heavenly guidance.

Walking again, he turned right and went down another alleyway he hoped he had not yet explored. When he came to an intersection, he then went right again and continued down a slightly wider thoroughfare. His knuckles grew white clutching his blade's scabbard, and he pushed on. His body burned and his head ached, but there was no stopping. If he did not find whatever Rudra had sent him here for, all would be lost.

Just as Aleksi felt the urge to backtrack, he turned a corner and suddenly stopped; across the street stood the sagging remains of an old shop. Its windows were dark and its worn sign hung loosely above a boarded-up door. Aleksi crossed the street, unconsciously holding his breath.

He then saw it—the faded image of an upturned hand with a ball of green light inside its grasp. Despite the dirt on the carved sign, he could read the painted words clearly by the light of the moons: THE EMERALD PROMISE.

Aleksi let out a great sigh of relief that seemed to echo throughout the dark alley.

CHAPTER IV

Beck sighed as he watched Arva Vatana approach the officials' side gate to Mindra's Temple. Bathed in moonlight, the horse lord was followed by an orderly phalanx of his own Pa'laer bodyguards and the High Council Honor Guard dispatched to protect him. As the men came closer, Beck nodded to the sentries manning the temple's interior gate. They, too, were keenly eyeing Arva and his armed entourage. At Beck's command, however, the large gate slowly swung open with the sound of creaking metal.

Arva let his gaze drift across the manicured temple gardens as the gate opened upon grounds separated from the public parks. The officials' entrance was reserved for the council and other officers of state, and was surrounded by gardens of the highest quality. Beck assumed the Pa'laer horse lord was not used to such extravagances on his vast plains across Devdan's sea channel.

Beck cleared his throat and walked up to Arva. The Pa'laer lord still sat astride his stallion, and as he saw Beck a small contemptuous smile spread across the horse lord's lips.

"Lord Vatana," Beck said, slightly bowing his head. "I trust the tour of the city was to your liking?" Beck paused, but Arva did not respond. The large man's eyes fixed on Beck's scar, and his smile deepened. Beck's tone grew icy as he continued. "Mehail Bander, Chair of the

High Council, will greet you in the Council Hall. Please dismount and follow me."

Unwavering atop his horse, Arva continued to eye Beck as a Pa'laer guard approached. The soldier placed a steady hand on his lord's warhorse and Arva dismounted with surprising grace. Arva hardly acknowledged the other man's existence as he handed off the reins and strode toward the temple.

Beck grimaced. A man's decency could easily be known by how he treated his vassals. Turning, Beck led the small group under a large archway into the foyer entrance. As they approached, two sentries opened the temple's wide doors and saluted. Beck nodded to each man as he passed. They entered in silent procession and the doors closed behind them.

Illuminated by innumerable ever-burning lamps and a tremendously long chandelier, the column of men walked up the formal circular staircase known as Magistrate's Gallery. The many-story stairwell was wide and steep as it corkscrewed its way into the temple's heights. Deep-navy rugs stitched with ornate golden embroidery covered its steps, and paintings of renowned Eastern officials from ages past adorned the walls. The pictures hung in lavish golden frames that reflected the flickering flames of the chandelier that cascaded from ceiling to floor.

The Pa'laer men and the High Council Honor Guard remained a respectful distance behind Beck and Arva as they climbed past the looming faces of the long-dead Devdan magistrates. After slowly ascending to the cylindrical room's peak, the group emerged into the Officials' Hall. Breaking across the threshold, Arva paused and looked up at the great embossed golden ceilings. Hung with more chandeliers and embossed with silver mosaics to mimic the starry sky, the hall's dome caught the eye of all who entered.

Beck waited a moment before leading the group on through the cavernous expanse. The sound of the men's boots echoed against the arched ceiling as they strode on solemnly. After crossing the chamber, they went up another winding staircase and finally came to two large doors gilded with elaborate flowers. The doors opened up into one of the most famed possessions of Mindra's Haven, the Night Gardens.

To get to the Council Hall, one had no choice but to walk through these gardens and bear witness to their splendor. The flowers, and the large garden beds where they rested, were a renowned gift left by the Guardians. The blossoms that grew from these beds were the only ones of their kind in all of Terra, or so the scholars said. A "teaching gift," the luminescent Zenith dwellers had called them, given to help the council members contemplate their duty, role, and station.

Some of Beck's fondest childhood memories were in this elaborate garden. Beck's father, a former High Councilman, had often brought Beck to these gardens in his youth. Beck assumed his father had done it to inspire him to follow in his father's footsteps of leading the people of Mindra's Haven. And while some might say Beck had done just that, Beck often mused that his leading them into battle had not been his father's intention.

Beck opened the doors himself. Entering into the gardens, the group came upon rows and rows of elegant flowers surrounding a long marble path. In the middle of the room was an ornately carved fountain bubbling in the silence. Overhead, a crystal-domed ceiling was seemingly open to the sky above. During the Zenith's light of day, the room was pretty, but nothing particularly unique. At night, however, anyone could see that the garden's blossoms were spectacular. For under the light of the stars, the flowers of the Night Gardens bloomed and died in rapid succession over the span of mere seconds.

As a child, Beck thought it was incredible. If he came in the afternoon, the flowers would remain stoic and unchanging for hours and hours. But as dusk approached, the flowers would wilt, die, and then bloom anew right before his eyes. He could clearly recall the childish sadness he felt watching their petals fall to the ground, and then the eager excitement when a new bud would instantly grow underneath. Now, walking down the garden's path with Arva close in tow, Beck felt a measure of tension release from his body. It was impossible to not be affected by the flowers and their strange dance of death and rebirth.

"I have been to Mindra's Haven . . ." Arva recited the old saying softly, breaking his silence for the first time. The large man stopped at the splashing fountain and looked at the blossoms for a long moment. "I thought it was only a myth, but they are truly amazing."

"Indeed, they are," Beck responded, watching Arva's face closely.

"It begs one to wonder, however . . ." Arva paused as he picked up a newly wilted petal and watched it disintegrate in his fingertips. Brushing the dust from his hands, the large man looked at Beck. "What do you suppose the Guardians were trying to tell us?"

Beck watched the flowers bloom and die around them. The only sound in the room was the splashing water of the fountain. "If you are interested in such things, we have many scholars who have devoted their lives to that very question. I'm sure they would be happy to explain their theories—"

"I'm sure their answers would be fascinating and well versed," Arva interrupted Beck curtly. "But I am not asking them, General Beck Al'Beth, I am asking *you*."

Beck held the other man's gaze for a long moment before looking to the stars above. "I'm sure the Guardians' message was several fold, Lord. But if these flowers have taught me anything, it is that . . ." Beck met Arva's eyes with intensity. "We humans are not as important as we like to think."

Arva slowly smiled.

After several silent moments, the men exited the Night Gardens and continued walking. Moving through a wide carpeted vestibule lined by lanterns, they came to a large golden-ceilinged antechamber. As they approached the great double doors that led into the High Council's meeting rooms, Beck saw a platoon of High Council Honor Guard standing at attention next to a platoon of soldiers from Farden.

Beck nodded to both captains as he continued forward. Pushing the doors open, Beck could hear voices coming from within the grand chamber. Inside were Mehail Bander, Jaiden Zeer, and High Priest Trailen Kaftal. They were seated at a large table with an empty chair. The hall about them was exquisite. It had smooth marble floors wrought with gold inlay and a vaulted ceiling of crystal that clearly showed the moons and stars above.

Pausing at the door, Beck locked eyes with Mehail. Mehail stood and smoothed out his long councilor's jacket. Mehail's coat was made of a sheer grey material with modest gold inlay on the cuffs and low collar. It was unbuttoned, showing a formal yet unpretentious white shirt and grey pants beneath. Around his neck, Mehail wore an intricate pendant necklace of finely wrought metal. Other than the pendant, his attire was modest, which only did more to accentuate his striking features. Beck had never met a leader who commanded attention like Mehail. Within minutes of meeting the Chair of the High Council, people would do exactly as he told them to, thinking all the while it had been their idea in the first place.

Standing next to Mehail, Trailen Kaftal, High Priest of the Eastern Order of the Arkai, smiled at the newcomers. The priest wore ornate golden robes befitting his position and had long silvery hair that shone in the moonlight that cascaded down from the crystal ceiling above. Cinched at the waist by a belt of woven silver, his robes gracefully eddied about his body as they flowed down to the marble floor. Unarguably, he was the most powerful man in the room. One of Trailen's many duties was overseeing Mindra's Temple, and he was at these meetings to moderate and speak on behalf of the Eastern Guardians. Trailen was one of six living people to have a Rune that directly connected him to a High Arkai, thereby allowing him to possess a sliver of the being's mysterious power. The Rune was clearly visible on Trailen's brow now, penetrating deeply into the flesh of the man's forehead. His smile was warm, but guarded, as if he understood a difficult truth few others could comprehend.

At the other end of the table, Jaiden Zeer stood as well. Strikingly beautiful, she wore a long-sleeved black dress over black leggings and high boots. Inlaid with subtle dark-green scrollwork, the dress was both elegant and functional, with sleeves hanging over the backs of her hands, supposedly concealing two long daggers on either forearm. Matriarch of the Eastsouthern forests of Farden, Jaiden was said to be a perfect example of her people: she was extremely thoughtful and reserved, but when provoked, her wrath could be quite devastating.

This will be a tough group to find peace with, Beck thought as he and Arva approached the table in the center of the large chamber.

"Welcome, Lord Arva Vatana," Mehail said, spreading his arms wide. "I hope General Beck Al'Beth kept you entertained on your way here."

"He is a very cordial man, Mehail," Arva said with a thin smile. "In addition, he showed great wisdom by accepting my bodyguard requirements. Only on equal ground will peace be found in Devdan."

"I could not agree more. General Beck, please have the temple's fire lit to let the citizens know that we have begun."

Beck bowed deeply to Mehail and turned back toward the doors.

"Oh, and General: one more thing." Mehail came over and put his hand on Beck's shoulder. Together they walked halfway to the door. Mehail paused and carefully removed his necklace. Holding the intricate pendant in his palm, Mehail closed his eyes for a moment. When he spoke again, his tone was much quieter. "Take this for me, my friend. I no longer have need of it."

"My Lord, I've never seen this off of your neck."

Mehail had once told Beck that the pendant was a gift from the High Priestess of the Southern Order of the Arkai. He had been told that the pendant, given to Mehail when he was only a child, was an ancient Runic relic. It was not a gift given lightly, then or now.

"It might just be an old trinket," Mehail said, smiling, "but I've always felt safe wearing it."

"Lord, I cannot take this from you." Beck's voice was low, but there was intensity in his words. "We both know it is *no* trinket, and you need it now more than ever."

"You must take it, Beck. I cannot enter these meetings with thoughts of the old times plaguing my mind. Wars have been won and lost by the two leaders behind me. Our friends and countrymen have fallen to their blades and arrows for countless years. Sadly, these are not easy things to forget." Mehail's eyes traced the scar on his general's right cheek. "Despite this, I've prayed for peace my whole life. And now, with unification within my grasp, I cannot carry any lingering remembrance of the past which might threaten my blossoming hope for the future."

Beck looked down as Mehail placed the pendant into his palm. Mehail then closed Beck's fingers around the necklace. After gripping Beck's hand, he turned to walk back toward the others.

"Lord." Beck reached out and grasped Mehail's arm. "I still do not think it was wise to agree to Arva's demands."

"As you know, the High Council's eventual vote was unanimous, and with the Bankers Guild's looming insolvency, our decision is backed by the majority of the other Guilds, too."

"Eventual? So the *usual* voices in the council were able to sway all others?"

"Yes, both Councilman Larrl and Berath strongly urged us to agree to Arva's terms. But they have always wanted peace in our realm."

"Is it peace they have wanted, or capitulation to Asura's Northern Empire?"

"Beck," Mehail said with a sigh, "there comes a time when one must put down the warrior's sword so a palm can be opened in friendship and trust."

"Lord, I trust you and Adhira's solders with my life."

"Then trust me now and trust in the wisdom of Adhira's Council."

"Even if they can be trusted, without my men in the city we will be defenseless if something happens. If *anything* happens. There is a difference between trust and recklessness, Lord." Beck paused, weighing his words. "Mehail, no one will know if I bring several legions over the channel by the cover of night. With those extra men, we would be prepared if—"

Mehail placed a reassuring hand on Beck's arm, silencing him. "Nothing is earned without risk, my old friend. *Nothing.*"

Aleksi stood in the dark and stared at the apothecary's boarded door. The planks that barred the entrance looked old and half-rotted. The store's windowpanes were covered in a thick layer of grime and Aleksi wiped his hand over the hazy glass. Inside, the building was dark and dirty, possessing a few pieces of cloth-covered, decrepit furniture. The bookshelves were empty and there was nothing else distinguishable inside the otherwise barren room. There was no grand answer and no shining light at the end of the tunnel—only dust and memories held by people long dead.

I finally found it, Aleksi thought bitterly, *but what for? What am I supposed to do now?* Closing his eyes to fight back tears, the youth felt his gut tighten. The pain rekindled a sadness both familiar and raw.

Aleksi's last memory of Rudra flashed before his eyes. Bathed in the early morning light of the Zenith, the black-hooded silhouette of his once-beloved Master was walking away from the Eastern Academy in exile. The Masters had tried to execute Rudra after his trial, but Rudra's Runic power was too great and the council, unable to slay him, was forced instead to condemn the Southern Master to exile in Vai'kel. Although Rudra's final words to Aleksi had been a whisper, they had rung in the youth's ear like a deafening blast. "Do not be afraid, my Apprentice, for I will come back for you." It was five years ago that Rudra had been banished, and the memory was forever engraved in Aleksi's mind.

Where are you, Rudra? Aleksi felt his body tense with resentment and anger. *Why would you send me here for nothing? You wanted me to find what? This rotting store? Why didn't you come back for me like you promised! Why?*

The boy rested his head on the door of the dead apothecary. A silent tear ran down his cheek. Aleksi's breath was heavy and it blew back hot on his face. *What am I supposed to do? Break into this damn place and rummage through the drawers? I risked everything for you, Rudra . . .*

Through teary eyes, Aleksi looked up at the glowing stars. His throat was tight and his chest ached. *Why did you have to leave me?* Aleksi sucked in air through gritted teeth and clenched his fists.

"Why?" Aleksi felt himself punch the door. "Why? Why? Why?!" Aleksi struck the door harder and harder. On the final blow, he felt the wood splinter beneath his strike.

Aleksi stared down at a small trickle of blood dripping from his hand.

"To receive such punishment," a weathered voice casually said from behind Aleksi, "that door must have wronged you greatly."

Aleksi spun and his left hand flashed to the sheath of his blade as his right grasped its hilt. Aleksi saw an older man dressed in rags leaning against a building across the alley. He was slumped on the cobblestones and wrapped in a torn cloak. His eyes were a milky grey green and unfocused, and his face was spotted with unkempt scruff. A bottle lay in the man's lap—he was the epitome of unthreatening.

Aleksi shook his head and took a deep, ragged breath. "I'm sorry to have disturbed you, sir." Dropping his hand from his sword, Aleksi turned away. "Please excuse me—"

"I'm the one who's sorry, my boy," the man responded before Aleksi could take a step.

Although rough, the old man's voice was strong, despite his ragged attire. Free of a beggar's cant, his tone filled the empty alleyway and rang out as if it had once commanded attention and respect, albeit a very long time ago.

Aleksi turned around to face the man. His green eyes seemed to stare past Aleksi. *He's blind.* Taking a step forward, Aleksi could see that this man was no common vagabond. A drunkard, yes, but not the common drifter trash he had heard about at the Academy. Upon closer inspection, Aleksi noticed that although disheveled, the man was mostly clean. His clothes were free of stains or smell, and what had appeared to be common rags upon first glance was in fact an old military uniform from the Vai'kel Unification War. Any further details, however, were impossible to tell from its frayed state.

"Why are you here, old man?" Aleksi asked, his voice growing soft. "Do you have nowhere else to sleep other than the street?"

"Ha! Without anger like yours," the old man chuckled, "I bet I sleep better than you do, no matter where I lay my head. Come closer, boy, you sound like a youth with a purpose. What is it, I wonder, so late at night? Why are *you* here?"

"My purpose is my own," Aleksi said sharply, wiping the tearstains from his face.

The old man's thin lips stretched into a slight smile. "Ah, the joys of youth. So full of passion and purpose, and yet possessing so few manners . . ."

Aleksi's jaw tightened and he widened his stance, causing his right boot to make a slight scraping sound on the cobblestone.

"Easy now, son. No need to take offense. My Lord used to have a saying, 'Only a fool hears truth and becomes offended.' I take it that you are young, but no fool."

Aleksi remained silent.

"If you're looking for the owner of this apothecary, his name was Eamon. He died some years ago. He was a good man, generous and fair. He took me in after . . ." The old man then took a swig from his bottle and said no more.

"You know about this apothecary?" Aleksi asked carefully. "You knew the owner?"

"Indeed, I did, and quite well. He said my blindness was curable, although I never believed him. But he never believed how I was blinded, so fair's fair, I suppose."

Aleksi ran a shaky hand through his long hair. "I . . . I was told to come here, to find this place . . . I don't know why."

The old man precariously rose to his feet. Steadying himself on the wall behind him, he took an uneasy step forward. Aleksi leaned back in reflex, once again placing a hand on the hilt of his sword.

"No need for that, I just wish to *see* you." The old man slowly put his hands on Aleksi's face. They were soft and their touch was soothing.

The old man first felt Aleksi's cheeks and forehead, then his jaw, nose and eyes. "Saven?" The old man whispered. "No, impossible . . . Then you must be—" Suddenly, the old man gasped, jerking his hand away as if scorched by a flame. Stumbling back, he braced his hands in front of him as if expecting an attack. Aleksi took a confused step away as the old man cried out, "I'm sorry! I'm *so sorry!*"

"What? What are you—"

"I . . . I did everything I could," the old man stammered. "We never had a chance against him! *No one* did!"

"What? Against *who*? What are you talking about?"

The old man reached into his cloak and removed a half-broken pendant from beneath his shirt. "I . . . I always knew you both survived . . ." he said between gasps. "No one believed me, but I always knew he didn't kill you . . . Not even *he* could kill infants."

Tears were now openly streaming down the man's face. Seeing tears come from blind and unfocused eyes sunken in a face so full of memories and anguish disturbed Aleksi deeply.

"Who are you?" Aleksi asked softly. "What are you saying?"

The old man thrust the damaged pendant out and fumbled it into Aleksi's hand. Split down the middle and strung on a chain, half of a pendant choker rested weightlessly in his palm. What remained was carved with intricate Runes. It looked like a House Rune, but with half of the Rune missing, it was impossible to know for sure.

"Take it, boy. It is yours. Your *birthright . . .*"

The material was a matte black and like nothing Aleksi had seen even in the Masters' Academy. At its severed center, a circular black stone was split in half and somehow was miraculously suspended at the pendant's former core. The stone was solid like steel, but its surface was soft like leather. Somehow, Aleksi felt as if he remembered the touch of it. Distant and hazy, the memory floated in his mind and then disappeared. Try as he might to recall it, however, the sensation faded away like he had imagined it in a forgotten dream.

"Which one are you, I wonder?" the old man said. "No, it doesn't matter." Suddenly, he stood up and tried to leave.

"Wait!" Aleksi grabbed the man's arms with a power stronger than his years. "You *must* answer my questions. Where did you get this? What does this have to do with the apothecary and *how* do you know who I am?"

The old man winced as pain and guilt spread across his face. "No, not the apothecary. That's my story, not yours. But yours is not mine to tell. You must find your truth for yourself. Please forgive me, young lord . . ." The old man went weak in the knees and was held up only by Aleksi's firm grasp.

Aleksi slowly released his grip and the old man slid down the wall and hunched over on the cobblestones. Aleksi looked down at the pendant. A strange feeling clung at his heart. "Tell me, please," Aleksi whispered, kneeling down beside the man. "Did you know *my father*?"

The man wiped his eyes on his sleeve and raised his head. "Yes. It was he whom I served. Until Terra's Bane . . ." The man shook his head. "It is a miracle you survived . . ."

"Terra's Bane . . ." Aleksi murmured. "I've heard stories, but my Master never told me what truly happened."

"You must go to Vai'kel to find your answers. Follow the great scar of Terra's Bane to its end. In the valley of Vandeen's Grove you will find"—a look of nausea passed over the old man's face—"you will find the ruins of a cursed house. Although once beloved, it fell to darkness. And then, by the hands of the Howler, it met its death." The old man raised his hand as if to touch the boy's face again. "But you live . . . and your house is dead no longer!" A wide smile spread across his face, giving contrast to his wrinkled and tearstained cheeks.

"So, not for the apothecary . . . ," Aleksi whispered. "You are why Rudra sent me here—"

The old man cried out as if kicked in the stomach. Stammering, he fearfully pushed himself across the cobblestones, trying to get away from Aleksi. "That's why he took you . . . He claimed you for atonement? And now he has sent you here to enact your revenge!"

"You have nothing to fear, old man. I mean you no harm."

"*Fear*?" the old man cried, raising his voice. "Even the High Lord Asura fears that one!" The old man looked up, his dead eyes penetrating through Aleksi. "For even the *High Arkai themselves* fear the Howler!" The old man fumbled his way to his feet as he continued. "And so should you, Lord, for it was he who broke the world! It was he who—" The man stopped speaking suddenly and, frantically tracing his hands along the sides of the wall, ran away down the alley, falling over himself in his haste.

Aleksi slowly stood. His green eyes were unfocused and his mind was elsewhere. *Let the wounded blindly run away from his fears . . .*

After several long moments, Aleksi walked back up the alleyway. His bandaged and white-knuckled fist gripped the broken pendant. As he continued through the darkness, the sound of his boot heels rang in the cavern of his heart.

CHAPTER V

Pulling his hooded cloak farther over his face, Beck allowed himself to meld into the flowing crowds of Guardians' Plaza. Each year, the general was amazed at the sheer number of people that flooded the main boulevard for the festival night. Passing locals and foreigners alike, he saw citizens from every walk of life enjoying the festivities and splendors of the evening.

Weaving his way around the masses, Beck passed a group of bare-chested Western sailors. With icy-blue eyes, thick arms, large tanned chests, and long Zenith-bleached hair, the men were truly an impressive sight. A few paces behind and trying to seem inconspicuous, three local girls followed them. No doubt the girls would shadow the men to a bar or inn and try to find their way onto their laps and into their purse strings.

Continuing on past a rugged group of soldiers from Pa'laer, Beck felt grateful to be free of Arva Vatana. Arva, and the negotiations which were currently under way, had the possibility of bringing a new-found peace and military alliance between Adhira and its neighboring Eastern nations. However, if Devdan's age-old prejudices could not be healed, the negotiations would end in a deepening of the land's feudal discord—a circumstance that now left the entire continent weak to the great shadow of Asura's growing empire in the North.

After the Vai'kel Unification War, tensions emanating from the occupation of the Northern Empire's so-called Peacekeeping Forces had escalated. And over the course of the ten-year encampment, those tensions had spread across the map. With Asura's aspirations now broadening, the entire world was polarized: those who followed Asura, binding their will to his empire, and those who struggled to maintain their nation's Guardian-given independence. For despite conquering Vai'kel by force, Asura had used the political maneuvering of trade, treaty, and contract to bind Iksir and Kaymahn, the neighboring countries of Simn, to his mighty cause, thereby forming the largest empire Terra had ever known. And, having forged an alliance with several of the controlling factions of the Western Thalassocracy during the Unification War, Asura was steadily gaining control of Terra's major shipping lanes, too. It was now only a matter of time before Asura would use the naval might of the Western admirals to complete his growing monopoly over all international commerce in Terra.

Beck knew that once that was accomplished, Asura would undoubtedly impose greater tariffs and transport taxes with the aim to destabilize, and then eventually bankrupt Mindra's Haven. If Mehail, Arva, and Jaiden allowed that to happen, Asura could easily divide and overpower the bickering factions of the East, thereby claiming rulership over all of Devdan for himself. And if the East fell in line to Asura's drum, none would be able to withstand his mighty call. Even the High Lords of Neberu in their secluded cities to the South had to know that their strange lands, hidden by mountain, stone, and endless night, would not be far behind.

Beck spat in the street. Shaking his head of these troubling thoughts, the general continued on through the throng of people. Everyone around him seemed to be utterly unaware of the threat of destruction that hovered over their nation. Much to Beck's chagrin, the crowds were actually quite enjoying themselves. Men and women, both young and old, were eating, drinking, and dancing. Hawkers were showing their wares, and bards were singing tunes both classic and modern.

As Beck passed a large gathering, he heard a line from the ancient poem *Kalki Vanga* float over the din of the crowd.

"The incarnate darkness consumed all with its might;
Yet, bound not by fear, the Kalki sat upon the throne of
flame and cast forth the Zeniths' collective numinous light;
Purging from Terra that dark and evil blight . . ."

Beck frowned. Its translation into the common tongue butchered the verse terribly. It sounded so much better in the original prose, but now with the Guardian Age so long past, nearly none knew that ancient language except for the erudite few who could read Runes.

Suddenly, there was a collective gasp as a burst of flame erupted above the crowd. Instinctively, Beck spun around, drawing his sword in one swift motion. It was followed by an explosion of cheering and laughter, however, as the bard, standing atop a barrel, took a deep bow.

Fire breathing, Beck thought, as he sheathed his sword with a sigh. *Good thing Adler didn't see that. I would have never lived it down.* Beck then continued down the street, leaving behind several men and women who eyed him with a smile.

Beck was glad to have slipped away from the temple without his personal five-man guard. It was so rare for him to walk the streets alone. The feeling of melding into the throng of citizens as a civilian, with his rank of general unnoticed, was wonderful. Over the years, it had grown only more difficult for Beck to sneak off without alerting his sentries. And although they were completely loyal, there were times like tonight when Beck needed to act on his own. Adler, however, the most senior of his guard and captain of Beck's personal legion, constantly reminded Beck that it was his personal duty to protect his general. And this duty, more importantly, superseded any orders that Beck might give him. In the beginning, Adler had even tried posting guards inside Beck's personal bedchamber, relenting only when Beck said that his wife would surely kill them *both* if she could not sleep in peace.

Normally, there was just reason for his bodyguard to be present, and tonight even more so. With so many foreign soldiers in the city, no general should walk the streets alone unaccompanied by several swords. But tonight Beck had no choice, for this was no casual walk on a warm festival night. He was off to meet Domadred Steele, captain of the *Illusive Diamond* and single most notorious pirate in all the waters of Terra. Domadred, however, in addition to being outlawed in the Northern and Western Seas for thievery and smuggling, was also Beck's single most trusted friend, companion, and brother in arms.

The fact that Domadred was a hunted thief did nothing to affect Beck's respect for his comrade, for Domadred hadn't always been a pirate. Before Asura's maneuverings in the West, Domadred had argu- ably been the second most powerful admiral of the Western fleet, and many believed he had been next in line to become the prime admiral of the Western Thalassocracy. But, with his honor and pride stripped from him due to lies and deception, Domadred was forced to flee with his loyal crew and live a life of piracy and subterfuge on the high seas.

Snapping back to the present moment, Beck suddenly jumped to the side and dodged a large moving cart. The wagon looked to be laden with amala fruit from Farden, and its driver was obviously drunk on the festivities. Several other people on the street were not so lucky, however, and cursed as they fell to the cobblestones as the cart swept by. Beck shook his head. Festivals were always good for morale, but each year there were countless injuries from negligence or drunken debauchery. *All things have their price.*

Rounding a corner, Beck saw a group of street performers dressed in costume reenacting Mindra's historic battle with the Dark Ones. An obvious favorite during the night of the festival, the theatrical battle was enacted every year by numerous stage troupes throughout the city streets. Standing on high stilts and dressed in large multiperson cos- tumes, the performers would be split, half as Guardians and half as Dark Ones. The Guardians' costumes were covered in reflective mate- rials, mimicking their numinous light. And in stark contrast, the Dark Ones' costumes were jet black, painted with *kaala* coal from the mines of the South—a material that eerily soaked up all light around it. The troupers would mock fight in the streets as spectators cheered them on. As a boy, Beck used to love watching the shows. He always would cheer for High Arkai Mindra, who naturally had the most lavish of the costumes. Mindra was traditionally depicted as taller than the rest of the Guardians and had bright eyes that shone like gold. The Arkai would dance about with skill and grace as he held his mighty blade aloft, cutting a path through the Dark Ones in the street.

If only it were so easy. War between men is a terrifying thing. I can only imagine what it was like during the Guardian Age, fighting those horrible terrors.

Beck's gaze was then drawn to Mindra's Temple. Clearly visible above the city skyline, its central spire was truly magnificent. The orange fire in the temple's citadel still burned bright, pushing back the encroaching darkness.

Mehail, I hope you know what you are doing . . . Reaching under his shirt, Beck fingered the necklace given to him by his lord. Like everyone else, Beck could only wait for the temple's fire to turn blue, thus signaling that the three leaders had reached a decision and were ready to announce their verdict to the people. Whatever their decision was, it would decide the fate of all living on this curve of the world.

Eventually, Beck found the swinging sign of the Guardian's Flame hanging above him. According to local lore, this hotel was one of the oldest in Guardians' Plaza. It was also one of the few privately owned buildings in the East made of Guardian Stone—the seamless mineral that was said to be the Zenith dwellers' favored building material. Nearly all such buildings made of this secret stone were now owned, managed, and rented out by the state. Only a rare few were privately held, passed down through many generations back when the Dark Ones last treaded Terra with their black specter-like armies. Stranger still, the stone was said to have not been brought with the Guardians—instead, they manifested it into existence as needed. Such were the mysteries of Terra and her divine protectors.

Pushing through the large doors of the hotel, Beck was met with the extraordinary sight of a giant fireplace whose golden flame rose many stories high within the center of the building's expansive inner hall. This hall was long and cylindrical, hollowing out the center of the tall building, rising all the way to a crystal canopy overhead. Additionally, as the establishment's namesake, the hall's massive fireplace did not possess an ordinary flame, for it blazed no matter the season, gave off varying degrees of heat, and did not need standard fuel to burn. Most impressively, though, was the fire's great size and height—for the golden blaze rose past the hall's many floors of internal terraces and balconies as it licked its way up to the hall's lofty, crystal-domed ceiling.

As one of the many great wonders of Mindra's Haven, the grand circular hall was famous for not only possessing such a miraculous view but also having some of the best food in the city. Tonight, however, the hall's tables were nearly empty, for most were roaming the streets and enjoying the festival. Even so, Beck was sure that all rooms within the Guardian's Flame were booked. Drunken foreigners needed a place to rest their heads, especially if they entertained any hope of sharing that bed with someone sweet.

As Beck moved deeper into the hall, he felt the fire's fresh breath of air press against him. Somehow, it gave off different temperatures depending on the weather. Tonight, sensing the warmth outside, the golden flame gave off a cold breeze despite its ferocious size. Like most of the Guardians' works, its properties defied all logic and lasted through the ages as if not touched by the decay of time.

We should send an envoy to the Masters. If only we could use this power against Asura. But as soon as the thought arose, Beck dismissed it. The Masters' covenant, much like the Guardians', was not to interfere in world politics on any large political, social, or military scale. They believed that their might, so vast and powerful, would tip the tides, destroying the careful balance Terra had maintained for its many ages. Sadly, despite the fact that Asura had already broken that balance, no Master had yet to see reason to join the fight—except for one, *Master Rudra.*

A cold shiver ran along Beck's spine as he walked toward the inn's guest booth. *I still think that those who lead the Resistance are fools for trusting him. After what he did, I very much doubt he even trusts himself...*

Beck shook his head and looked around. Strangely, he saw no one at the entrance's guest booth to seat him. Scanning the tables, he noticed a young girl dressed in a short skirt and flame-embroidered jacket leaning against a table somewhat removed from the other guests. The girl was speaking with a hooded man who sat in an adjacent seat. She had a smile on her face, but her golden eyes spoke of a predator having found its prey.

"Carli, can't you see we have a guest?" The girl jumped at a voice that was both high and surprisingly loud even from across the hall. The young girl reluctantly turned to Beck and walked toward the hall's entrance. As she made her way over, she glanced back at the seated man, flashing him a mischievous grin.

"Welcome to the Guardian's Flame, sir," Carli said, now turning that same smile on Beck. "If you're looking for rooms, we are full tonight with the festival an' all. But we do have some space in the basement dormitories. They usually fill up on a first come, first served basis as patrons stumble in."

"No, thank you," Beck said. "I only wish a table."

"Oh my!" Suddenly, an older woman with a silver braid hanging below her waist came up to the booth. She wore a long grey dress with golden flame embroidery that swished around her legs as she walked. Although in her later years, the woman was elegant and possessed an ageless beauty. She gently pushed the young girl out of the way before continuing in a softer tone. "I didn't see it was you, my Lord. Welcome back to the Guardian's Flame."

"Katrina," Beck said, averting his eyes. "How are you? It seems things are quite busy with all the foreign traffic."

The hooded man at the table cleared his throat but Carli didn't seem to notice. She now had eyes only for Beck and the large scar that ran down his right cheek and crossed the corner of his mouth.

"Oh yes, quite busy," Katrina answered. "But I'm sure it's nothing compared to your duties, my Lord. What brings you here on such an occasion? Are you expecting company this evening?"

"I am only meeting one other, and he should be here soon." Beck lowered his voice and pulled his hood farther over his face. "I'm trying to be discreet."

"Oh, I know much about discretion," the woman said, eyeing Beck sideways as the general cleared his throat uncomfortably. "So, how are you?" Katrina continued. "It has been quite some time since I've seen you last. How are the kids, and Laiya? It must have been over three years since I have seen her. The poor thing was swollen with child, and I told her the name of the best midwife in town . . ."

In moments like this, Beck always wished a fight would break out near him. Anything was easier than trying to speak with Katrina and dodge her numerous references to their shared past. In Beck's mind, the ultimate goal was to withstand her onslaught long enough so as to be polite and then make a hasty retreat with the hope she would not rally.

After a few moments of trying to interject words edgewise and disengage, Beck noticed that Carli had once again gone back to the man in the corner. Seeing that he had Beck's attention, the man then lowered his hood, exposing his sharp beard, blue eyes, and Zenith-worn face. Domadred gave Beck a knowing smile and then winked at Carli.

"Katrina . . ." Beck sighed, turning his attention back to the hotel's owner.

"I remember the first time we met and that was before the scar on your face—"

"Katrina, I must—"

"You were just a young lieutenant, so full of honor and—"

"I must be going."

"Oh, and guess who is dining with us tonight? But I'm sure you were expecting him." Katrina then motioned back to Domadred, who now had Carli on his knee.

Beck sighed. "Oh my, you're right. Thank you, Katrina."

"Oh, of course, my dear." Her smile then faded as she looked over at them at the far table. "I hope he is careful, though. Carli's hands are as quick as a thieving magpie."

"Well, I'm sure whatever transpires," Beck said, "*she* will be the one surprised for it." Beck took her hand and Katrina's smile returned. Leaning in, the general softly gripped her arm and spoke under his breath. "Katrina, thank you for your hospitality, but more importantly, for your discretion."

"General Al'Beth," she answered with a slight smile, "all you must do is ask, for the Guardian's Flame is forever at your service. If you remember, my Lord, during the Red Riots . . ."

"Yes, yes," Beck said, nodding his head. "And I will forever be in your debt. But now I must go."

Finally breaking free, Beck made his way over to Domadred. Carli was still sitting on Domadred's knee and her hand was under his coat's lapel, idly stroking his chest. Domadred gave Beck a wide smile and squeezed the girl's bottom. Carli giggled.

Without sitting down, Beck cleared his throat and spoke. "Give it back, whatever you have taken. We have business to discuss."

Carli opened her mouth to protest. Upon her face was a look of feigned surprise.

Beck shook his head. "No, not *you*, girl. Him." Beck then pointed an accusing finger at Domadred, who in turn mimicked Carli's surprised expression. "He has pickpocketed you of whatever you have and has taken back whatever you tried to steal from him in the first place." A look of genuine surprise now washed over the girl's face.

"Oh, come now, Beck," Domadred protested, as his smile grew wider. "We were just having a little fun. Besides"—the captain patted Carli's bottom—"she started it."

Carli bolted up and her hands flashed to a secret pocket in her skirt. Finding it empty, her face turned bright red and she swung her palm to slap Domadred.

Domadred easily deflected the attack and deftly bounced her back down on his knee with a thud. "What's the matter, darling?" The captain laughed, jostling Carli on his knee. "You were enjoying yourself a moment ago when you stole my pearl pouch!"

Carli's eyes shone with golden anger and she exhaled sharply.

"Fine, fine," Domadred said, producing several black pearls and three large rings much too big to be her own. But as she stood up and took them, Domadred slapped her bottom with his other palm and Carli let out a screech. "You've got to watch *both* hands, my little bird. That's the trick."

She turned on her heel in a flurry, but before she could get away, Beck stopped her with a single word. "Wait." The general's voice was calm and low, but it commanded attention like only a leader of armies could master. "You have not been given leave to go."

Carli stopped to face him. Her eyes were downcast and genuine fear shone on her face. "My Lord," she whispered in an unsteady voice, "I—"

"All of it, Domadred, and make it quick. I don't have much time."

"My friend," Domadred said, "you know me far too well . . ." The sailor then produced a folded slip of paper seemingly out of thin air. The girl's face turned pale as terror washed over her. "It seems to be a secret letter, Beck. Shall we read it?"

Carli made a move as if she was going to grab the paper and run. But before she could, Beck put a firm hand on the base of her neck, keeping her in place. Through his grip, Beck could feel the girl tremble.

"No need to fret, darling," Domadred continued. "I have a feeling that the letter starts with 'By the coalition of Vai'kel's light, we stand firm against the Northern oppression.' Which means you're in good company."

The girl's eyes shot wide, her terror now replaced by shock. "Carli," Beck said, shaking his head, "the captain had you marked from the beginning. Your agent's message was meant for him. This is Domadred Steele, *the* Domadred Steele."

Carli blushed deeply, giving her most formal bow.

"No, no, dear. No need for that," Domadred laughed. "I'm glad to have made your acquaintance. You fit my knee well, and my hand fits your . . ."

Carli looked up from her bow and her eyes were angry once again.

"Well, thank you for the note," Domadred continued. "After I am finished with my friend, I will draft a response. If you like, you can help me with my penmanship . . ."

She bowed again, turning to leave. But as Carli walked away, she turned and looked back. Her smile had returned.

CHAPTER VI

As Beck sat, he began to open his mouth. Domadred, however, started talking before the general could speak.

"Katrina always surprises me," Domadred exclaimed. "She has a memory as long as the ocean straits! When I came in, she started recalling stories from nearly two decades ago verbatim. It's unbelievable! She really should be hired by the Hall of Chronicles. I'd bet she has a better memory than the prime chronicler *himself!*"

Ignoring his words, Beck leaned in and whispered fiercely, "Do you have any idea the disaster you could have created this morning with Arva Vatana on the docks?"

Domadred smiled. "But I didn't. More importantly, did you see Brayden? He played his part so beautifully. He even got one of Arva's rings! Someday, he will be better than his old man. Now that, Beck, *that* is what you should be worried about."

"Cursed by the Dark Ones!" Beck said, slamming his fist on the table. "If Arva Vatana recognized you . . . You've stolen enough of his goods to be a common name in his lands. I don't even want to tell you how much your head is worth in some circles!"

Domadred's eyes lit up and his smile grew wider. "With a well-orchestrated plan we could easily fake my capture and steal—"

"Domadred, this is not a joke! He would have had you killed on the spot and put your head on a pike for all to see!"

"But he did not," Domadred said nonchalantly. "Nor could he have, had he tried."

"And why is that?" Beck seethed. "Did you not notice he had an entire platoon at his back? He would have massacred you and your whole crew. The harbor would have run red with your blood."

"Impossible!" Domadred laughed. "For you never would have let that happen." Beck threw up his hands as the pirate continued. "More importantly, I know there are no odds we could not face together, my brother. Remember back during the Unification War? *Remember* the valley of Thurlow?" Domadred's eyebrow rose and Beck could not help but smile.

"Dom, you are too reckless. This is not a game, especially now."

"Oh, come on. Arva and his men are nothing to my charm and your . . . well, your hard work and determination."

"You take needless risks." Beck let out a great sigh. "You walk the precipice and someday you will slip. When that day comes, neither I nor anyone else will be able to catch you as you fall."

"We both know why I walk the path I do. Treacherous as it may be."

"You mean to say your chosen career of thievery?"

"It has little to do with choice, Beck. No matter how much you and your Eastern Council want to forget what happened after the war, we both were there. We both remember what Lenhal did to my men. What he did to . . ."

Domadred's words trailed off and Beck looked away. After a moment, Beck spoke.

"No matter our relationship, Domadred, you can't just keep sailing in here like this. None see you in your former glory. All they see now is an outlaw."

"A man of virtue remains as such, no matter how circumstance forces him to act."

Beck let out a sigh. "Your virtue would not protect your head from being rammed on a pike. There is no telling how much longer the Eastern Council will turn a blind eye to your presence. It pains me to say this, but things are not as they once were."

Domadred took a long drink from his mug. "Enough of this talk. Tell me of the Northern tariffs."

"They bleed us dry, but you know that. What is your point?"

"I had assumed the Eastern Council would never bend to forced orders from the North."

"Domadred, you know Asura controls taxes and trade within the Northern and Central Continents while also holding their armies in his hand. I am growing tired of your games. All know how dire this situation is. Why do you think these peace talks are so important? If the East is not united, we will *all* fall to Asura if he advances his forces."

A wide smile spread across Domadred's face. "It's not a matter of *if*, but *when*, which is all the more reason to join the Resistance, Beck."

"I wish it were so simple," Beck said, shaking his head.

"It truly is simple. Asura sends his agents across Terra and must be stopped. Surely you have felt his reaching tendrils here?"

"Not in Mindra's Haven, but there are rumors that Arva Vatana has entertained Northern ambassadors . . ."

"Arva is not to be trusted, Beck. Just look into his eyes. What more proof do you need?"

"Sadly, it gets worse." Beck fingered the necklace under his shirt. "Arva sent a letter to Mehail saying, 'With unequal numbers of men guarding us, how can we find the trust to build allegiance between our nations?' He insisted our guards be cut in half and our standing army be stationed on the far end of the southern bank before he would set *one foot* in Mindra's Haven."

Domadred's mouth fell open in astonishment. "Tell me Mehail didn't agree?"

"What choice did he have?" Beck grimaced and the scar on his cheek pulled tight.

"There is always a choice, Beck. The only thing which can lack is a man's will to make it."

"Well, the council believes we must unite, despite the risk. If the North invades, we face a force too great for a fragmented East to withstand. Now that Prime Admiral Lenhal has signed a treaty with Asura—committing nearly the entire force of the Western fleet to fight under the banner of the North—we truly *don't* have a choice."

Pain flashed in Domadred's eyes. "Lenhal has betrayed not just me but also my people. But fear not, in the coming months I will finally bring an end to his treachery."

"Rumor has it," Beck said, narrowing his eyes, "that Saiya Vengail, the newly proclaimed High Priestess of the Western Order of the Arkai, has gone missing. Don't tell me you had anything to do with that . . ."

"Then I won't say anything at all," Domadred said, then took a long drink from his mug. "Although I will mention I've heard the priestess has been found."

"I have heard no such thing," Beck said, carefully eyeing Domadred.

"Then tell me what rumors you have heard."

Beck ran a hand through his hair. "One story says Saiya tried to kill Lenhal and take control of the West for herself. Another says she has a fleet of great ships at her command ready to go to war on behalf of the Resistance. Oh, and a third tale says she seduced Asura and has become his queen of the Northern Empire."

"Oh my," Domadred laughed, "she's been busy for one so young. That last one seems a bit outlandish, though. You do know the priestess is celibate, don't you?"

"All I know," Beck answered, "is that Western forces are being used to search for her in unprecedented numbers. Reports say that even as we speak, there are numerous warship expeditions searching for her in the South."

"Indeed, I ran into one on my way here." Domadred took another sip from his mug. "What's left of it is now stationed in Kaamos for repairs."

"Well, I'm sure you are quite proud of yourself, then."

"Sadly, no. I had hoped to find Lenhal. Word has it that he has brought his personal convoy of ships to find his young priestess. My sources say he's combing over every port in the South searching for her. Little does he know, Saiya is not there."

"Don't tell me you know where she is?"

"Then I suppose I shouldn't tell you that she is resting quite comfortably in the hold of my ship."

"Are you mad?" Beck sputtered, nearly falling over in his chair.

Domadred shrugged. "No more than usual."

"So you sail in here like it's nothing, with a cargo which could *literally* burn a hole in your hull? These are peace talks, Domadred. Peace talks! She is a Rune Holder of the High Arkai, and you hold her captive in my harbor. That goes too far, even for you!"

"Calm yourself," Domadred said, looking around the hotel. "I had no choice. She is locked in the Dreamscape in a self-induced coma and needs special provisions. Besides, Lenhal was going to kill her."

"Kill her? And a coma? What are you talking about, Domadred? Enough games, tell me the truth!"

"Lenhal cannot use the Runes on his ship's altar to locate her while she dwells only in dreams. Remember, Beck, because Lenhal is the prime admiral, they share Runes."

"Does Lenhal know you have her?"

"I'm sure he has his suspicions, but—"

"You are mad *and* reckless!"

"It matters not, old friend. So long as I keep moving, they cannot track us, and even if they did, no one has *ever* caught the *Diamond*, no matter the circumstances. Besides, if I actually had the opportunity to find him—"

"But why, Domadred?" Beck interrupted. "Why would you do such a thing as to kidnap a High Priestess of the Order of the Arkai, a direct line to Aruna, the Western High Arkai himself? I understand your wrath against Lenhal, but have you no respect for the Guardians?"

"Beck, you misunderstand," Domadred said in a soft voice. "I didn't kidnap her; Saiya has joined us. She has defected to the Resistance. The young priestess has information that will be the key to destroying the alliance between the North and the West, and it could even end Vai'kel's occupation. That is why Lenhal was trying to kill her."

"Well then, be gone," Beck growled. "You will not bring his fleet down upon us and risk open war with the Thalassocracy. That is all Asura needs for a full invasion of our lands!"

"Do not worry, I wish to depart in all haste."

"Good, I bid you safe travel."

"But Beck . . ." Domadred paused before he continued. "I want you to come with me. That is the real reason I am here in Mindra's Haven. The Resistance needs you. I need you. We owe them for what we did to

Vai'kel—for what we allowed to happen during the Unification War." Domadred leveled Beck with a firm stare. "It is time to gather our strength against the occupation. You know I speak the truth."

Beck looked into Domadred's eyes for a long moment, not responding.

"After the voyage to Vai'kel," Domadred continued, "Saiya and I will meet with the various commanders of the Resistance. Her information will be a common flag and fuse their fissures and infighting. Join us, Beck. With your tactics, not to mention your support in the East, coupled with a newly united Resistance, we can strike a lethal blow to the Peacekeeping Forces!"

Beck did not respond.

"Beck, you must see the logic in it. If we push Asura's armies back to the North, the East will be safe."

"You really have Saiya?"

"Yes. Her betrayal leaves Lenhal waiting for the Warden Women's High Council of the Thalassocracy to revoke his position of prime admiral. Once Saiya can surface in Vai'kel, the admirals will have no choice but to denounce Lenhal and rescind both his titles and station. A minority wants it already, for many of the captains are not happy with this forced alliance with the North. Grab your boys and wife, Beck; we can cast off with the tide tonight!"

There was a moment of silence and Domadred's blue eyes stared into Beck's golden gaze. "This is not a choice I alone can make," Beck finally said, letting out his breath in a rush. "My loyalty and honor are bound to the East. They cannot be broken, especially now."

"My friend, duty, like moral law, does not always serve ethical justice. If the Resistance falls, eventually so will the East, no matter if you are united or not. This is a fight for all of Terra."

Beck shook his head. "There is nothing more I can say until we hear Mehail's words tomorrow and know the outcome of the peace talks. I will be leading the Honor Guard into Mindra's Square when the blue fire is lit. Come and hear the proclamation. In his words, we will hear the answer to your question."

Domadred nodded thoughtfully. "I wasn't planning on staying the night. But if they proclaim peace tomorrow, you will come with us?"

Beck paused for a very long moment. "If there is true peace in the East, then there will be no need for a general such as me to be here." Beck's words came slowly. "And if I were to come with you to Vai'kel, it would be easy to bring several legions of men in secret. It would take several days to arrange, but those numbers combined with the Eastern soldiers already stationed in Mystari . . ."

Domadred's smile grew wide and he raised his mug in a high toast.

"No, Domadred," Beck said, shaking his head. "I get ahead of myself. We must wait for tomorrow's proclamation. Until then, I can say no more."

Beck suddenly stood and gripped Domadred's forearm firmly in farewell. His eyes, however, were lost in thought and planning.

It was late, and Aleksi sat in the bright light of the unnaturally massive fire of the Guardian's Flame. He hoped the serving girl wouldn't come back again. Carli, he thought the hotel steward had called her. The way the young woman kept hovering about his table and eyeing Aleksi's bandaged hand made him nervous. All he had asked for was food and water, but even after Aleksi had finished eating, she repeatedly returned to ask if he needed anything else or had plans for the remainder of the evening.

The hotel was very nice, but honestly, anything was nicer than the streets of Old City. The main hall was large with many inner balconies connected by winding stairwells. More impressive, however, was the fire that rose up to the high ceiling. Although it had been made by the Guardians, similar effects could be achieved by a series of complex Runes. Empowering them, however, was the difficult part. The only Master Aleksi knew who might be strong enough to do it was Rudra . . .

Aleksi looked down at the pendant that lay softly in his bandaged palm. *Who was that old man?* Aleksi thought. *How had he known me? He knew my father, but he knew Rudra, too.*

"Where did you get that?"

Startled, Aleksi stood up and was shocked to be face to face with General Beck Al'Beth. Eyeing the man's scar and slipping the pendant back into his pocket, Aleksi spoke slowly. "I search for its former owner, Lord."

"That house was cursed in life and the same in death," the general said harshly. "If you travel the length of Vandeen's Grove, all you'll find of them has been burned to the ground. And for just cause, I might add." The general looked around the hotel. "Son, I suggest you lose that and not be seen with it again. Some would count you an enemy just because you possess it. And if they did"—Beck shook his head—"it wouldn't take much for me to agree with them."

Without further words, Beck turned and disappeared through the hotel's outer doors.

Vandeen's Grove, Aleksi thought, grasping the pendant in his pocket. *Burned to the ground, same as the old beggar had said . . .*

Aleksi lay dreaming on a rented bedroll.

He floated effortlessly in a vast expanse of murky darkness. As the youth moved his hands, it was as if he were in weightless water. Though he tried to inhale, Aleksi's lungs caught no air. Instead of being startled by this, he suddenly was confused as to what breath even was.

Abruptly, the horizon of the world shifted and Aleksi felt vertigo. He became disoriented and his senses blurred. As the faintness subsided, lights swirled in the aphotic distance. At first, they seemed hazy, like a series of colorful eddies on the horizon. But as they swam toward him, their glow became brighter and more vibrant. Swimming nimbly in the darkness, they darted to and fro until suddenly they were next to Aleksi. Wispily embracing him, they lighted across his vision and sang him sweet melodies. But as swiftly as they came, the swirling colors were gone. Once again, Aleksi was alone in the vast emptiness of soothing black.

Rapidly, memories flashed around him and he saw visions of people. Aleksi knew them but could not remember their names. Try as he might, he could not even recall who they were or where they were from. Aleksi's right hand throbbed as he saw a cloaked man appear. The man had shining white eyes and a face covered in Runes. As suddenly as he had appeared, the man was gone, causing the sensation in Aleksi's palm to quickly subside.

Next came a vision of a woman. She had yellow eyes, flowing blond hair, and a sweet smile. Aleksi felt warmth, love, and the memory of the rhythmic beat of a heart. But then she, too, faded, leaving him only with a familiar feeling of loss. Lastly, a man with long black hair materialized. His face was harsh and his green stare shone with a look of violence. As Aleksi looked into his eyes, the youth somehow knew the man was profoundly sad. Before Aleksi could speak, however, the vision disappeared and the youth was once again alone.

Suddenly, Aleksi felt nauseous and the soothing dark expanse around him contracted. It was as if the world around him were being forcefully invaded. Aleksi then saw two gigantic and terrifying eyes of green fire stare at him through the murky gloom. Once they appeared, Aleksi instantly felt as if he were being attacked from within his own mind. Realizing that he was dreaming, he struggled to wake himself up. Before he could, however, he heard a booming voice emanate from the green blaze—a voice that rumbled like a crashing boulder.

"DESPITE ELUDING MY SHADOW AT THE ACADEMY, YOU HAVE NOT ESCAPED ME, FOR I SEE THE GILDED PATH YOU HAVE BEEN GIVEN BY THE GUARDIANS. THE ARKAI ARE NOT INFALLIBLE AND BY YOUR DEATH I WILL DESTROY THEIR HOLY MACHINATIONS."

Aleksi's eyes shot open and he bolted upright in his bedroll. He was covered in cold sweat and gasping violently. Seeing a faint glow emanate from his palm, Aleksi frantically clutched his fist close to his chest to prevent the light from showing. Aleksi's head and Rune-laden hand throbbed, and as he looked about the dark sleeping hall, it was as if he could still see the burning eyes from his dream and feel their deadly promise.

High above the streets in Mindra's Temple, Mehail Bander, Arva Vatana, and Jaiden Zeer sat around a table with High Priest Trailen Kaftal at its head. The light of the moons trickled down on them through the gilded crystal canopy overhead. The moons' position said the hour was very late, yet the three leaders and their Guardian orphic seemed not to be affected. The ornate hall around them was large enough to admit the Guardians in the ages of old. Yet the table at which they now sat was relatively small. This allowed each of the Eastern leaders to clearly see their neighbors and easily argue their position and needs for Devdan's Covenant of Eastern Amity.

"Mehail," Arva continued, "I will not surrender one blade of grass. Not for you or for Jaiden."

"The lands in question, my Lord Arva," Jaiden interjected, "will not be surrendered, for they are not being sequestered. They will be explored and populated by all our peoples. As you know, nearly everything east of the Zenith Mountain and the Great Lake of Marhala is badlands. Yes, we each have borders there; however, the fell beasts that roam those wilds care little for the lines on your map."

"Regardless, I will not relinquish my territory—"

"Arva, be reasonable," Mehail interrupted. "We have been so busy fighting these past few generations. No one other than the Masters at the foot of the Zenith even knows what's out there beyond the ruins of Marhala. If we are to stand against the North, we must press farther to the great impenetrable wall of mountains at the eastern edge of Terra. Together, we can go right to the mountains' edge, right to Dagger's Veil, and gain a foothold to mine its resources. The forecasted bankruptcy of the Bankers Guild is looming before us. We *must* expand and replenish our storehouses of black pearls now, while there is still time!"

"A foothold, ha! Yes, you want a foothold at my back door so that you can invade whenever the season suits you."

"Is war all you can think of?" Mehail threw up his hands. "If we stand divided, we will not survive Asura's trade tariffs from the North. He knows this and intends to bankrupt this entire continent. We have no choice but to unite and expand past the Eastern Zenith to claim our rightful place on this land!"

"And expand I will," Arva said. "But my people don't need your help to do so. Whatever we find will be ours and ours *alone!*"

"Lord Arva," High Priest Trailen said firmly, "do not be filled with such false self-importance. It is well known that your riders fall in droves once they dismount and fight in the forests. Lord Jaiden of Farden will gladly attest to it. She deftly defeated you during your last invasion of her lands. The reason you have not explored the badlands in the Far East is simple. You are not able."

Arva didn't respond and a thick silence settled over the room. As Trailen continued, the Rune imbued into his forehead glowed with a shimmering light.

"I . . . I remember a time when *my* Eastern people held mastery over all the lands of this continent." Trailen's voice grew unnaturally deep and chilling, bristling the hairs on the back of each of the three leaders' necks. "In the Guardian Ages, leaders did not frivolously quarrel over their petty egos but fought as one against the darkness to protect the gifts I bestowed upon them!"

Trailen's voice rumbled now and his eyes shone with the same blinding light of his Rune. "Do not defile your people's honor, Lord Arva. Do not defile *me!*" Suddenly, the light on Trailen's forehead was gone, and as he shook his head, the glow in his eyes faded as well.

"My apologies, High Priest," Arva said, now in a respectful tone. "But please tell me why I must surrender *my* lands. The badlands stretch across each of our borders."

"Because yours are not as thickly overgrown," Jaiden answered. "Other than reckless adventurers, not my people, or even the Akasha Kwa'thari with their strange technology, dare go into the wilderness which borders us. We must start with your lands, for the vegetation is milder on the Eastnorthern plains. Then together, once we have a foothold, we can all move south. You will have an equal share there as well. This I swear to you, before the High Arkai Mindra himself."

"We just . . . ," Arva said, eyeing Trailen. "We just must come to an agreement on the terms. My borders *must* be secure."

"And come to an agreement you shall, Lord Arva," Trailen answered. "But do what is right for the people. For you"—he then gestured, including Mehail and Jaiden—"are all *children of Mindra*. Never forget that."

"Yes, High Priest," Arva said, nodding solemnly.

"I now must excuse myself, Lords," Trailen said, smoothing his golden robes as he stood. "I will return shortly." All three leaders bowed their heads low, each avoiding Trailen's Rune with their eyes.

Trailen walked to the hall's entrance and opened the great double doors that led into the antechamber. Nodding to the small army of guards who stood at attention on the other side of the threshold, he then walked through the large vestibule toward an arched hallway. Taking a turn through a small corridor, he continued down a thickly carpeted hall toward the washroom.

Passing ornate paintings and sculptures done in styles long lost to the ages, the High Priest frowned. His steps slowed as he came to a closed door on his left. This was not the entrance to the lavatory. Despite this, he stopped. Facing the door, Trailen then raised his right hand. He reached out with his mind, sensing and probing.

Trailen's frown turned to a scowl and he flung the door wide. The room was pitch black and the High Priest flicked his fingers open. In response, a brilliantly bright orb sprung into existence over his hand, illuminating the room.

"Thank you for joining me, High Priest," a supercilious voice said from the shadows. "I'm sorry to interrupt such important business, for that was quite the speech you just made. Very . . . *inspirational.*"

"You are a long way from home, Luka Norte," Trailen said, eyeing the man seated in one of several lavish armchairs at the far end of the room. Although Trailen's shimmering sphere cast light on the man, Luka's features were still strangely masked in shadow. "Speak quickly," Trailen continued. "What business does a Master of the Northern Academy have in Mindra's Temple?"

"Several things bring me to the Eastern Arkai's realm, High Priest," Luka said, steepling his hands. "But the most important for *you* is a warning from Kaisra, High Arkai of the North."

Trailen's eyes narrowed as he answered. "It is rumored your Northern lands have fallen under a shadow of darkness. So, then, I ask you, of what use is a dark omen to one who is still loyal to the light?"

"Yes, there is darkness in Terra," Luka said, shaking his head, "a darkness which obscures other nations from seeing their Arkai's radiance. I tell you, however, my path is true to my Arkai's will. A will that is bright enough to cast many a *jealous* shadow."

"Your *Arkai's* will?" Trailen's orb flared brightly above his hand. "Or the will of Asura?"

"No, High Priest," Luka answered, shielding his eyes. "This comes from High Arkai Kaisra directly. Please heed my words; it truly is important."

"Speak quickly."

"Soon you will be given power over all of Devdan. You must choose wisely, however, and remember your Northern allies if you wish the East to survive. We can protect your people, High Priest, but only if you let us."

Trailen let out a sharp exhalation and turned on his heel. The light over his raised hand winked out of existence as he stepped out into the hallway. The High Priest then slammed the door behind him, plunging the room back into darkness.

CHAPTER VII

Upon waking in the morning, Aleksi folded up his borrowed bedroll and left the basement dormitory. The Rune on his palm ached and his mind was filled with the dark visions from his dreams. Walking up the stone steps to the main hall, he saw Carli, the serving girl from the night prior.

"I didn't know Katrina found a place for you to sleep. Too bad, you and I could have had some fun last night." A mischievous smile grew on Carli's face. "If you're lucky, we can make up for it *tonight*."

Because the sexes were sequestered at the Academy to prevent distraction, the look in the girl's eye made Aleksi as uncomfortable as when facing Nataraja and training with live blades. "I . . . ummm . . ." Aleksi felt color running up his neck. "Have you seen Mistress Katrina this morning?"

"She's in the main hall." Carli then slowly turned and looked at Aleksi over her shoulder. "Come find me when you're done." The young woman then walked away from him, her hips swaying hypnotically.

Taking a deep breath and walking into the hall, Aleksi noticed that the large hotel seemed unusually empty. The main room held only a few patrons nursing away the aftermath of the former night's revelry. Walking past the massive pillar of white flame, Aleksi approached the guest counter. Katrina was talking with a wiry old man who wrote furiously on a piece of parchment. Aleksi stood a respectful distance away as he waited for them to finish.

After a moment, Katrina turned to him. "Why aren't you out at the square to hear the treaty proclamation? I take it you didn't get much sleep last night, eh?"

"No, Mistress, I had a busy night."

"Well, by the way Carli was eyeing you, I'm not surprised."

Again, Aleksi felt color flood his cheeks. "That was not my meaning, I—"

"Tell me, son," Katrina said, interrupting him. "What's your business in Mindra's Haven? You here visiting for the festival? It doesn't seem you're that interested in these so-called peace talks."

Aleksi's bandaged hand grazed the pendant in his cloak pocket. Although it was weightless, he felt its lingering pull. "Actually, I am here to find passage to Vai'kel. Nothing more."

"Hmmm. Well, you aren't a sailor, that's obvious."

"Indeed not, ma'am."

"Are you the son of a rich lord, then?"

"Sadly, no."

"Then good luck finding a ship, hon. This city is full to the brim, and I'd bet passage will cost you more than that pretty sword at your hip is worth."

Aleksi placed a callused hand on his hilt. "I assumed I could find passage as a hired blade."

"Well, if that sword is not just for show, you normally would have little trouble finding work as crew, although a boy your age would be tasked with hauling lines instead of fighting pirates. But now, with the festival, Mindra's Haven is saturated with all measure of men, and you would truly have to stand out to get any attention as sailor or swordsman."

"My abilities with the blade are not average, ma'am. I should have no trouble convincing—"

"Well," Katrina interrupted, "you'd have to prove it to the captain, and outside of starting a serious brawl, which would likely land you in the stockade, I don't know how else you could prove yourself. But you know"—the mistress smiled—"you could work here for a few weeks.

You're strong and cute and I'm sure you would be very popular with the highborn ladies. I would make sure you had enough coin to get across the sea in no time. I even know a few captains. I could get you a discount so you had some pearls left over for your travels in Vai'kel."

"Thank you for the offer, mistress, but I must leave immediately."

"Shame, I could use you around here." Katrina paused and scratched her head. "Well . . . there is another option, but I'm sure you wouldn't be interested."

"Please tell me, ma'am."

"Honestly, I'm surprised you haven't heard of the exhibition matches yourself. They take place in two days in the Great Arena as the festival's finale. If you get lucky and place in the top ten, you would get more than enough pearls and clout to be hired on *any* ship."

"I need something sooner," Aleksi said, shaking his head. "I cannot afford to wait any longer than I already have."

Katrina cocked an eyebrow. "You're not in any sort of *trouble*, are you, son?"

"No, ma'am, just in a rush to meet up with my teacher in Vai'kel. He does not take well to tardiness."

"Well, I'm sorry, but the arena is your safest bet." Katrina laughed, shaking her head. "But what am I saying, hon? You're only slightly older than a boy; best to just work here a spell. I've heard that some of the deadliest warriors from across Terra have traveled to Mindra's Haven just to fight for this festival. Those men are a dangerous lot. They've been perfecting their fighting arts their whole lives."

"So have I, ma'am. So have I . . ."

As Aleksi walked out of the hotel, he breathed in the fresh morning air and felt the warm rays of the Zenith on his face. The breeze smelled of the ocean, and he could hear the cackle of gulls overhead. Entering the street, he didn't need to ask directions—the flow of people forced him west.

Before Aleksi left, Katrina had told him that when he changed his mind, he was more than welcome to come back and work for her at the Guardian's Flame. And although Aleksi was interested in the life of the city—which was to say, interested in talking further with the serving girl, Carli—he knew he could not afford to waste time working at Mistress Katrina's hotel. Not only was Rudra's warning clear, but Aleksi's dream last night was profoundly disturbing. Aleksi knew that whoever wished him harm would soon be upon him. Because of this, Aleksi knew he would have to break another of the Academy rules—he would have to use his martial skill for profit and personal gain.

Seeing the congestion of the main boulevard, Aleksi let himself be swept along with the crowd down a side street. People were all excitedly talking about the pending proclamation of peace. Next to him, however, one young boy of about eight was speaking insistently to his father about the exhibition matches.

"Why do we have to wait two days, Da? I already saw him this morning. He's really here! Can you believe it? Nara Simha, the *Lionman*, is here! Is it true that he fights only with his fists and when he puts on his yellow war paint, he has the power of a Guardian?"

Aleksi saw the boy's father shake his head and laugh. "Son, you will learn in time that most rumors you hear are filled with more fiction than fact."

"But he won last year, Da. You'll see, he'll . . ." The boy's words were slowly overtaken by the noise of the throng as the waves of bodies at Aleksi's back pushed him forward.

After what felt like a very long time, the tightly packed crowd finally broke into Mindra's Square. From his vantage point, Aleksi could clearly see the Arkai's temple and great statue in the distance. Everything below the height of the statue's glimmering wings, however, was obscured by a wall of people many times greater than what the youth had seen yesterday.

Looking around, Aleksi saw an abandoned barrel at the mouth of a side street. He pushed his way past the bystanders to climb atop the container. Aleksi stood and drew a deep breath. Yesterday's preparations were now completed and a wide path that ran down the middle of the square was partitioned from the crowd. Beginning at the outer gate, it ended at the western foot of Mindra's Temple with a ramp and raised platform large enough to hold several legions of men. The platform was about a man's height off the ground and stood directly below the temple's main balcony.

Aleksi let his eyes scan the crowd. Yesterday, he had gotten a feeling for the size of the great square. But now, seeing it filled with people, he truly understood how large it was. The mob moved like a swirling mass, flowing through marked trails in the chaos and kept in check by guards and festival attendants. Many thousands of tents lined the paths.

Even all the high buildings adjoining the square had people waving in the open windows and balconies. All the people were enjoying themselves and it seemed that all of Mindra's Haven must be here, cheering and mingling with their fellows. Some, however, were silent and had steady eyes upon the balcony of Mindra's Temple. No doubt they were waiting for the temple's fire to turn blue so they could be of the first to see the lords of Devdan proclaim peace.

Suddenly, Aleksi caught sight of a unique flag flying over a large tent in the distance. Jumping down from the barrel, the youth made his way through the mob. Katrina had told him that the official arena tent had a flag of a silver gauntlet above its center pole. She had said that was where the arena fighters registered and typically congregated until the matches began. Aleksi had the feeling, however, that she had told him this with the hope that seeing the tent's clientele would shake his resolve. As he approached, Aleksi noticed that normal citizens kept a wide berth as they made their way around the tent. He assumed that was not because of its armed guards but more likely due to its notorious patrons.

Emerging from the crowd, Aleksi nodded to the guards and they gave him a dubious look. After walking under the tent's awning, Aleksi saw a scribe dressed in a formal uniform. He was seated at a table and writing in a large and ornate Runic ledger. Over a white shirt with a tight-cropped collar, the man wore a vest of black twill with a golden sash. As Aleksi approached, the scribe didn't bother to look up from his work, and Aleksi wondered what type of Runic technology was embedded in the book. Behind another set of sentries, Aleksi could see many rows of tables under the tent. Seated at the benches were all manner of warriors from across Terra. They were talking in small groups, all eyeing each other keenly.

Aleksi walked up to the scribe and, clearing his throat, addressed the man formally. "Sir, I would like to register for the exhibition matches."

"You could have registered here twelve hours ago, *boy*." Without further words, the scribe went back to writing in the Runic book in front of him.

Aleksi frowned. Katrina had neglected to mention any time limit on registration. "My apologies, sir," Aleksi continued. "Is there somewhere else I could register, then?"

"The festival started yesterday at Zenith-down and registration is therefore closed. Besides"—the man looked Aleksi up and down—"you're not missing anything, except possibly some broken bones or an untimely death. This place does not take kindly to *children*."

"Sir, if given the chance, I—"

"We are closed. Leave now, or I will have you forcibly removed."

Out of nowhere, a black pearl landed on the scribe's book with a thud. "I don't think you're closed just yet." The smug voice came from directly behind Aleksi. The official's eyes widened and Aleksi spun around to look at the newcomer.

The voice belonged to a tall man with blue eyes, sharp features, and a Zenith-tanned face. Under his bead-braided hair, he wore a wide-brimmed captain's hat and had a tightly cropped beard. The man had a somewhat gaudy sword at his hip tucked into a thick cloth belt held with a lacquered blue buckle. His amber arms were crossed over an ornate vest and he projected more self-assurance than Aleksi had ever seen. There was no mistaking the attire and cocky swagger—this was the same captain that Aleksi had seen yesterday at the docks talking to Arva Vatana and Beck Al'Beth.

At the captain's right side, a boy of about twelve stood mimicking his father's stance. To the captain's left, a young man in a faded red shirt and black pants stood with his palm resting on the hilt of his sheathed blade. All three had the icy-blue eyes and long blond hair of the Western Thalassocracy.

Before the scribe could say anything, the captain spoke again. "I've got a man on my crew who wants to enter. I've also got enough pearls to see him through."

"As I've said, we're closed." The scribe's eyes glanced at the iridescent Runic denomination inscribed on the pearl in front of him. "You must know of the Eastern custom. No man can enter the tournament after the festival has begun. You aren't asking me to defy the will of the Guardians, are you?"

Two more black pearls landed next to the original and the scribe's lips curled up into a grin. "Friend," the captain chuckled, "Mindra *himself* grants us his pardon."

"Well, I'm sure we would have his blessing to make an exception for ones as generous as you," the scribe said, picking one of the pearls up and twisting it between thumb and forefinger. He smiled again as the pearl Runicly split into ten equally sized replications of itself. The only difference between the replications was that each bore a numerical denomination of one-tenth of the original stack.

"And this one, too," the captain said, nodding to Aleksi. "Every man deserves a chance at glory."

The scribe looked at Aleksi doubtfully as he closed his fist around the cluster of black pearls, causing them to Runicly reform back into a single stacked orb. "I don't think—"

"Kefta," the captain interrupted, turning to the young man at his left, "give the scribe your information. Let us be done with this before the proclamation is given."

The young man in red stepped forward. "Kefta Vanarus, and make sure not to misspell anything; I want my champion decree to be legible."

"Champion, aye?" the scribe said, opening to a fresh page in his ledger. "You do know Nara Simha is here, don't you? They don't call him the Lionman for nothing."

"Just write down my name."

The captain smiled as the scribe shook his head and added Kefta's information in the Runic ledger.

After a moment, everyone's eyes went to Aleksi.

"And you, *boy*?"

"My name is . . . Astya."

"*Surname?*" the scribe said with a sneer.

"Astya is enough."

The scribe looked back and forth between Aleksi and the remaining pearls on his desk. Muttering under his breath, he started writing again in his ornately bound book.

After another moment, the scribe instructed Kefta to sign his name on a blank page and then place his hand over the signature. As soon as Kefta's palm touched the open book, his handprint darkened on the page. After the biogram was complete, the scribe made additional notes next to the newly formed moniker before repeating the process on a blank page for Aleksi. Aleksi was careful to use his left hand, keeping his bandaged palm out of sight.

The scribe then flipped to the back of the book and carefully tore out two pages filled with printed information. He handed one of them to Aleksi and the other to Kefta. Each page was personalized, outlining their names, heats, and fighting information.

"Be at the arena in two days," the scribe said with a sigh. "Find the flag with this first Rune on it. That is where you wait. The second Rune is for when you will fight. If you make it past your first round"—the man eyed Aleksi doubtfully—"a new Rune will appear, which tells you your next heat. Oh, and remember, no fighting until your appointed time. If you break the arena pact, the punishment is quite severe."

When the scribe was done, the captain tipped his hat and began to walk away with his entourage in tow.

"Sir," Aleksi said, calling after him, "what is your name and how can I repay you?"

The captain turned and looked Aleksi in the eye. "The name's Domadred. And how about this, if you win the tournament, I get half the earnings?"

"Agreed," Aleksi replied instantly. "But only if you can take me to Vai'kel immediately after the match." The boy next to Domadred snickered and Kefta put a hand to his mouth, trying to hide a smirk.

"Astya," Domadred laughed, "if you place even in the *top ten*, I will take you anywhere you wish to go in all of Terra. That, my boy, is a promise!"

"Agreed and well met, Captain Domadred." Aleksi placed his hands together at his heart and then to his forehead, bowing deeply. "I then swear by the Guardians, you will have half of my winnings upon safe arrival to Vai'kel. Find me when the final matches are over. I look forward to our journey together."

Domadred's eyes narrowed. "I haven't seen that bow in a while. Well, it's a deal, then, son. I think I just made a very good investment."

As Domadred turned away, Kefta raised a hand and spoke to Aleksi over his shoulder. "I'll see you soon, but you need to remember one thing: no hard feelings, alright?"

Aleksi didn't respond and turned back to the table. He saw that the black pearls had vanished from in front of the scribe. The man's head was down and he was already busy writing once again.

Passing several rows of empty tables, Aleksi made his way farther into the fighters' tent. Before him were nearly fifty men and women, all bearing weapons and armor as different as the lands they hailed from. The classic weapon of Terra was a two-handed, slightly curved sword called a *blade*. Measuring longer than a man's arm, this was the same weapon that Aleksi wore at his hip. Masters of the Academy used these traditional swords exclusively, seeing all other edged weapons as utterly inferior. This same mentality extended to the aristocracy of each nation of Terra, who, no matter what corner of the globe they came from, preferred this curved blade over other assorted arms. Most commoners, however, did not have the opportunity to study the Masters' famed "art of the blade," and thus turned to other, less conventional weapons such as shields, maces, spears, and pole arms. Aleksi had even been taught of the rare Berzerker warriors in the North-Eastern Mountains of Iksir who used large two-handed axes during their hallucinogen-induced battle rages.

As Aleksi continued through the tent, he saw a hooded Southerner polishing a heavily curved scimitar. Its dark material seemed to soak up the light in the tent as the sickly pale man from Neberu worked it with an oiled cloth. On his left, Aleksi noticed a group of what looked to be North-Western Kaymahn mercenaries. They wore the traditional leather mail of their people and leaned on their long pole arms as they talked in a small circle. As Aleksi continued on, the youth then saw the red-flecked brown eyes of a South-Easterner look at him dubiously from under his ceremonial headdress scarf. The Salbatan man's dark skin was mostly concealed by his sand-colored cloak, but the series of curved daggers tucked in his belt was plain for all to see.

What impressed the youth most of all, however, was a group of men surrounding the largest warrior Aleksi had ever seen. Over a head taller than most all the others, the man had broad shoulders laden with rippling muscle and crisscrossed with innumerable deep scars. His striking green eyes with yellow flecks marked him a North-Easterner by birth, hailing from the high mountains of Iksir. In addition, Aleksi noticed that the man wore no weapon and instead carried two long, oversized steel gauntlets strapped to a thick leather belt.

"Don't be fooled by him, boy," a female voice with a thick South-Western accent said from behind Aleksi. "He's nothing but show."

Turning, Aleksi saw a woman lounging on an adjacent bench. She had the striking turquoise-flecked amethyst eyes of a Sihtu native. Possessing a long whip at her side, the woman was scantily clad in leather and chain mail. Her dark and semicovered body was lithe and strong, showing a multitude of intricate tribal tattoos scrawled across deep olive skin. Aleksi thought her armor probably did more to highlight her feminine assets than actually protect her in battle. As Aleksi continued to glance over her body, the woman smiled amusedly.

"Pardon?" Aleksi asked, averting his eyes from her curves.

"I saw you admiring the so-called *Lionman* over there. You should know, Nara is nothing but a glory-seeking entertainer. Not a true warrior of Terra."

"I'll . . . be sure to keep that in mind."

"All will see him fall by my hand in two days. But then again, many wish to take the title of champion from him." She paused, eyeing Aleksi with a wry smile. "Son, you're very cute, but aren't you a bit young for the arena?"

There was a short silence before Aleksi responded. "Age, like many things, can be deceiving. A similar question could be asked of a woman who thinks to challenge a warrior as renowned as the Lionman." Aleksi looked over at Nara. The giant of a man had his back to them. The youth could see Nara's massive shoulders tense and relax, the muscles heaving, as he laughed on the other side of the tent.

"I hope you are not implying that I am weak because I am a woman," the warrioress said, crossing her arms over supple breasts. "While that's a fatal mistake most men make, they make it only *once.*"

At the Academy, men were not heralded as more powerful or more able than women in any way. However, without the proper training, the gap in physical strength was very difficult to overcome. But this Sihtu woman before him was lean and strong, and Aleksi had a feeling that whatever she lacked in raw power, she made up for in dexterity, skill, and cunning.

"That's exactly my point—" But before Aleksi could continue, he was interrupted by a voice behind him.

"Oh, I'm sure Astya's implication is clear, madam."

They both turned to see Kefta, the red-shirted fighter whom Domadred had just registered moments before.

Kefta made an elegant bow before continuing. "Women have many wonderful talents and traits, but strength in battle is *certainly* not one of them."

"No, that's not—" Before Aleksi could continue, he was cut off again.

"Is that so, little sailor boy?" the Sihtu woman said, standing up as her accent grew thicker. "I doubt *sea trash* such as you knows anything of a woman. Other than the price he must pay to bed one, that is."

"I'm sure that is a bit of knowledge we both share in common," Kefta said with a grin. "Although I'm certain you're on the *receiving* end of it, so to speak."

The woman's hand gripped her whip tightly and her turquoise-and-amethyst eyes flared.

"And you truly fight with that toy?" Kefta continued, gesturing to her whip. "Who has ever heard such nonsense as fighting with a *whip*?"

"Then you have not heard of the Pa'alna or of their wrath!" the woman said harshly. "But I would be happy to—"

"I have," Aleksi interrupted, taking a step forward. "You hail from the South-Western Isles of Sihtu, correct? And your capital island of Pa'alna is named after the color of your people's eyes."

"You know of my people?" the woman asked, surprised.

"Yes, my teachers speak very highly of their martial prowess and valor."

"Come now," Kefta said. "I don't care what backwater fringe island you come from—a woman can never stand against a man in combat, especially when facing the greatest warrior this age has known. Besides"—Kefta smiled wide—"all know Nara would rather fondle that pretty body of yours than fight it."

There was a very uncomfortable silence as the woman gave Kefta a murderous glare.

"A thing in which he has much experience, or so he told me. For isn't that why Nara didn't fight you at the Southern games? If memory serves, he forfeited the final match, saying he would not fight a Sihtu *whore*."

"Hold your tongue, sea trash, lest I rip it out," the woman growled. "I care not for the arena's pact. I will take pleasure in killing you here and now!"

"Ahh, so his words were true. I guess women do have a way to win battles, eh? It's not just how they make their money, but how they fight their wars, too!"

The woman grabbed her cloak and stalked toward Nara, who was still engaged in conversation on the other side of the tent.

Aleksi looked at Kefta, aghast.

"What?" Kefta said innocently. "You should be thanking me. They have some bad blood and I'm just thinning out the top competition." He gave Aleksi a wink. "No hard feelings, remember?"

Aleksi shook his head and followed the Sihtu woman as she made her way across the tent to Nara. The large man was midsentence in conversation with an old soldier who wore a short sword and shield.

"Kendell," Nara said to the man, "you aren't fooling anyone dyeing your hair black. Don't you think you're getting a little old for the arena? The crowd will notice, friend."

"I'm young enough to best you when I get the chance," Kendell growled back. "You are nothing without your Berzerker war paint, Simha! And the crowd will notice, alright—notice who is standing above you when you fall!"

Nara threw back his head and laughed. Raising a massive arm, he flexed his bicep, and thick veins bulged from his muscles as he spoke. "Kendell, I have more strength in a single arm than you have in your entire body. Lest you wish to be sent to an early retirement, I suggest you leave now." Kendell glared at Nara but strode away.

Wasting no time, the woman from Sihtu stalked up and spoke in a commanding tone. "Nara, do not continue to pretend to not remember me!"

Startled, the Lionman looked the woman up and down. He took a deep breath before speaking. "My dear Fa'ell, you are not easy to forget and harder still to find. I will have you know—"

"I won't let you humiliate me and shame my family again," Fa'ell interrupted. "You will fight me this time, or I will take my family's vengeance *here and now*."

Nara raised his hands and a look of unease washed over his face. "Fa'ell, you must know I truly had no idea—"

"No!" Fa'ell shouted. "No more of your pretty words. Now even sailor trash mocks me. You have dishonored my people and broken my house. But I will regain what is lost. Give me your word, or we fight now!"

"You know the rules, Fa'ell; we cannot fight until the arena." Nara lowered his voice and cast a nervous eye about the tent. "I'm profoundly sorry for what happened, but it changes nothing; I still—"

Fa'ell flicked her wrist and, like a swift clap of thunder, the sharp report of her whip cracked above their heads. "No excuses, Nara," she snarled. "Give me your *word*!"

The man ran a callused hand through his short blond hair. "You have my word, Fa'ell. But—"

Before he could finish, Fa'ell stormed out of the tent.

Letting out a great sigh, Nara looked around and saw many eyes and a few knowing smiles. Amid the sympathetic chuckles of amused men, the conversations in the tent slowly started again. Nara then saw Aleksi silently watching him from several paces away.

Catching Aleksi's eye, Nara spoke. "Well, son, I hope you enjoyed that more than I did. Some call me a performer, yet that's not exactly the kind of entertainment I'm known for."

"One man's sorrow is another man's glory," Aleksi said, approaching Nara. "Is that not the way of the arena?"

"Well said, son. Sadly, it is." Nara paused, studying Aleksi's face. "I do not know you, but your eyes are green and true. From where on our great Northern Continent do you hail?"

"I have the eyes of the North, sir, nothing more."

"I bet not, son, for unless you are a fool and know not who I am, you must have the courage of a Northern heart to speak to the Lionman. Especially on the tail of such an awkward incident."

"I can guess who you are," Aleksi answered, "but more importantly, I know where you are from. Yet I beg to wonder why you are axeless." Aleksi paused. "Should I assume, then, lion of Iksir, that you mix your paints alone?"

A frown spread across Nara's face and he answered curtly. "For one not from the Northern Continent, you seem to know much of her customs."

"Just because I do not live on her soil does not mean I do not know of her people."

"Well, son, some questions are best left *unasked.*" Nara gestured to the mass of humanity outside the tent and his demeanor changed. "But what of you, my boy? Here to perform for the crowd and claim the fabled mantle of victory?"

"I do not perform for show."

"Ah, not one for glory," Nara said, rubbing his massive hands together. "You're in it for the money, then. You've come to test your luck for the prize of pearls and make your fortune, I take it?"

"I have been taught that there is no luck on the battlefield, sir. Only choice and fate." Aleksi paused, looking up at the giant of a man that was Nara Simha. "And apparently, mine has brought me here to you."

Before Nara could say any more, Aleksi walked away with his left hand lightly resting on the hilt of his blade. Leaving the covering of the tent, Aleksi looked skyward and wondered what Nataraja would think of him participating in an arena like this. *To fight for money . . . There is no greater shame for a warrior.*

A feeling of dishonor flooded through the youth as he made his way into the crowd. Continuing to stare upward, he saw that both moons,

Rahu and Ketu, were high in the sky. Their blue light was drowned out by the Eastern Zenith, but still they rested graciously in the heavens— stoic and enduring.

I have little choice. Please, Arkai, grant me forgiveness.

CHAPTER VIII

The eastern side of Mindra's Square was filled with eager people. The only open space was along the western edges of the market, which abutted the city's main gate and high wall. The imposing doors had been closed for some time in ritual preparation for the grand entrance of the military. Traditionally, the march had been made up of Adhira's soldiers only, signifying the might of Devdan's former capital of Mindra's Haven. However, there were whispers in the crowd that a legion from each Eastern nation waited outside the barred doors.

Cutting through the cacophony below, a regal blast of fifty horns suddenly sounded from atop Mindra's Temple. All stopped what they were doing and looked up to the great balcony on the eastern edge of the square. From across the pavilion another blast rang out. This time, the noise came from atop the high outer walls. Again, the crowd turned. All eyes were now looking westward to the main gate that led to the harbor. Next came the metallic moan of heavy chains, followed by the groaning rasp of metal hinges as the mammoth gate slowly opened inward.

With the light of the Zenith brightly shining before him, General Beck Al'Beth led fifteen legions of soldiers—totaling 1,875 men and women—into Mindra's Square. The crowd cheered in a deafening roar, welcoming their beloved national heroes into the festival grounds. Beck wore full-body plate armor, each steely silver plate edged with hammered gilt leaf. His breastplate had high collar guards and the golden crest of the High Arkai Mindra embossed upon its center. It shone bright amber as it reflected the Zenith's glare. Beck's hands and arms were adorned with intricately crafted gauntlets and his lower body was armored with full leg plates. An elegant purple cape fringed with gold flowed behind him as he marched. Despite the formal dress, Beck's head was bare. He held his ornate helm tight under his right arm, and his left hand rested on the pommel of his sheathed blade.

Beck and his procession of soldiers ceremoniously marched through the square. The convoy was made of three rectangular formations of warriors. Six hundred twenty-five of each nation's finest men and women marched beside their feudal neighbors. In addition, renowned Pa'laer and Farden generals flanked Beck on either side. These seasoned leaders also had their helms removed and squinted against the Zenith's rays.

Directly behind their generals marched each legion's standard-bearer. Each nation's emblem flew high on its bearer's pole, rippling proudly in the warm ocean breeze. The Rune of High Arkai Mindra was featured at the center of each ensign, yet beyond that, the flags were as different as the lands they represented. All in the East worshipped Mindra, but in the Modern Age, Pa'laer and Farden had their own variant of the Eastern Arkai's Runic standard. In addition, both neighboring nations had little love for Adhira's banner, for it was Devdan's ancestral flag, reminding all of the historic claim of Mindra's Haven to political supremacy and divine right.

Flying to Beck's left, the flag of the Pa'laer of the Eastnorth was blood red. It was embossed with yellow plumes and a golden stitching that shone in the light of the Zenith. Scrolled in ancient Runic text surrounding a much larger Rune of Mindra was an account of their nation's history in the Modern Age, including the lineage of their ruling houses. The horse lord's history showed many a battle won over their neighbors, and as the Pa'laer warriors marched, the people of Mindra's Haven looked up at the banner keenly. Many likely remembered friends, parents, or even grandparents who had fallen in defeat to the notoriously vicious war riders of the Eastnorth.

To Beck's right, the Eastsouthern forest nation of Farden had a banner of green, instead of red, with a similar yellow stitching. Their flag also had an account of their nation's history and lineage. Standing out among the domains listed, however, was a Rune all knew and many feared. Patterned in silver stitching instead of gold was the House Rune of the fallen Akasha people. After their crash on the face of Terra by the hands of the Dark Ones so many long ages ago, their sacred descendants chose to live on what remained of their organic starfaring tree ship, Kwa'thari. The giant tree now rested in the impact crater it had made upon its hard fall to land. It was said that much of the large tree was submerged in a great lake, for the ship had, upon impact, struck an underground reservoir. After the Kwa'thari took root in the fertile soil, the Akasha had then stayed hidden in the mountainous and secluded forests of the Eastsouth for many ages. Although occult and strange, that one branch of the great Akasha had made Terra their home, mingling with the people of the Eastsouth in trade, friendship, and, when necessary, military allegiance.

Finest of all and directly at Beck's back was Adhira's great standard banner. It was larger than the other two nations' flags, and its material was made of a Runicly gilded fabric sewn with molten gold stitching which shone of its own accord. When the crowds saw the great banner, it was understandable why the other nations of the East felt inferior to Mindra's Haven. Legend told that this flag was given as an honorific gift by Mindra himself to an ancient High Priest of the Eastern Order of the Arkai, a man notorious for his valor in combat against the Dark Ones. The banner had then been passed down through the generations of Adhira's mortal protectors ever since, inspiring her people with faith in the Guardians' might and virtuous promise. It was said that any army which marched with this flag at its head would never fall in defeat, for it had the divine protection and power of the Eastern Zenith itself. This had yet to be proven wrong.

The rays above shone off Beck's polished steel plate with blinding intensity as the progression moved forward through the square. The sound of 1,875 pairs of boot heels rang out through the large plaza, inspiring awe and admiration. The generals, along with their respective five legions, were dressed in the soldiers' arms of their nation.

Behind Beck, the legions of men and women belonging to Adhira were dressed in less-ornate plate mail and equipped with long blades strapped to their belts. To Beck's left, the Pa'laer warriors of the Eastnorth were dressed in tan leather armor banded together by sturdy belts and buckles. Both male and female heads were bare, but their necks were protected by thick leather gorgets. While reinforced leather was not nearly as strong as steel plate or chain, it allowed the Pa'laer warriors to ride their warhorses with the utmost ease and lethal speed. Without their horses today, the soldiers marched in line with their short bows strapped to their backs and their wickedly curved swords secured at their hips.

To Beck's right marched the Farden soldiers of the Eastsouth. Half of the soldiers were men armed with long axes and carrying shields on their backs. The men were dressed in green tunics cinched over chain mail that covered their entire bodies. The other half were women dressed in thin green and brown leathers and armed with a belt of sheathed daggers. Known for keeping to themselves and their thick woodlands, the people of Farden fought most battles in the seclusion of tree and canopy. The men would fight on the forest floors with their axes while the lightly armored women would wait, camouflaged, in the canopy above. Once an enemy was fully engaged with the heavily armored men in mail, their swift, acrobatic wives and sisters would swoop down upon their prey, wreaking havoc before retreating again to the cover of leaf and branch above.

As the column of soldiers marched through the center path of the square, Beck looked up to the great shimmering statue of Mindra and smiled. Although Beck had been given several hours' notice of his lord's having reached a decision with the two other nations' leaders, his chest still felt giddy from their proclamation. And while the announcement had not yet been made public, Beck could see that even just this formal show of military unity was doing much to inspire the onlooking citizens.

Mehail Bander had told Beck, "The people must see the military force of each Eastern nation bending knee as one, showing fealty to a new, *united* rule. We must inspire harmony through unity. Therefore, the commendation ceremony will pay homage to our new alliance, proclaiming true peace throughout *all* of Devdan."

Mehail was right. United like this we can stand against Asura. Beck looked up at the giant statue of their patron Arkai, and for the first time in many long years, he felt joy in his heart. *I wish I could see the grin on Domadred's face.*

Across the square and close to the temple, Domadred stood with a hand on his son's shoulder. "Can it be true?" Brayden said, looking out across the crowd. "They march as one? This can only mean one thing!"

"Indeed," Domadred answered, smiling wide. "Beck Al'Beth and his men will sail with us when we return to the Resistance."

Behind them, Kefta weaved through the crowd. After making his way to the pair, the young man spoke. "Well, I'm sure you're happy, Captain."

"The Guardians have smiled upon us and our cause." Domadred then paused, giving Kefta a sideways glance. "What kept you? You didn't get into any trouble, did you?"

Kefta gave an innocent smile. "No, Captain, just opening some old wounds. If we have to stay in Mindra's Haven, I plan on *winning* this tournament."

"Don't worry, you will place well. Although if I was a betting man, which I am, I still would put my pearls on the Lionman as this year's champion."

"In light of your recent success with Beck," Kefta said with a wry smile, "care to make a wager?"

Before Domadred could answer, Brayden spoke with an incredulous tone. "Kefta, you *seriously* think you can beat Nara Simha?"

"When you have something greater than two tiny copper nuggets in that little-boy purse of yours," Kefta said, as Brayden's face turned red, "you can start making wagers as to who will win. Until then, leave it to the *men* to talk of their speculations."

"Why should I bet more?" Domadred answered. "I'm already several stacks deep on you, and those are black pearls I plan to make back with very high interest when you receive your winnings."

"Yes, yes," Kefta said, waving his hand. "There is no doubt we will make good earnings in the semifinals. I'm talking about a *side bet*."

"I'm listening."

"Not only do I make it to the final round of four," Kefta said, "but that hooded *boy* we met at the arena tent, Astya, does not make it past his *first* heat with me."

"And your wager?"

"Ten more stacks. And I want five-to-one odds."

"Done," Domadred said with a smile. "In addition, when I win, you take Brayden's cleaning chores for a *month*."

"Why?" Kefta asked, confused.

"Because you're a rude ass."

Aleksi pushed his way to the front of the crowd as people cheered for the soldiers nearing the platform. Never in his sixteen years living at the Academy had he seen people so expectant and eager.

The youth watched Beck and his marching procession make their way up the ramp onto the platform directly in front of the temple's high balcony. The group halted when all were atop the wide stage, more than a man's height off the ground. Maintaining rank and file, the warriors then fell into a stationary formation in wait. As his men stood at attention, Beck turned to face them, and out of the corner of his eye he caught Brin Al'Beth, his son and a most talented young soldier, glancing aside.

Beck flicked a gauntleted finger across his steel thigh plate and it rang out with a pure metallic clang. When Brin's eyes were slow to snap front and center, Beck saw why—the graceful form of a dark-skinned South-Western woman from Sihtu standing at the edge of the crowd with her elegant arms folded over her cleavage. Scantily clad in tight leather armor that revealed more than it protected, she would be able to turn any young man's head and captivate his attention.

Beck gave Adler a nod and the veteran leaned close into Brin and whispered fiercely, "What is it, boy? Do you think the sweat that drips off her breasts would taste sweet? Or is it the olive skin and jet-black hair? Perhaps you want to trace her tattoos to their *source*?" Brin swallowed hard as Adler continued. "Or maybe it's the bullwhip she uses. Would that keep you in line, do you think?"

Brin's face was bright red as Beck approached. Beck, too, had once been young. He had also been distracted, but not today. "Son, you are damn good with that sword, but this is a momentous occasion and I cannot afford the minds of my men being any less sharp than their blades. Keep focused and act a man."

Brin nodded and Beck looked at the two opposing generals on either side of the large platform. He had fought wars against these men and had killed and lost many a soldier in the process. Gazing back at the faces of his warriors in formation, Beck raised his voice and addressed them all.

"*Children of Mindra*, today we represent our country as the foundation of a unified continent. Let us show the people why it is in us they put their *faith and adoration!*"

In response, his five noble legions of 625 soldiers pounded their gauntleted fists on their breastplates twice before letting out a guttural roar which echoed throughout the square. To their left and right, many a Pa'laer and Farden face turned to them, remembrance of the battle cry shimmering in their eyes.

Suddenly, there came the call of trumpets from the temple high above, and all stood in stillness. For a moment there was complete silence throughout Mindra's Square. Beck then heard the rush of a fire being ignited on the pavilion high above. The orange flame of the temple's bastion now burned a raging cobalt blue. In one smooth motion, all fifteen legions dropped to their knees with a metallic clatter. A second later, in a rippling wave, the massive crowd behind them did the same. Lowered down in preparation to give honor to a newly unified realm, all looked to the balcony, waiting.

The moment stretched on as Beck watched the azure plume of smoke above the temple bastion rise high into the sky like a lazy wisp. The Zenith shone hot overhead and several drops of perspiration had developed on Beck's forehead. Despite this, he remained stoic and unmoving. Far off in the distance, a gentle breeze blew off the ocean. It softly caressed Beck's face in the eager stillness.

Finally, Mehail Bander stepped out onto the balcony. He was followed by Arva Vatana and Jaiden Zeer. Instantly, a deafening roar rose from the crowd. Beck glanced around the multitude and saw elation on their faces. He let the feeling wash over him.

He's done it. Devdan is whole once again.

Mehail Bander looked down at the crowd below. The sea of people stretched out to the end of the square and their jubilant chorus rang in his ears. They were illuminated in the light of the Zenith and their expectant eyes were locked on him through its glare. The councilor breathed in slowly, feeling both Arva Vatana and Jaiden Zeer several steps behind him. Mehail knew they were watching him closely. The two leaders had not been easy to satisfy, but peace was worth the price.

Mehail smiled and raised his arms. The cheers were silenced. "My friends and fellow citizens, I speak to you at the height of a most auspicious day." Mehail's voice was loud and booming, projected out into the square by the Runic power of Mindra's Temple. "We have all felt the drains of these last years. Many across the sea foster rage in their hearts, and even within our great walls we taste fear with every bite of bread. Yet, while our world approaches an uncertain time and faces the prospect of global war, I tell you now, whatever trials we face from this day forth, we of the East will face them *together*. For we, the people of Terra's great Eastern Continent of Devdan, are now once again *united*!"

Again, the crowd burst into cheers, women held their children up to see their lords, and men wept openly at the thought of a unified realm.

Beck squinted. He could have sworn there had been only three people on the balcony a moment ago. But now, two more men dressed in the livery of the Honor Guard slipped behind the three Eastern lords. Silently, one man stepped behind Jaiden Zeer and the other behind Arva Vatana.

Beck raised a gauntleted hand and called out, but his words were drowned in the din of the crowd's cheers. In one smooth motion, a dagger appeared in each man's hand. Crimson red blossomed from Jaiden's cut throat and Arva Vatana struggled violently as the second assassin tried to kill him as well. The cheers of the crowd turned to gasps.

After slaying Jaiden, the unencumbered assassin charged Arva with his knife. The lord of Pa'laer, still wrestling with his original assailant, turned at the last moment and avoided the man's blade. Before the assassin could strike again, Arva grabbed the man's wrist. With one flush movement, the horse lord threw his original assailant over his shoulder with a hip check, while still deftly grasping the second assassin's arm.

Mehail, still facing the crowd and knowing nothing of the commotion behind him, heard a voice boom out through the square. Imitating the voice of the Chair of the High Council of Adhira, it cut through the hushed gasps of the crowd.

"For with the deaths of these charlatans, we of Mindra's Haven, the true Eastern rulers, will reclaim our *rightful* place of power and dominion over all of Devdan!" The temple then stopped projecting the sound from the balcony and Mehail turned in astonishment. He saw one of his own guards trying to force a dagger into Arva's heart and another man lying broken at the horse lord's feet.

On the platform below, Beck shouted out as each legion fell into its respective battle stance. "Hold, men, there is some confusion! This is not what it seems. Our lords have declared peace!" Each nation's soldiers eyed one another fiercely, but none moved. Beyond the platform, the crowd stood frozen in shock, breaths held in a collective gasp.

High above on the balcony, Arva twisted the blade from the assassin's hand. Before Mehail could move to help, Arva drove it into the assassin's neck. Blood squirted over Arva's clothes, and the large man eyed Mehail with a vicious glare. As the assassin's now-limp body slumped to the ground, Mehail looked back into the foyer and heard the violent clash of blades.

"I *knew* you were incapable of sharing power!" Arva shouted as he gripped the assassin's knife with white knuckles. "This was all a ruse. Asura was right about you!"

"You cannot believe that this is my man," Mehail said, raising his hands numbly. "This peace treaty has been my life's *greatest* achievement! You must see it; this has to have been Asura's plan all along, that you—"

"*Lies!*" Arva shouted.

Without another word, Arva charged and drove his knife into Mehail's stomach. The force of the blow thrust the two men against the hip-high railing. Arva looked deep into Mehail's eyes as the councilor reached for something around his neck that wasn't there.

Feeling the long blade slide deep into his gut and scrape past his spine, Mehail closed his eyes and whispered, "Guardians, please protect our people."

"Your death," Arva shouted as he lifted Mehail up into the air, "will set them *free!*"

Arva then heaved Mehail's body over the balcony railing and sent him hurtling to the flagstones of the pavilion below.

In his last instant, Mehail felt himself falling through the air with the sound of the Eastern wind rushing in his ear. A silent tear sheared from his face and then his body hit the ground with a wet smack.

Numbness enveloped Beck as he stared at the broken body of his lord lying mere paces away. For a moment, silence held the square with the tight grip of disbelief. The only sound Beck could hear was the drip, drip, drip from Arva's blood-soaked dagger. It seemed to echo throughout the entire pavilion with a callous countdown to inevitability.

Then chaos erupted in Mindra's Square.

CHAPTER IX

"Avenge our fallen lord, Jaiden Zeer!" The call came from the Farden general and his shout cut through the screams of the fleeing crowd. It was answered with a torrent of throwing knives aimed at Beck's legion of soldiers. While most of the warriors of Adhira were well protected from such an assault in their plate mail, some had yet to don their helms. The sound of whistling sharp steel thunking into several of Devdan's less fortunate warriors gave Beck the fleeting childhood memory of throwing daggers at melons with his father on the beach of their ocean-side estate. Pushing the memory away, Beck continued to stare down at the mangled body of Mehail Bander as another salvo of knives whizzed by.

"General! What are your orders?"

Broken from his trance, Beck slammed his helm onto his head. "Unit defensive formations! All men, repel the attackers."

At the order, the five legions of Adhira moved as one. They drew their swords and created five tight-knit formations, each poised to strike at their aggressors. As his soldiers moved, Beck called out to the Farden general over the shrieks of the escaping throng of citizens.

"General Tora!" Beck pleaded. "We need not fight. End this now and peace is still within our grasp. This disastrous tragedy is a mistake!"

In response, the foreign general threw a dagger at Beck's head. Beck dodged and the dagger whirred by, then embedded itself into a captain of the Pa'laer army behind him. The general of the Eastnorth raised a leather-banded hand, commanding his men to draw bow as he shouted to the balcony above.

"Lord Arva Vatana, what is your command?"

Arva leaned over the balcony with the bloody dagger still held tight in his fist. "Kill them! Kill them all!" Arva then threw the knife into the crowd of citizens below. "Even the women and children! Burn Mindra's Haven to the ground!"

"You heard Lord Vatana," the Pa'laer general shouted, raising and then dropping his hand. "Fire at will! Sack this traitorous city."

At his command, many hundreds of bows released in a violent twang, sending a dark flurry of arrows into civilian and soldier alike. The crowd surged in pandemonium. Looking for any way to escape, men and women trampled each other underfoot, and it was impossible to discern if more died by their fellows' boot heels than by enemy blade or bow.

Arva turned from the balcony and stalked toward the tower's terrace veranda. As he entered the gracefully decorated foyer, he was met with bodies strewn about the floor. The fallen were guards hailing from each of the three Eastern nations, yet their blood was indistinguishable as it soaked through the elegant carpets of the temple. Standing above the corpses was a group of similarly dressed men with swords drawn. At first glance they, too, seemed to hail from differing Eastern nations, yet despite their uniforms, they had obviously worked together to cut down those who were now strewn about their feet.

Confused, Arva addressed the man at the head of the group. The soldier was missing his left ear and wearing the uniform of a Pa'laer guard. "What is happening here? Who are you?"

Upon seeing Arva, the soldier smiled and wiped the blood from his sword. Slowly walking toward Arva, he spoke to a High Council Honor Guard beside him. "After the explosion, take the rest of the men and find General Beck. Make sure he is dead. I will deal with this one and then we *burn* this city."

Far below, Beck scanned the sea of fallen Eastern citizens and raised his sword high. "In the name of Mindra, full advance! We fight now to protect our families, our homes, and our nation. Purge this *faithless filth* from our walls!"

In response, there came the deafening crash of gauntlets on breastplates, followed by guttural roars as Devdan's legion rallied. "Legions five and three, engage the soldiers of Farden!" Beck shouted. "Legions four and two, engage the men of Pa'laer! And legion one, *with me!*"

At their general's command, the heavily armored legions of Adhira split rank and charged at either side, crashing into their opposing forces with the devastating fury of their two-handed blades. Their swords deftly hewed the warriors in their path, cleaving first through their leather armor and then flesh and bone. In one fell surge, all but the Farden men dressed in their heavy chain mail were easily overwhelmed and the legions of Devdan were able to push the foreign forces off both sides of the raised platform.

Suddenly, there was a blinding light beneath the men's feet and a thunderous explosion tore through Beck's ranks.

Beck felt himself flung high and hurtled through the air from the blast. Finally, he landed hard with a crash of splintered wood and heavy armor. Battered by the fall, he could not see and it took him a moment to shake his mind free of the shock.

Orienting himself, Beck could feel that his beaten body was lodged in what seemed to be broken wood and ripped cloth. Beck groaned as he removed a whipcord sheet that was stuck on his helm.

Looking around with eyes clouded in blood, Beck saw that the explosion had thrown him into a tent stall and his body was wedged inside of a large wheelbarrow filled with pelts of textile. The wheelbarrow had broken his fall and likely saved his life. Beck saw the tent was one of many in a long row of what must have been one of the festival's countless thoroughfares. Only several moments ago, it no doubt had been filled with hawkers and merchants alike. But now, instead of their ruckus calls, Beck heard only the screams of civilians and the steely crashes of battle coming from the makeshift streets around him.

Trying to move, Beck let out another moan as sharp anguish shot through his rib cage. He raised a gauntleted hand to his chest plate and felt a severely deep dent over his left breast. Fighting through the pain, Beck lifted his head. All about him, people were running through the tent-lined lanes in terror. And off in the distance at the base of Mindra's Temple, Beck could see orange-tipped tongues of flame coming from the wreckage of the raised platform.

As he dislodged himself from the debris of the tent, Beck saw countless mangled bodies strewn about him on the flagstones. In addition to slain citizens, there also were soldiers who had been caught in the brisance of the blast yet had not been as lucky as he. Sadly, the majority affected were Adhira's own. While most had been crushed by their armor, many were also burning inside their mail, filling the air with the scent of charred flesh.

Beck lifted himself up over the lip of the wheelbarrow. Fighting past the strain of broken bones, he collapsed over the cart's side and sprawled out of the tent and into the flagstones with a metallic clatter. Lifting his head, Beck then saw one of his men lying prone several tents away. The soldier was still alive. Catching Beck's eye, the man raised his gauntleted hand and let out a raspy moan.

Abruptly, a Pa'laer captain appeared over the soldier. Firmly placing his foot on the man's neck, the captain then plunged his sword through a kink in the soldier's armor. The man let out a throaty death rattle as the captain twisted the blade.

Turning, the captain removed his sword from the fallen and a sheen of blood ran from its tip. As Beck fought through his pain and tried to roll over and sit up, the Eastnorthern captain called out to his three-man unit. "It's Beck Al'Beth! Take his head and we will dine with Lord Asura *himself!*" The captain let out a wordless scream and, raising his sword high over his head, rushed at Beck.

The captain closed the gap between them in a blaze. As the man's sword came down through the air, Beck raised his gauntlet in defense. The captain's sword landed hard, embedding itself in Beck's forearm bracer with a hollow thud. Beck felt the sharp, steely bite of the sword through his armor, and his gauntlet instantly pooled with the warmth of fresh blood.

Beck grabbed the man's blade, still stuck in the plate mail, with his other gauntleted hand and pulled his attacker off balance. The captain, still holding on to his sword, fell forward toward Beck. With tremendous force despite his wounds, Beck heaved both of his armored boots up, striking his attacker in the gut. The Eastnorthern captain let out a deep grunt as he was knocked back several paces and fell to the ground.

Wheezing, the captain clambered to his feet. His three other unit members then came up beside him, falling into formation. Beck gritted his teeth and grabbed the hilt of the sword. He pulled it free from his bracer with a groan. The blade came away slick with blood. Unable to stand, Beck pointed the sword's tip at the captain's face and spat.

Regaining his breath and balance, the captain smiled wickedly as he drew a long curved knife from his belt. Before Beck could act, however, a flash of movement cut across his vision faster than his eyes could follow. A man in a sleeveless cloak slammed the captain's blade back into its sheath and struck an explosive blow centered on the captain's solar plexus. Its force dropped the captain to his knees, causing him to gasp for breath.

As the captain hit the ground, the second soldier in formation barely had time to respond before the hooded man was on him next. The Pa'laer soldier thrust his sword in an attempt to impale his hooded attacker. Without slowing, the man stepped aside so that the blade pierced only air. Then, with a flick of his knuckle, the hooded man hit the soldier in the throat. The warrior fell to his side, wheezing as he clutched his broken windpipe.

The hooded man turned to face the third soldier. The soldier was midcharge, his blade aloft and poised to strike. The soldier brought his blade down with immense force but struck nothing as the hooded man stepped sideways. Moving closer, he then drew back his cloak to expose a sheathed blade of his own.

Without drawing his sword, the hooded man grasped his scabbard and thrust the hilt of his weapon up, slamming it under the soldier's chin. There was the loud crack of steel on bone and a deep grunt of pain as the now-unconscious soldier went down with a stream of blood and teeth oozing from his shattered jaw. The hooded man then turned to gaze at the last remaining warrior. The ensuing silence was broken as the soldier turned and ran, leaving only the captain, who was still doubled over in pain.

Beck gaped in astonishment as the cloaked man threw back his hood. This was not a man at all, but the youth from the Guardian's Flame! Beck guessed he was in his midteens at best, and certainly younger than any of those under Beck's command—and yet at the center of the youth's cloudless green eyes swam the cold strength of a deadly warrior.

Staggering to his feet, the Eastnorthern captain drew his knife and charged at Aleksi's back. Beck called out but the youth stood motionless, watching the incoming attack over his shoulder. At the last second, Aleksi spun, stepped aside, and deftly grabbed his opponent's hand as the knife stabbed air.

The captain threw himself against Aleksi, desperately trying to gain advantage with his greater weight. Taking another step to the side, Aleksi twisted the captain's wrist past the breaking point, forcing the captain's hand back on itself with a loud snap. In response, the captain's other hand shot out like a claw, seeking to rip out the youth's eyes. Aleksi instinctively twisted away and rammed the captain's own knife into his throat.

The captain fell to his knees, gagged once, and then collapsed backward into a dark-burgundy pool. The man's eyes were locked on the azure sky as blood flowed from his gurgling neck. As the captain's heart stopped, the stream subsided and Aleksi looked down at the man's body as if surprised by its lack of life.

Runic pain suddenly surged through Aleksi's bandaged hand. It dug deeply into the bone of his arm, causing the youth to clutch his throbbing fist close to his body. Despite his agony, Aleksi bowed to the fallen and then turned his eyes to Beck. The general saw that what had been a gaze of cold strength was now filled with anxious doubt.

Grimacing, Beck hoisted himself up onto his elbow and looked Aleksi in the eye. "You have my deepest gratitude."

"There is no need," Aleksi responded, bending to kneel over the general. "Your people love you. That love is not a thing Terra can afford to lose. Now we must—" The youth's words were cut short as Beck coughed and blood splattered across his breastplate.

"Don't move." Aleksi reached under Beck's deeply dented chest cuirass and undid the armor's buckles. Beck let out a ghastly moan as Aleksi slowly removed the chest plate.

"I think this is it, son," Beck wheezed, laying his head on the ground. "I feel the Guardians' call . . . If only the Vashyrie still came for our people . . ."

"No, Lord. With a wound like this, you should be dead already." Aleksi gently lifted the armor off Beck's body. "Whatever is keeping you alive needs . . ."

Aleksi's words trailed off as he peeled away Beck's cuirass and saw his ghastly wound. Under the dented plate, Beck wore only a sodden cloth undershirt that clung to a deep indentation that once had been his left breast. This truly was a thing no man could survive naturally. At the center of Beck's battered chest, however, a dim glow shone under his shirt.

"Son," Beck said roughly, as a series of screams cut through the square, "tell my wife . . . tell her . . ."

Aleksi didn't respond. Instead, he pulled a dagger from Beck's belt and cut open the general's clammy shirt. Peeling the cloth away revealed a glowing amulet bound to a silver chain. The amulet, with a circular latticework of ethereal Runes dimly radiating from its gossamer surface, lay fixed to the center of Beck's crushed chest.

"Where did you get this?"

Glowing with each pulse of Beck's heartbeat, the amulet's light suddenly weakened. "Mehail," Beck whispered roughly. "He . . ."

"No, don't speak. You must—"

But it was too late. The light of the amulet faded into darkness and Beck's eyes grew dim with its passing. Beck's chest then let out a great sigh and did not rise again.

"No!" Aleksi shouted. "No, no, no!" The youth placed his bandaged hand over the amulet. Hearing the clash of swords behind him, Aleksi focused his mind and all sound faded from his ears. As he did his best to ignore the raging pain of his Rune, Aleksi's arm shook violently and he focused all of his concentration into the amulet.

Aleksi could feel power flow through his body as the amulet blinked back to life. The pain of his Rune surged up the nerves of his arm and threatened to consume him, but Aleksi knew that if he held it back, Beck would die. Pouring the energy of his Rune into the amulet, Aleksi opened himself fully, allowing his Rune to dig its metallic tendrils deeper into his arm.

Despite Aleksi's efforts, it was not enough—Beck's chest still remained broken. Deep blues and purples marred the general's crushed torso, and breath had not returned to his ruined lungs.

Desperately refocusing his mind, Aleksi directed everything he had into his Rune. The veins of his arms bulged as his Rune's light began to shine out through his fingers, causing the amulet's faint glow to grow stronger in response. Aleksi felt as though the bones of his arm burned with holy essence and he let it flow through him into the amulet. Absorbing Aleksi's power, the amulet shone even more brilliantly.

Suddenly, surrounded by a web of interconnected Runes which floated in the air, ethereal tendrils emanated from the amulet and worked their way through Beck's skin and into his lungs. Aleksi continued to pour himself into the amulet as its numinous power then reknitted Beck's flesh and bones under his now-shimmering skin.

Beck's back arched violently and his chest heaved with breath. As the general blew out a rattling exhalation, Aleksi was astonished to see that though bruised, Beck's chest was now no longer concave. Due to the Runic power of the amulet, it had miraculously regained its normal shape.

As the light of the amulet grew faint, Aleksi fell backward and cradled his bandaged fist against his chest. The pain under his flesh was profound, as if his bones were on fire and his flesh were melting away. Tension gripped him as the searing pain surged deeper into his shoulder—and then was gone. Head spinning, the youth rolled to his side as sound violently returned to his ears. With a look of disbelief, Aleksi stared at his bandaged hand. Somehow, both the pain and light of his Rune had disappeared.

Behind him, Aleksi heard a guttural roar and turned to see Nara Simha holding a Pa'laer lieutenant aloft by the neck. Scattered bodies were strewn at the Lionman's feet, and the paving stones were slick with their blood. Nara's massive right arm suspended the lieutenant, and the Berzerker's gauntleted fingers were wrapped around the man's throat in a death hold. Nara's upper body was flexed and his multitudes of deep scars stood out clearly on the striations of his rippling flesh. Aleksi had never witnessed such an outward sign of pure muscular strength.

The Pa'laer lieutenant struggled violently against Nara's grip. The man soon became still, however, and his eyes rolled back into his head. Nara tossed the soldier's body aside and turned to Aleksi. The youth was now standing over Beck and his right hand was deftly gripping the hilt of his sheathed blade.

"It looks like you have some secrets of your own, boy," Nara said, as he stretched his massive arms wide. The Lionman had several smudged lines of yellow paint on his arms and his eyes were slightly dilated. He wore plain brown pants held up by a thick leather belt. This, combined with his bare chest, clearly showed the size of his monolithic frame. Two large steel bracers adorned his hands and forearms, and other than several small pouches attached to his hefty belt, Nara had nothing else with him.

Aleksi's eyes narrowed as Nara continued. "That was a pretty bit of Rune work you did there; however, those soldiers would have cut you down if I had not intervened."

Aleksi's right hand twitched on the hilt of his sword as Nara calmly took a step forward.

"Fear not," Nara continued. "I mean you no harm. If I did . . ." The colossal man gestured to the mangled soldiers dead on the ground. "You would already be lying there next to them."

"Then . . . I thank you, sir." Aleksi glanced down at Beck.

"They were after the general, no doubt," Nara replied. "But it looks like you have saved him. You do need to get him to safety, though. I'm sure more will be here soon."

Although the makeshift lane of tents about them was empty, Aleksi heard sounds of carnage as foreign soldiers butchered the fleeing citizens of Mindra's Haven close by.

"He should be able to move, but just barely." Aleksi knelt down over Beck but still kept his eyes on Nara. "Nara, will you help me?"

"I remember you," Beck suddenly wheezed. "Son, what is your name?"

"My name is Aleksi."

"Last night," Beck continued in a rasping voice, "you had that forsaken pendant at the Guardian's Flame . . ."

"Ever more interesting, aren't you, Aleksi?" Nara said, crossing his immense arms.

"Nara Simha . . . When did you get here?" Beck tried to sit up unsuccessfully. "I . . . I feel weak. What happened?" Beck's eyes scanned the bodies strewn about them.

"Concussion," Aleksi said, eyeing Nara. "You blacked out."

"Well, thank you . . . Thank you both, but I must return to my men." Shrill cries echoed off of the high buildings at the edge of the square. "Please help me out of my armor. I am too weak to move while encumbered by this heavy mail."

"General," Nara said, as Aleksi knelt down and unbuckled Beck's steel plates. "Sadly, from what I saw, there was not much left of your legions after the blast."

Beck grimaced as Aleksi removed the gauntlet on his right hand. But as the guard came off, Beck looked down at his forearm in confusion. Instead of a gaping wound, he had only a thick scar where the Eastnorthern lieutenant had slashed him.

"You must get out of sight and to safety," Nara continued. "I have been patrolling these makeshift streets looking for one of my traveling companions, and I have seen several of these death squads. They are scattered all about."

Eyeing the disarray of the tents around them, Beck scowled. "Damned Arva Vatana, I knew he would betray us."

"No, Lord," Aleksi said, removing the last of Beck's armor. "Although dressed to play the part, these men are not Pa'laer plainsmen." Beck looked at Aleksi in confusion as the youth continued. "They are Hanval and hail from the—"

"Northern capital city of Erithlen," Nara said, finishing Aleksi's words as he looked at the boy in astonishment.

"How do you know this?" Beck's gaze flicked back and forth between Nara's and Aleksi's green eyes.

"Some of these men fight the dance of the Northern Hanval," Nara continued. "And they are a surreptitious group that never shares their techniques with outsiders. I, Lionman of the North-Eastern Mountains of Iksir, have fought these men my whole life, but I do wonder how young Aleksi knows of the Hanval . . ." Aleksi averted his eyes and Nara grinned wide. "Now it seems that *you* prefer that certain questions be left unasked."

"Questions can come later," Beck said roughly as he struggled to stand. "All that matters now is that Mehail is dead and I must regroup with the rest of my men and protect the city."

"General, I don't think you understand." Nara came over and helped Beck to his feet. "Whoever did this did it well. Your men are dead and you must go into hiding."

"We will go to the temple, then. The acolytes and High Council Honor Guard should be dug in awaiting reinforcements." Before Beck could say more, several figures came running down the path.

Domadred Steele led them, and upon seeing Beck, he sprinted even faster, causing his strands of beaded braids to swing violently. Kefta and Brayden followed him closely. Each had his sword drawn, blood glistening on the blades.

"Release him!" Domadred snarled as he ran at Nara with sword raised high.

"Domadred, no!" Beck exclaimed. "They saved me."

"Aleksi fought the first wave and I the second," Nara added. "The general is safe, but not for long."

"Aleksi?" Domadred said, sliding to a halt. "Just several hours ago this youth told me his name was Astya." Aleksi looked away sheepishly and Domadred eyed Aleksi, Nara, and then the multitude of bodies that lay at their feet. "Beck, can Mera Dalh be trusted?"

Beck frowned. "No, Domadred. She is traitorous filth, dead more than ten years. Stop speaking in code. These men truly did save me, if that is your real question."

"Fair enough," Domadred said, sheathing his blade. "Then, regardless of your real names, you both have my highest thanks."

"How did you find me?" Beck asked as Domadred came over and shouldered his friend's weight.

"Luckily, I had my eye on you when the explosion hit," Domadred answered. "I am truly amazed you survived the fall." Nara looked at Aleksi, but the youth remained silent.

"I haven't survived yet," Beck said, slumping as he tried to turn his body back toward Mindra's Temple. "I still feel very weak . . ."

Trying to take a step, Beck sagged and lost the strength in his legs. But as he began to fall, Kefta rushed over and grabbed the general's other arm. Brayden came beside him and a profoundly concerned look shone in the boy's moist eyes.

"Regardless," Domadred said, leading Beck toward the docks. "Once we get you back to the ship, Doc Marlen will take care of you."

"No, Dom," Beck said, struggling against his friend's grip. "We must regroup with my men at the temple. We have to fight and retake the city."

"This is no fight, Beck." Domadred's words were soft. "This is a massacre, and the enemy is the victor. You have men across the channel. With them at your back, you have a chance. Without them, you are only throwing your life away. There is no other choice but to return to the *Diamond*."

As Domadred and Beck continued to debate, Aleksi walked over to the man he had killed just moments before. Kneeling down, Aleksi gazed at the soldier's lifeless body and then at the Rune under his bandaged palm. The youth then took a deep breath and reached out timid fingers, gently closing the man's eyes.

Nara came over and put one of his massive hands on the youth's shoulder. "You fought incredibly well, son. I saw it from afar. Your first kill, I assume. It's hard. But it gets easier. I also saw what you—"

Suddenly, Aleksi doubled over, once again clenching his bandaged hand as it momentarily surged with pain.

"Were you cut in the fight? Let me see." Nara reached over to inspect Aleksi's arm, but the youth flinched away.

"No, I . . . I'm fine. It's an old wound and nothing serious." Aleksi swallowed hard. "It must have reopened. I should keep it bandaged."

Nara nodded slowly.

"Hey, Lionman," Domadred called out, hoisting Beck up higher on his shoulder, "how does safe passage to somewhere other than here sound?"

"Captain," Aleksi said, before Nara could answer, "if you are headed that way, I still need passage to Vai'kel."

"Don't worry, Aleksi. I remember," Domadred answered. "I'm counting on you to watch my back as we head for the ship. I just want the Lionman to watch our front."

"I will go with you on one condition," Nara answered. "We don't leave without my companion."

"Do what you must. But we are headed straight for the ship to set sail for the other side of the channel the moment my boots hit the deck. You are welcome to join us and will be compensated very well for your trouble. However, if you have more pressing matters, I will leave you to them."

Nara frowned but nodded an agreement as a woman's scream cut across the square.

"Domadred," Beck exclaimed, "we must stand our ground and fight for the people! They are getting slaughtered. We must go to the temple!"

"The East," Domadred answered, "cannot afford to let you throw your life away out of some misguided love for Mehail. You *must* live so that you may continue to serve. The people need you now more than ever."

"But Brin . . ." Beck's voice grew hoarse with emotion. "He was on the platform. I . . . I can't leave him."

"Beck, your son is strong and able. We will find him. But if we don't get your men who are waiting across the channel, that will be impossible. If your soldiers are at the temple as you say, they will be dug in tight, desperately awaiting reinforcement." Beck dropped his head.

"Enough of this talk!" Kefta exclaimed, pulling Beck even faster. "We have to get to the ship, *now!*"

"And hope to High Arkai Aruna it's not burning," Domadred added. "Let's go."

As the rest of the small group made their way down the makeshift alley, Aleksi knelt and picked up Beck's battered breastplate. He ran his hand over the unnaturally massive dent on its center curve. Out of the corner of his eye he could see that Nara had turned around and was looking at him keenly.

Aleksi then set the breastplate down on the bloody flagstones and took his position at the rear of the group.

CHAPTER X

Scanning the empty alley of stalls before them, Nara slowly led the group down a makeshift lane. Lining both sides of the trail were tents and marquees of all shapes and sizes. The interlocking maze of paths weaved through the massive square with seemingly little rhyme or reason. Aleksi noticed that the tents' vivid awnings of blue, gold, purple, and green stood in stark contrast to the splattered crimson from Adhira's citizens.

Behind them Aleksi could hear the steady cries of carnage as the foreign soldiers ransacked the city. Looking back, he saw that several of the tall buildings of Guardians' Plaza were burning. The vivid imagery combined with the sounds of battle were deeply unsettling. Drawing his eyes away from the flames, Aleksi saw debris of the mob's panicked retreat strewn about his boots. Even worse, every few meters or so, the youth came across a fallen body lying among the refuse. It seemed that the majority of the fleeing citizens either exited the main gate to the harbor or were routed east around Mindra's Temple through the central boulevard that led through the heart of the city. This left the western edges of the square relatively barren and disconcertingly quiet.

"Horrible," Brayden said, eyeing a corpse ahead of them. "I can't believe . . ."

His words trailed off as the group approached the broken body of a teenage girl sprawled out next to a pile of trash. She was facedown and her hair was splayed out unnaturally. The girl's dress was torn and a thick pool of dark blood had congealed around her head. As the group passed, Brayden looked closer and saw that the back of her skull had been gashed open by the slash of a sword.

"Who could do this? What kind of man could kill a . . ." But Brayden couldn't say any more. His words were choked back and his eyes welled with tears.

"Oh, my son," Domadred said consolingly. Although the captain was still supporting Beck's weight, he reached out and pulled Brayden close to his chest. "These are not men any longer. They have fallen to darkness, and the Guardians will treat them as such."

"Then where are the Guardians?" Brayden looked up at the towering, luminescent statue of High Arkai Mindra in front of them. Its great shimmering wings were spread wide, casting flowing shadows of light around them.

"Mindra works in mysterious ways," Beck answered. "But protect the people he shall. Just hold hope in your heart, for his grace will save this city and vindicate the fallen—this I swear to you."

Brayden nodded solemnly and looked back at the girl's lifeless body lying behind them.

As the group moved westward through the square, they came closer to the gigantic statue of Mindra. Looming above them, its incandescent surface shimmered in the light of the Zenith. Rounding another corner, they came to a path that led to a break in the tents near the foot of the statue. Although it was still some ways off in the distance, they could hear the sounds of men fighting and yelling in the small clearing near the statue's base.

"We should go around." Domadred started to walk Beck down an alley away from the commotion.

"No," Beck said firmly, planting his feet. "There is no way to know that there won't be more down that way, too."

"And no way to know how many are out there in the open. We must stay out of sight, go around and stick to the tented alleys."

"We go straight and cut them down," Beck growled. "The less of this filth on my streets, the better."

"Beck, I applaud your determination, I truly do. But you are in no condition to argue, let alone fight. If you had your feet under yourself and a blade in your hand, things would be different. Sweet Akasha, if that were so, we could even storm Asura's great citadel in the North. But I'm sorry, old friend, with you wounded we are vulnerable and it's just too dangerous. We must go around."

Suddenly, the sharp crack of a whip echoed through the square. It was soon followed by the throaty shriek of a man. Nara's eyes shot wide and he sprinted across the paving stones toward the great statue of Mindra.

"Damn the darkness! What is he doing?" Domadred exclaimed, watching Nara dash down the tent-lined path. Close behind him, Aleksi flew past the group, running after Nara. "What? Not you, too?"

"Meet us at the base of the statue," Aleksi shouted over his shoulder. "Please, just trust me!"

As Aleksi tried to catch Nara, he saw the Lionman slide his gauntlets over the flesh of his arms and chest. The motion visibly tore at his skin, reopening old scars. Nara then reached back to a pouch on his large belt and plunged both his hands inside. Picking up speed, Nara pulled his hands free and slid his fingers along his arms and chest, coating the freshly opened wounds with a thick yellow paint. Smearing the remainder of the paint on his face, Nara surged forward and let out a horrifying roar.

Nara's heavy legs pounded the flagstones and he tore into the clearing around the statue with the force of an unshackled bull. He slammed into the first Pa'laer soldier before the man could even look over. One tremendous punch of Nara's gauntleted fist shattered the left side of the man's head. The blow sent the warrior rolling across the paving stones, leaving a bloody streak in his wake. Nara was on top of the next soldier almost instantly. The Lionman picked him up with both arms and hurled the man into a nearby tent, where he landed with a loud crash of timber and torn canvas.

Aleksi was still some distance down the path and could not tell how many men were in the clearing. He did, however, hear several more sharp reports of a whip, answered by howls of pain. After killing a third man, Nara looked over as Aleksi continued running. The enormous man's eyes were fully dilated, for the euphoria of the stimulant-induced battle rage—used only by the adrenalized North-Eastern Iksir Berzerkers—was now coursing through his bulging veins.

Letting out another guttural roar, the Lionman engaged a fourth man. Aleksi watched as Nara waved away the soldier's sword with his gauntlet and grabbed the man's skull. The Lionman let out a terrifying growl and squeezed. Nara's muscles bulged, protruding from his form in a way Aleksi had never seen, and his mighty grip crushed the soldier's skull. Throwing away the pulpy mess, Nara charged across the square in a blinding rage toward a nearby group of soldiers.

Aleksi broke through the mouth of the alley and saw Fa'ell fighting several Pa'laer soldiers some distance away. She seemed to be protecting a handful of huddled civilians at the base of Mindra's statue. The soldiers circled her viciously, however, closing in with blades drawn. Aleksi ran past Nara and his bloody melee and rushed over to Fa'ell just as the soldiers simultaneously lashed out at her.

Fa'ell hit the closest warrior in the eye with a sharp strike of her whip's cracker. The man's eye exploded and he fell to the ground, clutching the socket as blood spurted out through his fingers. Another soldier slashed out with his sword but Fa'ell acrobatically dodged the blade and her whip struck again. The cracker raked the man across the throat and his face convulsed in a wordless scream as he fell to the paving stones.

As Aleksi entered the fray, another soldier heard his hurried footfalls and spun. The man swung his sword, trying to slice the youth from forehead to navel. Just like he had been taught at the Academy, Aleksi slid to the side of the strike, rushing out of the blade's way as it cut through the air. Aleksi then reached out and followed the sword's arc of movement to completion. When the blade reached the bottom of its strike, Aleksi used both hands to deftly grip the man's wrist and hilt in a powerful joint lock. Using the hilt as a fulcrum, Aleksi then flipped and rotated the soldier's sword vertically. This brought the blade's tip up so it pointed to the sky with its cutting edge reversed back at the man.

The soldier, now facing the blade of his sword, tried to wrestle himself free. Aleksi held him firmly, however, and the man's wrist threatened to break under his own strained movement. The soldier tried to kick out at Aleksi, but as he did, Aleksi cut down with the sword. The movement first snapped the man's wrist with a loud pop and then embedded the soldier's own blade into the thick of his skull. Blood squirted out from the man's forehead and splattered on Aleksi's face.

Startled, Aleksi released the hilt of the sword as the soldier staggered back. Wide eyed and terrified, the man numbly fumbled at the blade as he fell over onto the paving stones. Aleksi watched in horror as the soldier's eyes raced wildly and blood flowed from his head. "Sweet Akasha . . . ," Aleksi whispered, looking down at the man's cleaved face. The sword was still deeply lodged in the man's skull and his fingers clutched at it futilely as he died.

Suddenly, another soldier charged, forcing Aleksi to spin and evade an attack at the last second. Before the soldier could swing again, however, there came a swift rush of wind and the tight knotting sound of leather. The man went motionless and his eyes grew bloodshot. The long fall of Fa'ell's whip was wrapped securely around the soldier's neck. The man clawed at his throat and tried to free himself, but Fa'ell pulled back on the whip's thong and yanked him off his feet. The soldier fell to the ground and soon stopped struggling as his face turned purple and bloated with dark blotches.

Aleksi looked over at what he had thought were huddled civilians. In truth, they were only corpses. A wave of nausea rolled over him as the pain of his Rune flared. The man with the missing eye then stumbled to get to his feet and tried to run. Fa'ell's whip struck out again. It caught the fleeing soldier's neck in a stranglehold. She then pulled the man off his feet and he fell back. The soldier's remaining eye rolled up into his head and he clawed at his neck, breathless and dying.

With no remaining soldiers near them, Aleksi looked over to Nara at the base of Mindra's shimmering statue. Where there previously had been ten Pa'laer soldiers, now only two remained standing. They had Nara at either end, however, and the speed with which the large man had once moved was gone. As a side effect of his *soma* paints, a sluggish torpor replaced the Lionman's battle rage.

One of the soldiers swung down and slashed Nara's side with his blade. Even at a distance, Aleksi saw the slice cut a clean gash in Nara's external obliques. Nara seemed unaffected by the blow, however, and struck the man in the mouth with an attack that followed through with the full force of his enormous body. The soldier's jaw was bashed off by the strike, causing a gooey mess of blood, bone, and teeth to spray from the man's mangled face.

The other soldier slashed next, and the attack carved Nara across his shoulder blades. Enraged, the large man let out a terrifying howl, and as he spun around, blood squirted out in a ninety-degree arc from his back. Now fully facing his attacker, Nara parried another blow from the soldier's sword before grabbing the man by the throat and lifting him off the ground. Nara then squeezed. The muscles in his massive forearm clenched and his mailed fist audibly broke the soldier's neck with a series of hollow cracks. As Nara threw the lifeless man aside, he scanned the square with eyes that blazed with the fiery, drug-induced mydriasis of soma battle madness.

Seeing no more soldiers, Nara stumbled toward Fa'ell and Aleksi. He was clumsy in his stupor, however, and tripped over himself after only several steps. The large man fell down hard on his side with a solid thud. Struggling to get to his knees, Nara had a look of confusion on his face. His eyes were dilated and unfocused and drool flowed copiously from his mouth.

"You damned fool," Fa'ell shouted, cracking her whip. "You will die of overdose!"

Nara's head reeled and he tried bracing himself on the ground with a massive hand, but it seemed only to destabilize him more. He looked beseechingly at Fa'ell as he floundered in a growing pool of his own blood and saliva.

"He is bleeding badly," Aleksi said, rushing over. "We need bandages!"

"Wait! He might lash out, you must let me." Fa'ell held her whip's thong deftly as she stalked toward the large man.

"Ff'al . . . Brronn paain . . . ," Nara mumbled as he pulled himself across the stones and left a streak of blood and spit in his wake. "Brroon paainn . . ."

Fa'ell came next to him, and Nara fumbled his hands toward her blindly. Just as he was about to grasp her in his massive arms, however, she lithely leapt over his shoulder and thrust her fingers into one of the pouches on his belt. Her hand came away slick with a dark-brown paint, and she smeared it over the deep gash on his back. Next she spread it on his side and then over his self-inflicted wounds on his arms and chest.

At first, Nara protested. Blindly flailing his arms, he tried to swat her away. But soon he stopped and lay back onto the paving stones as a wide grin spread across his face. His eyes were locked on the glittering statue of High Arkai Mindra, and a steady stream of drool ran from his smiling mouth.

"I've heard stories of the Berzerkers," Domadred said, as he, Beck, Brayden, and Kefta made their way over to the statue. "But seeing the real thing in action is actually quite terrifying."

Hearing the captain's words, Fa'ell spun on her heel. She raised her whip high, poised to strike. "Fa'ell, it's OK," Aleksi said from next to her. "They are with us." Fa'ell eyed the four newcomers suspiciously and seemed to not recognize Kefta.

"My lady, I am General Beck Al'Beth of Mindra's Haven," Beck said, trying to stand tall. "We mean you no harm."

"I know your face, General," Fa'ell said, eyeing Beck's massive scar. "I'm sorry. I tried to help your people, but . . ." Her words trailed off as she looked at the fallen bodies of the citizens of Mindra's Haven lying in pools of their own blood. "They were praying at Mindra's feet when the soldiers attacked. I tried to save them . . ."

Beck swallowed hard. "They will be avenged."

Brayden gripped the hilt of his sheathed sword in a white-knuckled fist as he looked at the piles of bodies. Casting a wary eye at Fa'ell, Kefta left Beck's side as the group made their way to the statue's base. The young man then went over to the fallen bodies and crossed their hands over their hearts.

Aleksi knelt down over Nara's painted body and looked into his delirious eyes. Although still dilated, they were now focused, staring at the glittering statue above them.

"Will he be . . . OK?" Aleksi asked.

"Oh, I'm quite sure he's enjoying himself," Fa'ell answered. "But with such a high dose, he should be dead. Lucky for him, I was able to get the counteragent into his blood nearly instantly courtesy of the sword wounds from the dead soldiers over there." Fa'ell then pointed over to the pile of bodies. Her finger lingered over the man whose neck was bent at a very unnatural angle and then the other who was missing half his face. As he followed her gaze, Aleksi's stomach turned over and he felt another wave of nausea flood through him. He clenched his bandaged fist and, trying to suppress his nausea, focused on the sharp tendrils that dug into the flesh of his hand.

"I've heard the brown paint acts as a coagulant and sealant," Domadred added. "It will stop the bleeding and keep his wounds closed, correct?"

"Yes," Fa'ell answered, eyeing Domadred keenly. "And depending on how much blood he has lost, he should either die very soon or awaken quite shortly."

"Damn good thing," Kefta said, as he finished performing the last rites to the fallen civilians. "There is no way we can drag him to the ship. He must weigh over a hundred and fifty kilos!"

"You!" Fa'ell spun to face the young man. Recognition shone in her teal-flecked amethyst eyes and she cracked her whip. "You *filthy* piece of sea trash. I will kill you for your insults!"

"Whoa there, little lady," Domadred said, jumping in between them with his arms held out. "Whatever your issue is with Kefta, which I'm sure is justified and well deserved, you will have to settle it on the ship. He is a member of my crew, which means that by the Law of the Sea, he can be sentenced and put to death only while aboard my vessel. And if such a judgment is passed, just make sure you kill him above deck."

"Captain, that is *not* funny!" Kefta said, moving behind Domadred.

"You are no captain of mine," Fa'ell hissed. "And there obviously will be no arena fights, so he will pay his debt here and now! I think a *hand* will suffice." Her whip then lashed out over Domadred's shoulder and caught Kefta by the wrist. Kefta cried out in pain as a trickle of blood ran down his arm.

"What's that, little boy?" Fa'ell asked, laughing. "Not so cocky now, are you?"

Before Fa'ell could do more, Domadred reached up and grabbed the taut whip in his fist, wrapping it around his own forearm. "I really must insist," Domadred said firmly, as he drew his sword. "If Kefta has wronged you, he will atone for his actions. But an issue with one of my crew is an issue *with me.*"

"I can attest to it," Aleksi said, walking toward them. "I was there. Kefta slandered her honor and her people. It was unprovoked and unwarranted, which means *he* broke a Thalassocratic law while at port in Mindra's Haven." Kefta shot Aleksi a vicious glare but remained silent.

"Then, m'lady, I am sure this man owes you penance," Domadred continued. "Penance which he will pay, but it will happen on the deck of the *Illusive Diamond* and nowhere else."

Fa'ell's eyes flashed a cold rage, but before she could say anything, a slurred voice spoke behind her.

"Fa'ell . . . the sailor is a worthless boy," Nara said, pushing his massive frame up onto his knees. "Leave him for now. We will sort this out on board their ship."

"What ship?" Fa'ell shouted, tightening the tension on her whip and pointing an accusing finger at Nara. "And what is this *we*? I'm not going anywhere with you!"

Domadred wrapped another cord length of the whip around his arm as Nara continued. "Fa'ell . . . for nearly two years I futilely scoured Terra just to find you. And once I had given up all hope, you show up cursing my name and refusing to listen to my words. Then I had to hunt through this bloodbath of a square just to find you again. I nearly died for you, my lo—"

Nara cut himself off. A look of pain passed over the Lionman's face as he stood up on unsteady feet. "I nearly died . . . to repay my debt to you. So please, listen to reason. All you need do is look around; this city has fallen." Nara removed one of his gauntlets and put a callused hand through his short blond hair. It smudged the paint on his now-pale face. "We must get to safety, and this captain has offered us passage. Drop this pettiness and release them now."

"You are a fool, Nara, and you should be a dead fool." Fa'ell then gave two flourishes of her whip that first untangled Domadred and then Kefta. "But even worse, you *still* do not know how to speak to a woman."

CHAPTER XI

Due to his wounds, Nara now led the group significantly more slowly as they moved past the statue and through the weaving maze of tents. As the small party continued on to the great outer doors of the city walls, they encountered no soldiers along their way. They did, however, continue to see the horrible aftermath of the invaders' carnage strewn about them.

As they came to the large city gates, the light of the Zenith dimmed into artificial dusk and Aleksi looked up at the guard towers high above. Whoever had been stationed there was now nowhere to be seen. Looking out through the open gate, Aleksi saw fire flickering among the docks.

Suddenly, three sharp peals of a horn cut through the eerie calm of the square. The call was answered by another horn in the pavilion behind them. Instantly, it was followed by the sound of over a hundred people slamming gauntleted fists on breastplates and cheering out in one triumphant voice.

"A legion of Adhira's soldiers!" Beck exclaimed in joy. "But how?"

Aleksi looked up at the guard tower and saw a lone soldier with a horn at his side. The man was gazing down at them from the wall high above, saluting his general. "Up there, Lord," Aleksi said, pointing.

Beck looked up and saluted the man before turning back to the square. After a short moment, several rows of men and women in shining mail rounded a corner through the tents. The soldiers marched forward in quickstep and the sound of their boots rang off the flagstones like rhythmic claps of thunder. Armored in full plate mail and helms, they shouted out a guttural "ha!" with each fourth step they made. The booming call reverberated against the city's high walls as they marched onward.

"Blessed be the High Arkai Mindra!" Beck said roughly, with emotion. "There is hope yet!"

As more of the legion rounded the corner, they could see High Priest Trailen Kaftal holding the great banner of Mindra aloft by its large pole. Its glorious Runic stitching shone brightly in the fading light of the Zenith.

"By the grace of the Guardians . . . ," Domadred exclaimed.

As the legion got closer, Adler and Brin broke formation and ran to Beck at full sprint despite their heavy armor. Unaided by Domadred, Beck managed to take several steps forward as they approached. Reaching Beck, both Adler and Brin removed their helm and fell down to their knees, breathless. Eyes locked on the ground, Brin was the first to speak.

"Forgive me, Father, I—"

Beck said nothing but placed his fingers under his son's chin, gently raising the young man's face to meet his own gaze. Brin looked up and saw tears welling in the eyes of the great general of Adhira.

"Forgive me, Lord," Adler said, still kneeling beside Brin. "We tried to find you."

"There is no need for forgiveness," Beck answered, wiping his eyes. "Instead, you have my thanks. Both of you, please stand." Despite the fading light, Beck could see that their armor was badly marred by the blast and ensuing battle. "Tell me what happened out there. How did you escape the explosion?"

Adler stood. "Lord, we assisted the legion that pushed the Farden men off the platform and the blast was kind to us. The others . . . were not so lucky."

Brin stood and looked past Beck's shoulder to the battle-worn group behind him. "Father, how did *you* survive?"

"I was saved by these brave souls," Beck said, gesturing to Domadred and his companions. "They were agents of Mindra's divine will, no doubt. They are the only reason I draw breath."

Nara glanced at Aleksi with a glimmer of a smile on his pale lips. The delirium of his paints still held his green eyes, but his expression was filled with knowing. Aleksi looked at Nara pleadingly and the large man's smile grew wider.

"But how?" Beck continued, looking over the approaching legion of men dressed in perfectly shining mail. "How did you get reinforcements?"

"High Priest Trailen brought a legion of men through the south-western gate. I have no idea how he knew, but we were able to rout the enemy away from the temple." Adler paused. "And then we broke pursuit to find you."

"The enemy is still out there?" Beck said, aghast. "They are raiding the city, yet you brought the reinforcements here to find *me*?"

"Lord, we found your armor abandoned some ways back . . . We feared you were captured." Adler dropped his head. "I gave the order for only a small task force to continue searching for you, led by me and Brin, but—"

"And you should have followed through with that order!" Beck said furiously. "Why would you ever bring these men to an abandoned square while foreign forces burn our city?"

"For we followed a *higher order*," Trailen said firmly, walking up behind Adler and Brin. The High Priest still held the glorious banner of Mindra. In addition, the Rune on Trailen's forehead burned a molten white and complemented the banner's magnificent glow.

"Finding you was a *direct* commandment from the High Arkai," Trailen continued, as his eyes filled with his Rune's searing light. "Lord Mindra's will is mysterious and occult. And while not even I can fathom why he would allow such an atrocity to befall his magnificent city, his grace and power are *eternal*. I follow his orders as a dutiful child—an order to find and protect *you* at all costs."

"Blessed are we, his children," Beck said formally, placing both hands across his heart in ceremonial salute to the High Priest. "May we serve faithfully to earn his love and grace." Beck then bowed low with both arms extended, palms up.

"Faithfully serve, you have," Trailen said, as his voice boomed louder so even the legion behind him could hear. "And because of it, Lord Mindra has decreed that you, Beck Al'Beth, will act as an agent of his divine will! For he commands that *you* shall be his holy High Protectorate over all of Devdan!"

"High Priest," Beck said, shock clearly showing on his face. "May the Arkai's divine wisdom guide my heart and hands . . ."

"Guide you, he shall," Trailen said, eyes still blazing in the growing darkness. "For with Mehail Bander's tragic death and the city in chaos, the council has declared martial law. Lord Al'Beth, not only does that make you High Protectorate over Adhira, but High Arkai Mindra tasks you to once again reunite the East under *his* holy rule! Devdan will be a unified realm once again."

"Yes, High Priest," Beck answered, bowing low. "May I earn in the days to come the great honor that High Arkai Mindra has bestowed upon me."

"High Lord Al'Beth," Trailen said solemnly, "I trust you shall. Now please prepare yourself, for we must march immediately to save our people."

For an instant, Trailen's luminous stare locked on Aleksi and he looked as though he were about to speak again. Aleksi felt his Rune pulse and clenched his bandaged fist, but the High Priest did not hold the gaze. As he turned, the light of Trailen's eyes then slowly faded as he walked back to the legion behind him, leaving Adler and Brin looking at Beck in awe. Likewise, Domadred and the rest of the group also gazed at the new High Lord, similarly amazed.

"High Protectorate over all of Devdan . . . ," Adler said in a voice that was hardly more than a whisper.

"Father, I . . ." Excitement clearly showed on Brin's face despite the darkness.

"Status report!" Beck said firmly, ignoring their words. "Where do we stand, *General* Adler Karll?"

Adler's eyes lit up at the words, and when he spoke, his voice was once again clear and strong. "We have a full legion of one hundred and twenty-five soldiers here, *High* Lord. We must hold out until the other ten legions arrive from the far side of the great river at Zenith dawn. Also, I am not sure how, but the enemy has many more soldiers than we first saw during the commendation ceremony." Adler paused and his tone grew grim. "We are greatly outnumbered, and members of the enemy are masquerading as civilians and rallying the general population to riot and plunder. Even worse, some are dressed as the High Council Honor Guard. I am not sure how, but they must have infiltrated our city some time ago—"

"The . . . High Council Honor Guard?" Beck scowled. "Do we have any within our *own* ranks?"

"None that we have found, Lord. The legions of Adhira are loyal to her people."

Beck nodded. "Then this city has a chance, for no one else knows the streets of Mindra's Haven like her legions! Get me a suit of mail, for we now march to *battle!*"

"Yes, sir!" Adler and Brin said in unison, saluting. They then turned and jogged back to the legion with the heavy clang of armor following each step.

Beck turned back to Domadred. The captain wore an impressed look on his face. Seeing it, Beck smiled.

"Congratulations," Domadred said, as he crossed his left hand over his heart and extended his right arm, fingers wide. Beck placed his fist across his own heart and firmly grasped Domadred's forearm in salutation. As Domadred clutched Beck's arm, he could feel that Beck's hand was shaking.

"Sadly," Beck said, "you must now go." Domadred opened his mouth to object, but Beck didn't give him a chance to speak. "We have no way to know when Lenhal's Western fleet will arrive, and with things as they are, we are not even able to protect ourselves, let alone you and your crew."

"The *Diamond* can protect *herself,*" Domadred protested. "And we can help shuttle soldiers from the mainland."

"You cannot risk your cargo. Too much hangs in the balance. Especially now."

"But it is a balance which you will turn in our favor," Domadred answered. "For after I rally the Resistance, I'm sure that the East will now finally recognize our cause. I hear it's convenient when one's friends are *High* Lords."

"We will soon fight together once again, my friend." A faint smile spread across Beck's lips. The High Protectorate then looked around at the disarray and destruction of the square. "That I promise."

"Watch your back," Domadred continued. "I feel the waters which swirl about us are dark and treacherous, possessing currents within currents."

"I have been to Mindra's Haven," Beck said, reciting the old saying. The captain was about to open his mouth, but Beck stopped him. "Domadred, the Guardians saved me once, and I will trust in them to do so again."

Domadred nodded solemnly and Beck turned to Aleksi and Nara. "I cannot thank either of you enough. You both now share my heart and hearth, for I forever will be in your debt."

Nara bowed his head, wincing as the movement pulled on the crusted wounds on his back. The large man's green eyes were still dilated and somewhat wild but his smile was genuine. Beside him, Aleksi placed his palms together. The youth touched his thumbs first against his forehead and then against his heart.

"Yes, I thought so," Beck said, looking at Aleksi. "Keep Domadred safe. His cargo is more important than you could possibly know." Beck then leaned closer and whispered in Aleksi's ear. "He also can tell you much of that pendant of yours. Just tread on those grounds lightly, son, lest you wake the restless dead."

With that, Beck nodded to Brayden, Fa'ell, and Kefta, and then abruptly turned to rejoin his men as they prepared to retake their besieged homeland.

Under the shimmering light of the great statue of Mindra, High Protectorate Beck Al'Beth, his noble legion of men, and their High Priest Trailen Kaftal marched back through the square toward the temple. As Domadred's group watched them depart, a slight breeze picked up and the last of the Zenith's light disappeared into darkness. Once the torch-lit glow of the legion's armor disappeared into the night, Domadred and his group turned and looked out the great double doors to the harbor beyond.

"An escort to the ship would have been nice," Kefta said disdainfully. Fa'ell shot the young man a deadly look.

"Kefta, not another word until we board the *Diamond*." Domadred did not break his gaze at the harbor. "Those soldiers will be forced to fight over the corpses of their countrymen to retake their fallen city. Their numbers will dwindle building by building, until there is only a handful left. The hope of reinforcements at dawn will be the only thing which keeps them from succumbing to the darkness of the night." The captain then turned his head, eyeing Kefta. "The last thing on their mind is a mouthy sailor like you. Now let's *move*."

As the group walked through the great double doors of the city's outer walls, it soon became clear that the harbor was in worse shape than the square behind them. While Mindra's Square had been mostly empty of living people, Aleksi could now clearly see the chaos of both locals and foreigners fighting and rampaging across the docks. The riotous people moved in droves, raiding warehouses and burning ships unlucky enough to still be moored.

Looking out into the harbor, Domadred saw hundreds of flaming boats floating aimlessly into the night. It brought back a memory of the historic Red Riots of Mindra's Haven and their destructive wake of blood and flame. "We will have to move quickly," Domadred said, turning his eyes back to the long thoroughfare that only hours before had been revered as the great center spoke of the wheel of Eastern trade and commerce. "I tell you, the *Diamond* is holding strong, but I can't say for how long. We must make all haste before these fires spread. Although her hull won't burn, the *Diamond's* sails and rigging will catch easily if any one of these flaming ships gets too close."

"Where is your ship, Captain?" Nara asked, scanning the crowds as the group moved forward.

"The *Diamond* is moored at the foreign trading docks," Domadred answered, looking down the long stretch of disarrayed harbor before them as he walked. "She's a three-masted barquentine schooner, and last I left her, she was riding on spring lines. While I am not sure what she is flying now, at full sail she is gaff rigged, fore and aft, with one large set of squares on her foremast and an assortment of staysails at her bow."

"She doesn't look like anything else in the harbor," Brayden added. "You won't be able to miss her."

"The *Diamond*," Fa'ell said slowly. "You keep saying that name. You can't possibly mean the . . . *Illusive Diamond*?"

"One and the same, my darling," Domadred replied with a theatrical flourish of his captain's hat.

Fa'ell's eyes grew wide and she stopped abruptly on the dock. "Then you're Domadred Steele, *the* Domadred Steele!"

"At your service, m'lady."

Fa'ell turned an accusing look on Nara. "Did you know this, Nara?"

"Yes." Nara continued walking and scanned the various groups raiding the remaining ships. "Now, Captain, how far—"

"You knew this man was a pirate, and yet you still agreed to board his ship?"

Nara paused and looked back at her. His eyes were still dilated, and although his wounds were now crusted shut with medicinal brown paint, it was obvious they pained him greatly. "Although I have never personally made the good captain's acquaintance, I am aware of his exploits and reputation. It's one of the reasons I agreed to—"

"He is a hunted man!" Fa'ell blurted out. "You have us bedding down with a bloody pirate?"

"Well, this is the first I have heard about bedding anyone," Domadred said with a smile. "However, I assure you that whatever reputation you know me by has been exaggerated. Unless it's favorable, of course; then it's a gross understatement."

"I will *not* consort with pirates!" Fa'ell protested, ignoring Domadred's words.

"Look around you, Fa'ell. What choice do you have?"

Fa'ell looked at Aleksi. "What about you, boy? You're comfortable with these men's *reputation*?"

"I am not familiar with the reputation of the *Diamond* or her crew," Aleksi answered, looking at the multitude of burning ships in the harbor. "But not only do we have little choice, I do in fact trust that Captain Do—"

"You've *actually* never heard of the *Illusive Diamond*?" Domadred asked incredulously. "Where have you been hiding yourself, son?"

"I have not traveled much," Aleksi answered. "But—"

"Well, when you step aboard the *Diamond*, all that will change! But let's take that step in haste, shall we?"

An explosion rocked one of the ships burning nearby. It sounded like an ammunition barrel bursting, and Kefta and Brayden both gave their captain a pleading look.

"Domadred has done nothing to betray my trust," Nara continued, eyeing Fa'ell derisively. "And if High Lord Al'Beth trusts him, it speaks only greater of Domadred's character. I, for one, will sail on the *Diamond*. You may stay here on the docks if you wish." Nara once again began walking down the wharf. Fa'ell shook her head but her protests ceased.

As they continued on, the group passed several gangs of marauders. However, when the clusters saw the bare-chested and bloodied Lionman leading as vanguard, they thought better of starting any trouble.

As the group approached a long stretch of empty dockage, the *Illusive Diamond* finally came into view. Brayden was right; the *Diamond* looked like no other ship in the harbor. Her pristine sails were pure white and her elegant hull was built for speed. She had a complement of twenty cannons—nine on either side, and a chaser at the bow and stern. With a square-rigged foremast and fore-and-aft rigged main and mizzen, the majestic ship stuck out amid the smoke and turmoil of the pier.

Containers were strewn about the dock along with a mob of citizens and soldiers. It appeared they were petitioning the *Diamond*'s crew to allow them to board. The ship's men, however, held drawn swords and were keeping the rabble at bay. As Domadred and his small group came closer, they could see that a wharf building farther up the dock was burning brightly and cast long shadows across the crowd trying to get passage aboard the *Diamond*. In addition, the crackling blaze highlighted several squads of armed soldiers in glinting plate mail.

Something from deep inside the building behind the mob exploded. Even from afar, Aleksi could feel the blast reverberate in his chest. The detonation jettisoned bursts of flame and wood onto the docks. Although the *Diamond* was outside the eruption's radius and unharmed, the majority of the crowd on the pier fled from the explosion. Billowing smoke rose up from the building's wreckage, its thick black column illuminated by the fires below. The flames cast looming shadows about the remaining soldiers who continued to demand passage on the *Illusive Diamond*.

As Domadred came closer, he could see the soldiers were dressed as the retinue of the High Council Honor Guard. They were also holding torches, threatening to burn the ship if they were not let aboard. Several of the soldiers then extended a long plank to the *Diamond* and tried to clamber over. Members of the *Diamond*'s crew, however, grabbed long pole arms to knock the soldiers into the water.

Coming within earshot, Domadred gave out a piercing whistle and yelled, "Rihat, cut the spring lines and come about to me!"

Rihat, the ship's quartermaster, looked over to Domadred and smiled wide. He then ordered the ship's crew to cut the docking lines and upturn the plank, with several High Council Honor Guard already halfway across to the ship.

The armored soldiers fell into the water with a heavy splash as several of the *Diamond*'s sails unfurled. Instantly, the sails caught the night's breeze and urged the great ship into motion.

As their comrades sank into the dark waters below, the soldiers on the dock shouted and about half tried to jump across the growing gap between pier and ship. The other half split rank and ran down the dock toward Domadred and his group. Of those who jumped for the ship, about three-quarters made it and clambered up the gunwale, drawing swords. The others, however, hit the water with muffled splashes.

As the *Diamond* coasted toward Domadred and his companions, the ship's crew engaged their bulky attackers with the harsh clash of steel on steel. Domadred could see his men fighting fearlessly; however, the High Council Honor Guard clearly had the advantage in combat, for they wore heavy armor which far outstripped the sailors' cloth clothes.

"Push them over the side!" said a Northern-accented voice aboard the ship. Domadred had never heard this man before, and he strained his ears to listen. "You there, grab ahold of this other end."

A man dressed as Northern nobility came into view and passed a thick weave of *teraf* rope to several of the deckhands. Together, they drew it tight. The sailors charged the majority of the High Council Honor Guard, clotheslining them off the side of the ship. There came a loud splash and the attacking soldiers' numbers were greatly diminished.

Domadred watched on as the man dressed in formal Northern attire fought alongside the ship's men, personally slaying a great many of the High Council Honor Guard.

As the *Illusive Diamond* coasted adjacent to the dock, Domadred once again cupped his hands and called out to his quartermaster. "Have six men tie in with catch lines, and on my mark, have them swing out!"

Just then, there came another furious explosion from the wharf behind them. This one was much larger than the first. The blast hurled a great deal of debris into the air, including numerous barrels that landed on the dock and in the water with a fiery combustion of *pancera* oil. Wherever the oil touched, flames instantly ignited. The fire stretched across wood and water alike, and its oddly multicolored flare cast eerie shadows about the harbor.

Domadred watched as several of the barrels landed in the *Diamond*'s path. They exploded into rippling flames on the waves in front of the ship's bow as she came to rescue her displaced captain and crew.

Seeing the firelight across the water, the helmsman called down to Domadred. "Sir! Orders?"

"Cut her in close, then push out hard and *hold true!*"

The helmsman followed his captain's instructions and spun the wheel hard to avoid the worst of the flames. But as she was rounding the pier, the *Diamond* nearly struck a large mooring post protruding from the dark water. The helmsman then spun the wheel the opposite direction and evaded the bollard by just a millimeter as the ship slid up and approached Domadred and his small group.

The ship came in with such force and speed, however, that the *Diamond*'s starboard bow struck the dock with a great crash. The ship scraped the mooring with a screech of grinding wood and twisted metal. A shower of sparks and splinters was cast into the burning waters as the *Diamond* finally came aside.

With armor and swords glinting in the flames, the remainder of the High Council Honor Guard engaged Domadred and his party. They came in at full charge but were met by the Lionman's mighty fists, Fa'ell's cracking whip, and both Kefta's and Brayden's swords. Aleksi, too, met them in battle, but instead of drawing blade, he fought with open hands, using joint locks to throw his attackers over his hip and into the water. Despite the group's skill, however, the High Council Honor Guard were too many. The party was pushed back, unable to board the *Diamond* as it skidded its way along the pier with a mournful groan.

Domadred called out to his crew, and six sailors swiftly swung down from the *Diamond*'s rigging and slammed both shoulder and sword into the attacking men. This sent the majority of their assailants sprawling out onto the dock. The sailors were tied to their lines by the waist, and on each rope's meter-long tail was attached another man-sized noose. The sailors had numbered off, and upon landing, each tied his line to his appointed person of Domadred's party.

First came Kefta, then Fa'ell, Aleksi, Brayden, Domadred, and finally the massive Lionman. After the sailors had secured their lines, they each shouted out and the crew pulled the man and his accompanying party member up onto the moving ship as the Diamond continued to grind past the pier.

The struck soldiers, however, were quick to recover. After only Kefta, Fa'ell, and Aleksi were drawn aboard, one of the High Council Honor Guard lashed out at Brayden, cutting his rope and killing the sailor who was to rescue him. Seeing this, Nara went over to save the boy, but Domadred called out.

"No! Everyone get on board, that's an order!" As the words came out of Domadred's mouth, he cut his own rope and threw himself on top of his son's attacker. The ship then pushed away from the flaming pier, and three men struggled to pull Nara up and away.

Struggling under the force of the soldier, Brayden freed a small dagger from his belt. As Domadred did his best to wrestle the guard off his son, Brayden stabbed the knife into the man's gut under a gap in his chest plate.

Domadred flipped the dying man off Brayden and tied his own rope around his son as the *Diamond* pulled farther away from the dock.

"Pull him in!" Domadred called out as he parried blades with another relentless wave of soldiers. "And helmsman, *hold true!*"

"No!" Brayden screamed. But then his line was pulled taut, and with a violent snap he was wrenched off the dock, nearly hitting the flaming water as he was hoisted onto the *Diamond*. Twenty meters away and growing, the great ship then picked up speed as it soared away on the burning waters.

Domadred, now alone on the dock with the High Council Honor Guard, fought off five soldiers at once. His blade flew furiously as he shouted back to his crew. "Now throw me the—"

A line with a weight tied to its end hit the dock at his feet with a hollow thud.

"—sounding line," Domadred finished, looking back at his ship in astonishment. Kefta stood on the quarterdeck holding the line's end, a wide grin on his face.

Just then a blade swung across Domadred's periphery and he lunged. The captain deftly rolled across the deck with the sounding line firmly grasped in his hands. After sheathing his sword and running at a full sprint down the pier toward his ship, Domadred wrapped the line around both of his wrists and called out as the High Council Honor Guard chased at his boot heels. "Wait till the *Diamond* clears the fire, and then *pull me up!*"

With that, Domadred leapt off the end of the pier with a mighty dive and plunged, fists first, into the flaming waters below.

CHAPTER XII

Domadred awoke vomiting seawater. Strong hands propped him up and he wretched on the planks of his ship, surrounded by crew and friends alike.

"Give him space," Kefta yelled out, pushing back the sailors on the dim, lantern-lit deck. Opening his eyes, Domadred had just enough time to see Brayden lunge into his arms. Brayden was sobbing as he clung to his father's soaking body. Mustering all the strength he could, Domadred raised shaky hands and held his son tight.

"Thank the Guardians . . ." The murmurs of the crew echoed in Domadred's ears as he looked about in the darkness. Domadred could see that the *Diamond* was just passing the harbor's breakwater jetty and he was encircled on the ship's quarterdeck. With Brayden still in his arms, the captain rubbed his swollen eyes. He saw Nara, Fa'ell, Aleksi, and his crew all standing with looks of relief upon their faces.

Feeling the lull of the *Diamond* as the current coasted them out of Mindra's port of Azain, Domadred heard an unfamiliar voice. "Blessed are the Guardians"—it was the same Northern accent as before—"may they forever protect us in our time of need . . ."

In unison the crew completed the oath's response: "We vow to forever be worthy of their grace and love." The sailors then turned and eyed the fancily dressed man as he came forward.

"Captain," the sailing master said, stepping in front of the Northerner, "this man fought for us when we were boarded. If it were not for him . . ." The officer's words trailed off.

"Well then, you have my thanks," Domadred replied as he stood upon shaky feet and smoothed out his dripping hair. "Although now is not—"

"No need for thanks, Captain." The Northerner gave an elegant bow. "I am only happy you are safe. That was an outstanding feat you just performed. I am nothing short of impressed. Truly."

"Yes, well, I—"

"My name is Luka Norte and I am an ambassador from Simn, currently serving Vai'kel's ruling council. I won't bore you with the details now, but I wish to meet with you and personally deliver an urgent message. Seeing that our departure was so . . . *hurried*, I feel time truly is of the essence."

"Well . . . Luka," Domadred said, coughing the last of the seawater from his lungs, "I'm sure you can understand there are things I must attend to as we set forth from the harbor. I look forward to speaking to you further and hearing your message at a more . . . *appropriate* time."

"Indeed, Captain," Luka said, throwing his ornate green cape over his shoulder. "I shall then await you with great anticipation." Luka then strode to the foredeck at the front of the ship, leaving the rest of the crew with Domadred on the quarterdeck at the *Diamond*'s stern.

"Northern bastard," Domadred said with his eyes locked on Luka's back. "Lucky for him, he will fetch a good ransom." Domadred then looked about his crew. "Rihat, report. How is our *cargo*?" There was no answer, and no one met the pirate's eye. The captain continued in a low voice. "Where is the quartermaster?"

"Captain," Marlen, the ship's doctor, said, swallowing hard, "the cargo is safe. But the quartermaster is . . . dead, sir."

Domadred scanned the crew, inhaling deeply. When he spoke, his voice was no more than a whisper. "Where is Narem?"

". . . The master gunner is also dead, sir."

Domadred put a shaky hand to his eyes. "Who else did we lose, Marlen?"

"Five other seamen, sir."

"Damn the darkness!" The captain lowered his hand, clenching it into a fist. "At Zenith dawn we will have a proper service for the fallen. And then . . ." Domadred's voice faltered. "We will vote in our new officers. Crew dismissed."

With Domadred's final word, the seamen broke away to their stations. Left on the quarterdeck were the *Diamond*'s remaining officers, which included Kefta and a handful of other sea-worn men. Nara, Fa'ell, and Aleksi stood several paces behind them.

Domadred took off his dripping vest as he addressed them all. "Men, we have some new guests. These three here"—Domadred gestured to Nara, Fa'ell, and Aleksi—"have earned passage as trusted friends and allies. And while the lady Fa'ell and our own mate Kefta have some important business which will be taken care of at Zenith dawn, our new friends are to be given their own quarters, free rein of the ship, and whatever supplies they need. As you can assume, we left Mindra's Haven in a hurry and they will need provisions. That one, however," Domadred said, gesturing to Luka, "will be a valuable war asset to the Resistance and will be held prisoner until we dock at Port Rai'th, in Vai'kel."

"Captain," the ship's boatswain said, "permission to speak, sir."

"Granted, Valen."

"Sir, Quartermaster Rihat had given Luka Norte permission to board before the riots broke out. Rihat had similar thoughts to your own but was awaiting your return to make the final decision. But, sir"—Valen's voice grew soft—"Luka saved my life, sir, along with many others. He fought nobly to protect—"

"Noted, Valen," Domadred said sternly. "I saw much of the fight myself." The captain shook his head as he continued. "I will decide his fate soon. Until then, I want a two-man guard on him at all times. Kefta, you are in charge of security until a new quartermaster is . . . nominated."

". . . Understood, sir," Kefta said, swallowing hard.

Domadred then turned to Brayden. "Relieve the helmsman, Son, and take us out into the channel's current."

"Yes, Captain," Brayden said, taking the wheel.

"Once we are out into the open current," Domadred continued, "I want all officers to meet me in my cabin. Until then, I will be cleaning up. Dismissed." The officers bowed and went about their duties as Domadred looked at Nara, Fa'ell, and Aleksi. "Please follow Doc Marlen; he will tend to whatever wounds you have and then show you to your quarters. I trust you will find your accommodations to your liking. If you need anything, don't hesitate to ask."

"Thank you, Captain," Nara said, but Domadred had already turned and disappeared through the door to his cabin.

"Please come with me," Marlen said, looking over Nara's wounds and Aleksi's bandaged hand. "I will patch you up in the infirmary and then show you to your quarters. I trust you are tired from the day's . . . festivities."

The three guests followed the ship's doctor toward the stairs that led down to the main deck. As they walked, Aleksi noticed that Marlen was the only member of the crew who lacked the telltale blue eyes and long blond hair of a Westerner. Instead, he possessed black hair and the bright-green eyes of Northern descent.

"Actually, if it's alright," Aleksi said, pausing on the deck, "you can tend to Nara's injuries and then show him and Fa'ell to their rooms. My hand needs no further attention and I would like to watch us depart Adhira."

"As you wish," Marlen said, looking slightly surprised.

Marlen then went belowdecks and Nara gestured for Fa'ell to go first. As she passed, the Lionman placed a large hand on Aleksi's shoulder and nodded with a knowing look of compassion. Aleksi looked down but returned the nod. The massive man then turned and, ducking his head, walked through the passage that led under the quarterdeck.

Down the stairs, Aleksi could hear Marlen's voice. "Lionman, I can't count how many years it's been since I have seen a Berzerker from Iksir so decorated with wounds yet still able—" But then the doctor's voice was gone and all Aleksi could hear were the rush of the wind in the sails and the splash of waves against the *Diamond*'s bow.

Aleksi looked up through the filled sails to Terra's great dome of stars overhead. The moons had yet to rise, but the youth noticed that there was a bright amber light in the distance behind them—Mindra's

Haven was burning. Visions of the massacre from Mindra's Square flashed through his mind and the nerves in his hand pulsed painfully. So many people had died—so many had been murdered. And while Aleksi had not drawn his blade in anger, he, too, had killed. The Masters' Vow was to protect, yet who was he protecting when he had killed? Beck? Rudra? Himself? All Aleksi could see were the hollow eyes of the men he had slain. Their empty gazes looked at him accusatorily as the pain in his palm grew stronger. Aleksi shook his head and pushed the bloody images away.

Turning away from the burning city, Aleksi walked forward on the dimly lit deck and let his eyes wander across the vessel. As he took in the shipboard activities, the crew eyed him harshly, and as one deckhand passed, Aleksi was forced to quickly sidestep so as to not be knocked over.

"Watch your step, *Green Eyes*," the man said gruffly. "I'd hate for you to fall overboard so far from your Northern shores."

"There would not be a blue-eyed tear shed for your loss," another sailor responded with a laugh, "that's for damn sure."

Aleksi clenched his bandaged fist but didn't respond. He did, however, make sure to stay out of their way as he continued moving forward. Each sailor seemed to intimately know his place and position aboard the *Diamond*, and all moved in unison as the ship prepared to enter the mouth of the great channel. Topmen climbed into the rigging and out onto the spars. Deckhands stood at the booms and manned hawser lines. Officers stood at attention, observing everyone's movements with critical eyes. It was a harmony of movement and motion choreographed on instinct alone.

Trying to soothe his agitated mind, Aleksi let himself be lulled by the rhythmic flow of the ship. Below his boots the youth could actually feel the *Diamond* as she cut through the water. He felt her sails draw breath as her body swayed with the metrical pulsing of the sea. All about him there was a musical creaking of wood, canvas, and taut lines. A soft breeze blew across him, and despite its warmth Aleksi shivered. Coming to the edge of the ship, Aleksi turned away and looked out into the dark water flowing ahead. The tips of the waves softly glistened in the star shine for as far as his eye could see. Aleksi took a deep breath—he felt exhausted.

Letting out a sigh, Aleksi leaned against the gunwale and reached into the pocket of his cloak. He fingered the letter from Master Rudra, that fateful message committed to memory from many long hours puzzling at its occult meaning. All he had to do was close his eyes to picture Rudra's carefully scripted words. He felt himself mouthing his Master's prophetic message like a mantra.

> *Aleksi,*
>
> *I sense your Rune has finally begun to awaken. Others can feel it, too. Dark assassins have been sent to corrupt or kill you—to steal your Rune for their own or to prevent its power from entering this world. If they succeed, you will become the catalyst of the Guardians' destruction, for it will be by your hand, or lack thereof, that Terra's salvation will be plunged into darkness.*
>
> *To flee the grasping shadow, you must go to the city of ruin that the Guardians neglected. At the precipice of eternal ignorance, turn from the edge of darkness, for if at any time upon your journey you take a life in anger, you will fall willingly into the hands of those who hunt you. As the repercussions of your rage burn through your body, drink deeply from the light of Mindra—his power of compassion and healing is freely given if you can but open your heart to his eternal song.*
>
> *Next, find the ancestral place of healing which was once dedicated to the Northern light. As you search, give not into your temptation, but remember the Masters' Vow. Once you arrive, let the wounded blindly run away from his fears. As you bear the token of your father while seated by a cold flame, a soon-to-be-resurrected leader will tell you to forsake your lineage. Save him from both flame and steel, for he will lead you to your safe passage before giving the children of Mindra a new hope against the looming shadow.*

*As you search for your past, your house, and its fate-
ful ruin, you will cross the sea on a ship of many facets.
When torment returns, the myth of the moons and their
holy birth will temporarily cleanse your wounds. As your
mettle is tested, please remember: the truth is never as simple as a deceiver would lead you to believe. Contemplating
your choices from the loft perched in light, do not unveil the
truth of the noble, for the leader must seal the fate of his
people untainted, lest he condemn us all to shadow. Finally,
when you find Vai'kel's last hope in dire need, give her your
strength and trust in your heart, for it will be love that will
save you both and awaken your true power.*

*Most importantly, however, never forget that only I can
teach you how to harness your Rune and protect yourself
from its devastation. Until you have it mastered, you are
a threat to both friend and foe alike. But fear not: your
fissured heart will lead you to your answers, and then,
finally, to me. I know that you have great faith but also
great doubt—remember that both are needed, yet it will be
great determination which will allow you to transcend to
salvation.*

*When you are well on the path, I will send word again.
But remember to make all haste, my Apprentice, for shadows follow your every step. Never forget that if at any point
on your journey you choose to fall prey to its alluring power,
then its corruption will reign over Terra, eternal.*

~Rudra

How could he have known? Aleksi thought.

Just then, Aleksi heard the deep swoosh of sails above as the *Diamond*
turned into the channel's strongest outgoing current. This flow of water
moved profoundly fast and would carry the *Diamond* to the sea quickly
despite the great distance traveled. As the ship came about with her
jibs unfurled and ready to catch, the massive sails snapped with the
solid sound of canvas and wind, then filled in the strong breeze as the
Diamond surged forward on the swifter-than-natural artificial current.

Suddenly, dual hallowed blue lights crested on the horizon before them as the twin moons began to rise. The *Diamond* moved in to meet them and entered into the slot of the channel where the racing combers crested and then broke into white water.

Both moons had now risen high into the sky, and after changing into fresh clothes, Domadred had joined his son at the wheel. Together, father and son read the fast-moving currents as the ship was propelled along the channel toward the sea. Brayden was a wave-born seaman, and he kept the *Diamond* on a perfect line even as the extreme waters bucked and shuddered the ship stem to stern.

Nearing the end of the channel, the boy conned the wheel perfectly as the ship's keel caught in a churning crosscurrent two fathoms down. The *Diamond* then shot out into the open ocean. She pushed past the headland and entered into the great Eastern Sea, where the waters ran fast and clean.

Despite the late hour, Aleksi was still gazing out at the water. Suddenly, he felt his Rune pulse frantically. He looked to his right and saw Luka Norte approach the gunwale. He was dressed in fine clothes with woven gold and jewels sewn into the fabric; everything about the man seemed burnished in the glowing light of the moons.

"Do you mind if I join you in your contemplation of the ocean's beauty?" Luka asked.

Aleksi eyed the man without speaking and rested his bandaged hand on the hilt of his blade. Up close, the nobleman's mocking green eyes were filled with dark secrets. As the land slowly disappeared into the distance, a cutting wind picked up and chilled the air.

After a short while, the nobleman turned to Aleksi a second time. "We pass the point of no return," he said with a thin smile. "Wouldn't you say, *Aleksi*?" Without waiting for a response, Luka turned away and disappeared belowdecks.

Aleksi watched the man's back as he left. His youthful eyes then grew wide. *My name—how does he know my name? Did he ask the captain or crew? Did Domadred even tell anyone?* Aleksi gripped the hilt of his sheathed sword and winced as the sharp tendrils of his Rune dug deeper into his flesh. *Could it really be possible that Luka knows who I am? But if Luka were an assassin, wouldn't he have tried to kill me instantly? No, he must have overheard my name somewhere . . . He must have . . .*

Trying to calm his mind, Aleksi drew a long breath as he once again gazed out to sea. As Adhira faded from view, the sea seemed to swallow Aleksi's last sense of security.

Aleksi stood in a small guest berth lit by a wall candle and desk lamp. His quarters had their own porthole, and through it, Aleksi could clearly see one of Terra's two moons resting in the sky. But whether it was Rahu or Ketu Aleksi did not know. The youth's berth contained a sleeping hammock, an empty chest, and even a desk built into the wall next to a series of hooks. Upon one of the hooks hung his long black cloak and hidden pendant.

Aleksi leaned against the desk and slowly drew his blade from its scabbard. The youth inspected the layered steel and checked its edge. He then sheathed the sword and lay back in his hammock. Able to rest for the first time in countless days, he stared up at the ceiling's wooden timbers and tried to force his body to relax into the rhythmic yawing of the ship. It was no use; fear still clutched at his heart.

Although I'm finally bound for Vai'kel and one step closer to finding Master Rudra, if Luka truly knows who I am, then I'm no safer than when I started. But with my Rune continuing to grow, I have even greater problems. Let's see how much time I have left.

Aleksi slowly removed the bandage wrapped around his right arm. Almost ceremoniously, the youth raised his hand to the light of the moon. The majestic Rune etched into his right palm shimmered in the moonshine. It had grown considerably.

The black Rune flowed in an intricate circular pattern over his palm, and its glow of power radiated out from under his skin. Aleksi had borne this Rune for his whole life. For nearly the entirety of that time, however, the Rune had lain dormant. Now, it had finally begun to synchronize with his body and was clawing its way through his nervous system, leaving many darkly bruised lines behind as it painfully crept toward his shoulder.

Clenching his fist, Aleksi felt the new metallic tendrils in his hand and forearm pulse with a strange, foreign power. He then flexed his biceps and winced as the sharp ends of the growing Rune dug into the muscles of his upper arm. The Rune's tendrils were still working their way up his peripheral nervous system—but Aleksi knew that if he did not find Rudra soon, he would not survive when the Rune's metallic links reached his spine and entered his central nervous system and brain.

Somehow, channeling Beck's amulet drained the Rune of its energy stores. Although I felt that same searing pain when it dug its way deeper into my upper arm, I think saving Beck bought me some time. Aleksi let out a sigh. *If only Rudra were here to tell me how long I have until its power replenishes and the Rune fully synchronizes with my body.*

Closing his eyes and focusing on his breath, Aleksi felt his mind wander over the events of the past two days. Coming to the carnage of Mindra's Square, Aleksi's mind grew uneasy. He deliberately forced himself to move on. Relaxing, he then came to Luka, the nobleman . . . his smile . . . those eyes. It was the look of dark power—the smile of caged violence.

Aleksi knew that look *all too well.*

Nataraja's eyes were fixed on him, cruel and calculating. They were in the Academy training yard.

"Come at me again!" the man said, as his long hair flowed in the wind. "How do you expect to purify yourself when you succumb to fear?"

The child Aleksi snarled, letting his passion rise in his chest as he ran at Nataraja. The boy's wooden sword flashed out, lunging high toward his teacher's right shoulder. As Nataraja's practice blade came up in an easy parry, Aleksi let his weight carry him forward to attempt his real strike. Aleksi felt time slow as his right foot swung out to side kick his mentor in the ribs.

Nataraja, however, easily slid inside the strike, catching Aleksi's leg in midair. The Master forcefully pushed up and Aleksi saw the sky rush below him as he was thrown backward. His young body then hit the ground, and the wind was knocked out of him in a painful gust.

Aleksi felt his chest sting bitterly and he rolled over, trying to recover. Nataraja's practice blade then slammed point first into the boy's sternum. Bolts of searing pain shot outward from Aleksi's rib cage. Instinctively, the boy curled his legs up and tried to reclaim his breath. In response, Nataraja only pushed down harder, pinning Aleksi to the ground.

"Tame your anger like the animal it is," Nataraja said, shaking his head. "You must become its master and establish dominance, or you will never come close to awakening your true power." Nataraja removed his sword, allowing Aleksi to roll onto his side.

Wheezing, the boy crawled onto all fours and silent tears fell to the ground. "Why . . . why are you so hard on me?"

"It is only through the purification of pain that you can achieve clarity of mind and emotion."

As he clutched the earth with his hands, Aleksi's voice was rough. "But you don't even treat the older students like this! Why me?"

"You know you are not like them, Aleksi. Because of your Rune, you must become an Apprentice soon, despite your age. Although the demands are strenuous, you have no choice but to prepare yourself for your Runic training. You are deeply underprepared and already behind schedule."

Still lying on the ground, Aleksi looked at the dormant Rune embedded on his right palm. "I *will* be ready for Rudra when he comes for me."

"Rudra?" Anger leapt across Nataraja's face and his voice was thick with hatred. "That murderous betrayer will never return here; this I swear to you!" Taking a deep breath, Nataraja recomposed himself. "I am your Master, for only I can ensure that you will not fall to failure and disgrace like that *outcast* Rudra. But regardless of your delusions, if you do not burn away your weakness, you will not be ready to

Apprentice under me, or *any* Master. So wipe away your tears, channel your anger, and come at me again!"

Rage welled in Aleksi's chest as he rose to his feet and snatched his practice sword from the dirt. "Rudra is my *true* Master and I *will* be ready when he comes back for me!" Nataraja's eyes narrowed as the boy wiped the streaks from his face and held his training blade high in defiance. "For neither you nor anyone else will *ever* see weakness in me again!"

"Yes. Now that you feel your anger's strength, cage it! Only through mastery of self will you awaken that which separates you from the others. There is power in your anger, beyond what you could ever know. Let it rise and then become its master!"

Aleksi felt his rage expand as he attempted to order its direction and flow. Standing in the wild current, he felt the hairs on his skin rise in anticipation as the Rune on his palm pulsed painfully for the first time in his life. Shudders of energy suddenly climbed up his spine as Aleksi sensed the power of his Rune awaken within him. Somewhere deep in the core of his essence, there was a raging fury ready to burst forth and devour him.

"Yes . . ." Nataraja's voice was only a whisper. "It's finally happened."

Aleksi let himself go and a tortured scream rang in his ear as he lunged forward. Faster than he had ever dreamed, he attacked Nataraja and drove the Master back. Nataraja's smile slowly widened as he was forced to take one, two, and then three steps backward. With every parry and counter, Nataraja's green eyes glimmered with anticipation.

This is it! Aleksi thought as he parried Nataraja's sword close to his own body, creating an opening. And then, for the first time in one-on-one combat, Aleksi struck his mentor, slamming his elbow into Nataraja's stomach. Nataraja gave a muffled grunt as Aleksi's Rune sent a surge of pain up his arm. Then, in one continuous movement, Aleksi cut down with his sword—it was aimed directly at Nataraja's head.

Time suddenly seemed to freeze. Aleksi watched as Nataraja miraculously slipped to the side of his strike and grabbed his right arm. In slow motion, Aleksi then felt himself wrenched forward with extreme force. The boy looked down and saw Nataraja's knee rise and slam into his chest.

Time sped up again. Aleksi's feet left the ground and he felt his ribs crack from the powerful blow. He then hit the dirt and agony flooded his body. The pain was from Nataraja's strike, however, for the Rune had gone dormant once again.

"Become master of your rage, my student." Aleksi felt the tip of Nataraja's sword lie softly against his neck. "You play with a fire which will consume not only you, but potentially the whole world. Domination of your anger is what will set that power free and save us all—for it seems that *my* Master was right about you."

A knock brought Aleksi back to the present. "Hey, Green Eyes, Captain thought you would be hungry from the day's *events.*"

After draping a blanket over his arm, Aleksi opened the cabin door to reveal a small man holding a platter of dark meat, cheese, and bread. There was even a small bowl of soup and a mug of what looked to be spiced wine.

"Thank you," Aleksi said, taking the tray. The sailor grunted before turning to depart.

I hope it's not poisoned. I'll have to take the risk, though, because I can't starve myself for this entire voyage.

After eating, Aleksi lay back in his hammock and sank into the rhythms of the ship. The movement slowly lulled him to sleep.

It was then that Aleksi saw *her*. The young woman rose out of the depths of the dream into which Aleksi was falling. They passed one another, each riding their own current in the psychical waters. Aleksi cut off his dive to return to her, wanting. She seemed to do the same, deftly soaring back through the shifting colors and feelings of the shadowy ether.

Her youthful eyes were magnetic, and Aleksi felt pulled to her and her power. She was ethereal and unique but also *alive.* A light glowed upon her forehead and he tried to get nearer to her but was pushed back. An invisible barrier was keeping him away. Her lips moved but Aleksi heard nothing but a beautiful melody of the heart. The sound seemed to come from across a distant horizon.

Aleksi read her eyes. The young woman seemed to warn him, to beckon, to plead. She came closer. Her hands pressed against the invisible wall as her surreal beauty shone out in the darkness. Again, her lips moved wordlessly.

What is she saying? But then the young woman was closer and Aleksi no longer cared. Her eyes drew him in. He breathed in the scent of her body and felt the warmth of her breath. Suddenly, she swirled and came apart like paint on a canvas. Only her eyes remained. Unchanging and stoic, they were like fire and water flowing together in darkness. They were beautiful—and then she was gone.

Suddenly awake, Aleksi fell out of his hammock and groped for her in the darkness of his mind. He tried to cling to the memory of her eyes as he grabbed the wall to steady himself. Aleksi continued to feel her gaze and it pierced his heart painfully. He put a shaky hand through his hair. It came away damp with a sheen of cold sweat. The young woman was more than a dream. He *knew* it.

Aleksi went to the desk. Illuminated by the blue light of the moons, he took a leather-bound notebook from a shelf. With a charcoal pencil, Aleksi drew her eyes on a blank page—just her eyes.

Over and over again Aleksi drew them until at last he lay back in his hammock, falling into a deep sleep with the young woman's eyes gazing back at him.

CHAPTER XIII

Aleksi awoke with the glaring rays of the Eastern Zenith streaming through his cabin's small porthole. He had never slept in a hammock before and as he unsteadily descended from its intricately pleached netting, he felt his neck ache. Rubbing the sleep from his eyes, Aleksi looked out the window. Through the thick glass, he saw endless sea stretching out before him.

Aleksi blinked his eyes several times in surprise. In addition to the light of the Eastern Zenith behind the ship, Aleksi saw another glare shining on the horizon before them. *Sweet Arkai, of course, that's Vai'kel's Zenith!* Because of its great distance, it was hovering just above the horizon line, but the sight of it caused Aleksi's breath to catch in his throat. Although it did not rise as tall as its cardinal brethren, the Central Zenith of Vai'kel, according to legend, commingled its light with each of the other four Zeniths at the very center of the world—the Yad'razil Island. Never before had Aleksi seen anything other than the Eastern Zenith, and witnessing this glowing orb so low on the skyline was astonishing. Aleksi took a deep breath as he watched the waves glisten with two sets of morning light as they rolled out into the distant horizon beyond.

"So vast," Aleksi whispered as he turned from the porthole. Back at the Academy, Aleksi had often gazed from his dormitory window out to the great sea past Adhira. He had always wondered what it would be like to leave the high towers of the Academy and sail off into the endless unknown.

Nataraja said he would take me to each corner of Terra if I chose him as my Master. He said that there would be nothing we could not see together—nothing we could not do. But at what price was his offer extended, and to what purpose? Nataraja, just like all the other Masters of the Academy, was only interested in me for my Rune. What would he have done had I pledged myself to his command? How would he have used my power? How would he have used me? Is Rudra any different?

Inside Aleksi's quarters, brilliant-white dust motes floated in the air. As the youth got dressed, he still had a lingering sensation from his dreams. What they had been of, however, he could not recall. All Aleksi could remember was the piercing blue gaze of a young woman and his own deep longing. Pushing the feeling away, he finished dressing.

Pulling on his boots and cinching his blade to his belt, Aleksi felt his eye rest upon his long black cloak that hung on the wall. Even though he could not see it, the pendant resting in the cloak's pocket tugged at his mind. Aleksi stepped toward the cloak and reached into its pocket. At first he felt only smooth fabric, but then his probing fingers grazed it. It was like touching thickly braided leather—soft, yet firm. Aleksi closed his eyes and rubbed the broken pendant between his fingers. Touching the etched Runes, he felt their talismanic murmur, a familiar melody of a near-forgotten song. Before he could remember its source, however, the sensation was snatched away, leaving in its place the hollow feeling of a lost memory.

Aleksi let out a sigh as he retracted his hand. *Just more mysteries. I've waited this long; what is another few days?*

Making sure the bandage that wrapped around his Rune-covered hand was snug, Aleksi rested his left palm on the upper scabbard of his sword and opened the door to the hallway. He locked the door behind him, glancing down the dimly lit and small passage beyond. Walking down the narrow hallway which led to the ladder to the deck, he realized that getting used to living in such close quarters was not going to be easy. The ship was at a slight angle and gently swayed with the rhythmic yaw of the ocean. At first, walking on a slant was strange, but after reaching the ladder, Aleksi felt his body naturally adjust to the ship's movement and tilt.

Aleksi ascended into the morning's bright light and fresh sea air. Shielding his eyes from both Zeniths' rays, he looked about the ship and saw that the crew was up and working. In fact, they moved tirelessly. Walking the deck and climbing the shrouds, they flowed over the ship in a symbiotic harmony.

In the darkness of the night prior, Aleksi had not been able to see the full majesty that was the *Illusive Diamond*. Now, in the bright light of day, he could clearly appreciate the true splendor of the three-masted ship. He took in her grandeur as she cut through the waves, spray splashing at her bow. Looking up at the cloth canopy above, the youth saw that the regal ship flew with full sails catching the morning wind. Her strong spars and tight rigging creaked and moaned as she cut across the water. The soft groaning of the tackle sounded odd to his ears, but he assumed it would soon become second nature.

Closest to the bow, the *Illusive Diamond*'s foremast had five large square-rigged sails that rode on horizontal spars, which were perpendicular to the midline keel of the ship. The other two masts were fore-and-aft rigged; however, each possessed two massive sheets fitted to long booms that were set along the line of the keel, rather than perpendicular to it. In addition, much like a schooner, both booms of the latter masts could swivel freely. This gave the *Diamond* profound maneuverability with the added trait of being able to sail nearly directly into the wind. With this suite of fore-and-aft rigged sails, Aleksi assumed that the *Diamond* could be operated with relative ease and efficiency, while the single foremast offered long-distance speed and dramatic appearance at both sea and port.

"She's a beauty, isn't she?" a voice said from behind Aleksi.

"She is at that," Aleksi responded, turning toward a sailor with blue eyes. The man's garb was slightly more ornate than the clothes of the majority of the seamen, and the numerous beaded braids in his hair signaled him as an officer. Instead of going shirtless or wearing simple cottons, he bore a loose-fitting embroidered V-neck vest tucked into an elegant belt. He had the same baggy pants as the crew but instead of being barefoot like the many of others, he tucked his pants into knee-high brushed-leather boots.

"Sixty meters long, nine and a half wide, and thirty-six tall," the officer said proudly, his thumbs hooking into his belt. "She's got just shy of thirty crew, and with a strong wind her one thousand square meters of sail can fly us faster than any on Terra."

"Sir, are you the boatswain?" Aleksi asked.

"Indeed, I am," the man responded in a thick Western accent. "The name's Valen. It's a pleasure to meet you, Aleksi. Welcome aboard the *Illusive Diamond*."

Suddenly, the ship hit a large swell and Aleksi had to take a step backward to steady himself. "The pleasure is mine," Aleksi continued, as salty spray noisily rained down about them. "The boatswain . . . that makes you in charge of deck activities, rigging, and the handling of the sails, correct?"

"Indeed. It is my duty to reconnoiter the ship every morning, inspecting her lines, sails, and other equipment to make sure there was no damage in the dark of the night prior."

"You even take note of the supply stores, correct?"

"You know a lot for your first time at sea, m'boy. Especially for a *green eyes*," Valen said, chuckling. "The captain was right about you, it seems."

"Oh, well, I read a lot . . . and—"

"No need for explanations, lad," Valen said, patting Aleksi on the shoulder. "When each of us joined the *Illusive Diamond*, our pasts were forgiven *and* forgotten. A man makes his own destiny upon the open ocean."

"Thank you, sir."

"But I'm sure you are hungry," Valen continued, his tone lightening. "Let's find you some food before the captain draws us all together and begins the service for the fallen."

After Aleksi finished eating, he joined the large gathering assembled on the main deck. Most present were standard seamen, but Aleksi also saw the crew's officers along with Fa'ell and the wounded Lionman, too. All present were waiting, with an air of silent rumination, for Domadred to emerge from the navigation room.

Coming closer, Aleksi saw Marlen, the ship's doctor, standing above the corpses of the fallen. Each was wrapped in fresh sailcloth, yet their faces were left exposed to the morning air. Through the crowd, Aleksi could see several of the dead men. Their skin was pale and their expressions were blank. One corpse had a wide gash in his face from one cheekbone across to his opposite jaw. The wound, however, was closed and a series of stitches rejoined the dead man's carved flesh.

Aleksi swallowed hard. An image of Mindra's Square and the soldier with a blade embedded in his skull flashed through the youth's mind. A wave of nausea quickly followed, and, clenching his bandaged fist, Aleksi forcibly pushed the memory away.

Looking up at the intricately carved wood of the navigation room's windowed double doors, Aleksi saw movement from within. Opening the doors, Domadred deliberately strode out of his cabin. The captain's folded knee-high boots rang on the wooden deck with each step. He held an elaborately bound book and, in the manner of the Thalassocratic fleet, wore an ornate dark-blue vest inlaid with silver stitching.

Pausing at the quarterdeck, Domadred cast a compassionate eye over his crew standing at attention. Aleksi saw Kefta was slow to turn, however. The young man had been looking at the corpse with the slashed face, and Aleksi thought he saw tears glisten in Kefta's eyes as he turned to face his captain.

"Men," Domadred said in a strong voice, "this is a dark day despite the warmth of the Zenith rays. We have lost brothers. Brothers who gave their lives defending the *Illusive Diamond*—their family and their home. All of the fallen were with the *Diamond*, with me, before Lenhal stole our honor away. Our seamen Ranet, Vanmar, Yaeral, Warr, and Kail, and even Narem, our master gunner, and"—Domadred's voice faltered and his eyes flashed to Kefta—"and Rihat, our quartermaster.

"High Arkai Aruna has once again taken more members of my family into his eternal embrace. And regardless of whether it was Pa'laer treachery or Asura infiltrating the Eastern High Council

Honor Guard that killed them, I take full responsibility. However, I also will not waver from our noble mission. We *will* purge Lenhal and his wretched filth from our great fleet, and the *Illusive Diamond will* retake her rightful place in the noble Thalassocracy of the West!" The crew cheered openly, bitterly cursing Lenhal, the prime admiral of the Thalassocracy. Domadred allowed their shouts to go on a moment before he continued.

"But *first*, we must turn our attention to our fallen brothers. Together, we must usher their souls into the waiting arms of High Arkai Aruna on the Western Zenith." Domadred solemnly walked over to the seven men wrapped in sailcloth. Aleksi felt the mood of the ship shift as the crew bowed their heads and folded their hands over their hearts.

Domadred read aloud from his ornate book. "High Arkai Aruna, preserve these souls in your holy abode atop the Western Zenith so that they may rejoin the great ocean that is Numina. These mortals faithfully served your will, dying valiantly to protect their holy home of Terra. So we call upon you today, like countless days before, to hold true to your promise made so many ages past. We beseech you, holy Guardian and divine father of the West; please lead these souls back to their rightful home."

With hands still crossed over their hearts, the sailors bowed low. As they stood back up, they stretched their arms toward the corpses. With their palms facing the fallen, the crew spoke in unison. "We cast your bodies back to the sea from which they came. But your souls, brothers, ride on Guardians' wings to the Western Zenith . . ."

When the chant was complete, several deckhands ceremoniously stitched the sailcloth over the corpses' faces. One by one, they slid the bodies over the ship's side. The cloth bags were weighted with a cannonball each and entered the water with a hollow splash before disappearing beneath the cobalt waves.

When the last body was ritually cast into the sea, Domadred turned to face the crew again. "It saddens me deeply, but now we come to the business of voting in new officers. As you know, we have two openings—the position of master gunner and that of quartermaster. Like always, the officers and I will make our nominations, and the crew will shout their vote. If any say *nay*, a new nomination will be deliberated and presented for your approval."

The officers walked up and stood at Domadred's side as he continued. "First we will vote the master gunner." There was a long pause before Domadred continued. "A knowledgeable master gunner is essential. We have chosen a man who has served as gunner on the *Diamond* for battles aplenty, and nominate seaman Mareth Yerana for the crew's consideration!"

There was much nodding and whispering among the crew, and a sailor Aleksi assumed to be Mareth came forward. He was an older man, hair bleached by the Zenith or just white with age. Mareth's face seemed to have weathered many a storm at sea, and his hands were permanently stained black from his long use of fire powder. His blue eyes, however, shone bright and clear, and as the sailor stood proudly facing the crew, Aleksi could see this was a man of noble character.

"What *say you*, men?" Domadred shouted. "All for, signify by saying aye!"

"Aye!" The vote came in one thunderous roar of unanimity.

"Mareth," Domadred said officially, "you have been charged with the commanding and safekeeping of the *Diamond*'s guns and ammunition. Do you swear to lead the gunners in times of battle and of peace?"

"I do, Captain!" Mareth said in a voice strong and throaty.

"Then before the divine eye of Arkai Aruna, I, Domadred Steele, captain of the *Illusive Diamond*, so declare that you, Mareth Yerana, are now an officer of this mighty ship, serving as her *master gunner!*"

In response, the crew gave a wild shout.

"Now," Domadred continued, "we must choose the *quartermaster.*"

The crew hushed and all eyes flashed to Kefta. The young man stood awkwardly off to one side with his face downcast. The seamen then returned to their places and Mareth went over and stood next to the other officers. There was a long silence before Domadred spoke again.

"Words cannot describe the loss we suffered when Rihat fell. He was a brother to me and a brother to you all. However, to his apprenticing mate, the quartermaster was more than just a brother of the sea—he was a brother by blood. As you all know, Rihat and his young apprentice were born of the same mother and father. Men, this youth's loss far exceeds our own. For other than the family of this crew, Rihat was the last kin this lad had—the last of his blood."

Domadred paused before continuing. "We all knew that one day this young mate would succeed Rihat. And I know in your hearts you were proud to see that so. But I also know what you are think-ing now. You are thinking it's too soon. The lad is too young to have such responsibility. And men, sadly, you are *right*. It is far too soon for him to ascend to this role. In truth, this sailor is a brash and foolhardy youth, and I'm certain he has gotten himself into more trouble due to his sharp tongue than any three men aboard combined. Despite this, I'm also certain there is no better sailor to replace our former quarter-master than his own apprentice."

Domadred then turned to face Kefta. "Men, it was *Kefta* who saved my life yesterday. It was that young sailor who knew my thoughts before I could even speak them. By throwing me the sounding line, Kefta showed us all that he knows his captain and ship as deeply as he knows himself. This is what we need from a quartermaster. We need a man to whom we can implicitly entrust our lives. A man who is fearless and persevering, and whose mind is as sharp as a *diamond*! I say Kefta Vanarus is that man. Therefore, I submit him as my recommendation of new quartermaster and acting *second-in-command* of the *Illusive Diamond*!"

The crew was silent. There were only the sounds of wind and wave as Kefta stepped forward and approached the other officers. Kefta's eyes were still downcast, and the hush stretched on as the young man glanced over to where the body of his hewn brother had lain only moments before.

Finally, Kefta turned to face the crew. A look of fierce pain was etched into his youthful features and two silent tears ran down his cheeks. Kefta swallowed hard and slowly stood to his full height. The young man's face suddenly changed. It grew stronger and more assured—more confident. His blue gaze then scanned the crew before him. Although red from his tears, Kefta's sharp eyes glistened in the Zenith's light. They were piercing and powerfully beautiful. As Kefta looked at the men before him, most of whom were double his age,

Aleksi saw in the young man's gaze the awakened strength of a leader of nations.

"So what say you, crew?" Domadred shouted, shattering the silence. "Aye or *nay*?"

There was no hesitation, not even a second's falter—the entire crew shouted a unanimous "Aye!"

Kefta's face lit up as he choked back more tears. The men then surrounded the new quartermaster and embraced him with congratulations and cheers. Although his face bore a smile, it was obvious that all Kefta could think of was his brother, Rihat. As the crew and officers of the *Illusive Diamond* surrounded him in their loving embraces, the young man broke down into sobs, mourning the death of one true brother.

"We have yet to swear him in," Marlen, the ship's doctor, shouted. "Get back in formation, men!" The sailors reluctantly stepped back, leaving Kefta to face Domadred with swollen eyes.

"Kefta," Domadred said in an official tone, "you have been granted a very important responsibility. You hereby are charged with maintaining order on the ship, settling quarrels, and distributing work, prize, and punishment. You are to oversee the crew's hand-to-hand and bladed combat training and lead all boarding parties. You are to act as witness to any and all duels, ensuring that they are fair and just. You are to uphold the Thalassocratic Law of the Sea and, when needed, administer punishment to the guilty. Kefta, do you vow to do these things? To be my right hand and honor this ship as your own?"

"I do, Captain!"

"Then before the divine eye of High Arkai Aruna, I, Domadred Steele, captain of the *Illusive Diamond*, so declare that you, Kefta Vanarus, are now an officer of this mighty ship, serving as her quartermaster and my first mate!"

Once again, cheers went up from the crew, but Domadred silenced them all with a sharp whistle. "Quartermaster Kefta, your first order of business is to provide retribution to Fa'ell, our honored guest from the South-Western Isles of Sihtu. In accordance with the Law of the Sea, I expect you to oversee punishment to the one who sullied her honor and instigated dissention in a port in which the *Diamond* made berth."

The crew looked at the captain confusedly but Kefta nodded his head.

"Lady Fa'ell," Kefta said, looking over to her and Nara, who stood by the starboard gunwale. "Please come forth and aid me in the administration of punishment."

Fa'ell looked at Nara uncertainly but Nara nodded with a slight smile. Fa'ell then slowly walked to Kefta with her hand gently resting on the whip strapped to her leather armor.

"Men," Kefta continued, "please prepare the mainmast for a lashing." Four deckhands quickly laced two lines through a metal ring that hung on the mast. They then tied nooses on the lines' ends where the punished's wrists were to be bound. Holding the lines, they awaited the whipped to be called forth.

"Lady Fa'ell, as you are the party wronged, I will trust in your judgment as to the severity and duration of the whipping." Fa'ell nodded slowly. "And, as you are a proud warrior from the Pa'alna clan, I trust in your martial ability to administer the punishment in my stead. Show no mercy or quarter. Is that understood?"

Fa'ell nodded again as murmurs rippled through the crew. "Dr. Marlen," Kefta continued, as he walked to the mainmast and removed his shirt, "please come and oversee the lashing. It will be difficult for me to see from behind." As Kefta inserted his wrists into the nooses, several members of the crew protested.

Marlen came to stand beside Fa'ell as Kefta shouted out to the crew. "At attention, men! As your newly appointed quartermaster, I hereby sentence myself, Kefta Vanarus, to a lashing for unprovokedly sullying the honor of a lady, while also creating dissention and discord in a port where the *Diamond* was moored. Under article twenty-three of the Thalassocratic Law of the Sea, I thereby sentence myself to the appropriate punishment!"

He turned around and offered his back to Fa'ell. What had once been confused protests from the crew turned into shaking heads. "Men," Kefta continued, "pull the ends of the lines taut so as to prevent the whipped from falling." Kefta then put a biting block in his mouth and raised his arms.

The deckhands pulled the lines, and Kefta's chest was drawn to the mast with his arms locked straight above his head. "Lady Fa'ell!" Kefta shouted through his biting block. "You may *commence!*" The sound of tethered whip or cracker did not come. Instead, there was only the silence of the sea. "Lady Fa'ell," Kefta shouted again, "I implore you—"

But before he could say more, there was a sharp crack and Kefta's back arched violently. Red blossomed on the young man's shoulder blades, and Domadred slowly nodded.

"Son," Domadred whispered under his breath as crack after crack cut through the morning breeze, "your brother would be proud. You have truly earned the right to call yourself quartermaster. Welcome to the ranks of the *officers.*"

✳❮●❯✳

After the whipping ended, Kefta supplied Fa'ell with additional apologies and the crew went back to their daily responsibilities. As Marlen finished cleaning Kefta's lash wounds, Domadred walked to the mizzenmast.

"Well done," Domadred said, helping Kefta to stand.

"Thank you, Captain. You have given me a great honor."

Domadred chuckled. "Well, there was no way you were going to make good on our bet with the lousy salary I pay low-ranking mates."

Kefta looked at Domadred with wide eyes.

"I jest, son. I jest! The crew chose you because we know not only what you are capable of, but more importantly, what you have already done to prove yourself. You have earned this, Kefta—*all of this*, actually." Domadred then reached behind Kefta's back and inspected the young man's bloody lashings. "But from here on out, let's try and keep the contravenes to a minimum, OK?"

"Yes, sir. I'm sorry."

"No need to be sorry, son. You paid your debt with honor. This not only makes the *Diamond* proud, but makes me proud to be her captain. But even more important than all of that, Kefta, your actions have made your brother Rihat proud."

CHAPTER XIV

Finding he had little to do aboard ship, Aleksi explored the upper deck. From bow to stern, the *Illusive Diamond* had four open decks—the foredeck, main deck, quarterdeck, and even a small stern deck above the navigation room and captain's cabin.

Aleksi walked along the main deck and moved forward toward the bow. The main deck was home to the mainmast and was by far the largest of the four upper decks. Possessing much room for the crew to move about and tend to their duties, its long surface spanned the middle of the ship and also took up much of the *Diamond*'s length as well. As Aleksi kept moving, he saw a crew member go down a hatch. Although Aleksi had yet to see most of them, he assumed the lower decks within the ship each had specific multiuse purposes, providing multiple levels on which the crew could work, store tools and supplies, or congregate and lounge.

When he had boarded, Aleksi had noticed that directly below the main deck was the gun deck. He remembered seeing nine gun ports on the starboard side and assumed there were an equal number on the port side as well. Aleksi had read that the gun deck was a large open space where the crew spent the vast majority of their time when not on duty. Usually it housed not only the armaments but also the crew's sleeping hammocks. In addition, there were typically collapsible tables and benches for eating and leisure. Beneath the gun deck, there were always additional layers of cargo holds, housing barrels of water and various other compartments for goods and payloads, too.

Making his way along the starboard side of the ship, Aleksi saw four seamen pull a line that was suspended over the edge. The line was taut and—he guessed, from the straining of the sailors—tied to something heavy. Approaching the gunwale, Aleksi looked over the side and saw a suspended officer. The man wore a rope harness and the seamen were keeping him in place as he performed work on the ship's exterior. The officer was rubbing a strange flat-edged tool on the ship's hull, spreading a paste that Aleksi assumed was some sort of caulking. The man was working on the same location where the *Diamond* had scraped her hull during the rescue the night prior. Now, however, there was hardly a scratch showing.

Seeing that Aleksi was watching him, the officer called up to his men. "Alright, that's good for now. Hoist me up and let's take a break."

The men shouted, "Heave-ho!" and pulled the officer back up to the deck. After the officer deftly scaled the gunwale railing, the four other crewmen looked at Aleksi's eyes and dispersed, grumbling. As the last crewman walked past, however, he forcibly bumped his shoulder into Aleksi, causing the youth to stumble. Aleksi spun at the man, clenching his fist. The man laughed and, looking back at Aleksi, said, "Watch your step, Northern dog!" His three companions chuckled as they walked away.

Aleksi clenched his fist even tighter, causing sharp pain to flood through his arm. Trying to suppress his anger, he turned back to the officer still standing by the gunwale. The man wore the same clothes as the other officers, yet his dress was slightly more worn, the colors faded. He had a thick blond beard and a kindly face, and when he smiled, it warmed his blue eyes.

"Hello, there. The name's Levain."

Aleksi nodded in response but glanced at the four sailors who had just accosted him.

"Don't pay them any mind," Levain continued. "We have been fighting your kind a long time."

"Northerners are not *my kind*," Aleksi responded curtly.

"Whatever the case may be," Levain answered, "you are here now, Aleksi, so well met, and welcome aboard the *Diamond*."

Aleksi bowed his head. "I feel at such a disadvantage. You all know my name . . ."

"That's what introductions are for, son," Levain said, chuckling. "Besides, our names are the least of your worries. There is much to learn if you want to be a proper crewman."

"Oh no," Aleksi said, readjusting the bandage on his arm, "I think you misunderstand. I am only here for passage."

"Whatever you say, son," Levain answered, rubbing his hands together.

"I saw you were mending the ship from the run-in with the pier last night," Aleksi said, eyeing an elegant tool on Levain's belt. "But what were you doing, exactly? I have never seen—I mean, *read*—of a tool like that. It looks Runic."

"Pretty observant, aren't you? Well, this is something special we use to mend the ship. The *Diamond* is made of *yalmalrah* wood from the Western capital island of Skadra in the heart of Delebat."

"I know of yalmalrah," Aleksi replied, nodding. "All admirals of the Thalassocratic fleet have ships built of yalmalrah. It's strong and can even mend itself if given enough time. I just have never read about that tool you have there."

"Yes, well, that's because there are not many of these tools around anymore. We don't ever tell our passengers about such things, though, son." Levain paused and ran a hand over his thick straw-colored beard. "But if you want to learn the ways of the *Diamond* in hopes of becoming one of the crew, I doubt the captain would mind if I shared a little more information . . ."

"I would greatly enjoy learning more, sir. Although I make no promises about—"

"Well," Levain interrupted Aleksi before he could continue, "I was with the captain back before . . . well, for a long time. And we were gifted this tool by the prime admiral for our valor during the Unification War. It's a highly coveted object, able to help coax—well, actually *persuade*—the yalmalrah wood to bind with itself more quickly. So, when the hull gets anything from a small nick to a large breach, we just overlay some new yalmalrah, apply some Runic encouragement from this tool, and then the hull is well on its way to being mended. With just a little love and time, she is even stronger than before!"

Aleksi looked down at the man's belt, fighting back a strong urge to reach out and grasp the tool.

"It's kind of funny," Levain mused. "Each time the hull is mended, the shade of the new wood comes out slightly different. Damned if I know why, though. But the *Diamond* has been banged up and fixed so many times, that's where she gets her name!"

Aleksi cocked an eyebrow in confusion.

"Because if you look closely at the hull, it has a million different shades of wood—just like the many facets of a diamond. Get it?"

"Ahh," Aleksi said. "I had no idea."

"You can't see it unless you look closely, but it's there. There are many wonderful things to see when you take the time to look."

"Interesting. What then was the original name of the *Illusive Diamond*?" Aleksi asked.

"That, my boy, is a question for another day. Here, come with me." Levain strode toward the foredeck and Aleksi had to jog to catch up.

The foredeck housed the galley, or kitchen, below its planks, with the square-sailed foremast protruding above. Following Levain, Aleksi passed the foremast and then one of the *Diamond*'s chaser cannons. Coming to the bow gunwale, Levain gazed out at the sea.

"There's nothing like it, son," the weathered man said. "I come out here every morning and gaze at the horizon before us. So much vast opportunity with the whole of Terra at our fingertips!"

The rays of the Zeniths, one low on the horizon before them, the other high in the sky at their stern, lit up the water around them. Aleksi watched the waves sparkle like a million tiny sapphires as a salty breeze blew back his shoulder-length hair.

"I know our crew has a bad reputation," Levain continued. "It helps with our current profession. But the captain has a favorite quote from the *Kalki Vanga*: 'So long as he stays true to his heart, a man of virtue remains as such, no matter how circumstances force him to act.' Despite what they say, son, we raid only capital ships, never civilian vessels. And the ones put to the sword, well . . ." Levain paused. "They *deserve* it, and that's the truth."

"Lord Beck Al'Beth spoke very highly of your captain," Aleksi said. "If he trusts you, then I have no reason not to. And Trailen, the High Priest of the Eastern Order of the Arkai, just promoted Beck to High Protectorate, so his word holds even more sway now."

"Ahh, yes. I heard about Beck's promotion. 'Tis a wonderful thing. It was well over fifteen years ago now, but I served with the general on this very ship back when he was just a lieutenant. He is a good man and well deserving of the honor. That was before I was an officer, but Beck didn't seem to care. He still treated all us low-ranking seamen with dignity. I will never forget that—or what he did for us in the Battle of Thurlow." There was a long pause and Levain just looked out at the ocean, eyes locked on the endless horizon before them.

"When were you voted into the officership?" Aleksi asked, breaking the silence.

"Oh, during the end of the war. The former carpenter took some wooden shrapnel to the throat. It splintered off from the hull during a cannon barrage." Levain stroked his beard with an odd smile. "Fitting way for a carpenter to go, eh?"

"I . . . suppose."

"I was sworn in the next day and have been the ship's carpenter ever since." Levain shook his head. "We were running low on yalmalrah wood at the time, with the war and all. So my first task as an officer was to dig what little I could from out of the old codger's throat. We needed the shards to repair the hole in the hull that killed him. It was a *messy* first day's work."

Aleksi grimaced. "When the crew votes in a new officer, is it always so easy to get unanimous agreement? What happens if someone says *nay*?"

Levain looked at Aleksi strangely, but then a wide smile spread across his face. "Oh, we just throw the dissenters overboard, and then *unanimity* is restored."

"You can't be serious!"

"Oh, come now, son," Levain said, chuckling. "I'm just joking. This crew is a family. We all know our fellow man better than his own mother ever did. We entrust our lives to the captain and officers, and we all know who is, or who is not, deserving of such responsibility. Only once was there a vote against one of the captain's nominations." Levain cast a glance amidships.

Aleksi followed Levain's gaze to the green-eyed Doc Marlen, who sat slumped against the mainmast. A half-empty bottle of whiskey was loosely clutched in the man's fingers and he seemed to be passed out.

"So this yalmalrah wood," Aleksi asked, purposely looking away from Marlen, "how often do you have to resupply?"

"Well, now that's a tricky business. Since we are outlaws, the Western High Council does not welcome us into her home port with open arms, you know. But"—Levain paused and a sly smile spread across his lips—"there are other ways of obtaining yalmalrah planks, if you catch my *drift.*"

"Ahh . . . I see."

Levain patted the youth on the shoulder. "Sadly, the captain has got some kind of *special* cargo and now won't tarry even for a banker's pearl ship. Unfortunately for you, that means that this voyage should prove to be less than interesting." Levain then turned and looked back to the main deck, where his small team was already waiting for him. "Well, time to get back to work."

Such an odd assortment of men, Aleksi thought as Levain walked away. *Truly they are not how I expected pirates to be. They are nothing like the stories . . .*

Suddenly, Aleksi felt very tired. The youth sat down and leaned his back against the chaser cannon. Lazily, his focus drifted up to the sky and his eyes became heavy. Slowly beginning to soften, Aleksi's gaze became lost in the infinity of azure above.

The blue of the sky began to look very familiar and a memory from the night prior tugged at his mind. The blue eyes in his dreams—*her* eyes. As he basked in the warmth of the Zeniths, Aleksi's gaze lost focus.

Gradually, he was lulled by the ship and waves and pulled into a deep and restful sleep.

Aleksi floated in an infinite blue. As he looked around, he actually could feel the color, not just see it. It felt deep and heavy—cold, yet comforting. It was not a normal blue but was more of a profound sapphire or a powerfully dark cerulean. Stranger still, it did not just envelop Aleksi; it was inside him. He was breathing it, drinking it, made of it.

And then *she* was swimming next to him. The young woman was unclothed, seemingly made out of the same lazuline essence they both floated in. Her youthful features were undefined except for the soft glow on her forehead and her striking blue gaze. Once again her eyes shone out, piercing Aleksi with their poignant stare.

Aleksi tried to swim closer, but his hands came up against the same barrier as last time. He placed his palms against the invisible wall and she came to him. The young woman then stretched out her own hands, and Aleksi was almost able to meet her palms.

Her lips moved, but Aleksi could not hear what she said. He strained to listen, yet the young woman's flowing face was too beautiful and her eyes were overwhelmingly captivating. Aleksi tried to keep focus, but he felt himself slipping into her gaze.

Despite the barrier between them, it was as if he could feel her skin on his and touch the softness of her lips. As Aleksi gazed into the young woman's shining eyes, he was filled with the intoxicating scent of her—almost able to taste the sweet musk of her body.

Suddenly, the young woman's eyes went wide with alarm and a look of fear flashed across her face. She mouthed one final warning and her body sheared apart, returning back to the ethereal waters from whence it came.

"I would have thought *he* had trained you better than to let your guard down, boy."

The condescending remark woke Aleksi. Seeing Luka standing above him, Aleksi's hand flashed to the hilt of his sword. The Zeniths' light had faded considerably and it seemed to be nearly evening already.

"Who are you and what do you want?" Aleksi asked, standing up, readying himself to strike.

"Don't be too hasty with that blade; I'd hate for you to hurt yourself prematurely."

"Answer my question!" Aleksi gripped the hilt of his sword even tighter as the pulsing of his Rune grew frantic.

"Well, you heard the answer to your first question yesterday," Luka said, crossing his arms over his chest. "The answer to the second question is a bit more complicated. Ultimately, however, I want what everyone wants—peace on Terra."

"What does that have to do with *me*?"

"A more relevant question than you could possibly know, but one which will not be answered today." Luka let out a great sigh. "Although tedious to extract, there is some important information I must ascertain from Captain Domadred before you and I can properly discuss your *situation*. In the meantime, I had hoped to see how your training had progressed. I'd be lying if I told you I was anything but disappointed. Luckily, that is a thing which can be remedied."

"Enough of this," Aleksi said, feeling his anger turn into rage. "If you are here to harm me, make your move! If not, tell me what you want, and tell me now."

"Calm yourself, Aleksi. In truth, you have no idea how lucky you are. This all will play out soon, and if you choose wisely, the tide will actually turn in your favor. If not . . ." Luka smiled wickedly. "To put your mind at ease in the meantime, however, I will tell you this—if I personally wanted you dead, you would be so already. So you are safe . . ." Luka's smiled widened. "For now."

Before Aleksi could open his mouth to respond, Luka turned and walked away toward the main deck. Desperate rage flooded through him as he clenched his bandaged fist. In response, Aleksi's Rune dug its tendrils farther into his bone, causing shuddering pain to surge up the nerves of his forearm.

Damned by the darkness! What am I supposed to do? He says he is a Northern nobleman, but he obviously is more. What is going on and what does he want? Rudra, why did you send me on this ship! Is this included in your letter? If so, I don't understand.

The look in Luka's green eyes as he had smiled was frozen in Aleksi's mind. Aleksi turned and cast one last glance out past the bow of the ship. The waters had grown murky with the fading of the Zeniths. Aleksi could not help but feel that the horizon beyond held innumerable perils hidden in the darkness—and worst of all, that he had no choice but to just keep moving forward.

Feeling restless, Aleksi went aft and headed back to the main deck. He ran his hand on the gunwale, hugging the port side of the ship. As Aleksi walked, he looked up and saw several sailors climbing up the shroud's symmetrically netted riggings. Seeing him, one of the sailors scowled. The sky was illuminated with a rosy hint from the Zeniths, and the dark ratlines stood starkly outlined in the late-afternoon sky. In the fading light, the men looked like bugs caught on a long slice of a spider's web that was strung from the deck to the mast's crosstrees. The thought made Aleksi shiver.

What is Luka? A Master from the Northern Academy? An assassin? Either way, what am I to do? Attack him unprovoked even though he is unarmed? Try to forcibly question him on deck? Break into his room and search for clues? If I did any of those things, the captain would throw me in the brig. And even worse, if the crew got their say, I'd be thrown overboard instead. No, I need more information—I need to speak with the captain and find out what is going on. Beck also told me to ask him about the pendant . . . Rudra, why did you curse me so?! Arkai, what did I do to deserve this?

Trying to calm his mind and release his tension from Luka's ominous words, Aleksi continued farther down the main deck until he approached its mast. At its base, Marlen was still slouched in the same position he had been in hours before. Aleksi cast a careful glance at the old man. He appeared to be sleeping, yet he still clutched his bottle.

Passing under the shrouds of the mast, Aleksi continued on and came to a wide set of steps which led up to the raised quarterdeck. Beneath these stairs was a berth entrance that led under the quarterdeck through a long hallway. This was the same hallway that housed Aleksi's cabin, along with the officers' and guests' quarters as well. Instead of going down, Aleksi looked up the steps and saw the quarterdeck proper.

Aleksi had read in *Gairu's Companion to Seafaring* that the quarterdeck was arguably the most important location on a ship of the

Western fleet. The captain and senior officers navigated and controlled all activities on the vessel from this one location. In addition, it held special significance in the Western honor code, and traditionally, only officers or special guests were granted permission to set foot upon it.

At the center of the quarterdeck was the helm. The helm, a massive wheel, was the steering mechanism of the ship, able to adjust the angle of the large rudder at the *Diamond*'s stern. Next was the mizzenmast, which rose slightly behind the wheel. Farther past that, the quarterdeck led to the great double doors of the navigation room and captain's cabin beyond. This slightly elevated position provided the captain and officers a superior vantage point to observe the operations of the ship as they plotted her course and commanded her activities.

As Aleksi approached the stairs to the quarterdeck, he could see that Brayden was at the wheel with Domadred standing beside him. Aleksi stopped at the foot of the stairs and called up to them. "Captain, may I have permission to join you on the quarterdeck?"

Domadred looked down at Aleksi, seeming surprised. "Granted, son," he said, running a hand over his tightly cropped beard. "You may approach."

Aleksi walked up the small set of stairs and slid his bandaged hand along the smooth railing. Next to the wheel, there was a large golden binnacle. It was rounded and raised to waist height. No doubt the binnacle was Runic, possessing many useful instruments within its case of brass and carved crystal. Most ships only had traditional binnacles that held navigational tools such as the helm compass, sand timer, and possibly even a small glow lamp for ease of reading. Additionally, most would be mounted in gimbals, allowing them to stay level while the ship pitched or yawed from waves and wind. A ship like the *Illusive Diamond*, however, undoubtedly had many Runic relics passed down through the ages, and the binnacle would be a prime candidate. As he came closer, Aleksi could see that under the carved crystal, there were several glowing Runic objects whose purpose he could only speculate about.

"Welcome to the quarterdeck, son," Domadred said with a smile. "How can I help you?"

"Captain, I wished to ask you about Luka and what you plan on doing with him."

"I have not decided the fate of our Northern prisoner." Domadred paused and stroked his beard. "But even if I had, tell me, young Aleksi, why should I tell *you*, someone whom I just met yesterday—and under an alias no less?" Brayden chuckled as Domadred continued. "Although I try to not be a bigoted man and judge one on the color of his eyes, I have no choice but to see that yours are Northern green as well. Does that have anything to do with your asking?"

"Sir, I meant no disrespect," Aleksi said, averting his eyes. "Luka troubles me. He seems to be hiding something and not telling the full truth about why he is on this ship."

"Yes, and Luka is not the only one."

There was a long silence and Domadred watched Aleksi closely as Brayden continued to steer the ship. Aleksi nervously glanced at the massive Zenith Mountain at their stern; glowing red, it was the only thing on the horizon behind them other than cloud and wave. In addition, Aleksi noticed it now rested lower than yesterday when seen in Mindra's Haven.

Taking a deep breath, Aleksi spoke again. "Captain, I am sorry. It is none of my business. This is just my first time at sea and I am trying to learn the ways of your ship so as to better understand her rules."

"Son, you seem to already know more of our customs than you let on."

"Only what I have read, sir."

"Well, you seem to have read a lot." Domadred paused again, this time letting out a great sigh. "How is your *map* reading, however?"

"Poor, sir,"

"Excellent, I'm glad to see you're still *human*. As mysterious as you are, I was beginning to think you were one of those strange Akasha people from Kwa'thari in Farden."

"Sir, you can clearly see by my facial structure that I am most certainly *not* Akasha."

Domadred's eyes narrowed. "I have been told that what they *truly* look like is a mystery because none but the Masters have seen under the Akasha's ceremonial face masks."

Aleksi was silent and once again averted his eyes.

Domadred chuckled. "Well, trust, much like knowledge, is a thing earned through hard and diligent work. So if you truly wish to learn the ways of sailing the high seas, then tomorrow afternoon at second bell, I want you to meet Brayden and Kairn, the sailing master, up here in the navigation room for lessons. But do *not* test my hospitality, for I do not want to hear another word about our *guest* Luka Norte. Have I made myself perfectly clear?"

"Yes, sir, I—" But before Aleksi could say more, he was interrupted by Brayden.

"Da!" the boy blurted, full of indignation. "You can't seriously mean that he will be joining my—"

Domadred turned to his son with a look of sharp anger. Seeing it, Brayden was instantly silenced.

Regaining his composure, Domadred spoke again. "In fact, Aleksi, come here. Your first lesson begins *now.*" As Aleksi approached them in the fading light, Domadred then looked back at Brayden. "Step aside, Son, and allow Aleksi to take the wheel."

Brayden glanced up at his father and a look of shame shone in his eyes. "Yes, sir." The boy then released the helm. As Aleksi reluctantly took the wheel, Brayden spoke again. "Permission to leave the quarter-deck, *Captain?*"

"Granted." Domadred's response was curt, but his eyes followed Brayden as the boy walked to the shrouds of the mainmast and slowly ascended into the dark rigging above. Domadred was silent for a long moment as Aleksi held the wheel and felt the strong pull of water below and wind above.

Aleksi looked at Domadred, saying, "Captain, should I—"

"You're doing fine, son," Domadred interrupted. "We have a good wind, so just hold her steady." There was a pause before Domadred continued. "I'm sorry you had to see that. There are times when Brayden forgets who his father is. Or rather, *wishes* his father were someone else. No doubt he would like to speak openly to me like a normal son would. When we are alone it is fine, but when we are on deck it's . . . complicated."

Domadred let out a sigh and ran a hand through his long hair. Its captain's beads clinked softly as he continued to look at his son. "When he was young, things were different. But now he is a member of this crew and wants to be respected as such. Much like trust, respect is earned, however, and the other crew members still remember him as the young captain's boy who got special attention. It's difficult to break such memories in men who have been hardened by the sea"— Domadred chuckled and finally looked at Aleksi—"for they are as stubborn as the *old bitch* of an ocean that birthed them. But I'm sorry for boring you with such talk, Aleksi. It's just the idle musings of a father, I suppose."

"Was he born on this ship?" Aleksi asked as he looked up at Brayden in the rigging. The high spars were illuminated in the last rays of the Zeniths and shone red against the dark sky beyond.

"Yes, according to custom, Brayden's mother bore him during a calm spring morning back before . . . well, a good many years ago now." Domadred let out another sigh. "His mother was beautiful, smart, and well respected in the Warden Women's High Council. Something that worked out to be in Brayden's favor—for he looks nothing like his old man!" Domadred then winked at Aleksi with a smile. "High Arkai Aruna seems to have saved him from such a fate."

"If I remember correctly, Western custom dictates that after two years at sea, children and their mothers then return to land, yes?"

Domadred nodded before answering. "Indeed. After his two years, Brayden spent the rest of his childhood in Skadra. But when he came of age, he returned to the ship. After that, the ocean was his cradle, the sky his roof, and his mother watched over us both from her Runic altar."

There was a long silence as the evening sky became dark. Outside the creaking of the spars and the hum of the wind, silence now prevailed on deck as the seamen lit the lanterns. Aleksi then looked back and saw that only in the East, where the Zenith rose high into the sky, did the dying light of day still show itself as a faint glow of velvety red.

"Brayden wants so badly to be a man," Domadred continued. "He tries to kill his innocence before he's ready for its death. There are days I wish I could give this all up to allow him the childhood he deserves."

The pirate gave Aleksi a melancholy smile. "He practices incessantly with his sword, but yesterday was the first time he actually ever killed. He has yet to speak of it, but I am sure yesterday's carnage troubles him greatly. To be quite honest, yesterday's events trouble *me* greatly. I can only hope and pray that Beck and his men are faring well back in Mindra's Haven."

"Brayden has a right to practice," Aleksi said slowly. "You must run into many dangers on the open sea."

Domadred laughed. "I suppose we do, although I was once told by a man smarter than either you or me that 'a sword will cut its way through many men only to leave you to die at the feet of a beautiful woman. But'"—Domadred grinned—"'with the right words and a smile, you would instead have that woman in your bed, and the very same men bringing you breakfast in the morning.'"

Aleksi tilted his head and looked at the captain. "I know little of women and have been taught only to trust in the sharpness of a blade and the truth it exposes in one's heart."

"Just wait until you meet *your* woman, my boy," Domadred said, as his smile faded. "A blade may *cut* the heart, but only the love of a woman can truly *open* it." The captain's tone grew soft. "In my opinion, until you've found that, son, you are little more than a walking corpse."

Aleksi didn't reply. With the last of the Zenith's light gone, the rays of both moons shone on the deck about them as Domadred continued. "But enough of this wistful talk; what about you? What rude manners I have. Through all the commotion, I don't even know your full name. Where do you hail from and what is *your* story, Aleksi?"

"I was given a surname in my youth, but it is not mine to carry." As Aleksi's hands firmly grasped the wheel, he suddenly became very aware of his Rune pulsing in time with his heartbeat. Aleksi swallowed hard and looked out into the dark horizon ahead as he continued. "I am an orphan, sir."

"I am sorry. Lineages are not what they once were."

"Actually, Captain, one of the reasons I travel to Vai'kel is to learn of my house and fath—"

But before Aleksi could continue, there came a sharp snap from a line in the mainmast's rigging and then a hollow thud as a body fell to the deck.

"Damn the darkness!" Domadred cursed loudly. The captain then let out a piercing whistle and ran down the quarterdeck steps toward the huddled mass. Midstride, Domadred called back to Aleksi. "Hold the helm true, son, and pray to whichever Arkai you favor that whoever fell is not dead!"

CHAPTER XV

As Domadred ran up to the huddled figure on the deck, there came a deep moan of pain. Doc Marlen and several other seamen rushed over as well. Through the gathering crowd, Aleksi saw the fallen sailor begin to move and clutch his mangled leg in the lamplight.

Wasting no time, the doctor went about the painful work of aligning the dislocated joints. Aleksi heard a series of hollow pops followed by groans of anguish. The sound was harsh and throaty—too masculine to be a boy's voice. Aleksi let out a sigh of relief; it was not Brayden who had fallen.

Nara and Fa'ell came on deck. They must have heard the captain's whistle. As they emerged from the entrance below the quarterdeck's stairs, Aleksi could clearly see that innumerable stitches laced Nara's day-old wounds.

The Lionman glanced over at the small group still setting the fallen sailor's broken bones. Hearing the man give out another cry, Nara shook his head and walked up the stairs to the helm. When the large man saw Aleksi at the wheel, he smiled.

"They don't waste their time, do they?" Nara said as he strode up to the youth. "I would have thought they would have at least waited a few days before putting you to work."

"Oh, Nara," Fa'ell said curtly as she walked behind him, "your stupidity betrays you. Acting as helmsman is hardly *work* on a ship."

"Come now, Fa'ell. They are just trying to snare the boy in," Nara said. Fa'ell frowned as she followed Nara over to Aleksi. "Mark my words," the large man continued, "if this goes on, our young warrior here will be hauling lines within the week!"

Fa'ell shook her head and looked at Aleksi. "Son, the captain saw what you did yesterday. He wants that sword arm of yours, and I don't blame him. You have no need to worry and should instead take his trust as a compliment. Manning the helm is an honor reserved for officers and mates, not petty deckhands."

"And what does a crew's sword arm do when there is nothing to swing at, I ask? It *washes* the deck!" The giant of a man let out a great laugh and his muscles rippled in the moonlight. "And my darling Fa'ell," Nara continued, now speaking more softly and winking at Aleksi, "I'd watch who you call *petty*. Remember, my dear, we ride on a vile pirate ship manned by outlaws and thieves!"

Fa'ell rolled her eyes and walked closer to Aleksi, who continued to stand, awkwardly silent, at the helm. "Pay him no mind," Fa'ell said, running her hands across Aleksi's shoulders as she walked behind him. "In only a few days, that *oaf* over there will not only be stupid but also foaming from the mouth and speaking even worse nonsense."

Fa'ell leaned closer, and Aleksi felt her supple breasts press against his back. "And then, Aleksi, there will be no one to keep me company on this long and lonely voyage." Aleksi felt the warmth of her breath on his neck. "No one but *you* . . ." Her hands then slid across Aleksi's chest, feeling the crevices of his muscles.

Aleksi swallowed hard and tried to step away from Fa'ell's advance. But Fa'ell only moved in closer, pinning him between the wheel and her soft chest. Aleksi looked up at Nara and saw a dark expression grow on the large man's face. Nara was not watching him, however—the large man's gaze was locked on Fa'ell.

"And you fought so skillfully with such finesse and dexterity," Fa'ell continued, meeting Nara's glare but still speaking to Aleksi. "I'm sure with a little encouragement, you could please a woman wonderfully—"

"Enough!" Nara said loudly. "Oh, how I have missed your little games, darling."

Fa'ell took a step back, but Aleksi felt her hands linger on his body. She then gently squeezed his buttocks as she walked back in front of the helm. "Oh, don't be jealous, Nara," Fa'ell said, smiling sweetly. "I only speak the truth. Your soma withdrawal will be quite bad this time around. And with nothing to ease your letdown, dear, I do believe you will die."

Fa'ell then put the back of her hand to her forehead in mock lament. "And then, my brave Lionman, who will protect such a frail woman like me from these vicious pirates?"

"Don't be ridiculous, Fa'ell," Nara said, frowning deeply. "My withdrawal will—"

"You have no more paint?" Aleksi interrupted, swallowing hard and purposely avoiding Fa'ell with his eyes. "What will you do?"

"Same thing I did last time," Nara answered, putting a large hand through his hair. "Weather the storm . . ."

"*Last time*," Fa'ell said angrily, "I had dried soma leaves to wean you off with. Now you have only the last crusted dregs from your pouches!" Emotion leapt across her face. "You're a fool, Nara, and by my guess, soon to be a dead fool!"

"Fa'ell, that is *quite enough*!" Nara said sternly. "I'm growing tired of—"

"Oh, won't it be a funny song sung by the bards!" Fa'ell then threw up her tattooed arms like a songster. "The mighty Lionman, brought to the Zenith not by the Vashyrie in battle but by his own stupidity, drooling at the mouth and shitting himself!"

"Listen, woman!" Nara said, jabbing a finger at Fa'ell. "I would have been fine with two full pouches, but I decided to rescue you from nearly twenty armed men. And this—*this*—is the thanks I get for saving your life?"

"I *never* asked for your help—or for you to kill yourself!"

"Well, no one asked you to be such a vindictive *bitch* of a woman, but that's not stopping you, now is it?"

"After what you did not only to me, but also my family," Fa'ell said, gripping her whip tightly, "you have the gall to call *me* vindictive?!"

"Sweet Akasha!" Domadred said loudly, walking up behind them. "You two bicker better than my wife and I. And trust me, that's truly saying something." Domadred put a firm hand on one of Nara's massive shoulders. "How long have you two known each other? It took us over twenty years to build up a banter like that!"

"I've known him long enough to know how much of a fool he is," Fa'ell said, as her turquoise-and-amethyst eyes burned harshly.

"Well," Domadred continued, "I had wanted to invite you three to dinner in my cabin tonight. I had wished to celebrate our new officers and officially honor you for your help yesterday—and if we all think we can keep it cordial, I would still very much like to do so. But Nara and Fa'ell, tell me now if having you together in the same enclosed space is a mistake."

"It would please m'lady and me greatly to attend," Nara said with a deep bow to the captain. "However, Fa'ell and I have not seen each other in some time and our history runs quite deep. Please grant us a day or so to sort things out, and I guarantee you that we will not dishonor your table with our petty trifles." Nara's former ire had completely vanished, but Fa'ell still glared at the large man's deeply scarred back.

"Then we shall postpone the dinner to accommodate your reunion," Domadred said with a wry smile. "What about you, Aleksi? Care to dine as an honored guest of the *Illusive Diamond* in two days' time?"

"Yes, Captain," Aleksi answered. "I would feel privileged to do so."

"Splendid. In addition, once we reach the Grya Sea, the crew will be having their own party for the officers. Sometimes drunken merriment is the best way to relieve the tension of losing your brothers." Domadred paused and cast a knowing glance at Nara and then Fa'ell. "For all our sakes, I would greatly appreciate if you two followed suit and likewise *relieved* your own tensions sooner rather than later."

Before Nara or Fa'ell could respond, Domadred turned and walked to the carved double doors that led into the navigation room and captain's cabin beyond. After opening one of the windowed doors, however, he turned around. "Oh, and Aleksi, someone will relieve you on the helm shortly. Thank you for your help."

"Yes, Captain," Aleksi said, deliberately avoiding eye contact with Fa'ell and Nara. "But do please tell me, how is your crewman?"

Domadred turned around, still clutching the door handle. "Thank you for asking, son. He is OK, but his leg is badly broken and he will not be walking much until we get it healed up. It was a series of clean breaks, though, so it should mend well once we get him to a temple of the Arkai in Vai'kel."

With Domadred gone, Fa'ell quickly went below and Nara stalked off to the ship's bow. Soon after, a mate came to relieve Aleksi from the helm, and the youth retreated to his cabin. Entering his small room, Aleksi locked the door and let out a deep sigh. Life outside of the Academy was much more tumultuous than he was accustomed to.

What am I supposed to do? Domadred won't let me ask about Luka, and how am I supposed to broach the topic of my pendant? Beck told me to tread carefully, and with everyone so high strung, I am left unable to say a word. Aleksi squeezed his fist and winced as his Rune's tendrils burrowed deeper into his flesh. *Damn you, Rudra, what have you done? Where are you?*

Although Aleksi was quite hungry, it did not seem to be mealtime, so he sat at his small desk and lit the lamp. He was seated close enough to his cloak that he could faintly see the outline of the pendant through its pocket. Aleksi let out another sigh.

There was a strange feeling nagging at him, but he could not quite place it. Pulling out the leather-bound notebook from the night prior, he tried to conjure up the images from his dreams. His recollection of the previous night seemed murky, however, and he could not clearly recall what had happened. But when he opened his notebook and saw the drawing of the young woman's eyes, the feeling of her came flooding back in an emotive rush.

Yes, how could I forget her?

Even in his dreams it had been hard to clearly see the girl, so when he tried to picture her now, all that came was her shining blue gaze. And while the young woman's face was unclear, the feeling of her was vibrant within his heart. It was almost as if instead of seeing the girl, he *felt* her.

Suddenly, a knock came at the door. Jumping out of his chair, Aleksi slammed the sketchbook shut. "Green Eyes," an older man said, "supper is ready—beef, steamed carrots, and potatoes."

Aleksi unlocked and slowly opened the door. Outside stood a sailor he had not met. By his look, Aleksi assumed the man was a kitchen hand.

"Thank you," Aleksi said, as his stomach growled and the smell of warm food wafted into his cabin. The man nodded and gave Aleksi the tray before turning and walking back down the hallway without another word.

Aleksi relocked the door, slid his notebook across the desk, and set the food down. After saying a prayer, he began eating and reopened his notebook. Aleksi flipped through the pages between bites and saw countless renditions of her eyes. Each showed different emotions, but they all had the same depth and majestic beauty. However, none of the images contained a completed picture of her face—none captured the totality of her enigmatic essence.

Aleksi had grown up drawing. It was his favorite artistic pursuit outside of wielding his blade. But these pictures were different; this girl was different. She was no figment of his imagination and no idle fancy of his mind. There was something disquieting about her stare, something which spoke to him *through* her youthful eyes. Deep down in Aleksi's heart, he knew this girl was real.

After finishing his meal, Aleksi unlocked the door and placed the tray in the hallway. He closed and relocked the door, then lowered the desk lamp's flame and sat on the smooth wood of the floor. Aleksi felt his heart crave to look back at the pictures, but he knew he must regain himself. For no matter who she was, or how badly he wanted to know her, Aleksi could not lose control of his own mind.

Craving is the path of ignorance and suffering—not the path of a Master.

Besides, wherever she was, Aleksi knew she was not here, and if he ever wanted to find her, he must maintain focus on the path that was laid out before him by Rudra.

Taking off his leather boots and thick wool socks, Aleksi folded his legs and rested both feet on opposite knees. Aleksi repositioned his sword and laid his hands in his lap, palms up. Looking out through his porthole, he made note of the location of the moons. Aleksi then half closed his eyes and cleared his mind.

Finding the gentle ocean of emptiness in his breath, Aleksi focused on the circular pattern of his breathing. It flowed in and out, and his mind followed its rhythmic waves. The young woman's presence did not leave him, but after some time, it no longer agitated his mind. Achieving one pointed concentration, Aleksi just sat.

A good while later, Aleksi opened his eyes and unfolded his legs. They were stiff and he had to massage feeling back into his calves. As his feet tingled like a million tiny needle pricks, he looked out through the porthole to the vast star-laden sky above. The moons had moved considerably.

Standing, Aleksi tightened his belt and repositioned his sword. Unlocking and opening his door, he looked down the hallway. His tray was gone. Seeing no one outside, Aleksi silently walked down the hall to the washroom. Stalking down the hallway at night reminded him of his many years living in the Masters' Academy dormitories. Aleksi had not liked being seen then and desired it even less now. After he finished, he reentered his room and locked the door.

Removing his blade from his belt, Aleksi propped it up in the corner near his hammock. As he undressed, his eyes went to his sketchbook. Pushing away the desire to flip through the pages, Aleksi snuffed out his lamp and walked to his hammock. Lying back on its netting, he wrapped himself in a thin blanket and looked out through the porthole window.

Suddenly, images of the fighting in Mindra's Square flashed before his eyes—fire, blood, and dead bodies. Why the images assaulted his mind now, Aleksi did not know—but lying on the flagstones in a pool of blood, the soldier with a sword embedded in his forehead stared into Aleksi's eyes accusingly. As the man's fingers futilely clutched at the cold steel in his skull, Aleksi's stomach churned and he felt the Rune embedded in his bandaged hand painfully erupt to life.

Aleksi felt excruciating pain as the growing tendrils of his Rune slithered under his skin and penetrated deeper into the nerves of his arm. Light streamed out from the Rune and Aleksi clenched his fist close to his chest in desperation. The youth did all he could to calm himself and push the violent memories away, but the bloody images would not relent. His arm burned with a fiery fury as another wave of nausea passed over him. Trying to rely on his training to calm his body, Aleksi focused his gaze on the sky in hopes of quelling his growing torment.

Understanding suddenly sprang into Aleksi's mind. Outside the porthole, the moons shone brightly and Aleksi desperately raised his head to get a clearer view. As the moonshine fell on his face, the pain that burned through his body, and the memories that clutched at his heart, were slightly subdued. Aleksi triumphantly thrust his glowing arm into the silver shaft of moonlight and felt the divine blessing of the two former High Arkai Rahu and Ketu slowly bestow itself upon him.

Concentrating his mind on the moons' pure radiance, Aleksi felt both the carnage of Mindra's Haven and the fury of his Rune subside. Doing all he could to open himself to the blessing, Aleksi mentally recited the story of Rahu and Ketu—the story of Terra's moons and the god who had ignited them innumerable ages ago.

Legend told that it was Rahu and Ketu's love and forbidden union that had destroyed the balance of celestial power, thereby shattering the Arkai's divine accord held since time immemorial. For according to myth, Rahu and Ketu's union had birthed the omnipotent deity of Numina. An otherworldly war had then been waged over the infant god, plunging all of creation into bitter darkness. The battle between the corrupted Dark Arkai and the pure Arkai of Light had raged on, but in the end, the corrupted Dark Ones grew too many in number. At the brink of defeat, the infant deity Numina had tried to escape with his few remaining Arkai across the vast expanse of stars. The Dark Ones, however, pressed their attack, and just as all was to be lost, Rahu and Ketu sacrificed themselves to enable their holy child's safe retreat through the cosmos.

After escaping the worst of the Dark Ones' danger, Numina then created Terra and her many peoples out of lamentation for his slain parents and their eternal sacrifice. Serving as a beacon of hope and rebirth, Terra and her citizens were said to be an homage to love and creation. Sadly, however, much like Numina himself, the peoples of Terra were cursed and pursued by the Dark Ones across the vastness of space. So, to protect his new and vulnerable children, Numina raised the deific bodies of his parents, Rahu and Ketu, high into the sky, where they could watch over Terra in protection and divine benediction. Even in this Modern Age, as Terra soared ever onward through the endless sea of stars, the Dark Ones were said to still follow close behind as the moons and their Guardians shone out their eternal light and pushed back the ever-approaching darkness and destruction.

The Masters would always finish the story by saying that when the moons were once again united in love, scripture told that Terra's savior, Kalki, would be born. Upon hearing the Masters recite this, however, Aleksi had always thought it was strange that love both had caused the seemingly eternal struggle between the Arkai yet also was Terra's only hope for true protection.

How could the thing that caused so many of the High Arkai to fall to darkness and corruption also be the key to Terra's salvation? Aleksi inspected his Rune-covered arm, no longer paining him so profoundly, in the moonlight. Although its light had subsided, it still glowed softly in the darkness of his cabin. *But then again, what do I know of love?*

Almost in response, the Rune under his bandage pulsed—this time not with pain, but instead with a soft, pure warmth, much like that of the moonshine itself.

The moons' light, the drawings of the girl in his notebook, and the images of the blood and death of Mindra's Haven—it all brought a strange reminiscence to Aleksi's mind. The recollection of a feeling he had experienced only once before: his most notable memory of Master Lina DeLuth.

Lina had been one of Aleksi's empowerment teachers at the Academy. She was the only person, other than Nataraja, that could separate Aleksi from his past. She was able to see beyond Aleksi's Rune and his association with Rudra, knowing that behind it all he was nothing more than a scared little boy. Both gentle and kind, Lina had been an advocate for Aleksi in his early years, but some time ago, she had been sent out on a mission to hunt for fallen Masters and had never returned. Deep down, Aleksi felt she was still alive. Where she was, however, and why she had not come back to the Academy were just more mysteries.

Aleksi's clearest memory of Lina was a conversation they had had one night after he had gotten into a particularly bad fight with several of his student dorm mates. Aleksi had been only eight. That night, four boys had jumped him after a blade-training class. Earlier in the day, Aleksi had beaten each of them in matches without being struck a single time, and they had wanted revenge. Looking back on it, Aleksi understood they, too, were in pain—the Masters' training was designed to weed out the weak, and Aleksi was making them look bad. It was a cruel system and Aleksi knew he was an easy focus of his fellow students' desperate anger. But at the time, Aleksi could not see past their constant antagonizing and his own desperation.

The boys would usually just jeer and push him around. But that night, one of them snuck up behind Aleksi and, snatching his practice blade from his belt, threw it to the floor. When Aleksi tried to pick the sword up, another boy hit him in the face and knocked him over. Before Aleksi could fight back, the first boy climbed on top of him and wrapped his fingers around Aleksi's throat.

"How do *you* like it?" the boy said, strangling him. "Not so good without your sword, are you?"

And then, on that fateful night, something inside of Aleksi *snapped*. A fury engulfed him, and just like he had been taught in hand-to-hand combat class, Aleksi broke the boy's arm at the wrist and elbow. One of the other students then kicked Aleksi and tried to push him back down again, but Aleksi struck out with his legs and cracked three of the boy's ribs. Regaining his feet with a snarl, Aleksi then grabbed his wooden practice blade from the floor.

The other boys ran, screaming for help. Looking back on it, Aleksi felt embarrassed about hurting them. But it had made them stop and had brought him closer to Lina. In the end, it had been worth it. Once he got his wooden blade back, Aleksi chased the remaining two boys all the way into the dorm Master's apartments. As the children were banging on the door for help, Aleksi cut down with his sword. He swung hard and fast, just like he had done so many times before in the training hall. His strike split the back of one of the student's skulls with a hollow thud. As the boy fell to the floor, blood started to seep from his broken skull.

Aleksi was about to do the same to the other, but the door swung open. It was Master Lina DeLuth. As Lina rushed over and healed the hurt boy with her Runic powers, she looked at Aleksi knowingly, and Aleksi remembered dropping his sword and breaking into sobs. The wooden blade clattered to the stone floor as Lina's Runic casting made the student's skull whole again. Aleksi remembered seeing through his tears the other boy cowering in the corner, soaked in his own soil. His shame had prevented him from meeting Lina's eyes.

Luckily, the wounded students were able to be mended in time and suffered no lasting physical injuries. They never bothered Aleksi again, however, and only one of them ever actually matured into his next student grade. What had become of them after that Aleksi did not know for sure, but he assumed they had suffered the same fate as all other unascended Academy students—death.

After tending to the wounded, Lina had taken Aleksi into her apartment. He thought he was going to be severely chastised, but instead, she made him tea. Aleksi remembered his hands were shaking as he timidly took the glass cup. But the tea was soothing *grathmala*, and as he drank it, his nerves settled considerably.

"Well," Lina said, "they certainly have learned a valuable lesson tonight." Aleksi stared at her with a look of blank surprise, saying nothing. She smiled as she continued. "Do not corner a wolf lest you desire its teeth upon your flesh."

Aleksi remembered being astounded. When a student was not in active training, there were profound consequences for drawing another student's blood, breaking joints, or splitting bones. That night he had done all three. But instead of punishment, he was receiving tea and compliments.

"This, however," Lina continued, "is also a lesson for you, too. Do not let your *rage* overpower you, lest you unconsciously rend the flesh of others. For that, my little cub, is the path of a fallen Master—a path that leads only to darkness, suffering, and death."

"But Nataraja . . . ," Aleksi remembered saying meekly, "Nataraja says I should channel my anger."

"I'm sure he does. And he, although a vindicated Master of the Academy, has had his own dance with darkness . . ."

Their conversation had continued for many hours that night. It had been the first time anyone other than Rudra had actually shown interest in how he was feeling. It was a rare cherished memory among his many harsh experiences living at the Eastern Academy. At the end of their exchange, Lina had then told him something that Aleksi had carried close to his heart from that day forth.

"You can't even begin to imagine the gift you possess, Aleksi," she began, pointing to the fledgling Rune on his right hand. "It is a magnificent blessing and not a thing to be ashamed of."

"But everyone *hates* me for it," Aleksi said. "It's a *curse*, not a blessing!" Aleksi then dropped his cup and it shattered on the floor. Fumbling, he tried to pick up the pieces. He cut himself in the process and only added his own blood to the fallen mess of glass and tea.

As his blood slowly dripped onto the floor, Lina clicked her tongue and took his hand in her own. Aleksi watched in reverence as blue light emanated from her palms and the cut on his finger began to heal. His skin quickly re-formed itself until it was whole once again.

"They are just *scared* of you," Lina said, making a motion with her fingers. In a Runic orb of light, the broken cup then reconstituted itself from its once-fragmented pieces. "The path to becoming a Master is a *very* arduous one. The things we put you children through . . . Sometimes I wonder if . . ."

Lina's voice trailed off as she refilled his cup. She took a deep breath and continued. "Those boys know they will never be able to compete with you and your Rune. No matter how hard they try, you will be chosen over them as an Apprentice. To be honest, I don't blame them for their feelings. *Many* are jealous of you."

"But I don't want any Master that would choose them," Aleksi remembered saying. "Rudra is *my* Master and I will apprentice under him, and him alone!"

"Aleksi, you must never repeat those words, because that is *exactly* what scares people the most." Lina had shaken her head. "You and

Rudra represent something that is very challenging for us Masters of the Modern Age. Other than Rudra, none have been imbued with a Rune for many long ages, let alone born with one. That combined with what Rudra did . . ."

Lina's voice trailed off, and there was a long silence before she continued. "Regardless, Numina chose you for a reason." She then reached out and ruffled his hair. "Numina chose *you*, Aleksi, and no one else. That is powerfully important beyond anything you could possibly know at your age. Why you have been imbued after so many years of Guardian inactivity is a mystery to even the Masters' Council. But to be born with a Rune, that is truly a numinous miracle of Terra! A miracle to everyone except Rudra. But that is another matter entirely. Right now, Rudra's actions are not important—you are what is important, for you are *my* student. And, if you choose it, you can also be *my* Apprentice."

Lina looked at him expectantly, but Aleksi remained silent and gazed at the ground. He noticed that his blood had begun to congeal on the stone floor at his feet. "Aleksi," Lina continued, raising his chin to meet her gaze, "ultimately the choice is yours. You are powerful and all can feel it. Unfortunately, the sad truth is that throughout your whole life, not only will people resent you for it, but more importantly, they will do everything in their power to use you for their own selfish ends. Rudra most of all."

Lina then placed one hand on either of his shoulders. "With the right tutelage, you will grow to be not just a renowned swordsman but a very powerful Apprentice. And then, once your training is complete, you will become an *incredibly* influential Master, and most likely a *High* Master serving on the Masters' High Council. But despite all of this, you must always remember that underneath all that power you have a beautiful heart that shines with a brilliant, pure light. And if you let your heart guide your choices, you will then never be cast astray— no matter the path you are forced to walk."

Lina smiled, and her eyes were filled with compassion. "So, no matter who you choose to be your Master, you must promise me, Aleksi—promise that no matter how alone, afraid, or abandoned you feel, you will never forsake the wisdom of your heart. Promise that you will never forsake *yourself.*"

"Yes, Master Lina. *I promise.*"

And with that, she sent him to bed. Master Lina DeLuth.

Where are you now, Master Lina? Aleksi thought as he held his glowing Rune-covered hand up to the moonlight. *I wish both you and Rudra had never left. But no matter where you are, I will find you. Lina, we will meet again.*

As Aleksi gazed at the moons and drifted off into sleep, he could feel the eyes of the young woman from his notebook watching him. Drifting into dreams of her shining gaze, Aleksi felt his heart gain a tiny measure of peace.

CHAPTER XVI

Aleksi woke with a start. His night had been filled with dreams of the young woman, and as he climbed from his hammock, his heart ached from her absence. Even despite the invisible barrier that separated them in the dream world, he could nearly touch her skin. In those moments, he felt permeated by the very essence of her, but when he woke, she was wrenched from him and all that was left was emptiness in his chest.

Each dream of the young woman was different, but she always seemed to be trying to tell him something important. Whatever her message was, however, it was lost to him, for he could not hear her words or understand her meaning. So instead, Aleksi just reveled in her beauty, enjoying the fleeting moments before she disappeared again.

Yawning, Aleksi stretched his arms over his head. *Whoever she is, she is not here.* His eyes wandered to his coat pocket and the pendant inside. *And I must not get distracted from my mission—or Luka's threats.*

After getting dressed and sliding his blade in his belt, Aleksi made his way down the narrow passage. As he came to the wide stepladder that led to the deck above, Aleksi could already smell the fresh sea air.

Despite the early hour, the crew was hard at work. As both Zeniths' light intensified, Aleksi watched the seamen work on the deck and climb about the vast latticework of rigging and sail above. Although it seemed that only a third of the crew was on duty, they nearly covered the whole ship, moving constantly. Without saying a word, men hauled lines and raised sails as if locked in a unity of thought and action.

As Aleksi walked forward across the main deck, he saw that several men were coiling long stretches of line on the port side of the ship. In addition, on the starboard side, two other sailors were scrubbing the deck's planks. Upon seeing him, both men gave Aleksi dark looks. Aleksi sighed. He had wanted to practice his sword work in the morning light but needed to find a clear space to do so.

Aleksi soon realized that the ship's remaining spaces would not take kindly to swinging blades. Each mast had its own fife rail used to belay the ship's halyard lines firmly to its base, and Aleksi knew that one stray swing of his sword would cripple the sails. In addition, if he moved too close to the gunwale, he would hit the shrouds that ran up the sides of the ship. The only place that looked somewhat suitable was the stern deck. This deck, however, was directly above the navigation room and captain's quarters, and Aleksi did not want to go there without permission. Aleksi abhorred missing morning blade training, and he had already skipped several days due to his traveling.

Sighing, the youth decided to continue walking forward and explore the foredeck at the ship's bow to see if he could find any space at the ship's tip. Aleksi knew that if he was unable to find an adequate training area, this voyage was going to be torturous. Feeling anger swell in his gut, Aleksi turned around sharply and nearly bumped into Kefta.

"*Whoa*, there!" Kefta exclaimed, taking a step back. "Good morning to you, too!"

"Oh, I'm very sorry."

"Not a problem. It takes a few weeks to truly get your sea legs. You probably won't stop wobbling about until we make it to Vai'kel."

Aleksi frowned.

"What are you doing up so early?" Kefta continued. "Most *guests* usually try to sleep away as much of the day as they can. You're not trying to learn the crew's duties, are you?"

"Actually, I was hoping to perform my morning training. The ship, however, seems very busy."

"Well," Kefta chuckled, "open space is not a thing we have in ample supply here on the *Diamond*. We train in shifts on the main deck so as to not interfere with work. Also"—Kefta looked at the sword on Aleksi's hip—"we use training blades so we don't cut anything important."

Aleksi followed Kefta's eye to his own sword and noticed his left hand was clutching the blade's upper sheath. He removed it.

"As per my new duties, however," Kefta continued, "I will be teaching a training session today before the midday meal. I would be happy to have you join in for my lessons. You fought well in Mindra's Haven and I wouldn't be against having you train alongside us."

"Thank you for the offer, but I prefer to train alone."

"Oh, come now," Kefta said with a wry smile. "My brother used to push the men hard, and I won't be any different, but that doesn't mean you should be intimidated. I'm sure our training is nothing *you* can't handle."

"Oh, I'm not worried about that."

Kefta's smile faded. "We're not up to your standards, then?"

"No need to take it personally," Aleksi replied, once again scanning the ship for a place to practice. "As I said, I train alone."

"Well, suit yourself, Green Eyes. Still, I don't think you will find any free space on the ship right now. There isn't a good place to be swinging a sword around while the men work."

Aleksi looked aft and gestured up above the captain's cabin. "How about the stern deck? I have yet to see anyone go up there."

"For good reason," Kefta replied curtly. "Because of the swinging boom, it's very dangerous. *Especially* for people who don't know the ways of the sea. Or her *manners*."

"I'm sure I'll manage just fine."

"Well, you're going to have to get the captain's permission to go up there . . ." Kefta's smile slowly returned. "Sadly, he is in the navigation room with the sailing master going over maps and won't want to be bothered. But if you're truly set on training this morning, I suppose you can practice on the foredeck. That's up at the bow near the chaser cannon." Kefta pointed to the front of the ship. "Just *don't* cut anything. But for someone with your supposed ability, I'm sure that won't be a problem."

Aleksi nodded and walked away. Coming to the foredeck, the youth passed under the foremast's shrouds and found some open space surrounding the chaser cannon. The fore chaser, unlike the cannons below that fired from gun ports, was mounted on special sliding trucks. This allowed the cannon to be slewed across the deck on heavy metal rails that were embedded into the deck's planks. These rails, however, rose nearly three centimeters above the wood, which meant that maneuvering around them as he practiced his forms would be incredibly difficult.

As Aleksi looked closer at the cannon, he saw that it could not fire dead ahead from its centerline position. If it did, it would hit the bowsprit lines strung above the deck. The bowsprit's thick spar extended forward from the vessel's prow and provided an anchor point for the forestay sails, allowing the foremast to be stepped farther forward on the hull. This gave the *Diamond* much more sail coverage but also crowded the foredeck. Looking up, Aleksi realized that with the lines above and the metal rails at his feet, he hardly had any space to actually swing his long sword, let alone walk about without stumbling.

Kefta knew I wouldn't have enough room up here, Aleksi thought darkly as he continued looking at the lines above his head. *He is trying to set me up . . .*

"Be sure not to cut a line!" Aleksi heard Kefta yell from the main deck. "The last person who did had his sword taken away by the captain. If you don't think you're skilled enough to move around them, though, you can still train with us instead!"

Turning, Aleksi saw that Kefta wore a wicked grin on his face. It was the same smile Aleksi had seen back in Mindra's Haven when the young man had cursed Fa'ell in the arena tent. "Not to worry," Aleksi yelled back. "This will work *perfectly*! Thank you for your hospitality, Quartermaster!"

"You must truly be talented!" Kefta exclaimed. "I look forward to seeing the skill with which your blade leaves its sheath. I just hope it does not leave your side! Good luck!"

Aleksi turned and knelt down, bringing his left hand to his blade's upper scabbard. *Just watch,* Aleksi thought darkly as he placed his right hand on the blade's hilt.

With those final thoughts, Aleksi's mind became as still as a mountain pond on a spring morning and as vast as the virgin blue sky. There was no thought, just the sway of the ship and the roll of the waves. All the youth heard was the wind in the sails and the creaking of the masts. He felt nothing but the spray on his hair and the Zeniths' rays on his face. Aleksi's mind was *empty*.

Aleksi's sword then left its sheath. In a flash of light, the Zeniths' rays reflected off the elegantly curved steel. An instant later there came a swift swoosh as the sharp blade deftly cut the air. He cut again and again as the heavy blade flowed about him in a delicate dance of power and control. Aleksi spun with both grace and speed and his blade did not stop for a single instant. His eyes were unfocused, but he saw everything and he swung his sword around the sails and lines with both skill and confidence. Unhesitating, he felt both power and passion rise up from his heart. Aleksi loved his art—he loved his blade. When they danced, they danced as *one*.

After what felt both like an eternity and a mere instant, Aleksi allowed his body to stop moving. His breath came heavy in his lungs and he was covered in a sheen of sweat. Sheathing his sword, Aleksi looked back at the main deck and saw that nearly everyone was staring at him. Not just Kefta and the deckhands, but Nara, Fa'ell, the officers, Domadred, and Brayden, too. They were all gazing at him in a mixture of awe, surprise, and fear.

Aleksi then saw Luka. The nobleman was standing away from the others, and instead of awe he wore a different look on his face. The same look a cat makes when it has cornered a baby mouse.

A beautiful young woman stood atop an impossibly high mountain bluff overlooking the endless shimmering ocean far below. The Rune of High Arkai Aruna shone out upon her forehead with a powerful light. She was wearing a sheer white dress, and the sky overhead was a fathomless blue alight with the Western Zenith. Strangely, there was no curving horizon about her, only ocean, and sky, and forever.

She was in the Dreamscape—the land of dreams—and the scene around her was hazy and surreal, made of flowing sensations of thought and emotion. At the young woman's feet, there were innumerable kaleidoscopic flowers. Their blossoms shone in every color imaginable, and their hues changed as the wind blew across their petals. In a sudden gust, the breeze blew back her long blond hair and caused the strange flowers at her feet to change color in unison.

The young woman didn't seem to notice the wind. She was looking out across the sea toward a three-masted ship many kilometers away. Despite the great distance, she could see the ship clearly. Her attention was focused on a black-haired youth upon its deck. He had sweat on his brow and a sword sheathed at his hip. More importantly, however, the young woman could feel the soft glow of a dormant Runic power shining from under his bandaged arm.

He still does not know how important he is, the young woman thought, as she continued to gaze across the shimmering waves. *Nor does he know the danger he faces—the danger we all face if he does not act soon. Very soon . . .*

The young woman let out a sad sigh and looked down at her feet. *I must keep trying, for all our sakes. Please, Arkai, grant me forgiveness.*

The day went on slowly after Aleksi's training session. And while the crew went back to their duties as if they had seen nothing, everyone looked at the youth slightly differently from that moment onward. After Aleksi cleaned himself up and found some breakfast in the galley, he walked the ship trying to find something to do.

In the light of day, his cabin felt stuffy and oppressive, so he wandered the gently swaying deck under the warm light. Aleksi had tried going below to explore the gun deck and its long rows of cannons and hammocks, but after seeing the looks on the crew's faces, he quickly realized *guests* were not welcomed in their personal space. This relegated him to the decks above, and while he did yearn to climb in the rigging, it was not a thing he was going to do unbidden.

The youth soon found that there was very little for a passenger to do on a sea ship at voyage. And so, after getting his sketchbook from his cabin, Aleksi sat down against the gunwale near the quarterdeck and began drawing the young woman. In his mind's eye, her face came to him in flowing flashes, and although he tried drawing her over and over again, his mind could not grasp her full image.

Who is this young woman? Is she even real? Aleksi knew he already had so much to do. Finding Master Rudra and following his letter's cryptic clues in Vai'kel would be hard enough. He would not have time for idle fancy. This Rune, the pendant, his father, and Terra's Bane—he finally was on the path to find the truth of his past and could not afford any distractions.

But those eyes and her sweet smile . . . Aleksi felt a pang of emotion in his chest, a longing for something he had never known.

Just as Aleksi was about to clamp down his heart, the young woman's eyes flashed in his mind. They were pleading, asking, beckoning. He could not deny her. Not knowing what else to do, Aleksi allowed himself to soften and he breathed her in. The young woman's melody was soft and sweet—inviting and warm. He felt her call, felt her summoning him. He answered.

Almost of their own accord, Aleksi's hands reopened his sketchbook and he began to draw. This time, however, he felt as if he were in a trance. He didn't need to look down at the page; instead, he sensed it with his heart. His emotions and the silent longing in his chest guided his fingers. As his charcoal pencil raced across the page, he felt the touch of her skin and the sweet smell of her hair. The gentle curve of her smile and the warmth of her breath. The power of her eyes and the youthful passion of her heart. In that moment, her *essence* was laid bare and he swam in its warmth and beauty.

Aleksi's arm cramped but he did not stop. It was as if the young woman were next to him, urging him onward. He felt the flame grow in his chest and he channeled his emotion into the page. Everything fell away from him: the waves below, the Zenith above—everything. There was only the longing in his heart and her silent call, only the magic of her eyes and the beauty of her gaze. There was only *her*.

And then, suddenly, Aleksi stopped and looked down at the page in near disbelief. The picture of her was *complete*. He truly saw her face for the first time. The image was elegantly shaded—she was only slightly older than he, possessing high cheekbones and profoundly smooth skin. Her face was framed by long blond hair spilling over a supple shoulder. The young woman had full, delicate lips that were playfully pert, and she wore a faint smile that was sensual and secretive. It stirred a deep desire within him.

Aleksi then saw her eyes and his breath caught in his chest. Striking and enigmatic, her gaze possessed wisdom beyond her youthful years. As Aleksi looked down, her innate splendor shone out through the page, conveying an expression that was both regal and mysteriously powerful. With the full image of her now solid in his mind, Aleksi felt her call him again. The sensation of her was now truly intense. It was no longer a whisper, but a plea of the heart. Aleksi felt her pull at him. She was drawing him into the Dreamscape. Lulled by the sway of the ship below him and the warm rays above, Aleksi allowed himself to fall asleep into her essence.

Swimming in a half-asleep, half-awake state, Aleksi could feel his body sitting on the hard deck with his back leaning against the gunwale—but he could also feel her silent undertones pulling his mind into a dream. As Aleksi slipped deeper into slumber, he felt a difference in her summons. Instead of meeting him in *his* dreams like before, she now was trying to draw him into *hers*: into the Dreamscape itself.

Just as Aleksi was about to fully submerge into sleep, a sharp voice abruptly broke him from the trance.

"Captain, I must speak with you!"

Even half-conscious, Aleksi knew the voice. It belonged to Luka Norte.

Rubbing at his refocusing eyes, Aleksi heard Domadred say something too soft to carry beyond the quarterdeck. Judging by the look on the captain's face, however, his response to the nobleman was not favorable.

"My message," Luka continued insistently, "is of prime importance. I have been waiting long enough and only wish for a *moment* of your time."

Again, Domadred said something Aleksi could not hear. The captain's face, however, was growing angrier. Aleksi focused his mind, trying to listen. He still felt the young woman's silent whispers in his chest, however, and it took a good deal of effort to bring himself back to the waking world.

"Do not *misunderstand*," Luka said, holding a finger up. "I bear a proclamation of peace and terms of treaty!"

"And do not *misunderstand* me!" Domadred shouted, his voice now loud enough to carry across the entire ship. "You will not have your audience until I deem you *worthy* of my time." Everyone on deck froze and all eyes flashed to the quarterdeck as Domadred continued. "If you have a problem with that, Luka Norte, you are free to wait for me in the brig! Or, if you prefer, you can swim to Vai'kel! Have I made *myself clear?*"

"Perfectly," Luka said, storming down the steps from the quarterdeck. Despite his groggy state, Aleksi gripped the hilt of his sword tightly as Luka stalked down the stairs.

Seeing Aleksi, Luka sneered. "Don't worry, I will deal with you soon enough, boy." Then the man was belowdecks. Luka's eyes had been filled with a violent rage, causing Aleksi to shiver despite the Zeniths' warmth.

"Pay him no mind," Domadred said from the quarterdeck. "He is a pompous fool and nothing more."

Aleksi stood on shaky feet and gave the captain a small bow. Aleksi could still feel the young woman calling out to him. She urged, almost pleaded, for him to find her in the world of dreams. Aleksi tried with all his might to both hold the feeling in his mind and concentrate on the captain's words.

"Some time sulking alone in his cabin will cool his flames," Domadred continued, as the crew went back to work. "Whatever he has to say can wait. We have several days of voyage ahead and I have little interest in hearing his political pandering until I *truly* must."

The young woman's silent whisper was growing stronger, and it made Aleksi's waking mind feel foggy and unclear. As Domadred walked toward him, Aleksi had to forcibly suppress his heart so as to not become lost in her emanating waves of emotion.

"He was a fool for sailing with us to begin with," Domadred continued, as he walked down the steps next to Aleksi. "But then again, with
the riots, I suppose he had little choice." Coming closer, the captain
then eyed the youth's sketchbook. "Not just a sword fighter, but an artist, too?"

"I"—Aleksi paused, gripping the book tight—"enjoy drawing." The
feeling of the young woman was becoming too strong and threatened
to overwhelm his mind with its power. He *needed* to regain control of
himself.

"Well, if you draw half as well as you wield your blade," Domadred
said, chuckling, "your art must be stunning! We got quite a show today.
I can't say the last time I have seen a sword wielded so well by one so
young."

"Thank you, Captain," Aleksi said, bowing. As he came up from the
bow, Aleksi forced the feeling of the young woman away and reclaimed
his mind. Pushing her away was like tearing open his own heart, but he
had little choice.

"Actually, Captain," Aleksi continued, shaking his head slightly and
refocusing his eyes, "I wanted to ask you if I could train up on the stern
deck from now on. I know it's above your cabin, but I don't want to
interfere with the crew's duties or endanger the ship."

"Why don't you train *with* the crew tomorrow? I'm sure they could
learn a thing or two from your form, and they have a wealth of sailing
experience that might be of benefit to you as well."

"Captain . . . ," Aleksi said, then paused for a moment before continuing. "While I would be honored to train with them, I would truly
prefer—"

"No need to explain yourself. You have my permission to use the
stern deck at your leisure." The captain gestured to the stern of the ship.
"Just be careful, for when the ship comes about, the booms swing. And
if you don't jump down to the quarterdeck or hang over the railing,
you, my young friend, will be swept into the sea. We'd then have to turn
around and get you, and that is not a thing you would *ever* live down."

"I understand, Captain. Thank you."

"Well," Domadred continued, turning to look at the Zenith behind
them on the horizon, "it's almost time for you and Brayden to meet

with Kairn, the sailing master. So why don't you go into the navigation room a little early and introduce yourself. I think you two will get along very well."

Before Aleksi could answer, Domadred gave the youth a smile, then strode off, shouting critiques at a crew member high in the rigging.

Aleksi sighed. The captain had *not* been asking.

CHAPTER XVII

The young woman's call was all but gone now, and as Aleksi went belowdecks to drop off his notebook, her silent whispers disappeared altogether. Replacing them was a profound feeling of loss tinged with deep regret. The sensation stung at Aleksi's chest bitterly, and he pushed the feeling away.

What does it matter? Aleksi thought angrily, as he came back on deck. *Even if she is real, I am stuck on this ship. What could she possibly want?*

Walking up the stairs to the quarterdeck and past the helm, Aleksi saw that a new mate was on the wheel. Aleksi nodded at the sailor, and while the man did return the greeting, he did not make eye contact. Passing the mizzenmast, Aleksi then approached the great double doors of the navigation room.

The doors were made of thick wood with two large circular windows. Still feeling the sad ache in his chest, Aleksi paused to gaze at the door's intricate carvings before entering. Engraved into the darkly polished wood were hundreds of high waves all flowing into each other. They crashed angrily, surrounding an elegant carving of the *Illusive Diamond* herself. It was beautiful but also evoked an ominous sense of foreboding. The motif went well with the somber longing in Aleksi's heart.

The ship is surrounded by nothing but waves and danger, with only the moons to guide them. Not unlike me . . .

Aleksi took a deep breath and placed his hand on the ornately carved door handle in front of him. It was time to meet Kairn.

"Don't be timid, son," a voice said from inside.

Looking up, Aleksi could see a figure through the hazy glass of the door. It was an officer, but Aleksi could not see the man's face.

"Come on in," the voice said again. "You won't learn anything just standing there."

Aleksi pulled the handle and the door glided open. Inside, the navigation room was much as he had expected. Medium sized and possessing no chairs and many windows, the space was lined with high slanted tables built into the wall. These bore maps and Runic ledgers laid out flat so the navigator could see them clearly. Up above the tables and in between the windows, there were shelves filled with hundreds more maps. No doubt the *Diamond* had a chart for every meter of Terra's great ocean. Among the maps there were also various non-Runic navigational instruments and tools, too. Aleksi saw sextants used to measure the angle between visible objects and even very rare Zenith astrolabes. These specialized tools allowed the user to see a mechanical diagram of the Zeniths' locations and perceived height based on the observer's latitude, depending on the ship's position.

"Ahh, you have a good eye there, Aleksi," the voice said again, seeing the youth gaze at the astrolabe.

Looking up, Aleksi saw that its owner was indeed an officer. He wore a sky-blue vest and had a clean-shaven face, long bead-laden blond hair, and a neater presentation than the other sailors. The man also seemed younger than many of his fellow crewmates. His hand rested on a copper looking glass tucked into his belt and the corner of his mouth was turned up in a small smile.

"Welcome to the navigation room. My name is Kairn and I am the *Diamond*'s sailing master."

Aleksi closed the door behind him and bowed. "Well met, sir. It is a pleasure to both meet you and enter your studio."

"Studio? Both this ship and I have been called a great many things by a great many people, but no one has ever called my navigation room a studio."

"Oh, please excuse me . . . ," Aleksi said slowly. "I had read that sailing masters were also called sea artists, due to their role of being ship navigators and experts at reading and correcting charts. It was my understanding that it took the work of a talented artist to not only work with but, more importantly, correct the ever-changing sea charts of Terra. I am sorry if I have offended you."

"Ahh, yes," Kairn said, nodding. "No apology needed. That is from Olmarr's *Treatise on Sea Navigation*, correct? His theories on Terra's ever-changing coastlines and currents, and his proposed ancient united outer continent are fascinating; however, I cannot imagine Terra without the Thalassocratic Islands of the West. Either way, Olmarr was brilliant and I'll gladly accept his label as artist, for correcting the *Diamond*'s charts is no small feat."

"Indeed," Aleksi answered. "And from what I have heard, even just taking *zenars*, sir, is a very difficult art, too."

"Yes, and an art you cannot learn from a book, mind you." Kairn paused, shaking his head. "And I'm not even going to ask how you came by that text, son. I found it only after I had actually *been* a navigator for over five years. And after I found it, it cost me nearly a year's wage to actually buy the damn thing."

Aleksi looked down at his feet.

"But you were eyeing that tool over there. Do you know what it's called and what it's for?"

"Which, sir?" Aleksi pointed to each on its respective shelf as he continued speaking. "You have a sextant, astrolabe, compass, and a multitude of looking glasses."

"Good answer. The one which takes zenars."

"Oh, that's the Zenith astrolabe," Aleksi said matter-of-factly. "But you also have a sextant, and with some skill, I have heard even with that you can measure the height of the Zeniths and gauge their angle to approximate your position. But you must have the corresponding charts to make any sense of the readings. That's why the astrolabe is more helpful"—Aleksi paused, but Kairn nodded encouragingly and the youth continued—"because the charts have been miniaturized and etched into the various moving metal plates of the device itself. On a clear day, you can line the Zeniths' height and locations upon the tool, and calculate your location with a very high degree of accuracy."

"Well done!" Kairn exclaimed, wrapping his knuckle on one of the tables. "Back in the Guardian Age, sailors had many miraculous Runic tools at their disposal, but the Masters now confiscate the best of those ancient treasures and lock them away in their Academy fortresses. This leaves us lowly sailors relying on of the old ways of sea navigation. For those who can afford it, the astrolabe works well when you can see the Zeniths, but sadly, most ships outside the Western fleet don't even have a sextant." Kairn grimaced. "They are poor fools, if you ask me. For navigating Terra's deep currents with only a cross-staff and no charts to guide your way is nothing short of suicide—and that's during the daytime."

"I've been told that only fools would point their bow at the Zenith and sail straight, hoping for the best despite the risk with no charts," Aleksi replied. "My teachers said that with the shifting of the stars and no light of the Zenith to guide one's direction at night, ships that cannot navigate the glowing currents are easily cast off course. Best case is that they are merely lost in the maze of frothing waters and set back several days' sail; worst case . . ."

Aleksi's voice trailed off but Kairn finished for him. "Yes, son, they are cast to the wickedest of the currents unknowingly, then thrashed and destroyed by the unnatural waters which gyrate in Terra's deep oceans. Legends say that the currents did not used to be so perilous in ages past, but whatever the truth may be, the deep waters of Terra are anything but safe. Only those who can read the currents' frothy flow by day and navigate the water's glow by night have any hope of traversing the sea and living to tell the tale."

Kairn paused, eyeing Aleksi keenly. "Well, you seem to know much about nautical navigation theory already, so tomorrow meet us here at second bell to join Brayden in his lessons."

"I thought we were to have lessons today, sir?" Aleksi asked, confused. Just then, the door opened and Brayden walked into the navigation room.

"Ahh, right on time, my young friend," Kairn said, looking at the boy. "I was just about to tell Aleksi what the two of you will be doing for the next hour."

Brayden shot Aleksi a dark look but remained silent.

"Aleksi seems to know much *about* the sea, but not the sea *itself*. So, instead of looking at dusty old maps today, Brayden, you are to show Aleksi a real map of the ocean—the view from the crow's nest. And while you are up there, you can also show him the lines and help him learn the *Diamond*'s rigging."

"Alright," Brayden said, scowling, "let's go." The boy then left the navigation room and did not look back to see if Aleksi followed him.

Brayden wasted no time. The boy stalked toward the shrouds of the mainmast and Aleksi had to jog to keep up.

As they came to the mast, the pair passed Kefta, and the young man called out to them. "I see the children are going above to play. You are so kind, Aleksi; I'm sure Brayden must be happy to finally have someone his own age to frolic with."

"These," Brayden said to Aleksi, as he jumped up onto the long rope ladder, "are the shrouds. They are also called ratlines." Brayden did not look down as he spoke and was seemingly ignoring Kefta's words. "Follow me. I hope you're not afraid of heights."

"Be careful up there, boys," Kefta continued. "We wouldn't want anyone else to fall from the rigging!" Brayden glared down at Kefta and deftly climbed upward into the canopy of cloth.

Shaking his head, Aleksi grabbed ahold of the netting and also began to climb. At first, it felt clumsy—not from difficulty but due to the long sword at his hip.

"Hurry up, Aleksi!" Kefta shouted from below. "Or that child will leave you behind!"

Looking up, Aleksi saw that Brayden had gone nearly three-quarters of the way to the crosstrees. Aleksi growled under his breath and shot Kefta a dirty look. Repositioning his sword out of his way, Aleksi climbed speedily.

Despite Kefta's jeers, Aleksi marveled at the large sails around him. As he climbed, Aleksi could now clearly see these large sails close up. Never before had he seen such enormous sheets of fabric. They were full with wind and he could actually feel their reverberation as the strong breeze gave them life and movement. From afar they were stately, but up close the sails were not only regal but quite imposing, too.

Aleksi remembered reading that the higher one went up above a tall ship, the farther one was from its center of mass—so what felt like only a little rocking on the deck below would be profoundly more forceful high above. He soon realized, however, that knowing this and actually *experiencing* it were two different things entirely.

As he was admiring the sails, the ship surged over a particularly large wave. Hitting the crest, the *Diamond* leaned back sharply and then lurched downward as the prow dove into the wave's swell with a loud splash. Spray showered the deck below, and the shrouds swung from the movement of the masts. Aleksi had to cling desperately to the ratlines so as to not be thrown. Steadying itself, the ship rocked back again and Aleksi's boot slipped on the line. Losing his footing, the youth frantically reached out and had to catch himself with his hands. Unable to get a good grip with his boots, he was forced to scramble and climb up several rungs using only his arms. Finally, his heel bit into the rope and he got a better hold of the ratlines.

After the ship settled, he hooked his elbows around the ladder and looked around in amazement. His heart was pounding violently and his hands ached. There was a fresh sheen of sweat on his brow, and his breath came in ragged gulps. The other crew members in the rigging, however, seemed to have not been affected. They were busily performing their duties as if nothing had happened. Brayden, though, was looking down at Aleksi—and for a second, Aleksi thought he saw the boy's eyes shine with concern. But then whatever look had been there was gone and Brayden began climbing upward once again.

Aleksi swallowed hard. His hands burned, but he kept climbing. Because of the large sail coverage, he was unable to look out at the ocean, but his view below was unobstructed. As he ascended, he suddenly had the urge to glance down. Looking past his feet, he saw sailors working on the deck and hauling lines far below. They looked *very* small. Vertigo suddenly swept over Aleksi and the youth forced himself to look up. He knew he had no choice but to climb higher.

Trying to focus his mind on the large sails around him, he forced his body to move upward. As he continued, a gust of wind blew across him. The salty air pushed back his shoulder-length hair and his heart continued to furiously pound in his chest. Aleksi looked up and saw that Brayden had made it to the crosstrees and was gazing down at him expectantly. Aleksi hardened himself and moved on. There was a strange beauty to being in this cloth canopy and knowing you could fall at any moment. It added sharpness and necessitated a keen focus— much like training with a live blade.

As Aleksi came to the mast's large crosstree, Brayden nodded. Extending behind them was the massive boom that served to hold the top of the mast's enormous fore-and-aft rigged sail aloft. It was as thick as a medium-sized tree trunk and was held at an upright angle by massive hinges connected to blocks, tackle, and rigging. Despite all his studying, Aleksi quickly realized that no amount of reading could have prepared him to make sense of the ship's intricate systems of tackle, pulleys, and blocks.

Deftly holding on to the shroud with one hand, Brayden pointed to several hawser lines which ran up to the boom from the deck below. "I'll show you only a few now. I don't want to confuse you."

Aleksi nodded. Normally the boy's words would have irritated him, but there were so many lines just on this part of the mast alone that Aleksi knew he never would be able to remember them all even if Brayden did tell him.

"That is a *halyard*," Brayden said loudly, speaking over the wind. "It is used to raise the mainsail and control luff tension. Here"—the boy pointed to another line—"is the *topping lift*, which holds the boom aloft. This is the *guy*, which controls boom angle. And finally, there"— Brayden then pointed to a line which was attached to the bottom edge of the sail very far away—"is the *cunningham*. It also tightens luff." Brayden paused and eyed Aleksi keenly. "I hope you have a good memory because there are a lot more of them, too."

Before Aleksi could answer, the boy began climbing again. Brayden now scaled a much smaller set of ratlines, only a little wider than the width of his body. Aleksi followed, and as they ascended farther up the mast, his heart pounded even harder. Taking a deep breath, Aleksi tried to connect to the rhythm of the ship and let his body feel and absorb its movement. If he fell from this height, he would not be given a second chance.

Moving above the boom, they came to the mainmast's staysail. It was large and attached to both the mainmast and the foremast with a series of long lines. "The staysail is shaped like a rhombus," Brayden shouted over the wind, "and therefore needs no boom. It's used only when the winds are favorable."

Aleksi nodded and Brayden continued to climb.

Suddenly, the *Diamond* hit another large wave, but this time it did not take Aleksi off guard. As the ship lurched, he held on and let his body flow with the motion. As the ratlines swayed, so did he. Even before the ship settled itself, he began climbing again and was almost able to keep pace with Brayden. Despite this, his heart pounded in his ears.

When he saw Aleksi at his heels, Brayden's eyebrows rose. "We are almost to the top; just wait until you see the view!"

As they passed the main topsail and came to the mainmast's tops, Brayden climbed up onto the small crow's nest. The nest was little more than a small platform with a very low railing. Gripping the railing, Brayden sat and dangled his feet in between the rungs. There was just enough room for two people to sit, and as the wind blew about him, Aleksi hoisted himself up and took a seat next to Brayden.

Firmly holding on to the railing, Aleksi finally let himself look out at the water. In an infinite circle around them was white-tipped sapphire. Other than the *Diamond*, the sinking Zenith behind them, and the rising Zenith before them, there was nothing but endless ocean for as far as the eye could see. From this height, Aleksi could truly begin to grasp the sheer majesty of Terra's great ocean. It was beautiful and terrifying in scope and grandeur.

Aleksi felt the ship rock back and forth as it cut through the water far below. He looked down. Below him was a multitude of sailors working the decks and climbing in the rigging. From up above, the whole process looked very far away. He also could clearly see, outlined in light and shadow, the top of each sail and its respective boom and spar. Glancing behind them, Aleksi saw a long widening line of the ship's frothy wake stretching off into the distance. His breath came heavy in his throat—being in the crow's nest was truly exhilarating.

With the strong wind blowing his hair back, Aleksi looked at Brayden and smiled. The boy could not help himself and smiled back.

CHAPTER XVIII

Saying nothing, Aleksi and Brayden stayed up in the crow's nest for a long while. At first, Aleksi just gazed out at the ocean, soaking in its vastness. But then he sensed the familiar feeling of the young woman. Once again, her call was soft and sweet—a whisper of the heart. Aleksi opened himself instantly and his chest drank her in. Holding on to the sturdy railing of the crow's nest, he could feel her beckoning—almost pleading for him to listen. As the Zeniths shone down on him, the feeling of her grew in his chest until it permeated his whole body. He would not lose her this time. He knew he must go to her.

Aleksi turned to Brayden and the boy nodded, saying, "Alright, let's go back down." Brayden deftly swung over the railing and hopped back on the shrouds. As the boy descended, Aleksi had to struggle to keep up.

When Brayden reached the large boom's crosstrees, he waited for Aleksi. Once Aleksi neared, Brayden removed two thick leather gloves from the back of his belt. After putting them on, the boy took hold of a line connected to the top of the mainsail's boom.

"And this," Brayden shouted, jumping off the shrouds and sliding down the line, "is how I get down! Follow only if you dare!"

The boy then slid down the line to the boom and let go in midair, flinging his youthful body into the bowed mainsail. When Brayden hit, the sail made a hollow slipping sound of canvas on cloth as the boy slid down its long curve toward the deck.

Aleksi shook his head as he watched Brayden glide down the sail and finally jump and roll onto the main deck. *Nope,* Aleksi thought, as he slowly climbed down the shrouds.

As he descended, he could hear the young woman's whispers growing stronger. Her summons was powerful in his chest, her urgency clear. Climbing back down to the deck, Aleksi saw that Brayden was nowhere to be seen. The boy had left, no doubt, feeling his tour guide duties were completed. Aleksi returned to his cabin. He could no longer resist the young woman's call.

After walking down the guest hallway and entering his room, Aleksi locked the door. He then took off his boots and set his sword in the corner. Aleksi let his mind relax and opened his notebook to thumb through his countless renditions of the young woman.

At first, he saw the numerous sketches of her eyes. Sadly, they all seemed to lack the full majesty of her presence. But then he came to the completed picture of her face and froze. Seeing it took Aleksi's breath away. She was *gorgeous.* Her lips were full, smiling a secret smirk, and her skin was perfectly smooth, almost inviting him to touch the page. But her eyes—her eyes shone out at him, radiant and beautiful.

Looking into her, he felt the young woman pull at his heart. With her image now fully formed in his mind, she felt more solid and real. She felt alive. Yes, he could now find her in the Dreamscape—he could go to *her.*

Aleksi tried to remember what he had been taught about the Dreamscape. The first thing that came to mind was a vague lesson Rudra had once given.

"The Dreamscape is a great field of dreams," Rudra had told him. "But not all dreams are in the field of the Dreamscape." Aleksi had been a very young boy, but like always, Rudra's teaching had been obscure. "The Dreamscape should be thought of as one gigantic *shared dream*: the dream of Terra herself."

Aleksi remembered being very confused, and Rudra had laughed, saying, "It is a place both confusing and elegant, my student. And much like a woman, it is not a thing to be taken lightly. Instead, the Dreamscape should be respected and held in great reverence. For in this enigmatic land you will find profound splendor but also boundless danger. Luckily, these are things you need not worry about now. You have much to learn before you explore the etheric fields of the Dreamscape or the majestic mysteries of womanhood."

Aleksi pushed the memory aside and shook his head. There was so much that Master Rudra had *not* taught him, and it only made Rudra's disappearance all the more painful. Aleksi opened his sketchbook and flipped through the pages one last time. He would have to find his own gateway into the land of dreams—hopefully the image of the young woman and her emotive summons were enough. Either way, Rudra could not help him now.

After Aleksi lay down in his hammock, it did not take him long to drift off to sleep. He clutched his sketchbook in his arms, and as his breathing slowed, his grip on the leather-bound journal loosened.

He held on to only one thing—the beautiful feeling of *her*.

Much like when waking in the physical world, Aleksi transitioned into the domain of the Dreamscape slowly.

Aleksi stood on a beach. Behind him the sound of the ocean was clear and sweet. As each wave softly rode in, the water scraped pebbles and small shells over the sand before dragging them back out to the sea. The tender rhythm of the surf was soothing, and the shells sounded like twinkling bells as they rolled over each other on the beach.

As Aleksi regained focus, he saw the foothills of a monolithic Zenith Mountain. He was not sure how, but he intimately knew he was standing before the Zenith of the West. The massive peak towering above stung his eyes, and Aleksi had no choice but to shield his gaze from its magnificent rays. Looking around at the long grasses and sand before him, he saw that everything seemed bright—even the very air itself. It felt as if the Zenith's light were somehow a tangible thing here in the Dreamscape.

Aleksi paused and raised a hand to his forehead. His brow was furrowed, but why? He tried to remember. Had he been trying to find something? *Yes*, he had been searching for something important. *But for what?*

He looked down at his hands. His right arm was covered in a thin, gauzelike bandage and the lines that etched his left palm looked somehow older. At his feet, the sand seemed to shimmer and shift around his boots and everything appeared hazy and languid. Aleksi then realized he was *dreaming*.

The youth's gaze rose up his arms. They felt bigger—stronger. He flexed. Although the tendrils of his Rune were deeply embedded in his flesh, they no longer pained him. Additionally, the muscles of his biceps looked larger than he was used to. He even seemed taller here in the Dreamscape. Although he was not a grown man yet, he felt older than he had before. Aleksi was powerful, and it felt good.

Suddenly, a stirring sensation arose in his chest. Filled with yearning, Aleksi felt his heart open. Its whisper was subtle and yet alluring, like the sweet aroma of spring. Almost intoxicating, it was a delicate fragrance of the heart and mind, possessing beauty, elusiveness, and splendor. It was *her*.

Aleksi turned, and he saw her. The young woman's brilliant-blue eyes shone out to him and her forehead radiated with light and power. She was under a large willow tree some distance away. Its long branches stood sentry where the beach's sands met the grasses and trees of the mountain's foothills.

She was wearing a long, wispy white dress. The thin fabric shone lustrously in the shaded Zenith light, accentuating her exquisite form. Seeing her standing before him made his heart stir powerfully.

Despite the distance, Aleksi intimately knew her face. From his long hours of drawing her, he recognized every facet of her beauty. But seeing her now, even if it was only in the Dreamscape, was like seeing a thing of abstract magnificence *come to life*.

The young woman regarded him elegantly from under the tree's long branches. She raised her hand to her forehead and its light slowly disappeared. In her gaze there was wisdom beyond her years and an aloofness that spoke of responsibility, duty, and authority. The willow's canopy blanketed her in a patchwork of shadow and light, and her long blond hair swayed gently, framing her elegant face.

Aleksi quickly went to her. As he approached, her blue eyes watched him warily. Coming to the end of the sands, Aleksi crossed several stride lengths of tall grass until he came just under the canopy of her large tree. The willow's long leafy tendrils hung about them, creating a domed shelter from the bright light above. Aleksi raised his hand and touched the invisible barrier that separated them like it had so many times before. He firmly placed his Rune-laden palm, still bandaged, against the wall.

The young woman's lips moved, but again Aleksi could not hear what she said. Pressing against the unmoving barrier, he let out a great sigh. He could feel her on the other side and he ached to immerse himself in her radiance. She was so close, yet he could not touch her. Aleksi felt longing burn in his chest.

The young woman slowly tilted her head to the side and looked at him strangely, as if conflicted. As the golden beauty of her hair spilled over her shoulder, Aleksi felt her reach out to him, again trying to communicate her message. He felt a warning—but of *what*? He shook his head and pushed against the wall. It did not budge.

The young woman tried again and desperation shone in her eyes. Whatever she was trying to tell him, it was very important to her. He leaned his forehead against the barrier and a look of defeat spread across his face. She was right here before him, yet he could do nothing.

The young woman drew a deep breath and then hesitantly walked forward. With each slow step she took, the feeling in Aleksi's heart grew. He opened himself to her and breathed her in. He then felt something in her, something beyond just her message. He felt emotion stir within her, but it was conflicted and held tightly at bay.

Aleksi reached out, but the young woman bit her lip and looked away. He felt her emotions grow. It was a fledgling feeling within the young woman's heart, but it was masked by uncertainty and reservation. Aleksi pushed against the barrier and probed into her. *Yes*, there was something deeper there—she felt *something for him*.

The young woman paused for a long moment, trepidation clearly showing on her face. Finally, she timidly raised her hand to the wall. Instead of meeting it, her hand reached through. And then, very slowly, almost reluctantly, her fingers gently touched his.

The moment they touched, Aleksi's heart surged with desire. Nothing else in the world could feel like this, so wonderful, so powerful—and yet so *terrifying*.

Aleksi saw fear in her eyes, too. But the barrier then loosened, and she let her fingers slide between his. Aleksi reveled in her eyes. They shone brightly for him but were also filled with bashful uncertainty.

Aleksi now was able to feel her warning—but he also felt that *other* emotion. It was held deep within her, and she was guarding it carefully. Aleksi searched for it, probing and feeling into her. Suddenly, he found it. It was hidden away in her heart. It felt soft as the newly formed petals of a blossom, as sweet as the dewy nectar from a honeysuckle—as innocent as a young woman's new love.

Abashed, the young woman looked away in self-consciousness, but her fingers closed around his as if by their own volition. Embarrassment flowed through her. Or was it guilt? No, more like disgrace—as if Aleksi had unveiled a private shame.

Before Aleksi could probe deeper, however, storm clouds grew around the Zenith. Light began to once again shine from her forehead and the young woman's eyes flashed high above in fright. A strong wind picked up and she quickly retracted her hand.

Confused, Aleksi tried to reach through the barrier but he was suddenly forced back. He felt the feeling of her grow dim as the darkening sky obscured the light of the Zenith. Desperately, Aleksi tried to go back to her, but it was no use. A strong wind picked up and pushed him toward the water.

The young woman now felt very distant. As the beach around them descended into shadow, she placed her hand against the barrier. In her eyes was a look of sadness, loss, and shame.

He tried to call out to her, but it was too late. As full darkness came over him, Aleksi awoke.

Aleksi lurched in his hammock. His room was dark, with only the moons outside his porthole giving any light. He felt stiff and must have been asleep for a very long time. Aleksi rolled from his hammock and straightened out his hair.

What happened?

Slowly, memory came back to him. The young woman had been right there before him, and they had actually touched! The remembrance of her skin sent a wonderful shiver up his spine. Her eyes, her heart, her love—it was all so beautiful.

But why did I wake up? Why did she push me away?

Aleksi looked around his shadowed cabin. The air felt stale and suffocating. He dressed quickly and secured his sword to his hip. Grabbing his sketchbook, Aleksi left his room. As he walked down the dark hallway, he could not shake the last emotions he had felt from her. Her heart had been filled with longing but tinged with *something else.*

Aleksi paused in the hallway, trying to grasp the emotion. It was heavy like duty, but stained with humiliation. *She had been filled with a shame,* Aleksi realized. But why would she feel shame in her desire to be close to him? Was it not *she* who had beckoned *him*? And he had been so near to actually understanding her warning and supposed urgent message. Aleksi shook his head and continued walking. *Just more questions left unanswered . . .*

Ascending the ladder up to the dark main deck, Aleksi breathed the night's ocean air deeply. It was cool, moist, and refreshing. Overhead, the stars shone out in a great dome, making the moons look as if they were caught in a majestic canopy of diamonds. The ship felt different at night. There were still crewmen about manning lines and walking the deck, but their actions were slow and reserved, as if they moved in a mindful reverence.

As Aleksi walked to the front of the ship, the crew eyed him carefully but no one said a word. All that could be heard were the quiet creaks of the rigging in the wind mixed with the soft splashes of waves. Clutching his notebook tightly, Aleksi came to the ship's bow and looked out at the ocean beyond. Before him were peaceful darkness and glittering waves. Aleksi let out a great sigh and tried to allow the tension of his dream to leave him.

Whatever happened, she must have had her reasons.

Aleksi sat down against the chaser cannon and opened his sketch-book. By now, his eyes had adjusted to the moonlight and he could clearly see the book's pages. He longed to touch her again, even if only for another instant. After flipping to a blank page, Aleksi started draw-ing. He drew her full body now, for the image of her was clear in his mind. He drew her in an elegant dress with her lustrous hair blowing in the breeze. He reveled in her smooth curves and glittering eyes. The young woman's radiant essence was palpable on the page.

Suddenly, a voice broke the silence. "Are you drawing the *Diamond* or the sea?" Startled, Aleksi looked up and closed his notebook with a snap. It was Domadred, and the captain was standing near the bow with one hand on the gunwale's railing.

"Neither, sir." Aleksi stood and gave a small bow.

"Ahh, look." Domadred pointed out to the ocean. "The wind and currents have been extraordinarily favorable—we are entering the *luminescent sea.*"

Aleksi looked out ahead of the ship. As far as the youth could see, the whitecaps of the waves pulsed with tiny blue flickering lights. Amid the glowing waters there was also a clear sparkling path before the ship, signaling the edges of a swift-moving sea channel of currents. The flowing luminosity of the currents extended far below the water's surface, like a powerful corridor of light.

"I do so love the glow," Domadred continued wistfully. "The first time I saw it, I was a very young boy. It was the first time my father allowed me to cross the sea on his ship. Although she was flying dif-ferent flags, the *Diamond* was much the same as she is now. But to my young eyes, she seemed so very big."

"This was your father's ship?" Aleksi asked.

"Indeed. And when we came into the luminescent sea—the Western side, of course—I was held in rapture by the ocean's lights. My father, being a man of dramatism, timed it so we sailed through the beginning of it during the day. That way, when the Zenith's rays grew dim and night fell, we were well into the glowing waters as darkness descended over the ship. When full night came, my father brought me to the bow and the ocean exploded into a magical radiance before my very eyes. I will never forget that night."

Domadred turned back to Aleksi. "And to this day, every time we enter this part of the ocean, I come out here to watch the *Diamond*'s bow evoke that same radiant beauty again. Come here and stand at the gunwale—you will see what I mean."

Aleksi went to where Domadred was standing and looked over the side of the ship. As the *Diamond* cut through the waves, her bow wave was brightly illuminated in the water. The rippling light cast a long trail of afterglow on either side of the hull. Extending for over ten meters at a forty-five-degree angle, the rolling waves of light looked *magnificent*.

"This, and the flowing path before us, is but one of Terra's great mysterious marvels you will encounter while out on the open ocean," Domadred exclaimed, staring out at the glowing waters. "The magic of the Guardians is vast and powerful."

"I had no idea the algae's bioluminescence would be so stunning," Aleksi said quietly.

"*Algae?*" Domadred chuckled. "Son, you are mistaken. This is no algae but a gift from the Arkai! Terra's ocean lights up to give us sailors a path through the currents when we navigate at night with no Zeniths to guide us. Without the glow of the ocean water, we would be blind with nothing but the moons to light our way through the currents. But as you know, the moons move of their own accord, possessing no known rhyme or reason for their celestial path. So, under darkness of night, with only the Zeniths' outlines on a blanket of stars to ground our position, if we had no glowing aquatic path to light our safe passage, all ships at sea would undoubtedly drift off course and into a violent sea channel, which would very likely shatter both bow and body. Because of the innumerable currents and the erratic movement of the moons and stars, a dark ocean would be a fate cruel beyond words."

"What then do you do during a storm and harsh seas, Captain? Do not rough wind and water obscure the current's glow even deep under the ocean?"

"That occurs only in the hardest of storms, in which case we have no choice but to do what sailors have done long before we ever set our boats upon the waters of Terra . . ." Domadred paused and looked Aleksi in the eye. "We pray for safe passage."

"Please excuse my ignorance," Aleksi said, bowing his head. "I know only what I have read."

"There is so much in life that cannot be known from a book."

"Very true, Captain," Aleksi whispered, looking back to the shimmering brilliance. "A book could never do such a sight justice. This truly is a thing of beauty."

"I agree, son. I agree."

Aleksi nodded his head, but he knew the captain was misguided—at least in part—in his understanding of the ocean's light. The Masters taught that light such as this was chemically induced and came from within a living organism. In this case, the glow was coming from a tiny sea creature known as a *dinoflagellate* that, in turn, fed off the light of Terra's moons. Even young students of the Academy were taught that the glow of the ocean was a biochemical reaction, and nothing more. The real magic of Terra was the power of Numina, and the power exposed by that light was truly mysterious—just like Aleksi's Rune.

Both Aleksi and Domadred stood at the *Diamond*'s bow for what seemed like a very long time until Aleksi slowly turned to Domadred. "Captain, this might sound like a strange question, but have you ever seen a Runic pendant with a small black stone suspended in its center? It has to do with one of Terra's ancient houses, but I don't know any more than that."

"Why would you ask such a thing of me, Aleksi?"

"Before we left Mindra's Haven, General Beck told me you would know about it. He told me to ask you, sir."

Domadred took a deep breath before speaking. "Yes, a very old house, son. Beck and I knew its head well. Many did. But the house was brought to ruin by darkness and wiped from Terra by a mighty gale of anger and wrath. Such things are not meant to be revisited, son. Let the sleeping dead rest. They have earned it."

"Beck said something similar, but I cannot, sir. I must know the truth; it is very important to me."

"The truth," Domadred chuckled. "I wish *truth* were clearer than it seems to be these days. Only the Howler knows the truth of what happened that day at the great scar of Terra's Bane. And to one like the Howler, the truth must be a very *relative* thing. Besides, *his* truth is not something the minds of us mere men can fathom, son. It's best to just let it be."

"I cannot do that, Captain. Do you know a Master of the Academy known as Rudra?"

Domadred did not take his eyes off the ocean, but when he answered, his tone was harsh. "What business do you have with the Resistance, son?"

"The Resistance? None. My business is with Rudra, and its purpose is between him and me alone."

"Between you two and that pendant, I'm sure," Domadred said coolly. "Well, many wish to find Rudra for their own vengeful purposes—and for good reason. He has made many an enemy in Terra, and his head fetches a very high price because of his war crimes. There are times I wish I could even cash in the reward myself. But these are things I do not like to dwell on, son. I'm sorry, but I have no further information for you, regardless of what Beck might have led you to believe. Do not ask me again."

Both Aleksi and Domadred stood in silence until the captain let out a sigh and continued in a lighter tone. "Well, the hour grows late and I have a busy day ahead. Tomorrow we have the dinner celebration in my cabin, and I must get some sleep. You should get some rest, too, for it will prove to be quite the spectacle. That I guarantee."

Domadred began to walk to the main deck, but after taking only a few steps, he turned back to Aleksi. "Son, what brought you to speak of such things with Beck? It is not, how can I say, *normal* conversation."

"My life, sir, has been anything but *normal.*"

Domadred walked away without saying another word. As Aleksi watched him go, the youth saw the Eastern Zenith begin to give off its first early-morning rays in the far distance.

CHAPTER XIX

Aleksi awoke midmorning. He rolled from his hammock and stiffly stretched his arms over his head. He had yet to get used to sleeping on a woven net, and he felt it taking its toll on his body. After dressing, Aleksi swiftly left his room. Now that he had Domadred's permission to use the stern deck, the youth looked forward to once again falling into the rhythm of his morning trainings.

As Aleksi continued down the passage, his reverie with the young woman in the Dreamscape vividly sprang into his mind. Even now he could still feel the pulsing energy from when their hands had touched. Aleksi could not recall any dreams from the remainder of the night after he saw the luminescent sea with Domadred. Despite this, there was no mistaking what he *did* remember. Aleksi had felt a powerful passion—a passion for him—held deep within the young woman.

Just more mysteries... A slight smile spread across the youth's face. *But of all of the mysteries in my life, this young woman is by far the most exciting.*

As Aleksi climbed the ladder and came above deck, he felt a cool draft blow across his skin. The air smelled wet and salty. Looking above, he saw that there were clouds in the sky and the winds were blowing more strongly than yesterday. Moist and filled with ocean musk, the breeze caused the hairs on his arm to prickle.

Coming out from under the hollow of the ladder, Aleksi looked to the helm and saw Brayden at the wheel. Walking up to the quarterdeck, Aleksi nodded to the boy and Brayden nodded back without saying a word. As Aleksi passed, however, Brayden's eye hovered on Aleksi's sword. In the boy's gaze there was a silent longing—a longing Aleksi knew all too well.

Aleksi came to the large doors of the navigation room. Looking above the carved motif of the *Diamond*, he saw the seldom-used stern deck. From what Aleksi could discern, the deck seemed to be little more than a glorified roof, and the youth assumed that few ever went upon it, except possibly to fly the *Diamond*'s flags.

Letting out a sigh, Aleksi climbed up the railing and hoisted himself over the deck's lip. Coming onto the deck proper, he instantly saw the danger of the large boom. Currently held fast by its sturdy lines, the massive wooden pole was tied off wide on the ship's starboard side. When the ship turned and came about, however, the boom would have only a slight clearance as it swept across the deck. If he did not get out of the way as the boom came about, he would undoubtedly be swept into the sea.

In light of this danger, Aleksi had the space all to himself. Centering in the middle of the deck, he faced the bow and lowered into a kneeling position. Back at the Academy, his training sessions always began with seated meditation, and he was pleased he could finally get back into the practice of doing so again. Focusing his mind on his breathing, Aleksi relaxed his eyes into a soft focus. With his palms lying flat against his upper thighs, he felt his mind settle into stillness.

Concentrating on the rhythmic flow of the wind above, the waves below, and his breath within, Aleksi sat.

His hands slowly glided to his blade. Adroitly gripping the hilt with his right and the scabbard with his left, he inhaled powerfully and his sword exploded from its sheath. Aleksi took a sliding step forward with his right leg, dragging his left knee behind his body. Simultaneously, he used the opposing forces of his arms to swing his blade out in a horizontal slash with blinding speed. Aimed at an imaginary opponent's temple, the brilliant steel blade flashed in the Zeniths' light as it cut through the air with an audible swoosh. Aleksi immediately brought the sword's tip back around his left shoulder. The bottom of the blade faced upward to repel an opponent's retaliation strike. Then, raising the sword directly above his head, Aleksi firmly gripped the hilt with both hands.

Stepping forward with his right foot and left knee, Aleksi followed with a powerful downward swing. This mighty slash was intended to cleave the skull of his opponent. Aleksi could feel his back and triceps tighten as the heavy blade cut in a tight arc. There came a melodic swish as the edge once again sliced through the air. Next, using only one hand, Aleksi slowly tilted the tip of his sword to his right. He rose to his feet and brought the sword up and around his body in a wide arc. With the hilt of his blade now hovering at the side of his head, he then swung down with a diagonal slash.

This last movement was less of a cut and more of an on-guard swing which would prevent an opponent from counterattacking. It also helped to maintain one's focus after killing a foe. The Masters said that after splitting an opponent's skull with such a powerful downward strike, the muscles of the arm, or even the mind itself, would tense up from the severity of the blow. Therefore, they taught that one must release the tension from both the blade and the body in preparation for another attack. It also was hinted that the movement had the helpful effect of dislodging tissue, bone, and other viscous matter from the blade. Aleksi had yet to test that second theory, however.

Keeping the tip of his sword pointed at his fallen opponent, Aleksi switched his stance and slowly brought his left hand to his scabbard. The youth then extended his right elbow and, maneuvering his wrist, slowly slid his blade back into its sheath. As he did, he also lowered his right knee to the deck. This was done to offer a ceremonial bow to his fallen enemy while at the same time not compromising his own martial stance. Aleksi then rose and took several small steps backward, retreating from an encroaching pool of imaginary blood.

Despite the rhythmic rocking of the ship, Aleksi practiced that technique and many others over and over again. He felt his inner and outer states become one. His mental focus flowed with the movement of his blade's form as his body was united with the serenity of his mind's inner stillness. There were only the blade and his breath—nothing else.

Achieving unity in motion, Aleksi then let his attention expand. First, he reached out to the ship and felt its rhythmic sway. Slowly, his body's controlled motion of expanding and contracting muscles harmonized with the ship's steady movements. Next, Aleksi connected to the sea—the force that rocked the ship and gave Terra its life. He felt the source of the cavernous current of the ocean buried deep in Terra's heart. Pulsing in rhythmic beauty, Aleksi made Terra's heart *his* heart. Lastly, Aleksi connected to the wind—the force that drove the waves and gave lift to the Guardians' wings. He felt the numinous breeze blow across him, whispering of the mysteries of the great void beyond. Filled with awe and wonder, Aleksi saw that great mystery reflected in his own inner stillness. The sound of Aleksi's breath and the whir of his blade were united with the ship, the waves, and the wind's salty spray. There he selflessly dwelt, his mind unbroken in the fluid abiding of unremitting concentration—oneness.

The Masters' teachings are right, Aleksi realized. *You can't* become *at one with anything. For you already* are *at one with everything.*

During his training, Aleksi noticed that Brayden had been sporadically glancing backward from the helm. As Aleksi finished the last of his forms, however, the boy openly watched him.

Slowing his movement to a halt, Aleksi sheathed his blade and called down. "Your father says you practice very diligently with your sword." Brayden remained silent as he continued to look up at Aleksi. "I have finished my personal training for today. Why don't you come up here and join me? Now that Kefta is your teacher, I am sure you don't look forward to your training very much. If you agree to teach me the *Diamond*'s lines and sails, I would be happy to share my sword art with you."

"I must man the wheel," Brayden answered, biting his lip.

"Well then, maybe tomorrow . . ."

Suddenly, the doors to the navigation room burst open and Kefta surged to the helm. "Course correction! All hands, prepare to *come about!*" Shoving Brayden aside, the young man grabbed ahold of the wheel and spun it violently.

The ship's seamen ran to their stations and the *Diamond* abruptly cut across the wind. As the enormous ship turned, each sail momentarily luffed, losing the breeze. Kefta then looked up over his shoulder at Aleksi. Upon the young man's face was a wicked grin.

Suddenly, the ship's sails caught the wind from the other side and Brayden frantically pointed to the stern boom and shouted, "Aleksi, watch out!"

As the *Diamond*'s sails filled with air, the booms swiveled on their huge hinges. Although a number of seamen held each mainsheet firmly, thereby slowing the booms' movement, the massive stern spar picked up speed as it approached the stern deck. Before Aleksi could move, there came a loud snap as the stern boom broke away from its brake line. The sailors holding the line immediately fell to the deck and the boom swung toward Aleksi at breakneck speed. Kefta's eyes shot open in surprise and Aleksi had only a second to respond. Now free of restriction, the boom, thick as a tree trunk, hurtled toward the youth with blinding ferocity. Aleksi knew that if it hit him, it would surely break his legs before toppling him into the ocean.

Sprinting as hard as he could, Aleksi ran toward the front of the stern deck. Coming to its edge, he dove out to the left of the mizzenmast as the boom violently swept past him. Firmly tied to the fife rail were a series of vertical halyard lines, and as Aleksi flew through the air, he flung out his bandaged hand and grabbed one of the ropes. As his momentum swung him around the line, he clamped his left hand on top of his right to slow his speed.

Aleksi was over three meters above deck, and as he slid down the line, he felt the friction burn through his bandage. Once he was only a meter off the deck, he let go and deftly landed on the wooden planks next to the helm. Instantly, Aleksi's hands flashed to his sword.

"Kefta!" Searing pain flooded from Aleksi's Rune and green fury filled his eyes. As he felt his Rune grow and painfully dig deeper into the flesh of his arm, Aleksi used his left thumb to ease his blade several centimeters out of its sheath—readying himself to strike.

Kefta took several hasty steps backward before the navigation room's doors banged open.

"What in Aruna's name is going on out here?" Domadred shouted harshly. The captain's eyes flashed to Aleksi, Kefta, and then to Brayden and the rest of the crew beyond. Although the deckhands had finished tightening the sails and were just now getting the booms under control, they looked on with eager eyes.

"We had to come about, sir," Kefta said hurriedly. The young man's wide eyes did not leave Aleksi as he spoke. "I had only meant to jibe, but the mainsheet snapped, causing the stern boom to swing free."

"Never in all my years have I ever heard of a mainsheet snapping!" Domadred shouted. "Only through *sabotage* would such a thing happen."

"He nearly killed me," Aleksi said angrily, still clutching his sword. "I demand retribution!"

"I don't know what happened, Captain!" Kefta said, raising his hands. "I swear it! You know I would never sabotage the *Diamond*."

"No," Domadred answered. "You wouldn't sabotage the *Diamond*— only her guests." Domadred paused, eyeing both Aleksi and Kefta. "Whatever tensions you two have, duel them out. I will not have infighting aboard my ship."

"Gladly." A bitter smile crept onto Aleksi's face. With hands still clasping his blade, he took several stalking steps toward Kefta.

"*Not* with live blades, Aleksi!" Domadred said quickly. "I do not want to have to choose a new quartermaster so soon."

Kefta's eyes flashed to Domadred with a look of shame but he regained himself quickly and spoke. "We will settle this tomorrow morning, Captain. I want Aleksi to be well rested so that he does not have any excuses when he *loses*."

"Fine." Domadred's response was harsh. "See to it that nothing happens before then—lest I use Fa'ell's whip on the guilty party *myself*." The captain then turned around and slammed the door behind him.

Kefta followed Domadred but cast a disdainful eye at Brayden. "Oh, and no need to come to training today; I see you have found a *new* teacher. I hope he does not disappoint you tomorrow."

Aleksi's upper lip raised into a disdainful grin as he watched Kefta disappear back through the navigation room doors.

"Are you OK?" Brayden asked Aleksi as he retook the helm.

"I'm fine."

"I can't believe the mainsheet snapped," Brayden continued. "Kefta is an ass, but he would never cut a ship's line."

"Well, someone did."

"Still, your jump was incredible. Before the mainsheet broke, Kefta really thought he *had* you. He never expected that you could have swung out to avoid the boom even if it had only come across normally."

Cradling his right arm close to his body, Aleksi let out a great sigh. It seemed as if a tremendous amount of tightly held tension flooded from his body.

"Actually," Brayden continued, "neither did I . . . Aleksi, how did you move that fast?"

"I have spent a long time practicing my art. The idea to slide down the halyard line, however, I got from you." Aleksi forced himself to smile as he looked at the boy. "And a lucky thing, too; I would have destroyed my blade's sheath had I tried a jumping roll directly onto the deck from that height. I wish I had had your gloves, though . . ."

"Well, I bet you couldn't see it, but Kefta's look of disbelief was amazing!"

"Brayden, just wait until *tomorrow*."

The day continued slowly as Aleksi waited for the captain's dinner party. After getting salve from Dr. Marlen, the youth unwrapped his arm in the privacy of his own room. His palm had some mild rope burn, but his bandage had saved him from the worst of it. His Rune, however, pained him greatly and had grown considerably. The nerves of his hand looked infected with multicolored red, black, and blue lines spiderwebbing out from his palm. They nearly covered his entire hand, wrist, and forearm, but Aleksi knew the vast majority of the tendrils were hidden deep under his flesh and out of view.

Aleksi flexed his right bicep. He winced in pain as he felt the sharp ends of his Rune's metallic tendrils dig into the muscle of his upper arm. The external skin there was not as affected, but he could feel that the tendrils had reached nearly to the nerves of his shoulder. As he re-bound the covering, he had to wrap the gauze even higher up his arm. Within a matter of days, the Rune would reach his spine—if it was able to enter his central nervous system unchecked, all would be lost.

As Aleksi was about to leave his cabin, he heard a knock at the door. Opening it, the youth found a tray of food on the floor. He ate in silence.

Aleksi hardly tasted it.

After Aleksi finished his meal, he left his room and ascended the ladder. Kefta was at the helm and grinned when he saw Aleksi.

You won't be grinning tomorrow.

Aleksi settled himself at the bow. Leaning his back against the forward chaser, he opened his sketchbook. He wanted to think of better things than his anger at Kefta or his apprehension over Luka. Thoughts of *her* were infinitely better.

Gazing at the pictures of the young woman, Aleksi instantly felt a strong awareness of her fill his chest. She was real, he knew it. Despite this, Aleksi didn't know if he would ever be able to find her again. The thought made his heart ache.

What happened last night? And, more importantly, who is she? This whole thing doesn't make any sense . . .

Before Aleksi could start drawing, Nara walked up next to the youth. "What have you got there?" the large man asked, gazing at Aleksi's sketchbook. "Wow, she's a pretty one."

"Just some drawings." Aleksi quickly closed the book.

"She a friend of yours?" Nara asked, smiling.

"I'm not sure . . ."

"Women are a bit of a mystery, aren't they?" Nara sat down next to Aleksi. The youth didn't respond and Nara continued. "Quite an incident you had with Kefta this morning."

"You heard about that?"

"The whole crew did."

Aleksi shook his head.

"Tomorrow," Nara continued, as he idly scratched his stitches, "go easy on him, OK? The boy just lost his brother, and not all of us have had . . . *training* like you. Besides, I doubt that snapped line was his fault."

There was a long silence as they both gazed out at the distant horizon beyond. The morning's clouds had disappeared, and the Zeniths' afternoon rays now danced on the water's surface for as far as the eye could see. Aleksi felt his attention gravitate back to his sketchbook—back to *her*.

"Why is Fa'ell so upset with you?" Aleksi asked, breaking the quiet.

"That, my boy, is a very long story. But I will say this. It's surprising—the things people do for love. Those choices are not always easy to understand. Or, at times, *forgive*."

"I don't get it," Aleksi said slowly. "If someone loves you, then why would they push you away?"

"It seems as if you speak from experience." Nara gestured to the sketchbook in the youth's lap, but Aleksi remained silent. "The beauty is, son, you don't have to understand. You just have to respect the fact that they have their own reasons. And know that those reasons could be very important to them. Unfortunately, those reasons also might be more important *than you* . . ."

Aleksi looked at the large man expectantly, and Nara let out a great sigh.

"In my own case, the cause of Fa'ell's ire was something I did for love. Regrettably, my actions were something she could not forgive. Both in spite of, and due to, her own love—love for me and, more importantly, love for her family." Nara put a hand through his hair and smiled awkwardly. "But what of you, son? The young lady in your drawings, have you done something to wound her?"

"I don't know," Aleksi said, looking away. "It's hard to tell."

"Ahh, isn't it always?"

"This situation is . . . *unique*."

"Yes," mused Nara. "We all think that. Sadly, the troubles between men and women have been disturbing them both long before the Zeniths ever gave their first light. The *details* change, son, but, sorry to say, the themes themselves—they stay the same."

Aleksi tried to remember what Nara had said to Fa'ell back in Mindra's Haven, but he could not recall. "Nara, what are your *details*? Between you and Fa'ell, I mean."

"Remember what I said about certain questions?" Nara said, chuckling. "Suffice to say, it's a long story . . . and, more importantly, a story better told over strong liquor. Who knows, maybe someday I will tell it to you. But for now, I will say only one more thing. Despite my best intentions, the lady Fa'ell did not take kindly to several choices I made. Choices which, despite their great cost, most certainly saved her life."

"In Mindra's Square?"

"Oh no." Nara shook his head. "In her mind, I'm sure that only added greater insult. Our dilemma occurred several long years ago and on the other end of the world. Sometimes I wonder how our *situation* would have played out differently if we both had hailed from the same Arkai. Sadly, with my being green and gold of eye and from Iksir, and her having eyes of amethyst from Sihtu, our having children together is biologically impossible. This can . . . *complicate* a relationship."

"How long have you known each other?"

"Oh, a long while now," Nara said, his smile widening as he scratched his scars. "I'm actually a good deal older than I look. Although not nearly as old as our fearless captain."

Aleksi glanced over Nara's latticework of raised scars and grimaced when he came to Nara's newer wounds. The fresh skin was just beginning to rejoin around the dark stitches. The pink gashes looked strange next to the pale, muted flesh of the older scars.

Images of the bloodshed in Mindra's Square suddenly flashed in Aleksi's mind.

Would that be how the soldiers' wounds would look now, had I not killed them?

Aleksi did his best to push away the memory of the dead man's gaping wounds and blank eyes—eyes that stared into nothing as the soldier lay on the cobblestones in a pool of his own blood.

Are they still there now, lifelessly gazing at the sky? And what of my own eyes? Soon will they look like Nataraja's? Hard and cold—the eyes of a compassionless killer?

"Given time, they all look the same," Nara said softly. "They always do."

"What?" Aleksi's head spun to Nara in surprise.

"My scars," Nara answered. "You were staring at them. Marlen did a good job with the sutures. The new wounds look to be healing well. They will match the others and be a nice addition to my collection, wouldn't you agree?"

"Y-Yes . . . I suppose so."

Nara paused, then continued in an even softer tone. "There is something I want to ask you, Aleksi. Do not take offense." Nara cleared his throat before he went on. "The . . . *Rune work* you did for General Beck. Can you do anything for my withdrawal? Unfortunately, Fa'ell is right. In the next several days things will get very bad for me without my soma paints."

". . . I'm sorry," Aleksi answered slowly. "I cannot help you alone . . ." His words trailed off.

"I assumed as much," Nara said, letting out a great sigh. "Still, I thought I would ask. Regardless, I thought your kind were not allowed out of your Academies. Where is your Master and why—"

"A very good question indeed," Luka said from behind them. "Aleksi, what *did* your Master say when you left him? Did he not try to stop you?"

Both Aleksi and Nara spun around. Nara rose to his feet like a mountain of muscle, and Aleksi shifted onto his knees, hands flashing to his blade. Looking up at Nara's flexed shoulders, Aleksi was taken aback by the sheer magnitude of the man's taut might.

"Mind your own damn business, Luka," Nara growled.

"Strong words for a man knocking at death's door," Luka said with a smile. "In what stage is your withdrawal?"

"You would be wise not to tempt my ire," Nara responded, taking a step toward Luka, "for it's a *very* long swim back to the Northern aristocracy."

"Do not forget the punishment of assaulting a *guest* upon a Western ship."

"Guest? You? *Hardly.* More like a stuffed blouse waiting to be ransomed off to the highest bidder!"

"You cannot possibly imagine what I am, little kitten," Luka said, as his green eyes glittered.

"Have you had your audience with the captain yet?" Nara retorted. "Because it seems like you are still a prisoner aboard this ship. Is that not what *they* are for?" Nara motioned to the two men standing several paces behind Luka.

Luka's lips curled up into a sneer.

"Be off with you, Nobleman," Nara continued, as Aleksi's hands relaxed on his blade. "I, much like the captain, have little patience for the pandering of fools."

"Speak carefully, Nara." Luka answered. "I would hate for your own noble father, Raegnar, to hear your words, lest he come looking for you. It's been oh so long since you graced his halls in Iksir, or so I have been told . . ."

Nara's eyes went wide and Luka turned to Aleksi.

"And no need to answer my question now, boy. We can talk more about your *Master* tonight over dinner in the captain's chamber—for I have indeed been granted my audience. And, interestingly enough, you both have been invited to spectate. Our dinner together shall prove to be most interesting . . ."

Without another word, the nobleman turned and walked away. As Aleksi stood, he saw that Nara's face had gone pale. The large man remained silent and walked to the edge of the ship's prow.

As the Zeniths' rays turned a setting hue of crimson, Nara stared out at the horizon, lost in contemplation.

CHAPTER XX

Aleksi heard the sound of the ship's bell ring as he watched Nara gaze out at the ocean.

"Aleksi, you go on ahead to the captain's chamber for dinner." Nara's eyes were still locked on the sea. "I'll meet you there in a moment."

Aleksi nodded and turned toward the stern of the ship. As the youth crossed the main deck and approached the navigation room, Luka's question rang in his ears. *What did your Master say when you left him? Did he not try to stop you?*

Aleksi's chest grew tight as anxiousness rose up from his gut. *If Luka is a Master . . .* Aleksi's fear turned into panicked dread as he walked across the quarterdeck. He did not have time to ponder the thought further, however, for as he opened the navigation room's door, Kefta spoke suddenly from within.

"The crew are all very excited for our duel, Aleksi, so make sure you don't drink too much tonight; I would hate to have your mind dulled for our match." Before Aleksi could answer, Kefta turned to face Kairn as he continued. "And speaking of dull, I hope the sailing master does not bore you with his dusty old maps and navigation toys tomorrow morning. I don't know which would be worse, a hangover or a lesson with Kairn!"

"Oh, I have a feeling Aleksi will be just fine," Kairn said, as he stepped next to Kefta, "for he is a very smart lad." Kairn then slapped

Kefta hard on his back, directly on his newly healing whip wounds. "I truly wish I could say the same for you!"

Kefta tried his best to not flinch, but Kairn roughly rubbed his hand on Kefta's shoulders for emphasis. "OK!" Kefta yelled. "I yield! I yield!"

"Oh, come here," Kairn said, laughing as he embraced Kefta in a deep hug. "Welcome to the officership; you earned it—just like your lashing and duel tomorrow. Your brother will be greatly missed, but he is being replaced by a fine, although foul-mouthed, sailor. Just be careful with the booms next time, eh? I have a feeling you will be earning a few more welts because of it."

Kefta was about to respond, but Nara opened the great double doors to the navigation room. Instead of entering, the large man spoke. "I can hardly fit in here as it is. With you three blocking my way, I will surely knock over all those pretty maps of yours, and you will have only yourselves to blame."

"My apologies, Lionman," Kairn said with a smile. "Let us all enter into the captain's chamber together. The other officers are already inside."

As Kairn opened the door into the room beyond, Aleksi saw that the captain's large cabin had a surprisingly nice interior. The chamber was fitted with all manner of luxuries including festooned wall benches, fancily upholstered cushions, and even gilded lanterns that hung from the ceiling. The decorated benches were built into the walls and above them were shelves laden with hundreds of books and innumerable stacked scrolls. The floor was adorned with a finely emblazoned rug, and there was a good-sized carved cherry dining table in the center of the room. The table looked as if it could fit at least sixteen men if they sat snugly. Currently, however, there were twelve table settings and each was laid with the finest Western dining ware. Although tight by the standards of land dwellers, the cabin was undeniably elegant and truly befit an admiral of the Western Thalassocracy.

As he entered the chamber with the rest of the group, Aleksi's eyes were drawn to the back of the room. Past the dining table and the captain's writing desk, there was a gallery of five large paned windows that spanned the stern of the ship. The windows' burgundy curtains were pulled back, giving the cabin a perfect view from the *Diamond*'s stern.

Looking outside, Aleksi could clearly see the ship's frothy wake in the Zeniths' fading light. It glowed brightly from the churning of the bioluminescence and stretched out into the distant horizon beyond.

"Welcome!" Domadred said, as the small group made their way inside. "Please have a seat."

Domadred was facing the door and seated at the head of the table. Brayden sat to his right. Next to the boy was Levain, the carpenter, and then Mareth, the newly appointed master gunner. To Domadred's left was Valen the boatswain, and then Dr. Marlen. Other than Marlen, all seated at the table had the iconic blue eyes and golden-blond hair of the West. Despite the varying beard lengths and beaded hairstyles of the Westerners, Marlen stood out sharply with his black hair and green eyes.

Beckoning the newcomers to enter, Domadred stood and pushed back his chair. He then extended a hand to the remaining six open seats. Kefta and Kairn wasted no time in approaching the table. The other seated officers gave Kefta their congratulations as he pulled a chair out next to Marlen on Domadred's left. Kairn then sat next to Mareth on the opposite side and held a chair out for Aleksi. As he did, the door opened again and Luka entered. Without saying a word, the nobleman stepped past Nara and Aleksi and took the seat at the head of the table opposite Domadred.

"Welcome, Luka," Domadred said with a frown. "Please make yourself . . . comfortable."

"Oh, I intend to, Captain," Luka said with disdain as he sat. "I am honored to *finally* receive your hospitality."

"Nara, Aleksi, please sit," Domadred said, ignoring Luka's words. "All we wait for now is our lady of honor." Aleksi took the seat offered by Kairn on Luka's left, and Nara claimed the seat across from Aleksi.

As Nara sat, he looked at the empty seat between him and Kefta. "I knocked on Fa'ell's door on my way over. But she told me to . . ." Nara put a large hand through his hair. "Well, let's just say she told me to go on ahead without her."

"Not to worry, Lionman," Domadred exclaimed. "I'm sure we will receive her at any moment." Just as the words left Domadred's mouth, there came a knock on the door. "Please come in," Domadred answered cheerfully.

The door slowly opened and Fa'ell entered. Seeing her, Aleksi was astounded. She was wearing an ornately sewn indigo gown cut in the fashion of the Western aristocracy, and everyone's eyes grew wide as she entered the room. Her dress was faintly garlanded with an understated black lace that highlighted her olive skin and dark tattoos. She also wore a small black-chained choker around her neck from which hung a flawless teardrop sapphire. The stone shone in the lamplight and the dress accentuated her fit physique and supple curves.

"You look *splendid*, my dear," Domadred said, bowing as she entered. "I knew it would fit. You both have the same lovely figure."

"And you have my thanks, Captain," Fa'ell said, bowing her head. Her dark hair was not done up in the style of the West, but the dress fit her so well that none noticed.

"Oh, don't thank me," Domadred continued. "Thank my wife, Kalisa. She would have gladly given it to you, before . . ." Domadred paused. "It would have given her great pleasure that a powerful woman such as you could still enjoy the feminine fineries of life. Kalisa believed that a lady should wear armor for battle, but when it suited her, dress in elegance as well. For although she was unskilled with a whip, my wife knew her way around a blade, I dare say. If you have any doubts, I have *many* a scar I could show to prove it!"

Domadred then gave a wistful smile. "Despite her warrior's skill, however, Kalisa often said that most battles were won or lost while powers sat around a table. She felt that with swords sheathed at their hips, men thought better than when fighting at field or sea. And I must agree, for many a time it was her strategic mind and careful persuasion which got the angry admirals to listen to the logic of the Warden Women's High Council and thereby turn the tide for peace instead of war. But I digress, my dear—you look splendid." Domadred walked over and pulled out the last empty chair next to Nara and Kefta. "Please take a seat and join us. Trust us, the pleasure is *ours*."

As Fa'ell sat, she smiled at everyone at the table one by one, purposely passing over Nara on her left. The large man wore a complex look on his face as though multifarious thoughts swam behind his light-green, gold-flecked eyes.

"Horace, please pour for our guests," Domadred said, walking back to his seat. "I would like to make a toast."

"Yes, Captain." The short man came to Domadred's side and poured from a large pitcher. As the man went about the table and filled their goblets with wine, Aleksi glanced at Luka. The nobleman was resting his elbows on the tabletop and his hands were steepled.

Seeing the youth's gaze, Luka smiled and showed a set of pristine teeth that were unsettlingly white. As he held the man's gaze, Aleksi's heart grew tight in his chest. The youth's left hand instinctively went to the scabbard of his sword and he forced himself to look away.

After Horace filled all of the wine goblets, Domadred raised his own cup high and spoke in an officious tone. "Officers of the *Illusive Diamond*, not just two days ago we mourned our fallen brothers, but we have also welcomed trusted allies into our ranks. As always, it is with a heavy heart that our new additions, Kefta Vanarus and Mareth Yerana, take this office and honor. New brothers, may your minds be at peace and may you accept your duty well. For we, your fellow officers, vow to stand by your side in both war and peace, while the High Arkai Aruna guides you from within. May the wind forever fill your sails and the Arkai's grace stay strong in your hearts!"

The officers gave a hearty cheer and raised their goblets in praise before drinking their wine. As Aleksi drank, he once again cast his eyes at Luka. The nobleman was still looking at him, and a look of amusement whispered through the man's emerald gaze.

"Horace," Domadred continued, "please serve us." Horace carved from a cut of meat that sat on a serving table behind them. The short man piled slices onto a platter covered with an assortment of cheeses, fruit, and bread.

"Horace here is the best ship's cook I have ever encountered in all my days at sea." Domadred winked at Brayden. "He is the only man in Terra who can take the same few ingredients and create a taste that will *surprise* you every time." Horace muttered something under his breath as he continued to cut pieces of meat from the haunch. "And tonight he has cooked us a fabulous meal indeed! We feast on our finest meat and drink our best wine, for we not only dine with new officers but also with honored guests!"

Nara and Fa'ell nodded their heads to the captain and Aleksi did the same. Luka, however, did not move. His hands were still steepled, resting on the table as if posing for a sculpted epitome of superiority.

"Although for one who sits at my table," Domadred continued, casting his eyes on Luka, "I use the term *loosely*. However, Luka says he has a message of treaty—and it is a message, I might add, which will most certainly decide his fate. So for his sake, I hope the treaty's terms are *favorable*."

"I assume," Luka said disdainfully, "that that is a threat and my life is in danger despite the fact that I not only boarded your ship as a peace messenger but *also* saved the lives of your men?"

Domadred smiled. "You misunderstand, Lord. I invited you to this dinner to determine if I should treat you as a guest or as a prisoner. And I assure you this is not how we treat prisoners aboard the *Illusive Diamond*. So you are already off to a good start."

"*Splendid*," Luka said sarcastically. "I am so very glad, then, that there are no hard feelings between us, Captain."

"None that I am aware of as yet, but the night is young and we have not heard your message."

Luka shook his head and the muscles of his face grew tight. "Captain, I will tell you only one last time: I have been explicitly instructed to deliver my offer to you and you alone."

"And as I told you, Luka," Domadred answered casually, "if your message truly is so important, then the rest of my officers have a right to hear it as well."

"Over dinner?"

"Indeed. For as I told the elegant Fa'ell, it is around a table in discussion that angry hearts are soothed." Domadred paused, leaning in. "And let me be frank with you, Lord. Our hearts are not at peace with Vai'kel's rulership."

"So, if you keep your word," Luka asked, spreading his ring-laden fingers wide, "I have until the *end* of dinner before you make your decision in this matter, correct?"

"Indeed, Lord. I have been called many things, but *never* a liar." There was a pause as Domadred looked about the table. Seeing that Horace had finished serving everyone, the captain spoke again. "And so, let us all enjoy this meal."

As everyone began eating, none spoke. The only sounds heard were the muted clinking of dining ware and Horace's mumbling as he cut additional servings of meat. Soon, however, Marlen broke the silence.

"It's been some time since we had a good whipping," the doctor said between bites of meat. "And never before have I seen a woman wield a whip so well or seen a man receive his punishment so nobly."

"And I hope it is a long spell before he receives it again," Domadred said, looking at Kefta.

"Certainly, Captain." Kefta bowed his head to Fa'ell, who sat to his left. "My words were unwarranted and I wear the proof of that on my back. I am honored to have received your forgiveness, lady."

"I'm sure you are," Fa'ell said, smiling sweetly. "In the same vein, I look forward to seeing Aleksi deliver *his* forgiveness upon you tomorrow during your duel."

"Ahh, yes." Kefta took a sip of wine and looked at Aleksi. "What happened with the boom today was a grave travesty of circumstance. I just hope the boy does not disappoint you with his martial performance."

Aleksi remained silent but the Rune on his palm pulsed with anticipation.

"Nara," Domadred interjected, "I trust you were satisfied with Doc Marlen's skill in sewing? Although my memory of boarding the *Diamond* is slightly foggy—drowning will do that to a man—I do remember you were badly injured in the square."

"Indeed, I was, Captain." Nara scratched his scalp with a large hand. "But your good doctor stitched me up well, and my wounds will heal nicely. You both have my gratitude."

"And now you have another fine addition," Levain said, smiling, "to your famed collection of scars, Lionman."

"That mountain of a man," Marlen exclaimed, gesturing to Nara, "has more scars than any *twenty* men I have ever worked on. Probably more."

"Such is the price of using the soma paints, or so I have heard," Levain continued.

"And not the *only* price," Fa'ell said. "My good doctor Marlen, do you have anything on this ship which might help with our dear Lionman's withdrawal?"

"Withdrawal?" Marlen asked, obviously surprised. "I had assumed Nara brought enough soma reserves for the voyage."

"That would have been the intelligent thing to do."

Nara cleared his throat. "As you know, our departure was slightly . . . rushed."

"Unfortunately," Marlen answered, "we only have medicine which can ease the pain and help with the nausea and sickness. But if things get bad . . ." His words trailed off and the doctor took a long drink from his goblet.

"I am only slightly familiar with the North-Eastern Berzerkers," Domadred said carefully, "so please excuse my ignorance. But Nara . . . what exactly should we expect to happen during this *withdrawal*?"

"Oh, my good captain," Luka exclaimed, "I am surprised you are not more familiar with soma withdrawal. It is my understanding that you smuggle the drug out of the Northern Continent often."

Domadred ignored the nobleman and took a drink of wine.

"Well," Luka continued, "I have some experience with the North-East. Lord Lionman, if you don't mind, please allow me to impress the captain with my knowledge of the consequences of his illegal exports."

Nara frowned but did not speak.

"It is my understanding," Luka went on, "that our *Berzerker* here will suffer blackouts, delirium tremens, convulsions, and dysphoria. If he lives, that is."

"The nobleman exaggerates," Nara said, glaring at Luka and once again running a hand through his hair. "This is not the first time I have been through soma withdrawal, nor will it be the last. I will weather the storm, Captain. Have no fear of that. If I were to hazard a guess this time around, its effects will be little worse than what you see with severe seasickness."

"Preposterous!" Fa'ell interjected. "My dear captain, why do you think Nara is constantly putting his hand through his hair and scratching his scars? It's a nasty side effect of the soma plant called *scalp itch*. When he is on the paint, it's only mild—but when he is off and goes through withdrawal . . ." Her voice faded into a mock whisper and she put her palm to the rounded top of her bare cleavage. "Let's just say his pretty blond hair will be turning a slightly darker shade of red. And that's *just the beginning* . . . Next he will reopen the doctor's handiwork, and then, unless you bind his hands, he will tear at the flesh of his old scars, too."

"Fa'ell, please—"

"This is because soma is profoundly irritating to human skin," Fa'ell continued, ignoring Nara, "and when a Berzerker of Iksir uses the soma paints on open wounds, the active ingredient of the drug gets trapped in his flesh when the lacerations heal over. Without the counteragent applied regularly to balance the chemical reaction, the pain of the soma embedded in the Berzerker's scars is quite unbearable. Or so I have been told . . ."

"I see," Domadred said, frowning. There was a brief pause before the captain continued. "Speaking of blood and a long, drawn-out death, I have a question for Luka. Nobleman, I must ask, how goes the governance of the Central Continent? I have been quite curious how the Northern aristocracy views the Vai'kel unification. Is it everything you all had hoped for?"

"Well," Luka answered, ripping apart a piece of bread and dabbing it into the red drippings on his plate, "as you know, we of the North came to Vai'kel's aid at the request of the *Masters' Council*." Luka placed the dripping piece of bread into his mouth and, looking at Aleksi, chewed it slowly. "We liberated the people from their treacherous and warmongering rulers. And now women and children no longer die in the streets. So yes, Captain, I would say we have accomplished our goal. I would have assumed that you, however, being a veteran of that horrid war, would agree with our sentiment."

"And how have the people *responded* to their newfound safety?"

The nobleman paused, idly raising a finger adorned with a large emerald signet ring. "Some have gracefully received the gifts they were given, while sadly, others have been less than appreciative. Apparently, they would prefer chaotic anarchy over peace and prosperity."

"Peace and prosperity?" Levain laughed. "It's a bloody occupation. Your Northern lords are stealing the continent's wealth. They are the only ones who are prospering from this *so-called* peace."

Luka eyed Levain flatly. "You of all people should know, Carpenter; rebuilding a continent is quite expensive. Sadly, the venture has been a financial loss overall. But still we persevere. You may call it a public service to the greater good. The most tiring thing, however, has been putting down Vai'kel's numerous groups of bandits. They have proven to be quite persistent despite their small numbers."

"Bandits or *rebels*?" Valen asked. "I have heard that your so-called bandits are actually a cohesive *resistance*. A resistance united against *your* tyranny."

"Boatswain, you honestly think the Resistance is united? Ha! Hardly." Luka took a long drink from his goblet and held it up for Horace to refill. "They will fall soon enough. In all truth, a few misguided farmhands with fissured leadership are of little actual threat to the United Rulership of Vai'kel *or* the Northern Council."

"Northern Council? Don't you mean Asura, the supreme commander of the Northern Empire?" This time, it was Dr. Marlen who spoke, and his green eyes were filled with old anger. "All of Terra knows Asura manipulated the Northern common folk into overthrowing his competition, thereby making him high dictator of the North!"

"The people chose wisely," Luka answered. "And Asura merely holds the position until the time comes for him to grant leadership to the *true* leader of the Northern people—someone who shall rule by divine right, not some petty council."

"True leader, ha!" Marlen retorted. "Asura controlled the people, even in their rebellion. I was there when it happened. Asura had the rest of the council *slaughtered*! When it was over, every other member's estate had been burned to the ground with them and their families inside!"

"Careful, my green-eyed friend," Luka said, looking at Marlen. "You do not need more enemies than you already have. Many still remember what you did that day, and many still do *not* approve." Luka then looked back at Domadred. "The truth of the matter is that the people of the North grew tired of the council's tyranny and oppression, and

Asura rose up to protect them. Most importantly, however, the people now rejoice under his rule. From his leadership we of the North have become the most prosperous nation in the entire world. In turn, we have extended that prosperity to Vai'kel. So, to answer your question, we have given the people of the Central Continent a generous gift that only a foolish handful have rejected."

"It takes only a dedicated *few* to lead," Domadred answered, "for the many to follow . . ."

"Spoken like a true dissident," Luka said, laughing. "I must remind myself that you were involved in the assassination of your senior, the former prime admiral of the Thalassocracy."

"A fool's lie!" Domadred growled. "And you know it."

"Indeed, I do know the truth, Captain," Luka said nonchalantly. "And lucky for you, so does Lord Asura. We know of your innocence, and we also know of your involvement with the Resistance. Sadly, as far as your fellow Western captains are concerned, your innocence is nothing more than idle hearsay. They now know you only as a traitor, for you are stripped of your honor and outlawed even in your own waters. It is no wonder you are drawn to the Resistance, Domadred. You share their same sad fate and dire situation."

"I stand firm in the truth, Luka. And the Guardians will grant me both justice and revenge."

"Do not believe everything you tell yourself, Captain. You have no allies by sea, and the world has become tired of your piracy. More importantly, the Resistance's rebellion has failed and no deific gods have come down from the Zenith to aid them. While you are cast adrift, your so-called freedom fighters starve in the sewers and deep forests of Vai'kel. The Guardians have forsaken you both. But lucky for you, Asura is not only generous but also wise. Instead of rooting the Resistance from their hideouts and causing unnecessary bloodshed, he would prefer to end things amicably. He has an offer that will not only vindicate you but appease the Resistance leaders and end this needless conflict and loss of life."

Luka resteepled his hands and eyed Domadred over his fingertips. "If, however, you do not accept Asura's terms, I guarantee that you will not find your justice, Captain. Nor will your fellows in the Resistance live to see another season. For not only will the *Illusive Diamond* rest quietly on the bottom of the ocean, all who oppose the United Rulership of Vai'kel will share your fate."

"You are a fool to threaten a man while alone at sea on his ship."

"No," Luka answered with a thin smile, "actually, it is an offer—if you're not *fool* enough to reject it, that is."

Levain shook his head. "It's been a while since we had Northern nobility on this ship. I had forgotten their way with words."

"If I remember correctly," Kefta chuckled, "the last one ended up gagged and in the brig. I do believe he was there for nearly a month before we ransomed him off. He started off all haughty with noble fire, but by the end, his words were not quite so *eloquent*."

"I trust you do not cage peace doves, Quartermaster," Luka said calmly. "Especially ones who risked their lives to save your ship and crew only days prior. You possibly don't know, but it was I who slayed your brother's killer. More importantly, I am here to offer you both *pardon* and *peace*, so do not insult me more than you already have."

"Yours is the offer of a man's dying breath," Domadred said, as he looked about the table, "for it seems that we all have finished the food before us." Domadred paused, idly stroking his beard before he continued. "But, lucky for you, I enjoy some whiskey and a cigar before a meal has reached its fateful end."

What is Luka's ultimate goal? Aleksi thought, tension gripping his heart. *If he knows who I am, then how does the Masters' Academy fit into his and Asura's plans? What do they want with me?*

CHAPTER XXI

As Marlen cleared everyone's plates, Domadred looked away from Luka and spoke to Nara, Fa'ell, and Aleksi. "I know my officers well—they all enjoy a strong drink and a good smoke. But what of my *guests*? Would you care to join us in some of the finest whiskey and tobacco that Terra has to offer?"

Nara raised his massive arms and, leaning back in his chair, placed his hands behind his head. "Captain, the only proper way to end such a fine meal with such interesting conversation would be for some single cask and a good rolled smoke. Sadly for the nobleman, I am a fast drinker."

"We have at least one taker," Domadred said, smiling. "Fa'ell, would you care to enjoy some whiskey and a cigar as we continue to listen to Luka's belittlement and condescension?"

"Only whiskey for me, Captain," Fa'ell answered. "The nobleman has been blowing enough smoke to cloud the room, so no need for me to add more."

"Spoken like a true lady. And the young Aleksi, what say you, son?"

"I am not particularly familiar with cigars . . . ," Aleksi answered, not taking his eyes off Luka.

"A whiskey, then, and half cigar," Domadred said. "I'm sure that Kairn will be nice enough to assist you in its lighting."

Lastly, Domadred turned his gaze to Luka. "And you, Northern Lord, do you wish to partake of these last gifts before I decide your fate?"

"A cigar and a good drink are wonderful companions to both peacemaking and killing, Captain. How could I possibly refuse you?"

With the table cleared, Marlen brought out an unmarked bottle of amber liquid and an ornately carved wooden box. Next he fetched a tray of unique glasses. They had a thick base but the actual hollow of the cup was only a small rounded bulb. Elegantly curving upward, the tapered mouth was just wide enough to fit one's lips and nose upon drinking.

Marlen set the glasses before each at the table and, as he poured the whiskey, Domadred opened the ornate cigar box. One at a time, the captain removed a cigar, cut its end with a snipping utensil, and then passed it around the table. Once nearly everyone had one, Domadred took out two much smaller cigars, cut them, and handed the first to Brayden and then the second to Aleksi.

"Marlen," Domadred said, putting his cigar into his mouth, "would you be so kind as to open the gallery?"

"Yes, Captain." Marlen moved to the rear of the room and then ceremoniously opened the large windows. Aleksi felt the cool ocean breeze glide across his skin. With the windows open, he could clearly see the silvery glimmer of the moonlight reflecting in the ship's frothy wake. Night had descended over the ocean and the view was profound. The moons' glittering brilliance atop the glowing blue-black waves seemed to stretch behind them into a dark eternity.

After pulling something small from his pocket, Domadred mysteriously lit his cigar with several strong puffs. The captain then handed the object to Valen on his left.

"A Runic *pocket flame*," Nara exclaimed. "I've never actually seen one up close!"

"They are quite rare," Domadred said, smiling. "We have others on board. But this one is my *personal* favorite."

"I would love to see it!"

"Please do. You all may use it to light your cigars."

Cigars were lit as the pocket flame was passed around. After a moment the Runic tool came to Luka. The nobleman held it up against the lamplight, inspecting its engraving. As he gazed at the ornate metal, his mannerisms were like a coiled viper's—the embodiment of control and deadly patience.

"Ahh, the craftsmanship of the Western Masters' Academy," Luka said. "What a wonderful piece; I do so enjoy the historic artistry of the Masters of old." Domadred nodded his head as Luka continued. "And although I am of the North, I have to be honest"—Luka's green eyes flashed to Aleksi—"I have a special fondness for the ones which hail from the *Eastern* Academies." Luka lit his cigar and passed the tool to Aleksi. "Here you are, son. I'm sure you know how to use a *Runic tool*, but you might want to ask the sailing master to help you manage that cigar."

Taking the instrument, Aleksi eyed Luka darkly. Before the youth could say anything, Kairn leaned in close. After a moment of coaching and a bit of coughing, the tip of Aleksi's cigar glowed with a fiery-red ember.

Soon all at the table except Fa'ell in her elegant gown held a lit cigar. The smoke wafted up but was carried out the windows by the evening's gentle, salt-laden breeze.

"Well, with that taken care of"—Domadred paused to take a long draw from his cigar, then blew the smoke before continuing—"what was it that you were saying, Luka? Something about an offer of Northern peace and pardon?"

"Yes, Captain," Luka answered before taking another sip from his glass. "But first, let me thank you for the cigar and fine drink. You are truly as generous as your reputation. And, if I am to fully understand the extent of your generosity, I do in fact believe that I have until the very *end* of dinner to speak of this offer. Before you make good on your threats, that is. Correct?"

"Indeed."

"Well then, before I speak further on the matter, I wish to ask the young Aleksi a simple little something."

"Excuse me?" The captain's cigar hung in midair.

"Well, the boy is a bit of a mystery, isn't he? He is so young and so skilled, yet so far away from his teachers. Terra is a dangerous place for a young student who strays from his elders, and I would like to know what he plans on accomplishing out here all alone."

Aleksi shifted in his chair, and although his right hand held his cigar, his left hand slowly crept to the hilt of his blade.

"You *must* be joking," Domadred said in disbelief.

"It's just that I'm confounded, Captain," Luka continued, blowing smoke up toward the ceiling. "And the boy's eyes are green, so I, a Northern lord, feel some responsibility for the lad and simply cannot help myself. Especially considering the fact that he has recently fallen in with outlawed pirates who threaten *peace messengers* at the dinner table." Domadred shook his head as Luka continued. "Honestly, I am very curious to hear his response to one simple question before, as your quartermaster stated earlier, things get *complicated*."

"Your time," Domadred said gruffly as he tapped ash from the tip of his cigar, "in fact, much like your life, is your own to use as you see fit. Do not waste it."

"Wonderful. Thank you, Captain." Luka turned his gaze to Aleksi. Aleksi's Rune tingled and Luka's eyes glittered as he continued. "So, son, what have you to say for yourself? Why have you forsaken your home and Master? And do not lie; I will know."

Aleksi remained silent and eyed Luka coldly as his grip on his sword's sheath tightened.

"Answer him, Aleksi," Domadred said curtly. "Let's get this *done with*."

Aleksi looked over at Domadred in surprise.

Domadred pointed his cigar at Luka. "Out with it, son; I am losing patience with this little game."

Aleksi cast his gaze back to Luka and spoke in an icy tone. "What makes you say, Lord, that I have forsaken anyone?"

"Just answer my question," Luka said with a slight smile as he tapped ash off his cigar onto the table. "As you can surely tell, we don't have much time."

"I would never betray my Master," Aleksi answered carefully. "He has taught me well over many long years. I don't know what you are referring to . . ." Using his thumb against the scabbard, Aleksi silently drew his blade under the table—after a centimeter, he stopped its movement. Having the blade removed from its sheath even a little would allow him a lightning-fast strike.

"Oh, certainly there is more to the story. Tell me *why* you left your school so suddenly if you had not also abandoned your Master."

Aleksi suddenly felt a strange feeling come over him. His body grew numb and his lips moved as if the words were speaking of their own volition. "I . . . I have been taught by many," the youth said, greatly surprising himself. "Yet there is only one I would ever call Master." Aleksi could no longer feel his hands and his head started to spin. "And it is *his* trust that I have never betrayed." Aleksi's focus blurred and he could hardly believe the words were coming out of his mouth as he continued. "In fact, I follow his bidding even now."

"Ahh. So I understand, then," Luka said, smiling. "You mean to tell me you did not flee your Master, you fled another whom *you* deemed unworthy."

". . . That is correct."

"Perhaps you have just not found the right Master, my boy. There are others out there who can teach you, and I promise they would not abandon you like the man you search for now."

Regaining control of himself, Aleksi remained silent.

"Well, it all makes sense, then; my curiosity is sated!" Luka raised his whiskey glass high in a mock toast to Domadred and took a long sip. "I am so fortunate that the Captain was generous enough to grant me several free moments so that I could understand the boy's motives."

"Enough of this, Luka," Domadred growled, standing slowly. "You walk a fine line and on either side you face your own ruin. The evening's entertainment is over."

"No, it is you, Domadred, who faces his own ruin. You are fooling no one but yourself!"

Steadily recovering his mind, Aleksi felt his Rune pulse and he deftly grabbed the sword at his hip. As his muscles coiled to attack, he suddenly felt a hand grip his shoulder. Surprised, the youth looked to his left and saw Kairn shake his head knowingly.

"Not yet, Aleksi," Kairn whispered. "Wait for the Captain's word."

"Damn it, Luka," Nara said, as he violently smothered his cigar into an ashtray. "If you have a proposal, come out with it! You are acting like a royal ass and even I am tired of listening to your drivel."

"Well, I am glad to know that you feel no need to protect me," Luka said, blowing smoke at Nara dismissively, "out of some lost sense of old honor, Lionman."

Nara folded his massive arms and clenched his jaw.

"Although, fallen son of Iksir," Luka continued with a smirk, "I suppose it would be very sad if you still felt you had *any* allegiance to the North after you were exiled by your father, Raegnar the High Lord of the North-East, with such disgrace!"

"You scrawny fool," Nara shouted, bolting upright and knocking back his chair." I will rip the tongue from your skull!"

"No, Nara!" Fa'ell said, jumping up and holding him back. "Not yet." Nara's light-green eyes blazed in anger and his massive muscles rippled—but the large man advanced no farther.

"You and Domadred make a fitting pair indeed," Luka said, smiling as he looked up at the monolith of muscle towering above him. "You both have lost so much but also have so much to gain if you accept Asura's offer."

"Luka, you have done nothing but show disrespect to my ship, my crew, and *now* even my guests." Domadred drew his sword, pointing the tip at Luka across the table. "You will die for your insolence!"

"Captain, wait!" Kairn said, as the other officers drew their blades. "We *must* hear him out! Even when he first boarded he spoke of a peace treaty—what if he is telling the truth?"

"This is your *final chance*, Nobleman," Domadred said with eyes ablaze and sword aloft. "Say your peace *now* lest I cut out your heart and cast you into the sea!"

"I am here," Luka answered, leaning back in his chair, "to offer a declaration of peace between the crew of the *Illusive Diamond* and High Lord Asura, commander of the Northern Empire. Asura offers to end all conflict with the Resistance of Vai'kel and vows to return you to your rightful position in the Western Thalassocracy. If you had met with me privately like I had asked, and not disrespected me so greatly, I would have told you of the offer *outright*."

"Offers made by a deceiver," Domadred said, making a small circle with the tip of his blade, "are as valuable as salt water to a sailor. Tonight, the leviathan will feast on your flesh!"

"Asura has done a great many things some deem unethical," Luka said, taking a puff from his cigar. "But he has *never* broken an oath. He, much like you, my good Captain, is no liar."

"My *ass*, he is no liar!" Marlen said, slamming his fist on the table. "He betrayed all of us and now rules the North with an iron fist."

"Marlen, you chose your own fate," Luka said dismissively. "Even now, Lord Asura does not understand why you betrayed him during the revolt and still hold such hostility in your heart."

"Only a fool does not understand Marlen's anger," Domadred said furiously. "Liar or no, it was Asura who stole everything from him! In fact, it was your lord who brought us all to ruin!"

"My lord did that?" Luka said in mock confusion. The nobleman shook his head and held up his arms with cigar in hand. "Captain, I thought it was *Lenhal* who killed the prime admiral, framed your crew, and then cast you and your men out of the Western fleet. Was it not *he* who bedded your wife, the chair of the Warden Women's High Council, before he had her killed?"

In a flash, Domadred threw a dagger with his left hand. All in the room leaned back in surprise as it flew through the air and thunked behind Luka, pinning his cigar to the wall.

"Nobleman," Domadred said coldly, still holding his sword aloft, "do not think that just because you offer treaty I will not gut you." Domadred wistfully waved the tip of his blade as he continued. "Like the morning catch, you will flail upon the planks of my deck as I spill your insides for all to see." Kefta drew a long, wickedly curved dagger from his belt and placed it on the table with a wide grin as Domadred continued. "Choose your words carefully, Nobleman, or the last thing you will hear is the gashing of your flesh and the throaty cheers of my crew."

"Was it not the saying of your former commander in the Unification War," Luka replied calmly, "that 'only a fool hears truth and becomes offended'?" There was a long and uneasy silence before Luka continued. "I speak the truth, Captain, and you know it. Therefore, do not take offense. Lenhal was the one who wronged you, not Lord Asura. In fact, my lord wishes to grant you justice and vindication—he wishes to grant you *revenge.*"

"I do not need Asura to kill Lenhal!"

"I wouldn't be so certain of that. However, if you accept Lord Asura's peace, not only will he allow you to exact your vengeance, but more importantly, once the deed is done, he will instate you, Domadred, as *prime admiral* of the Western Thalassocracy. A thing I guarantee that you could not do on your own."

"And why would he ever want to do that?" Domadred retorted.

"Captain, my mission is multifold. I have come to offer a truce not only between Asura and your crew, but also with the leaders of the Resistance. Moreover, Asura plans on using you as his negotiator—for who better to broker that peace than a member of the Resistance and prime admiral of the Western fleet?"

The officers at the table were taken aback at Luka's words, and both Valen and Mareth lowered their swords.

"You're lying," Domadred said softly.

"We all know that what happened to you and your crew was an atrocity, Domadred. Lord Asura wishes to make things right for you and your men. He also wishes to find peace in Vai'kel and end this petty squabbling with the Resistance. I would have told you all this sooner had you only met with me in private like I had asked. It's a shame you and your crew don't have better manners. Your years in exile have undoubtedly hardened you."

"Such an offer," Domadred said, swallowing hard, "comes at a high price, no doubt."

"The price is worth the reward, Captain." Luka turned and forcibly removed Domadred's dagger from the wall. He plucked his cigar from the dagger's tip and, covering its new incisions with his fingers, took a long draw. Luka blew smoke up to the ceiling as he continued. "As I'm sure you know, Lenhal searches for you even as we speak—with the fever of a corrupted Arkai, he hunts for Saiya. But, more importantly, Lenhal is not the only one who wishes to find the High Priestess."

Luka paused, taking another draw from his cigar. "Captain, I know you want revenge. If you agree to my terms now, I will, as a show of good faith, deliver Lenhal directly into your hands. And then, once I send word to Asura, he will have your name cleared and your ship and crew reinstated in the Western Thalassocracy. First, I only ask the whereabouts of—"

"It is *not* that simple!" Domadred growled.

"Captain, don't underestimate Asura's power and influence. You know what he is capable of. All you have to do is align yourself with him and agree to negotiate his peace with the leaders of the Resistance, and you will have your former titles restored and your riches returned. Even better, you will become prime admiral of the Western fleet!"

Domadred lowered the tip of his sword and the officers looked at each other keenly.

"There is one more thing, however," Luka said, sighing as he set down his mangled cigar. "It has come to Asura's attention that you know the whereabouts of Saiya. Asura wishes to know the High Priestess's location and then provide her safe passage to the Northern capital of Erithlen. There are some things Asura needs to discuss with her. In addition, he will provide her safe haven until everything with Lenhal has been played out."

"Discuss?" Kefta asked. "That sounds like a kind way of saying that you will harm her."

"Certainly not, boy!" Luka laughed. "Show some respect for your betters. Saiya is a young, celibate priestess devoted to High Arkai Aruna. Her safety is of the *utmost* importance, and neither you nor the Resistance can protect her from Lenhal and his searching fleets. It is only a matter of time before he tracks her with his Runes and kills her. Until Lenhal is dead, that young woman is simply not safe."

"But why the change of heart?" Domadred asked, shaking his head. "Lenhal and Asura signed a peace treaty just four short years ago. It just does not make sense. Why would Asura want him dead now?"

"You know full well that Lenhal has fallen out of public favor with the other captains in the Thalassocracy. He is not a born leader of men and all can see it. Many believe that he should never have become prime admiral in the first place. The whispers I hear say the honor should have been given to you. Well, Lord Asura agrees. He feels that you, Domadred Steele, honored veteran of the Vai'kel Unification War, would not only lead the West into a new era of prosperity but also have the ability to broker the Central Continent's much-needed peace."

There was a long silence and Domadred sat back into his chair. Still holding his sword, he tapped the flat of the blade on the table's edge, deep in thought. All at the table but Luka looked at him anxiously.

"I cannot speak for all Resistance leaders," Domadred finally said, "and therefore cannot guarantee peace—their motivations and constituencies are as numerous as the city-states they govern." Domadred stopped tapping his blade and looked Luka in the eye. "Let me be more clear. Many leaders within the Resistance will *never* declare peace with the North, no matter the offer Asura makes."

"Those few will then never reclaim their lands. But the ones who do align with Asura will be reinstated into the government of their city-state, able to once again have reign over their province and people. If you can sway just a critical mass, Domadred, that is enough to achieve Lord Asura's goal."

"For they have the people's hearts and will be able to still their ire and revolt," Kairn said, shaking his head. "And then *all* in Vai'kel will pay fealty and a hefty homage to Asura, no doubt. But I ask you, Nobleman, in truth, what is sovereignty if it is not free and unbridled?"

"Well, Sailing Master," Luka answered, "if the Resistance leaders prefer, they can stay in their sewer hideouts and deep-forest refuges. Or they can even live their lives as outlaws on the open seas like you—bouncing from harbor to harbor, hoping none will turn them in. However, Lord Asura has already infiltrated numerous factions of the Resistance, thereby finding their so-called *secret* locations." Luka turned his green-eyed gaze to Domadred and smiled. "For how do you think I found this ship, Captain?"

Domadred did not respond.

"Well, a *little bird* loyal to the North told me. I think you might know the one. You seemed to have enjoyed patting her bottom back at the Guardian's Flame in Mindra's Haven."

Domadred's eyes went wide.

"Lord Asura instructed me to make it clear to you that if peace cannot be found, he will have no choice but to mass a full-scale war against the Resistance. No matter the cost or sacrifice, he will root out insurgencies not just from Vai'kel, but throughout *all* of Terra. This includes your friend Beck Al'Beth in Mindra's Haven and your numerous allies in the Western isles."

Domadred stood and sheathed his blade. Taking a deep breath, he tilted back his head and drank the last of his whiskey in one fell gulp before speaking. "Well, Luka, we of the West do not operate in a dictatorship like your lord's empire, so I must discuss your proposal with my officers. You may wait in your guest chamber for my response. It may take several days, but I trust that you will find it more comfortable than the brig. While you wait, however, you will continue to have your two-man guard at all times."

"Thank you, Captain," Luka said, standing up. "May I assume that I have use of the deck by night? I would hate to miss the luminescence."

"So long as you are with your guard, Nobleman, you may move about as you please. But if you leave their side . . ." Domadred's tone regained its usual humor, and he winked at Fa'ell. "Our lovely lady will have another chance to display her talent for wielding a whip. And after she is done, you will have a *very* long swim back home. Have I made myself clear?"

"Perfectly," Luka said. "I hope you all enjoy the rest of your evening. I will now take my leave of you." Luka made a deep, flourishing bow. As he rose, his green eyes flashed to Aleksi. "Ponder my offer well."

As Luka exited the captain's chamber and the door was closed behind him, the room erupted in debate.

CHAPTER XXII

No one seemed to notice as Aleksi excused himself from the now-raucous captain's chamber. As he silently made his way through the dimly lit navigation room, the youth's right hand firmly grasped the hilt of his sheathed blade.

How could Luka have forced me to speak? Aleksi thought as he crossed the quarterdeck. *Only a Master could possess such ability—but if Luka is a Northern Master . . .* Aleksi didn't want to think about what that meant for him, for Domadred, or for the world. *Who, then, really is Asura? Is he a Master, too? And did Rudra know Luka would be on the Diamond as well? If so, why would he ever put me on this boat? I don't understand!*

Swallowing hard, Aleksi walked down the quarterdeck's stairs and stalked through the hallway that led to his room. No one was in sight and the youth quickly unlocked his door. After entering the cabin, Aleksi relocked the door and let out a great sigh.

The young woman in his dreams, his upcoming duel with Kefta, and now Luka—everything was happening too quickly and it was all too much. *I was only supposed to cross the ocean. It is not supposed to be like this!* Aleksi sat on the floor and tried to calm his mind. No matter what he did, however, the youth couldn't shake what Luka had said to him at dinner. *Perhaps you have just not found the right Master, my boy. There are others out there who can teach you, and I promise they would not abandon you like the man you search for now.*

Aleksi focused on his breath and desperately tried to force his mind to relax. It was no use, however, for his thoughts were flowing endlessly, like a river. So, just like he had been taught as a child, Aleksi relented and allowed his thoughts to drift by one by one as he focused on his breath.

Aleksi first saw Kefta's malicious gaze as the boom swung across the stern deck. Next were the eyes of green flame and the rumbling voice's deadly promise from his dream in Mindra's Haven. Aleksi then felt the young woman's passion—followed by her shame. Next, the youth saw the bloody faces and haunting stares of the dead soldiers in Mindra's Haven. Aleksi also felt Fa'ell's anger, Nara's deep scars, and Brayden's longing. Lastly, Aleksi saw Luka's eyes and heard his poignant statement. *"Perhaps you have just not found the right Master . . ."*

Rudra is my true Master! The thought burst into Aleksi's mind. *And I will kill you, Luka, if you try to stop me!* The idea surprised Aleksi greatly. *Kill Luka? Why? How? If he is a Master of the Academy . . .*

Suddenly, the young woman rose out of Aleksi's stream of thoughts. Clothed in the same water of the mental river itself, she beckoned Aleksi to join her in its flowing current. A shiver ran through Aleksi's body and the Rune on his hand pulsed painfully.

Opening his eyes in the darkness of his room, Aleksi looked down and saw light shining through the bandages on his palm, brighter than ever before. Agony shot through Aleksi's arm as the light seeped up the Rune's tendrils into his forearm. *No, not now!* The light was so bright he had to shield his eyes as the pain cut deeper into his shoulder. Curling up into a ball, Aleksi hugged his glowing arm to his chest. *Not yet, I'm not ready!*

As if in response, Aleksi felt the sensation of the young woman rise up in his chest. She was calling to him, urging him into the Dreamscape. Aleksi could not refuse her. Answering her summons, Aleksi closed his eyes.

Despite the burning pain, sleep took him instantly.

Aleksi was floating on his back. He opened his eyes and saw a sky of infinite azure. He felt the touch of the ocean encompass him—it was neither warm nor cool, just *there*. In the distance, the youth could hear waves washing against a coastline. He looked toward the sound and saw land. He swam for it.

Aleksi was at the shore in a heartbeat. Emerging from the water, he noticed he was dry. This did not surprise him. Looking up, the youth saw the towering Western Zenith. It shone out just like last time—watching, waiting.

Aleksi then saw *her*. The young woman was standing under the same willow tree. She was still clad in the same delicate dress, and its white fabric swayed in the warm breeze. Amid the green grasses, wisps of multicolored lights danced at her feet whimsically.

When she saw him, the young woman smiled, causing the light of her forehead to dim. The sight warmed Aleksi's chest and he rushed to her across the sand, rock, and grass. Despite the distance, he was at the tree nearly instantly. Before Aleksi could enter the canopy, however, he felt the same barrier push him back. He raised his hands and pressed against it.

The young woman shook her head. As she did, the soft amber strands of her hair wavered in the breeze. They framed her elegant face in a halo of spun gold. Aleksi sighed and looked into her eyes. They shone like brilliant glaciers, vibrantly illuminated in a frosty cerulean, asking a silent question.

Aleksi opened himself to her and the young woman raised her hand to the wall. This time, she did not hesitate. She reached through the barrier and slid her fingers between his. The moment they touched, Aleksi's heart once again erupted with emotion.

He gripped her hand and struggled against the wall. The young woman's timidness had returned along with her bashful uncertainty. Still, she grasped his hand firmly and pulled him through the barrier. Aleksi's breath caught in excitement as he felt the tree's canopy flow over him. As he passed through, the wall seemed to grow thicker and the young woman was forced to pull even harder.

Suddenly, Aleksi came free and the barrier released him quickly. Stumbling, he fell into the young woman and knocked her backward.

Before she could fall far, however, Aleksi pulled her close. The young woman held on to him tightly, and as she pressed her warm softness against him, he swallowed hard and looked into her eyes. They were illuminated with that same strong emotion he had experienced within her before. She felt something for him—something that had grown over their many encounters in their dreams.

She seemed to push her personal emotions away and again tried to tell Aleksi her urgent warning. Her lips moved, and while he could not hear her words, Aleksi could now feel their intention clearly. She was truly afraid of something—no, of someone.

Aleksi probed deeper and felt the young woman's meaning. This person she warned of was cunning and powerful, and if he did not get his way, he would take over the ship. This man was going to act very soon and *needed* to be stopped.

But how can she possibly know about the ship? How can she know—?

The young woman looked into Aleksi with her brilliant-blue eyes and forcibly grasped his attention to tell him more. This danger on the ship, he was sent by another who was much more powerful. This greater threat wished to reshape the world to his own desires by usurping the Guardians and stealing their holy power. But, more importantly, to realize his goal, he would need to kill Aleksi—and to her, *do worse . . .*

Aleksi felt the young woman's fear grow into terror. He then remembered the gigantic eyes of green flame and cold fury that had invaded his dreams in Mindra's Haven. Those eyes had rung with a voice of thunder that spoke as if a landslide had assaulted his mind. The voice had called for Aleksi's death and the destruction of the Guardians.

Alarm flooded through the young woman. *Yes!* That was the one who hunted them! That was the one who wanted to control her and wanted Aleksi dead. The young woman in Aleksi's arms was regal and noble, but she was also truly afraid. With her body pressed against his, Aleksi could feel her innocence, her fright, and the gentleness of her womanhood. He tightened his arms around her and held her in the shelter of his embrace.

The young woman's emotions changed. Her fear melted away and self-consciousness and abashment replaced it. Aleksi felt her breath grow heavy, causing her pert chest to firmly press against him. The young woman's desire to tell Aleksi her warning was gone—it was now replaced with a new desire and embarrassment of her youthful yearnings.

With one strong hand on the small of her back, and a confidence he had not known he possessed, Aleksi pulled her body even closer to his. The young woman blushed as she looked up at him. Slowly, Aleksi put his other hand to her cheek and gently touched her skin. It was so smooth and soft. He traced the lines of her brow and jaw with his fingers. He had drawn her so many times and he knew these lines so well. But knowing and *knowing*, Aleksi realized, were two very different things.

The young woman swallowed and her body quivered against him. Aleksi felt suppressed emotions rise up in her, and he then felt her desperately try to push them back down. The young woman now looked at him with a new fear. It went beyond youthful inhibition or even the nervous uncertainty of love. Her new emotion felt heavy like duty and honor. It felt as imposing as the responsibility of governing nations—as daunting as sovereignty over the lives of millions. The young woman was now not just fearful of her own love and humiliated by what it meant, but afraid of betraying something even greater than both of them. She was afraid of betraying not only her people—but also the holy divinity of Terra *itself*.

As Aleksi continued to look into the young woman's profoundly blue eyes, he felt her fear win out and she slipped away from him. Aleksi was also uncertain, and he, too, was nervous—but he was *not* scared. Not of the green eyes of fire or of the fury of the Guardians.

Gently, he brought his face to meet hers. Leaning in, Aleksi then kissed the young woman deeply. Her passion overcame her frightened inhibition. As the young woman's lips embraced his, her heart and tongue welcomed him into her warmth. She tasted salty, and sweet, and wonderful.

Aleksi swam in her emotive essence. It was a musk of sensuality and allure—a promise of connection, oneness, and joy. He felt both her fragility and her strength—the tenderness of her skin and the power of her passion.

The young woman circled her arms around Aleksi and pulled him closer. Aleksi felt her heart delicately open to him. With its opening, he tasted her beauty, her light, and her vast power. Awash in emotion, he felt the slenderness of her figure, but he also could feel her strength. The young woman's power was truly overwhelming.

Desire strongly built within him. In response, Aleksi pressed his firmness against the mound of her womanhood. Gasping, she dug her nails into his back and kissed him even deeper. All of her walls were down now. Reveling in their space of pure emotion, Aleksi experienced a connection to another in a way he had never before thought possible. He caressed her worries and celebrated her hopes—he nurtured her desires and guarded against her fears. He felt alive, free, and filled with joy—the joy of truly connecting to *her*.

Suddenly, the young woman pushed back and broke away from his embrace. Her eyes shone with pain, as if she did not believe what she had done. Aleksi reached out and touched her face consolingly, but the young woman shook her head. He felt anger within her. No. He felt shame, confusion, and, once again, *fear*.

The young woman's face hardened and an invisible force pushed Aleksi away. Everything around them then suddenly changed. The willow tree began to swing violently as a wild wind picked up. It pushed at Aleksi, forcing him back toward the water. Aleksi fought the torrent and ground his boots into the sand. In response, the wind blew even harder, and he had to use his bandaged hand to block his eyes from the gale.

Aleksi saw tremendous storm clouds building above the Zenith Mountain. As he struggled against the storm, he looked at the young woman pleadingly, but her eyes and the bright light on her forehead pierced him like sharp blue ice. The young woman's arms were crossed over her chest, and although her face was a mask of regal power and proud honor, her heart betrayed her.

Aleksi felt profound sadness well up inside of her, a sense of loss so strong it threatened to rip apart the world around them. He still felt her desire for his embrace, but while her longing and love flowed freely from her heart, they did not melt the ice of her eyes. Instead, they shone with pain and resentment.

High above, storm clouds obscured the Zenith's light. Everything about them was cast in shadows of grey and sadness. Even the ocean behind was afoul in anguish. Waves crashed angrily on the rocky shore, frothing their wrath across the coastline.

Aleksi tried to call out. But try as he might, the wind was too much. It pushed him farther away and his boots dug thick tracks into the sand. The sound of the gale rose in his ears—the wind was wailing the young woman's lament.

Her icy eyes commanded him to leave.

Aleksi did not yield.

Howling, the wind kicked up a squall of water and sand. Aleksi had to cover his face as a blast of gravel tore at his skin. Yet even as it ripped his flesh, he hunkered down and fought against the torrent. Through his fingers, he saw that the willow tree was gone and the young woman was now standing alone on a harsh, rocky bluff. What had once been soft grasses and gentle hills were now sharp boulders and desolate barrens. What had been a frail white dress was now a long, regal sapphire robe, ornate and commanding.

A radiant fury filled the young woman's eyes and forehead. The cold blue light streamed out into the darkness. She raised her robed arms high into the sky and called forth a tempest. The winds screamed about her, and rain and hail fell in icy sheets. The squall's cold shards tore into Aleksi's flesh, numbing his body and mind.

However, within Aleksi's heart, love still burned. Through the torrent of wind and ice, Aleksi saw that tears were running down the young woman's face. Amid the raging storm, sorrow flowed from her chest. There was grief, longing, and regret. There was regret of betraying Aleksi and herself, but what tore at her heart most of all was the regret of betraying her Arkai and her people.

In that instant, Aleksi understood this storm was not truly hers—the barrier was also not of her creation. Aleksi looked up at the Western Zenith. *There*, that was the seat of this fierce power. *That* was the cause of this violent storm. And while the young woman was not its captive, she was bound to its divine will.

Aleksi looked around in desperation as the icy tempest continued to slash at his flesh. *No! It does not matter. Nothing does. I will challenge the Zenith itself to be with her! I will not let my love be stolen from me, not even by a god!*

As the wind ripped at his face, Aleksi felt his right arm burn beneath his bandages. Then his Rune pulsed with fire and new life as crashes of lightning struck overhead. Blinding light illuminated the sky, and Aleksi's heart was ignited with an intensity that threatened to consume him.

Casting off his bandage, he raised his Rune-laden fist into the sky. A deafening boom of thunder echoed across the ocean. Here in the Dreamscape—the collective dream of Terra—scrawled from finger to shoulder, Aleksi's Rune was magnificent and fully formed! In defiance of the gale, he let out a wordless scream and called upon the *numinous* power of Terra—the power that was his holy birthright.

As he opened his hand, his Rune erupted with a brilliant light that shone through the rain and flying ice. Empowered with furious splendor, it cast long shadows in the murky, swirling darkness around him. Aleksi then thrust his fiery palm at the storm. Raging Runes swirled across his flesh and extended into the air around his arm as he pushed the tempest back. He forced *his will* upon the Dreamscape, challenging the Arkai itself!

Wind, water, and sleet frantically whirled around Aleksi's body as he pressed forward through the storm. Once again, raising his blazing fist into the sky, he channeled energy into his Rune. Aleksi then opened his palm and thrust his Rune-laden hand downward. Lightning cascaded from the heavens in a burning torrent of flame and electricity. Bolt after bolt struck the ground in sharp succession and their frantic explosions cast rock, sand, and *his fury* high into the air.

Aleksi's Rune burned with a ferocity that would have killed him if he had attempted to wield it in the waking world. But here in the ethereal Dreamscape, he was able to cast that untamed power at the Zenith's dark clouds above, undaunted by Terra's normal physical limitations. Raising his hand to the heavens, Aleksi channeled his attack through his mighty Rune, and crackling rage exploded in the sky.

As his wrathful passion illuminated the clouds, the young woman's eyes went wide—the force pushing Aleksi back had subsided. His Rune blazing across his arm, he sprinted to her over the barren rocks.

Moving with incredible speed and one-pointed concentration, Aleksi came to the invisible barrier and slammed his radiant fist against it.

When his glowing knuckles hit the wall, there was a deafening crash of lightning and thunder. Aleksi felt the barrier fracture from his blow, and large spiderwebbed cracks of light formed around the point of impact.

I will not lose her, too! I will not!

Filled with all the sadness and loss he had ever experienced, Aleksi raised his fist to the Zenith in defiance. Channeling his anger, he prepared to strike again. This time, he knew his blow would shatter the wall completely.

Suddenly, the young woman was right in front of him. She stood on the other side of the barrier with her hands pressed up against its surface. She was looking at him pleadingly, *begging* him to stop. Her love flowed freely and shone out through her heart and tearstained eyes.

Instantly, Aleksi's rage left him. He dropped his hand and his Rune lost its power. As its light faded, sadness, loss, and love flooded Aleksi's chest. His heart was filled with a deep and intense longing—a longing for *her*.

Profound sorrow shone in the young woman's eyes and she pressed her palms against the wall. It was the same place where she had pulled him through only moments before.

Raising his hand to hers, Aleksi looked at her beseechingly. In response, she mouthed two silent words.

"I'm sorry..."

Then Aleksi awoke.

Darkness surrounded Aleksi, and his body was covered in sweat. His Rune was once again dormant and his heart was numb. He rose from his hammock slowly, putting a shaky hand through his damp hair. Mindlessly, he walked out of his room, up the stairs, and out onto the ship's open deck. A hard breeze met him. It chilled the sweat on his body, making him tremble.

Aleksi walked past the foremast and continued onward toward the bow. The light of Terra's two moons washed over him in the darkness as he gazed out at the endless glowing ocean beyond.

Aleksi did not feel the moons' light, nor did he feel the wind's cold.

All Aleksi felt was *alone*.

CHAPTER XXIII

Aleksi awoke in his hammock and, groggily rubbing his eyes, looked out to sea. Thick clouds obscured the Zenith's light, and the water was murky. The scene matched his mood well. As he dressed, Aleksi could not shake the clinging sorrow of the previous night. It gripped his heart with icy fingers, freezing away what little glimpse of warmth he had experienced. The young woman's love was so real and so pure, yet she had cast him away with bitter fury.

Why would she deny her heart's own longing? Aleksi thought as he dressed. *What could be so important that she would forsake love? The Zenith? The Arkai? What?* Angrily, Aleksi thrust his sword into his belt and opened the door. Raw loss clawed at his chest as he strode down the hallway to the ladder. *Even worse was her message and the captain's dinner with Luka. What does she expect me to do? Kill Luka?* The thought caused a cold shiver to rise up Aleksi's spine. *If he is a Master, then he is much more powerful than I. I need to think—I need a plan! Rudra, why did you send me here? What am I supposed to do?*

Coming above deck, Aleksi saw that the overcast sky was even more oppressive than he had previously seen. The salty smell of the ocean was thick in the wind that blew across the ship. Without looking around, Aleksi walked aft past the quarterdeck. The youth knew there was only one way to dull the haunting ache in his heart—losing himself in the emptiness of his training.

With harsh determination, Aleksi ascended the ladder and knelt on the stern deck. He let his thoughts settle. As his mind became still, however, the pain in his heart only grew. It was now colored with dark anger. Anger at the young woman, the Arkai, Luka, Rudra—*everything*. Aleksi's hands then flew to his hilt and his blade exploded out of his sheath. In a rush of fury and passion, he swung his sword over and over again. As he practiced, his pain faded but only because his heart grew numb. Deep within him, a cold wrath steadily built.

Aleksi continued to train in isolation until he saw Brayden approach the stern deck. The boy wore a wooden training sword tucked into his belt as if it were a sheathed blade. Brayden timidly climbed the ladder and stood several paces away.

Aleksi let out a sigh as he sheathed his sword. Kneeling on the deck, he laid his palms flat against his thighs and nodded to the boy. Brayden came closer and copied his posture. Aleksi's hands floated to his sword and he moved slowly so the boy could follow.

Aleksi practiced the most fundamental technique, the drawing strike. He lightly gripped his sword's sheath in one hand and the hilt in the other. Slowly, he drew the blade as he leaned up onto his knees. In a sudden flash, Aleksi took a sliding step forward and, pulling back on the sheath, fully drew his blade in a cutting strike. With a vibrant swoosh, the edge cut through the air in a horizontal arc. Brayden watched with keen determination as Aleksi sheathed his sword and slowly sat back down on his knees.

Aleksi performed the technique again, this time even slower. After a couple of repetitions, Brayden followed along. The boy mimicked the motion of Aleksi's hands as he gently drew the training sword from his belt. Much like he had seen, Brayden then tried to step forward in a sudden surge and strike horizontally. The wooden sword, however, only clumsily moved through the air. Brayden's movements were forced and unrefined, for his efforts possessed all the vigor of youth but none of the sophistication of skill.

The sight of it reminded Aleksi of his many long years of training as a boy. He had been much younger than Brayden when he first learned this technique with Rudra. The memory was tinged with sadness and only strengthened Aleksi's buried emotions.

Pushing away his feelings, Aleksi nodded to the boy and they both continued to practice.

They trained in silence until Aleksi heard a voice come up from the navigation room below.

"Captain, the crew has already heard about Luka's offer." The voice belonged to Kefta and he sounded displeased.

"Yes," Domadred answered, "it seems that several of the officers have been swayed by the nobleman's words and wish to gain favor with the men. Personally, I have yet to decide."

Aleksi looked over at Brayden. The boy was concentrating on his sword work and didn't seem to hear the conversation below.

"You cannot seriously be thinking of accepting a pact with Asura?" Kefta said.

"Luka's is an offer not to be hastily dismissed. What weighs on my mind first and foremost is the safety of this ship. Next is my duty to both the Thalassocracy and the Resistance. If Luka can make good on his promises, this pact could very well ensure the protection of all three. Although it might not be a long-term solution, it would give us a few years of respite as we gather strength."

"But would the Resistance leaders ever agree to a treaty with Asura?"

"All but the most radical will agree to his terms after a good deal of negotiation—no one is as tired of an insurgency as the actual insurgents themselves. Asura undoubtedly knows this. An alliance with the North will not only bring peace to Vai'kel and vindicate us, but when combined with Saiya's help, will unite the Western admirals, too. In the end, we all come out the better for it."

"Yes, united under you. Captain, I feel you are being clouded by what you will gain in the deal. Remember, Luka said Saiya is to be taken to Erithlen. There *must* be more to Asura's plan."

"Undoubtedly there is, but Asura and Luka still do not know that she . . ." Domadred lowered his voice and Aleksi did not hear the rest.

Saiya . . . That name again; who is she?

"Besides," Domadred continued, "it does truly seem that the men like his terms—or the outcome, rather. They remember well what it was like when I was an admiral and would undoubtedly like to live that life again."

"Domadred, my brother would never have gone along with this. Asura is not to be trusted. Somewhere in this there is a trap; you must know that."

"If the crew agree to it unanimously, I would have to—" Domadred stopped himself. "I have yet to make up my mind. You'd best speak to each man individually and sway his opinion if you truly feel Luka's offer is to be denied. But before you go off politicking, I do believe you have your own personal business to attend to first. And a word of advice on that—be careful. I made that bet back in Mindra's Haven for a reason; Aleksi is much more dangerous than he looks. If it makes you feel better, I'm happy to void our wager—"

Suddenly, the doors of the navigation room opened and Kefta strode out onto the quarterdeck. The young man held two wooden staffs. They were slightly thicker than Kefta's thumb and stood nearly as tall as his shoulders.

"Don't fatigue yourself," Kefta said, turning his gaze up to Aleksi on the stern deck. "We still have our duel. Or are you too busy playing with Brayden?"

Aleksi sheathed his blade and, nodding to Brayden, descended to the quarterdeck in silence.

"It's obvious you are good with a sword," Kefta continued, tossing one of the staffs to Aleksi. "But let's see how you fair with this."

Deftly catching the pole, Aleksi ran his hands along its smooth surface. "At least it's well balanced," Aleksi answered coldly.

"Glad to see you can appreciate fine craftsmanship," Kefta laughed, walking down the steps to the main deck. "I made them *myself.*"

A crowd gathered as they made their way to the center of the deck. Brayden followed behind, and Aleksi turned and motioned for the boy to come closer.

"Brayden, please hold on to this for me." Aleksi then removed his sheathed blade from his belt, and Brayden's eyes went wide as Aleksi handed him the sword. "I'm trusting you to keep it safe for a moment. This shouldn't take long."

Taking the blade, Brayden nodded. The boy then clutched the sword close to his chest as he retreated back to the crowd of onlookers. Turning, Aleksi scanned the crowd. It seemed that most of the crew had come out to see the duel and all looked on expectantly, eagerly awaiting the fight to commence.

"Not having second thoughts, are you?" Kefta asked with a wide grin.

"Hardly . . ."

"Back in Mindra's Haven," Kefta said to the crowd of sailors, "I was going to win a good bit of pearls from the captain at the arena. Luckily, Domadred has been gracious enough to let our bet carry over to this match. And while I know you all are pondering an offer of another sort, does anyone wish to get in on this pot and make a wager on how fast Aleksi will fall? The captain has a large stack of black pearls at one-to-ten odds saying Aleksi will win. Well, I'm putting down an additional stack with Domadred that says this *boy* falls in the first thirty seconds. Who's with me?"

None raised a hand.

"No takers? The first *minute*, then!" Again there was silence. "Surely someone will bet on me winning the first blow, at least?"

"Enough with your talk, Kefta," a sailor called out from the crowd. "Get on with it!"

"Fine!" Kefta flashed Aleksi a look of dark resentment. Returning his attention to the crowd, the young man then called out in an officious tone. "All who are so interested may hold witness to this duel of honor between Aleksi, guest of the *Illusive Diamond*, and me, Kefta Vanarus, quartermaster of the same ship. Under the ardent eye of High Arkai Aruna, I hereby decree that after this duel is settled, all ire and resentment shall be absolved, with the victor receiving full honors over the fallen. The combatants may use staff, fist, and foot, and the first man to yield loses. Aleksi, do you so accept the terms placed before you?"

"I do." Aleksi's eyes shone with a cold green blaze.

"Then begin!"

Aleksi began swirling his staff. Switching it from hand to hand, he spun it in circles around his body. Kefta tried to follow it with his eyes but was unable. Aleksi's staff steadily picked up momentum until it blurred in a soft hum of movement and sound.

Frowning, Kefta rushed in to strike. Aleksi easily parried the attack and deftly kicked Kefta in the ribs. The young man staggered back with a grunt. A few of the men chuckled from the crowd.

"Ha! Looks like Aleksi has won the first blow," a sailor said with a rough laugh. "Glad I didn't take that bet. He didn't even hit you with his staff. Perhaps we should have sided with the captain and taken bets *against* you, Kefta!"

Scowling, Kefta swung his weapon high and rushed back at Aleksi. The hard crack of wood on wood reverberated across the ship. With increasing speed, the two fighters moved back and forth, their staffs connecting impossibly quickly. Strike, parry, counter, block—they danced across the deck locked in a deadly flow of whirling movement and harsh sound. As their tempo intensified, the peals of tempered wood rang out even louder, causing many of the onlookers to step back in fear of being struck.

As they continued to fight, Aleksi felt buried anger well up within him. It ripped at his chest with sharp resentment. Was it anger at Kefta, the young woman, or Luka? Or, really, was it *all* just anger at Rudra? In the end, Aleksi didn't know and it didn't matter. To his heart, it all felt the same.

Enough games; time to end this.

On Kefta's next strike, Aleksi raised his staff and deflected the blow. Stepping to the side and dodging Kefta's follow-up attack, he then struck out with his own counter. This time, Aleksi unleashed his rage.

He felt bottled anger surge through his body as he swung his weapon. His hands tightened around the smooth wood as it whistled through the air with blinding speed and connected with Kefta's upper thigh with a hollow thwack. Kefta let out a cry of agony as his leg went limp and he fell to one knee.

Aleksi rushed in and deftly slid to Kefta's side as the young man frantically tried to jab. Aleksi dropped his own weapon and grabbed Kefta's hand and staff. Forcefully, Aleksi twisted Kefta's wrist backward and bent the sailor's arm up and around in a wide arc. Pushing forward with his other hand on Kefta's weapon, the youth continued to rotate the sailor's wrist. Kefta let out a cry of pain as his body was forced around into a powerful joint lock. Holding Kefta's arm close to his body, Aleksi twisted Kefta's elbow and shoulder until they threatened to snap.

"Yield," Aleksi whispered into Kefta's ear as he slowly tightened his grip. Aleksi's heart stung with loss and abandonment, but across his face a small smile was growing. Hunched over and struggling against Aleksi's armlock, Kefta, however, remained silent.

Aleksi felt dark energy rise up within his Rune as he continued to constrict Kefta's trembling joints. The growing power drowned out the lonely longing within his heart. "Yield or I will *break you*," Aleksi growled so all could hear. "This is your final warning!" The dark power made Aleksi's body quiver as he twisted Kefta's arm even tighter. Energy pulsed through Aleksi's veins. It felt *good*.

Kefta let out a groan of pain and tried to strike Aleksi in the gut with his free hand. Aleksi felt the blow glance off his ribs, causing his dark rage and Runic power to erratically swell up within him. It blurred Aleksi's vision and threatened to take him over. As Aleksi tried to regain control of his body, however, his grip on Kefta's arm loosened.

Seizing the opportunity, Kefta attempted to push away and stand. Filled with fury, Aleksi allowed Kefta to seemingly regain his balance—but just as the young man got up, Aleksi forcibly stepped into him. Knocking Kefta off balance, Aleksi then swept his thigh behind the sailor's knees. As Kefta fell, Aleksi pivoted powerfully, swinging his upper body and elbowing Kefta in the face.

Aleksi heard Kefta's nose break, and the young man's head violently lurched back. Aleksi crouched and followed through with the blow, throwing Kefta over his knee with his outstretched arm. As Kefta toppled over Aleksi's leg, the youth then crashed the edge of his hand down on Kefta's ribs and slammed him to the deck with a loud thud. The breath went out of Kefta's lungs in a violent rush.

Aleksi felt the dark rage surge within his body and consume him. Letting out a wordless scream, he mounted Kefta's chest and hit the young man in the face with his fists.

"Yield!" Aleksi shouted, hitting Kefta again and again. "Yield, yield, yield!" Aleksi felt nothing but anger burning within him. His heart was completely blocked off. There was only rage, fury, and deep, deep suffering.

Strong hands yanked him back. Everything was blurry, and thick tears stung at Aleksi's eyes. Aleksi tried to wipe his face but he could not reach it, for someone was holding his arms back. Out of the corner of his eye, Aleksi saw that his hands were covered in red. He then saw Kefta's face. Blood was flooding from the young man's nose and mouth. It was pooling on his clothes and running in thick rivulets onto the wooden planks.

Aleksi's head spun. If someone had not been holding him up, he would have collapsed. Looking back at Kefta, Aleksi saw that Marlen was trying to stop the bleeding. It didn't seem to be helping. Suddenly, flashes of the carnage in Mindra's Square assaulted Aleksi's mind—the man with a blade stuck in his face, the dead soldiers' lifeless eyes, and the pool of sticky blood covering the cobblestones. It all was so real, so terrifying. Aleksi looked back at Kefta.

His blood runs red, too. In death, they all look the same.

Aleksi doubled over and vomited on the planks. The smell of it stung his nose. Strong hands then hoisted him to the side of the ship. Aleksi wretched over the gunwale—again, and again, and again. The vomit came out in heaving lurches and splashed into the churning ocean below. Filth was stuck in his nose and caught in his teeth. Aleksi tried to spit it out, but that only made it taste worse.

"All done?"

Someone then pulled Aleksi back up to his feet. Wiping his mouth, Aleksi looked over his shoulder. Levain stood behind him, and the large man rested a heavy hand on Aleksi's neck.

"Once you get it out," Levain continued, "you always feel better."

Whatever anger had been in Aleksi's body was now gone. Replacing it was a feeling of hollow exhaustion. Aleksi looked farther behind the large man and saw Marlen and Domadred huddled over Kefta. Aleksi tried to go over to him, but Levain held him firmly in place.

"Oh, I think you have done quite enough for now. Doc and Cap'n are patching him up, you just sit tight."

Tears welled in Aleksi's eyes again. "I . . . I didn't mean to—" Aleksi stopped short as Marlen swapped a sodden bunch of bloody rags for fresh bandages. Crimson quickly soaked the white cloth.

"I know, son," Levain said softly. "I know."

"Will he . . ." Aleksi's voice trailed off as he saw Fa'ell and Nara stand over Kefta. Fa'ell looked very concerned and Nara was shaking his head.

"Well, girls won't be calling him pretty for a good long while—but minus a few missing teeth, he should be fine. What about *you*?"

Aleksi looked up at the ship's carpenter in confusion. Levain motioned to Aleksi's hands. Looking down, Aleksi saw that his knuckles were bloody and gashed.

From Kefta's teeth . . .

Despite the bandage on Aleksi's right hand, blood was dripping down his fingers onto the deck. Before Aleksi had seen his knuckles, he hadn't felt a thing. Now, however, his hands throbbed painfully.

"He didn't yield," Aleksi said slowly, looking at his own glistening flesh. "Why didn't he yield?"

"At first it was pride," Levain answered. "But, son, you then knocked the wind out of him when you threw him on his back. After that, he couldn't have spoken even if he had wanted to." Levain looked deeply into the youth's eyes. "Aleksi, you're very talented in the arts of battle, but you need to learn to control yourself. Enraged as you were, you could have killed him had we not intervened. A fury like that will consume you, son. Not only will it make you kill others, but deep down, it will do even *worse* to you . . ."

Aleksi looked up and saw Luka smiling from the far end of the ship. The nobleman was looking directly at him, and Luka's green eyes glittered. The image was unbearable and Aleksi forced himself to look away. Aleksi then saw Brayden approach. The boy was still clutching Aleksi's sword. Timidly, Brayden came over and presented the blade. Aleksi slowly grasped the sword with his bloody hands. He could not bear to meet the boy's eyes.

Sliding the blade into his belt, Aleksi looked down at the small pool of blood below him. It continued to drip down his fingers and had left red streaks on his scabbard's glossy black surface. Aleksi felt numb—no pain, no anger, no sadness. Just empty. Empty and, once again, *alone.*

"Let's get you some bandages for your hands," Levain said, breaking the silence. "After you clean up, the captain will want to speak with you."

Aleksi slowly nodded his head and, despite his gashed knuckles, clenched his bandaged right hand. His palm burned and his Rune pulsed painfully. The youth could feel it slowly sending its black tendrils farther up his arm.

Rudra, where are you? Why did you leave me?

After the crew cleaned the blood off the deck, they once again went about their duties. An eerie silence then reigned over the ship as Aleksi was given a bucket of boiled salt water, salve, and some fresh bandages. To everyone's surprise, however, the youth took them down to his room and locked the door. After hiding himself away, Aleksi washed and bandaged his hands, taking extra care to roll the gauze higher up his arm to cover his Rune.

Aleksi then laid himself in his hammock and stared at the ceiling, waiting.

It took longer for someone to come than Aleksi expected. The youth didn't move as he waited. He just looked at the smooth planks of wood above his head, forcibly pushing away the feelings in his heart and the images in his mind.

Finally, a knock came at the door. Aleksi stood. Much to his amazement, however, when he opened the door, he saw Kefta instead of the captain. Aleksi instantly took a step back and his hand flashed to his blade.

"No, I'm not here for that," Kefta said. His voice was nasal but steady. "I just want to talk. May I come in?" The young man's face was badly bruised and he had two black eyes. His broken nose had been reset, but it was very swollen. Despite his wounds, Kefta wore a gentle smile. The dark splotches under the young man's eyes, however, made the smile look strange and foreign on his face.

Aleksi stood back from the door. Kefta entered, favoring the leg that Aleksi had struck with his staff. Aleksi's room had only one chair, and he pulled it out for Kefta. The young man winced as he sat.

"I just wanted to say—"

"I'm sorry, Kefta," Aleksi blurted, interrupting him. Aleksi bowed his head and dropped to one knee. "What I did was wrong."

"Hey, hey," Kefta said, pulling Aleksi back up to his feet. "I came here to apologize to *you*. You gave me a chance to yield, but instead, I hit you. This all was my own fault and I deserve what I got."

Kefta paused, motioning for Aleksi to sit on the hammock. "In addition, I want you to know that what happened with the boom was a horrible accident. Yes, I meant it to push you into the water and knock you down a notch in everyone's eyes. But I truly had no idea the main-sheet would snap. It could have killed you, Aleksi, and for that I am very sorry."

Aleksi remained silent.

"It's no excuse, but after my brother . . ." Kefta swallowed hard. "Rihat had been training me how to fight for a long time. But, other than Brayden, I'm the youngest on the ship. I wanted to rank well in the arena to make him proud and prove my worth to the captain and crew. But then everything went up in flames in Mindra's Haven, and when we got back . . ." Kefta's words trailed off. "My brother was gone and *you* were here. I don't know how you are so skilled. But when I'm around you, I feel like all the training I've done over the years has been for nothing. Rihat's death, my promotion, everything—it all feels like it's all just been for *nothing*. If I can't even beat you, a teenager, then what good am I, right?"

There was an uneasy silence.

"I wish I had a brother," Aleksi finally said, shaking his head. "Even a dead one. I may be good at fighting, but for what? You have a family here on this ship. You have something worth *fighting for*. All I have . . ." Images of Rudra's abandoning him and the young woman's icy stare flashed in Aleksi's mind. "I *truly* have nothing."

"Well, for as long as you want it, you have a home here on the *Diamond*." Aleksi felt his eyes began to sting and he looked down. Seeing the tears, Kefta hurriedly continued. "Well, my leg will be shot for a few days. That was a really good strike you did. Someday you will have to teach it to me."

"I hit you where the tensor fasciae latae merges into the iliotibial band," Aleksi answered slowly, still looking at the ground. "When done with enough force and in the right place, the strike renders the leg numb for anywhere from a few hours to a few days."

"Yeah, I can tell," Kefta, said chuckling. "My face hurts a bit, too. Although I think I know a little more about the technique that did that. The old *pin 'em down, right, left, repeat* is a classic on this ship when the boys have a bit too much to drink."

Aleksi looked up and couldn't help but smile. "Yeah, and my elbow into your nose helped, too."

"That it did," Kefta said, fingering his swollen face. "That it did." Aleksi looked down again, but Kefta reached out and touched his arm. "Aleksi, can we have no hard feelings—this time for real?"

"I'd like that."

Kefta nodded. "Well, do you want to get some food with me? Getting one's face mangled really works up an appetite."

"I think I'll just stay here for now." Aleksi looked into Kefta's eye. "Maybe . . . tomorrow?"

"Sounds good." Kefta slowly stood, bracing himself against the desk. Aleksi got up to help, but Kefta motioned him away. "Also, tomorrow the crew is having their sail-diving contest. It's a bit of a ritual on our ship. It starts midmorning. Brayden usually does pretty well; I'm sure he would appreciate if you came to cheer him on."

"I'll be there."

Kefta walked to the door. Opening it, he turned. "One last thing. Please keep teaching Brayden. He will be lucky even if you show him only a little of what you know. And if you'll take me, maybe I'll even join, too."

Before Aleksi could respond, Kefta walked into the hallway and closed the door behind him.

Aleksi lay back in his hammock, once again staring at the ceiling. The youth let out a great sigh. Slowly, he then unwrapped the bandage on his right hand. As he removed the gauze, his knuckles began to sting. Unrolling the dressings, he saw the dark tendrils of his Rune embedded in his nerves. They scrolled up his wrist and forearm, etching deeply bruised tracks in his flesh. Their lines were growing more defined day by day, and he could feel tingling energy pulse within them. Aleksi realized his Rune would soon fully awaken and consume him.

Aleksi did not speak to anyone for the remainder of the day. He ate alone in his cabin and, other than using the washroom, did not leave his room. All he could think of was Kefta's mangled face, the carnage of Mindra's Haven, Luka's green eyes, and the young woman's frozen tears.

Despite the images that flashed through his mind, however, Aleksi's heart felt numb. Deep within him there was only cold loss and a cavernous emptiness.

CHAPTER XXIV

The young woman was gone. At no time during the long night did Aleksi dream of her, and upon waking, he felt her absence sting his chest bitterly.

She has left me, just like Rudra.

After dressing, Aleksi exited his room. As he ascended to the main deck, he noticed yesterday's clouds had all but faded away. He looked aft, and the vibrant light of a distant dawn met him. *The Eastern Zenith now seems so far away.* Due to the early hour, the sky above was a dark purple with only an orangey-red hue coming from the Zeniths. Looking behind the ship, Aleksi saw that the Eastern Zenith was missing even more of its sharp mountain spire and burning lower on the horizon. He then looked past the ship's nose and saw that the Central Zenith before them had risen proportionately. *In several more days, the light from Vai'kel's Zenith will overtake that of the East . . .* Suddenly, Aleksi heard a loud splash and a cacophony of shouts. Startled, he turned his head. It seemed that the entirety of the crew was huddled around the foredeck's starboard gunwale, looking into the water. Aleksi hurried over and joined them. In the dark depths, he saw a murky figure clothed in a halo of swirling lights. As the sailor swam toward the surface, the luminescent glow slowly faded beneath the greater light of the Zeniths.

Breaking the surface, the man took a deep breath. He then grabbed ahold of a line tied to the gunwale and climbed up the side of the ship.

Once he was back aboard, everyone looked at Domadred, who stood atop a barrel near the gunwale. While hanging on to the shrouds with one hand, the captain raised the other and extended two fingers. The dripping man then shook his head, and the crew gave him consolatory pats on the back as he dried himself off.

"Next!" Domadred yelled.

All eyes went to the rigging above. Aleksi followed their gaze and saw Brayden climbing out onto the foresail's spar. The *Diamond's* sails were all lowered, and the ship's poles looked like a tree's barren branches in winter. The crew yelled both taunts and encouragement as the boy moved his way across the rounded beam. Looking down, Brayden saw Aleksi and waved. Aleksi waved back.

Brayden stood motionless for a moment, but Aleksi's breath then caught in his chest as Brayden raised his hands and sprinted to the spar's edge. Coming to the tip, the boy bent his knees and, using his upper body for momentum, lunged into the air. Tucking his arms around his legs and turning his body into a graceful, spinning pike, Brayden plummeted down to the water below.

Aleksi had a hard time counting how many times the boy flipped before Brayden stretched his body into a dive. The boy then hit the water with a silent splash and the crew shouted their approval. Aleksi could hear men arguing about how many flips Brayden had done. Some said four, but most agreed that three was the accurate number. As Brayden's glowing body came to the surface of the water, one man boasted that he could do better and climbed into the rigging.

In response to the banter, Domadred held up three fingers. Hoisting himself back onto the deck, Brayden nodded at the captain's verdict. Moving through the crowd toward Domadred and Brayden, Aleksi looked up and saw that the man in the rigging had made his way out onto the spar. As the sailor stalked across the beam, Aleksi noticed that the Zeniths' light was growing stronger and the purple sky was turning blue.

Aleksi reached Domadred just as the man above their heads ran and jumped. At first the sailor seemed to copy Brayden. With arms outstretched and tucking into a pike, he spun three times but then awkwardly came out of the flip and landed on his back with a loud splash. Domadred's face contorted into a grimace as laughter erupted from the crew.

"Fynn will be feeling that for a few days," Domadred said, chuckling. Seeing Aleksi, the captain smiled.

"Captain." Aleksi placed his hand on the barrel and looked up into Domadred's eyes. "I want to apologize for yesterday. What I did—"

"Say no more. You and Kefta settled your debt under the eye of Aruna and what is done *is done*. Besides, tensions have been high for everyone since Mindra's Haven. Thankfully, we have made very good time on our voyage, so lucky for us, we can afford a bit of fun!"

"Kefta mentioned the diving," Aleksi said, looking around at the crew. "But I didn't expect such acrobatics. Brayden did very well."

"Yes, indeed he did. He has had a good deal of practice, for it's an old tradition on the *Diamond*. We throw the anchor over to slow the ship's drift, and the man with the most flips and a successful finish wins a barrel of the captain's *finest*." Domadred then chuckled and used his boot to nudge Marlen, who stood next to the cask. "Good thing for the captain, however, he always wins!" Marlen muttered something unintelligible underneath his breath as Domadred continued. "Brayden currently holds the lead with three and a perfect dive. Care to test your luck?"

"I think I'll pass. Yesterday was exciting enough."

"No need to do any flips," Kefta said, approaching them. His face was still badly swollen, but he wore a warm smile. "Even just diving is quite invigorating, trust me."

"Come on, Aleksi," Brayden added, climbing over the gunwale. "You should at least give it a try!"

"I think I'll just congratulate you," Aleksi answered as the boy wrung out his hair. "Your jump was fantastic—there is no way I could hope to compete with such a performance."

"Then I guess it's my turn!" Domadred exclaimed, taking off his shirt. After kicking off his boots, the captain jumped on the ratlines and began climbing. As Domadred ascended into the rigging, the Zeniths' yellow morning rays shone brightly across his back. Despite his age, the captain's shoulders were strong and well defined, sculpted from his many long years of hauling lines and hoisting sails.

"Keep your eye on me, Aleksi!" Domadred yelled. "You won't want to miss this!" Aleksi watched as Domadred climbed atop the spar and easily made his way out onto its tip.

"For all his bluster and peacocking," Marlen said, climbing atop Domadred's barrel, "the captain never fails to deliver. Just watch."

High above their heads, the captain raised his arms and called to his crew. "No matter if I am made prime admiral or not, I'm still the best diver in all of Terra!" The crew gave a hearty cheer of agreement. Just as the boat came up on a swell, Domadred took a sudden sprinting leap and launched himself into the air. Grabbing the backs of his legs, he spun and descended in a blur. Right as Domadred was about to hit the water, he came out of the spin and entered the ocean with hardly a splash. The entire crew stomped their feet, shouting their approval.

As the captain swam back up, the water's luminescence barely cast off a glow due to the brightening Zeniths. After breaking the surface, Domadred treaded water and, holding up his fist, raised one, two, three, and then four fingers. Marlen nodded his approval and, while the majority of the crew was cheering, several only grumbled their congratulations.

"He's won again," Brayden said with a sigh as Domadred climbed out of the water. "The key is to time your jump just as the ship crests an upward swell. It's hard to do, but you can get added lift. Dad does it the best . . ."

"Well, I've had a good many more years of practice," Domadred said, hoisting his dripping body over the gunwale. "Brayden, soon you will get four flips. And eventually, I bet you will even be able to get *five*. Your grand'da could, and I have a feeling you will be able to as well."

Brayden's eyes lit up. Suddenly, he looked at Kefta, as if expecting a rebuke; however, Kefta only smiled at the boy. Although the dark bruises under the young man's eyes had grown worse, his expression was kind and genuine.

Domadred once again hopped atop the barrel and addressed the crowd. "I'm not the most talented with numbers, but I'm pretty sure I have won my own contest. Which means"—Domadred hit the heel of his foot against the barrel in sharp succession for emphasis—"we *all* drink tonight!"

The crew gave a raucous roar of appreciation. After the cheers died down, Domadred spoke again. "As many of you know, over dinner last night, the officers and I were given an offer. It is an offer you have no doubt already heard and have been pondering diligently. Well, I have another gift to aid you in your contemplative process. However, like all great prizes, it must be *earned.*"

The crew looked on with growing interest.

"So, I propose a deep-diving contest. Any man brave enough to go deeper than my last dive will win the crew another barrel of whiskey! I went so far that upon looking up, the *Diamond's* hull was no longer than my thumb, should anyone think to do better."

Many men called out saying they could easily beat the captain's dive. As the chorus of sailors died down, however, another voice spoke up from the crowd. "I nominate *Aleksi.*" A hush came over the crew and all eyes turned to Luka. The seamen parted as the nobleman made his way forward. "Kefta would have undoubtedly taken your challenge, Domadred," Luka continued. "But along with his dignity, Aleksi has also stripped away your young quartermaster's strength. So for honor's sake, I nominate Aleksi as his replacement."

"I refuse," Aleksi answered firmly.

"Are you scared, boy?"

All eyes looked at Aleksi. But before he could speak, Kefta stepped forward. "I dueled and was defeated. There is no lost dignity in that— only wounded pride. However, it seems that I have an overabundance of that, so I do believe Aleksi actually did us all a favor!"

The crew chuckled but Luka cut them off. "*Well,* you may not have lost your dignity, but Aleksi clearly showed us your incompetence as a leader. I wonder—"

"Enough, Nobleman!" Domadred interrupted. "The boy refuses and you are beginning to annoy me."

"Then I will raise the stakes," Luka answered. "We all know you will be giving the crew this barrel of whiskey regardless of who wins. Likewise, I merely want to see if our young swordsman has what it takes to jump from the spars. Therefore, I will offer a black pearl to every man aboard if this boy simply dives over. Sailors, think of it as a taste of things to come if you accept Asura's offer."

Using his thumb and forefinger, Luka flicked a single pearl into the sky. It seemed to hang suspended in midair as the Zeniths' rays glittered on its iridescent surface. As the spinning orb came back down to the deck, a sailor snatched it out of the air and pocketed it quickly.

Once again cheers rose up from the crowd and men shouted encouragement to Aleksi. "Go on, Aleksi," Brayden said. "No need to compete, just dive in! That's easy pearls for all of us!"

"Behind his eyes I see deception," Aleksi whispered so only Brayden could hear. "I'm sorry, but I will not do this." As the shouts died down, Aleksi raised his voice. "Nobleman, you are generous indeed. However, I must confess I am a poor swimmer and could never hope to compare with the captain. Sadly, I must decline your offer."

Everyone looked at Aleksi incredulously. "Just jump in," one man bellowed. "Who cares if you can't swim? For a pearl each, all of us will gladly jump over and pull you back up."

"I'm sorry," Aleksi said, with eyes still locked on Luka. "I will not jump."

Angry protests rose from the crew but Domadred's voice silenced them. "The youth has made his answer. Regardless, I will bring up another two barrels for the crew. It's not filled with black pearls, but pearls can't get you drunk. So, let us all get on with today's work so that we may enjoy tonight's revelries! Crew dismissed!"

Grumbling, the sailors dispersed. Many gave Aleksi dark looks as they walked away. Ignoring their ire, Aleksi watched Luka move to the stern of the ship. The nobleman turned and flashed Aleksi a smile before he disappeared belowdecks.

Despite the departure of the seamen, Brayden, Domadred, and his officers still remained on the foredeck.

"All you had to do was jump in," Kairn said, coming up to Aleksi. "What was your hesitation? Can you truly not swim?"

"Honestly," Levain interjected, "I'm relieved to learn there is something this boy cannot do."

"I can swim fine," Aleksi said. "I just don't trust that man."

"What was he going to do?" Levain said, laughing. "Cast some sorcery to drown you? Come now, don't be silly."

"It's just that I—"

"He comes offering peace from the *North*," Valen interrupted, looking into Aleksi's green eyes. "What ire could *you* possibly hold against him?"

Aleksi didn't answer and walked away. As he approached the stairwell that led under the quarterdeck, Aleksi saw the helmsman look at him disdainfully. Shaking his head, Aleksi went below to his cabin.

Darkness came early over the *Illusive Diamond*. Aleksi watched the last whispering glow of the Eastern Zenith fade through his porthole window and be swallowed by the horizon. After the sail diving, the youth had stayed in his quarters doing little but pace his room and ponder his situation.

Luka had proven himself to be profoundly distressing. Aleksi quieted his mind and tried to reach out and contact the young woman again, but all he found was an empty longing in his chest. Letting out a sigh, Aleksi looked down at his Rune-laden arm.

There are too many mysteries. I need more information . . .

When his food arrived, Aleksi ate lost in thought. After he finished, one of Terra's moons began to rise in the starry sky. Soon after it broke the horizon, Aleksi heard the sounds of drunken merriment drift about the ship. The sailors had begun to enjoy Domadred's whiskey.

Eventually, Aleksi heard a knock at the door. Opening it, he saw Levain standing with a mug in his hand.

"What are you doing here all alone?" the bearded man asked, leaning one hand against the door frame. "You should be drinking with us. Everyone else is, even that bastard Luka."

"I think I would rather just stay here."

"Naw, son. You're coming with me." Levain then reached over and playfully grabbed Aleksi by the arm. "I wanna find out who you are at the bottom of a keg of whiskey. Besides, you look like you need it!"

Despite his protests, Levain pulled Aleksi down the hallway and up the stairs. As they walked, Levain rambled on about who could outdrink who and what sailor was best known for starting drunken brawls. Crossing the main deck and entering a hatch down into the gun deck,

Levain told a story about a deckhand who was prone to weepy tears and bouts of hysteria whenever he had too much to drink. Aleksi tried to follow what the man was saying, but Levain seemed to be talking more for the joy of making noise than actual conversation.

As they stepped down the stairs to the gun deck, Aleksi saw that the seamen had set up rows of tables and benches in between the *Diamond*'s mighty cannons. The tables were crowded with sailors rowdily regaling each other with tales that undoubtedly possessed much more fiction than fact. Surrounded by warm lantern light, the men each had a mug in hand, and all seemed to have thoroughly begun their night of drinking.

As Aleksi moved deeper into the room, the sharp scent of man sweat, firepower, and alcohol stung his nose. On his left, he overheard one raucous table boasting about what they would do when they had shore leave in Vai'kel. Boisterous laughter rose up from the group as one man shook his head at his comrade's statement while simultaneously making an obscene gesture with his moving fist.

Levain put his hand on Aleksi's back and gave the youth a shove toward a table of drunken sailors. Approaching the group, Aleksi saw what must be one of the captain's whiskey barrels with several of the more dedicated drinkers seated around it. Passing Aleksi and coming up to the table, Levain slapped one of the men on the shoulder. In response, the sailor cried out in agony. Aleksi recognized the man as the same sailor who had disastrously flipped from the spar and landed on his back.

"Looks like *you* haven't had enough to drink yet, Fynn!" Levain exclaimed, laughing.

"Damn it, Levain," Fynn said, turning on the bench. "We were talking about Luka's offer and you startled me, is all. I swear if you weren't an officer, I would wipe that smile off your face myself."

"Let me know if you ever wanna try," Levain said, slapping the man again. "Just don't start anything with this one, eh?" Levain then pointed his thumb at Aleksi. Fynn looked at the youth and grumbled something under his breath before going back to his whiskey.

"Someone get Aleksi a mug," Levain continued, refilling his own from the barrel's spigot. From somewhere in the crowd a mugful of the dark liquor found its way into Aleksi's hand. "Alright, boys, hold 'em up!"

Liquor splashed across the wooden table as all mugs were raised.

"To Aleksi!" Levain shouted. "A young man who can beat our quartermaster bloody but can't stand the thought of a little water!" The crew laughed and smashed their mugs together. Aleksi then brought his cup to his lips. All it took was one sip to know that he did not want any more.

"Is that silver tongue how you lay your women, Levain?" The voice belonged to a bald man whose tanned head shone under the lamplight.

"At least I know something of women, Jesse," Levain rebuked, refilling his mug from the barrel. "With a face like yours, I'm surprised that your own mother didn't run faster than a stray cat the first time she saw you!"

"What are you talking about?" Jesse said, laughing. "She did! How do you think I came to be on this damn ship with the likes of you?"

The crowd laughed again. As the two men continued shouting, Aleksi saw Nara and Fa'ell across the room. Catching his eye, Fa'ell raised her mug to Aleksi in toast.

Slipping away from the crowded table, Aleksi made his way over to them. As he weaved through the men, he overheard two sailors speaking. "It just doesn't make sense," one man said to the other as they hunched over their mugs. "The way those Council Guards boarded us during the chaos in Mindra's Haven. It was like they were looking for specific people. They were singling out the officers and those from the old days. I just don't—"

Before Aleksi could hear any more, two men from another table stood up abruptly, nearly knocking Aleksi over.

"Ouut the waay," one of the muscular men slurred drunkenly. Once he saw it was Aleksi, however, the man eyed the youth's sword keenly. "Youu best waatch yourself, Grreen Eyyess, or you will be see'n how you faar against all of uus."

Aleksi quickly stepped away from the men and continued toward Fa'ell and Nara.

"Good evening, Aleksi," Fa'ell said, once again raising her cup as the youth approached. "It looks like you're making some new friends tonight."

Aleksi shook his head. Looking up at Nara, Aleksi noticed the man's face seemed much paler than usual. He sat hunched over the table, and he did not have a mug of whiskey. Aleksi opened his mouth, but Valen came over from another table and spoke first.

"Lionman, you're not drinking tonight?"

"Not tonight," Nara answered slowly. "I'm feeling a bit . . . seasick."

"Ha! Usually people say that *after* they have had the whiskey. What about you, Aleksi? Enjoying the captain's dregs?"

"Sadly, I don't have much of a taste for it."

"You and Brayden both. Just give it a few years, though; it will grow on you." Valen turned his eyes to Fa'ell and eyed her intricate tattoos. "M'lady Fa'ell, you deserve much better than this swill. The captain should be ashamed to give it to someone as beautiful as you. I, however, have some fine single barrel in my bunk if you're interested." Valen then flashed Fa'ell his best smile.

"Luka seems to be enjoying himself," Fa'ell said, ignoring Valen's words and gesturing to a far table. Aleksi followed her gaze and saw that the nobleman's face was flush with whiskey and he looked almost *jovial.*

"Once you get a few drinks in him," Valen answered, "he's not half bad. He's even losing over there and doesn't seem angry about it."

"Losing?" Aleksi asked, watching Luka keenly. "What do you mean?"

"They're playing *al'ath.* Luka has already lost a fair number of pearls, and the night is still young. Apparently he has never played before. I guess it's not common in the North. I'm surprised he's taking it so well, though." Valen then turned his smile back to Fa'ell. "My dear, have you ever . . ."

Aleksi stopped listening to Valen's words and continued to glare at Luka. Suddenly, the nobleman looked up from the table and caught Aleksi's gaze. Luka's eyes reflected the lamplight and he smiled, showing a row of perfect teeth. A shiver ran down Aleksi's spine.

"So, you all seem like you have made up your minds about this offer, then," Fa'ell said, once again ignoring Valen's question. "Are you sure that is wise?"

"Well, nothing's done until it's done," Valen answered. "But the idea of being back in the Thalassocracy, and at its head, no less, is obviously *very* tempting."

"And you think Asura will make good on his promises?"

"Either way, Lenhal will be dead, and with Sai—" Valen cut himself short. "What I mean to say is that either way we will be sitting pretty in the water." Fa'ell eyed him carefully and Valen looked at Aleksi as he continued. "You know, Aleksi, all you had to do was jump in the ocean this morning. Luka wasn't asking much. Some of the crew are actually pretty mad about it."

"Well, I'm sorry to have disappointed you . . ." Aleksi set down his mug and walked away from the table. Aleksi heard Fa'ell shout after him as he left, but the youth did not look back as he made his way past the rowdy tables.

As he ascended the stairs and walked out onto the main deck, Aleksi deeply inhaled the fresh ocean air. It felt wonderful after the thick scent of the drunken gun deck. Looking above, Aleksi saw one of Terra's moons high in the sky. It shone down on the deck, illuminating the *Diamond* and her billowed sails with a silvery-blue light. Looking out to sea, Aleksi felt a pang of sadness fill his chest.

Despite all of these people, I am still alone. Rudra, where are you?

Letting his eyes graze the deck, the youth saw Kefta standing at the starboard gunwale. Aleksi let out a sigh and approached him under the soft light of the moon. As Aleksi came closer, Kefta dropped something overboard. Coming to the ship's edge, Aleksi watched the object cast a glimmering trail of light downward as it sank out of sight.

"Had your fill of the drinking?" Kefta asked, still looking out to sea.

"I don't drink. You?"

"Not tonight. Although some whiskey might ease the pain my face is feeling right now."

"I'm sorry about that."

"I had it coming."

They both stood in silence, gazing out at the water. A nagging feeling grew in Aleksi's chest. "Kefta, is Domadred really going to accept Luka's offer?"

"I don't know. The crew want him to."

"I heard the men below talking about the boarding party back in Mindra's Haven. They said that the men who were killed seemed to be singled out, like there was some plan to the attack."

"Those that fell," Kefta answered slowly, "were some of Domadred's most loyal crew."

"What if . . ." Aleksi paused. "I don't know. It all just seems a little too perfect. I don't trust Luka. He's hiding something—something important."

"I already tried to talk to the captain about that. He does not want to listen to me and now neither does the crew. I may be the quartermaster, but with everything that's happened recently, none treat me like it."

There was a long silence as they both looked out to the dark horizon. "What did you just drop in the water?" Aleksi finally asked.

"Oh, that? Just some silly superstition."

Aleksi tilted his head. "If it's important to you, then it's not silly."

"It's a bit of a long story."

"I've got time."

Kefta let out a sigh. "Back before my father died, he was a Western captain. He wasn't an admiral like Domadred, but he had his own ship and my brother, Rihat, was his apprenticing mate." Kefta did not meet Aleksi's eyes and continued to gaze out at the water as he spoke. "This was back during the Unification War. They were stationed near Vai'kel's coastal city of Utarid, ordered to reconnoiter and patrol for enemy vessels. Well, when it came time for me to join him on his ship, my brother sailed back separately to pick me up. I was a young boy, no older than five or so, and was living back on Skadra with some family friends. I was very excited to finally meet my father again. I had not seen him or Rihat for years."

Kefta paused and leaned his weight against the gunwale. "But, as Rihat and I sailed to rendezvous with my father's ship, we heard that fighting had broken out off the coast of Utarid. When we arrived, much of the fleet stationed there was nothing more than driftwood, and only the *Illusive Diamond* and several others remained. With no home to go back to, my brother and I boarded the *Diamond* and joined the crew. But that's another story entirely. Anyway, after that, Rihat told me that if I wrote a message to my father, put it in a bottle filled with water, and threw it in the ocean, the High Arkai of the West would make sure my father got it. I was young, so I believed him. It didn't take long until we ran out of bottles . . ."

Kefta paused. When he continued, his voice was filled with a mix of old sadness and new anger. "When I dropped those bottles in the water, it really felt like my father could hear me. For years I would write him about our life. About how Rihat and I were doing, and how much I wanted to have known him. And now . . ." Kefta paused, putting a hand to his eyes. "With Rihat . . . with Rihat . . . dead"—tears leaked down Kefta's swollen cheeks—"I thought I should write . . . I thought I should write *him* now . . ."

Kefta leaned over the gunwale and his shoulders shook with silent sobs. Aleksi stood next to him, stoic and unmoving, as Kefta continued to cry. Aleksi looked up to the stars glowing in the sky and swallowed hard. Slowly, Aleksi reached out a timid hand and placed his palm on Kefta's shoulder. Aleksi could feel Kefta's lungs expand and contract as he silently wept.

For a long moment they both stood bathed in the light of the moon as the ocean's glowing water rippled before them and stretched out into the dark distance.

"I know this must seem silly to you," Kefta said, sniffing as he lifted his head. "But he was my brother . . . is my brother."

"You honor those you've loved and lost," Aleksi said, letting his hand fall from Kefta's shoulder. "There is *nothing* silly in that."

"When I was young, writing the letters made me feel better. Now . . ." Kefta looked at Aleksi. The circles under his eyes were badly swollen and his face was red and raw. "Now it only makes me feel worse. My bottle, the ceremony for the Arkai, Domadred and his big book, the chants, none of it will bring Rihat back. It's all just a waste."

"Giving respect to the fallen is never wasted," Aleksi answered. "I don't know the pain you feel, but I do know that the Arkai can do some wondrous things. If it is possible that your father and brother can hear you, don't you want to do anything you can to send them a message? To let them know you are thinking of them and that you love them?" Aleksi turned and looked at the floating orb of light in the sky. "I don't pretend to understand the mystery of the Arkai, but as the old saying goes, 'I have been to Mindra's Haven.' I have seen their power, Kefta, and faith in the Arkai's *promise* is never wasted."

"I suppose you're right," Kefta said, wiping his swollen face. "Still, it doesn't bring them back."

"No, it doesn't."

"It's been years since I've talked about those letters. I'm sorry for getting all emotional on you." Kefta dried his eyes and cleared his throat. When the young man spoke again, his tone had changed. "This is the first time you have seen the deep currents, right?"

"Indeed so."

"It's really something, isn't it?"

"It really is." Aleksi looked out across the sparkling water and gazed upon the many thousands of glow-capped waves before them. Terra's second moon then suddenly broke over the horizon and its light shimmered over the ocean, mixing with the luminescence. As the orb rose higher, it cast innumerable tiny flashes across the sea. Aleksi watched with rapt attention as the moon's light commingled with the water's pulsing glow. The sight truly was awe inspiring.

"The first time I saw it," Kefta said, letting out a great sigh, "I remember being comforted. I sat in the crow's nest all night, just staring."

"It's very impressive." Aleksi answered. "So much movement—so much life."

"Yeah, I think that's why I find it soothing. You can just get lost in it and disappear."

"I wish it were that easy. For me it's . . . overwhelming."

Behind them, Aleksi heard a group of sailors come up from the gun deck. They had mugs in their hands and joked noisily as they walked up to the mainmast's port shrouds.

"Go on, then, Malec," one of the men said. "Shut these men up with a song." A seaman then handed off his mug and hopped up onto the

shrouds. Holding on with one hand, he cleared his throat and began
to sing.

> "I rested my wings and can fly no more. My heart, once
>   strong, is now broken and sore.
> As I cast my gaze to the stars unbound, why doth my
>   soul yearn so profound?

> "The pain is clear, it does not fade. Why is there no end
>   to this evil charade?
> Oh, Guardians, shine your holy light down, for dark-
>   ness comes and circles round."

Aleksi looked at the man as he sang. The sailor was one of the crew's
younger members, most likely only a few years older than Kefta. As
the seaman continued, his long blond hair shone lustrously in the
moonlight.

> "I feel its pull penetrating deep. It says my soul it shall
>   safe keep.
> But I must not fall to its alluring song, for its promises
>   made shall break at dawn.

> "When will he come, the Chosen One? The Kalki,
>   Terra's savior and eternal son?
> Born of the moons, mother and father both, he shines
>   with love, which darkness loathes."

The young man had a clear voice and sang beautifully. Aleksi knew the
song well—everyone did. Aleksi looked over and saw that Kefta was
watching the young man intently.

> "When they touch again, their son reborn. Their light
>   commingled, their pain forsworn.
> Numen's gift, Terra he shall reclaim, his rightful seat
>   upon the throne of flame.

"But before his ascent, he must go forth and apprentice
under twin stars to find his worth.
Dual tutelage he will ascertain, learning a path both
light and dark, each filled with pain.

"Despite the trials, he shall prevail, and give the Dark
Ones flight back past the veil.
Yet I am only a lone child of grace, so I wait for the
Kalki and urge his haste . . ."

The sound of the man's voice slowly faded, leaving only the whisper of
wind and sea lingering in Aleksi's ear.

"What do you think about the Kalki prophecy?" Kefta asked, gesturing at the moons in the sky. "Do you think they will one day give
birth to some holy savior of Terra?"

"I don't know," Aleksi answered, "but my teachers thought so. They
said he would usher in a new age. But for that to happen, the Dark
Ones would need to return. Only when they walk again will Kalki be
born. At least that's what they said."

Kefta gave a short laugh and turned to Aleksi. "Well, I haven't
heard of any dark specters attacking our cities recently, so it seems like
Terra will just have to wait a little longer for its savior. But that may not
be such a bad thing."

Aleksi didn't respond and continued to watch the moon as it rose
higher over the horizon. *What if the Dark Ones do return? Could it
possibly be as bad as Terra's current age of stagnation and petty bickering?* Suddenly, Aleksi's Rune pulsed. *"Yet I am only a lone child of grace,
so I wait for him and urge his haste . . ."*

CHAPTER XXV

As Aleksi continued to look out at the shimmering water, he suddenly felt a hand grip his shoulder. Surprised, the youth spun and knocked the arm away, readying himself to draw against his assailant.

"Be aware of your surroundings at all times or not at all," Luka said, massaging his struck forearm. "But either way, you must learn to control yourself and not lash out, lest we have a repeat of *that*." Luka then gestured toward Kefta's swollen face.

"What do *you* want?" Kefta asked, eyeing the man disdainfully.

"I wish to have private words with Aleksi, Quartermaster. I suggest you leave now if you wish to keep that position."

"Is that a threat?"

"That's amusing coming from you. No, it's actually a suggestion. The men below speak openly of your failures as an officer. I advise you to go and talk with them if you have any interest in preserving your rank on this ship."

Kefta spat in Luka's face before walking away.

"And that," Luka said, turning to Aleksi as he wiped his eye, "is why people look down on sailors."

"I see what you are doing," Aleksi said, resting his hand on the hilt of his blade. "And I'm not the only one."

"You mean you see me trying to broker peace for a fissured nation by returning an outcast ship of war heroes back to a position of honor that was wrongly stolen from them? Maybe you are smarter than I give you credit for, Aleksi."

"No, when the *Diamond* was boarded, the crew said that officers loyal to the Resistance were singled out in the combat. It's all rather opportune—your boarding and their murder. You then fight off the lingering assailants to rally the crew's favor. It all seems as if it was planned from the beginning. Even the murder and chaos in Mindra's Square . . ."

"In some cases, sacrifices must be made for the greater good."

"Then you admit it's true?"

"Sadly, there is a price for everything, Aleksi. Even peace."

"Peace? The men who betrayed the leaders of the East were not agents of peace, they were assassins!"

"Open your eyes, boy," Luka said, shaking his head in the moonlight. "In Mindra's Haven, the upper classes rule the lower as if they were slaves. You must have seen it when you walked the city. That new Eastern treaty would only have subjugated the people further. The actual *people* of the East live as second-class citizens, and wrongfully so. Even as we speak now, those who reside in Old City are rebelling against the corrupt aristocracy of Guardians' Plaza. All Asura did was give the people a chance—nay, rather an *opportunity*—to claim their freedom. Asura merely lit the spark of revolution, son. The kindling of inequality has been gathering for over an age."

"Women and children dead in the street?" Aleksi growled. "That is no path to freedom! That's slaughter! If you are truly a Master of the Academy, how could you act in such a way?"

"Several of us no longer wish to hide in our arcane towers and watch the world decay before our eyes."

"So you don't deny it!" Aleksi said, taking a step back. "You *are* a Master. What of your vows?"

"My colleagues and I have chosen to save Terra from the putrid stagnation of the Modern Age. You are no different, Aleksi, for you chose to act, too—you abandoned your Academy. Sadly, you do not yet know what you fight for or what you even believe in. Instead, you blindly follow a man who is no different than those you condemn."

"I follow a Master who has earned my trust time and time again. You are nothing compared to Rudra! Rudra would never kill women and children to achieve his goal."

"Oh, Aleksi, how naive you are." Luka let out a great sigh and looked up to the stars above. "A tree's branches must be trimmed to allow new growth to flourish—especially when those branches have grown old and rotten. Rudra knows this better than any of us. If you only knew the truth of your beloved teacher . . ."

Luka paused as his gaze lowered to the sea. Shining out of the open portholes below, the gun deck's lanterns cast odd streaks of yellow across the glimmering water. As Aleksi watched Luka carefully, sounds of drunken merriment floated up from the gun deck beneath them.

"Lord Asura is the leader this world needs to regain its former beauty. Sadly, the path to redemption can be a bloody one. Much like he has done in the North, Asura will soon restabilize the East and give the power back to the people. But to do so, he has to trim back the deadwood. The same was done here on this ship. I needed the crew to be able to listen to the logic of my offer. Even so, you saw how hard it was for me to discuss peace with the captain, let alone have the opportunity to speak with him in the first place. It's all very sad, really."

"I'll tell Domadred!" Aleksi blurted. "I'll tell the crew that you are a Master of the Academy; I'll tell them what you have done! That you are a killer who has forsaken his vows."

"Vows?! Ha! What do you know of the Masters' Vow? No, even if the men of this ship did believe you, what would they do? You think they are any different than I? The ocean runs red with their savage piracy. Besides, they desperately want what I have to offer—vindication and power. And, more importantly, once they find out the truth about *you*, a truth I am happy to share with them, they will undoubtedly claim the hefty bounty that's on your head. Do you think your new friends would turn a blind eye to the fortune the Academy will pay for your return? A runaway student fetches a very high price, Aleksi, or have you forgotten that it is actually *you* who has forsaken vows? You and I are not as different as you would like to believe, son."

"I'm nothing like you!" Anger swelled in Aleksi's voice. "Killing to achieve one's goal is the path of a fallen Master. You and Asura have given yourself to the darkness. I will not allow it to continue! I will end this here and now!" Aleksi gripped his sword to draw but then stopped short as Luka laughed.

"Such hypocrisy!" Luka exclaimed, slapping the gunwale for emphasis. "You threaten to kill me because I am a killer? Your logic teachers must have taught you better than that! I am no more of the darkness than you, or any defender of freedom, for that matter. If you want proof, look at my eyes, boy. Do they look black to you? Aleksi, you killed in Mindra's Haven; does that make you *fallen*? No. There are times when you must kill to preserve life. That tenet is followed by Masters of each Academy. In fact, it is at the core of our teachings!"

"To kill *women and children*?!"

"Come now, son, even you know what happens to students who do not become Apprentices. The unascended are no more than children when they are culled, and for good reason. Child, adult, man, woman—it makes no difference, they are all the same. You do what needs to be done. *That*, son, is the path of a Master."

"So, then, what do you want with me?" Aleksi asked, watching Luka warily.

"Sadly," Luka continued, taking a step forward, "Asura has decreed that you, much like the unascended students, must also be purged. Now that you have fled your Academy, there are many who search for you, all hungry to fulfill his will. You are lucky it was I who found you first and not one of Asura's shadows. They are not as generous as I, nor as insightful into the nature of misunderstood Apprentices."

"I am ready," Aleksi said, thumbing his blade from its sheath in preparation to draw, "for them—and for you!"

"Do not force my hand against you, Aleksi. I had wanted you to live. Although clever, you overestimate your power against a Master. Besides, it need not end that way for you." Luka paused and placed both hands on the gunwale. He looked out at the shimmering horizon and took a deep breath. "Aleksi, I am not the monster you portray me to be. In fact, I am a fair man—a just man. Honestly, none of this is your fault. The fault lies with Nataraja. Nataraja and Rudra both."

Luka turned and looked into Aleksi's eyes. "Despite Asura's decree, I will give you a way to live. I offer you a choice. Swear fealty and train under me. Cast off your ties to Rudra and become *my* Apprentice. If you do, Asura will spare you—this I swear. In time you will reclaim your lineage's lost prestige and bring honor to your fallen house once again. With the right training, you can surpass even your father's legacy. More importantly, that is, with the *right Master*."

". . . I will never betray Rudra." Aleksi's words sounded weak even in his own ears.

"Such loyalty. Honestly, it's admirable. If you knew the truth about Rudra, though, I wonder if you would still feel so devoted. Aleksi, do you know how your parents died? Do you even know who they *were*?"

Aleksi shifted uneasily.

"You cling to a Master who has not only abandoned you but wronged you far worse than you could possibly imagine. You do not even begin to know the truth of your past . . . But I will show you."

Luka then raised his hand and took a step toward Aleksi. The youth tried to draw his blade, but his arm would not respond. Aleksi's eyes grew wide as he watched Luka's hand move toward his face.

"It's all there in your mind, Aleksi," Luka said, as a soft glow glimmered on his palm. "It's locked in your memory. You were there when it happened—you both were. All you need to do is *remember*."

Luka's palm touched Aleksi's forehead. Suddenly, Aleksi felt searing pain flood into his mind. Aleksi staggered back as his vision went blurry and the horizon spun with vertigo. Clinging to the ship's gunwale, Aleksi desperately tried to regain his balance.

"Go back to your room," Luka said, helping Aleksi to stand. "The *remembering* will take you shortly." As Aleksi tried to steady himself, he groped for the hilt of his sword. "Oh, come now, give it a rest. Go to your quarters and lie in your bed. I assume you do not wish the others to see you fall asleep on the deck. They will assume you are drunk, and someone will have to carry you down."

Luka guided Aleksi as the youth took several staggering steps toward the stairs that led below. "If you are as strong as you think yourself to be," Luka continued, "you will survive the forced remembering. It will cause you great pain, but as I said, everything has its price. For your sake, I hope to see you tomorrow. If you survive, I trust you will be a bit more open minded to my offer."

Aleksi's vision became blurrier with each step. The sharp burning in his head turned into a pounding throb as he stumbled down the stairs. Now alone, Aleksi was forced to use the wall to steady himself as he shambled to his room. As if reawakened by the throbbing, the Rune on his hand started to match the painful rhythmic pulsing in his head. Fumbling at the door handle, Aleksi breathed in jagged gulps. As he opened his door, deep fear crept into his heart. Aleksi knew he had to hurry.

Aleksi had heard about forced rememberings. The Rune had been outlawed by the Masters' Council as inhumane. As it provided only mild memory recall and possessed such a low rate of survival, the council had deemed its use ineffective and not worth its risk of fatality.

Clutching his throbbing head, Aleksi slammed the door behind him and groped at the lock. He latched the door and tried to sit down but instead fell onto the floor. Aleksi's sword clattered at his side as he tried to push himself back up onto one arm. The room was spinning violently and he forced himself up onto his hands and knees. He looked at his cloak. Cold sweat ran down his back as he crawled across the floor. His vision was so blurry that he had to use his sense of touch as he fumbled in his cloak's pocket for the broken pendant. Aleksi's fingers wrapped around its soft surface and his mind exploded with searing pain.

Clutching the pendant in his hand, Aleksi crumpled to the floor. His head and Rune pounded in unison. He lay on his back and gasped for breath; tears rolled down the sides of his face. It was coming. Everything grew dark and the pain faded as blackness took him. Aleksi felt death seep into his body as his mind entered the gloom of forced memory.

In his heart there was no fear of dying, only a longing for the truth.

Aleksi opened his eyes to glowing snow falling in darkness. The endless night stretched out in every direction as the pure-white flakes fell through the black. The snow was silently landing on his face, melting on contact. Aleksi took a deep breath and felt the cold air chill his lungs.

Where am I?

His head no longer hurt, but everything seemed dark and hazy to his eyes. He tried to move but was unable. He was propped up on his back, but his body felt small and weak. Desperately trying to focus his eyes, Aleksi could see the shadowed outlines of a massive chamber around him. Defying all logic, a ceiling formed overhead yet still the snow fell.

Suddenly, a dark, hooded figure approached from the distance. The man's face was obscured and he held a sword dripping with blood. As he silently moved forward, he left a thin trail of red in the snow.

Aleksi felt soft arms tighten about his body—he was being held. The embrace was warm and protective.

Mother?

Next to Aleksi, the darkness contracted upon itself and another man emerged. Although his face was blocked from sight, around his neck he wore Aleksi's pendant. It was whole.

Father?

Aleksi's father drew a Rune-covered sword and the blade ignited with life and color. In turn, the hooded man's sword also glowed with its own fiery light. Without looking back, Aleksi's father raised his sword and charged. The cloaked figure responded by swinging his own blade, and a wild blaze erupted from its edge.

Aleksi's eyes were blinded and a white afterglow lingered in the emptiness. Aleksi felt his chest grow tight. When his vision returned, he saw two separate halves of his father's body lying on the ground, split diagonally from shoulder to opposite armpit though there was no blood. Aleksi heard the sound of a baby wailing and the protective arms encircling him clutched even tighter.

Is that my voice? Aleksi felt himself gasp for breath as he continued to scream in the cold darkness.

The cloaked figure turned toward them and raised his radiant sword aloft. It cast a brilliant halo in the canopy of falling snow. The arms that had been holding Aleksi suddenly let go, and his fragile body was placed on the ground as a woman rushed forward. Aleksi heard his mother call out for mercy as the cloaked figure swung his blade.

Aleksi's mother's head toppled off and rolled away. As her body fell, gurgling burgundy pooled in the melting snow. The hooded man took another step as the blood misted around him.

Aleksi's ears rang with a high-pitched wail and his lungs stung from the cold. Strangely, he heard the sound most strongly in his right ear. The cloaked man then towered over him and Aleksi saw the man's face under the hood—it was covered in Runes.

Rudra!

Master Rudra then raised his sword and, once again, Aleksi's eyes were blinded with light.

The light was so strong Aleksi felt it burn into his mind. Suddenly, he was no longer a baby and was no longer screaming. Still, the pain pierced him to his very core. Through the glare, Aleksi saw the ceiling of his cabin back on the *Illusive Diamond.*

Still holding the pendant, he tried to make a fist and draw on the power of his Rune. Nothing happened—the Rune had gone dormant and the pendant didn't respond. His eyes grew dim. The pain was too great and he knew he was dying. Aleksi felt the breath go out from his body as his vision faded to black. As he died, only one final thought clung to his mind. It was not of his parents or of Rudra.

It was of *her.*

Aleksi awoke as bright light once again assaulted his eyes. Smooth silken sheets grazed his skin and he rolled over to avoid the Zenith's rays. Surprisingly, he could feel the softness of a bed beneath him. His mind felt foggy and his body ached. He tried opening his eyes, but the light was too much and he buried his face into a fluffy pillow. The pillow smelled sweet—like flowers, honey, and *her.*

Aleksi realized he was dreaming.

The youth forced himself up onto one arm. Using his hand, he blocked the Zenith's rays from his eyes. He was lying in a large canopy bed atop a high mountain bluff. In the distance, he could see the vast ocean beyond. It looked very far away. There was little else on the mountain's top other than some wildflowers, sporadic clusters of grass, and the vast view. Aleksi tried to look farther behind him but the glare was too bright. The Zenith felt unusually close and everything around him was imbued with its essence.

Then Aleksi saw *her*. The young woman was looking out over the ocean and standing with her back to him. The youth tried to call out, but his voice made no sound. Although only several meters away, she felt distant to him.

Despite the stiffness in his body, he pulled back the sheets and stood. The grass felt soft on his feet and he walked to her. The Zenith was reflecting on her back and illuminated her in a bright halo. She was wearing the same white dress as before, and her long blond hair blew in the warm breeze. Coming closer, Aleksi reached out with his heart. She still felt withdrawn and did not turn to face him.

As Aleksi continued, the bright Zenith rays seemed to permeate everything around him. He had to perpetually squint so as to not be blinded. Coming to the edge of the cliff, Aleksi got a better look at the vast ocean stretching to an infinite horizon. He was very high up, higher than should have been possible.

Am I atop the . . . No . . . He pushed the thought away as ridiculous.

Coming up behind the young woman, Aleksi paused for a moment. She stood with an air of majestic indifference and gazed out at the imposing vista below. Aleksi slowly reached out his hand. It hovered uncertainly in the air. Finally, he gently took her palm in his. Her skin was soft and warm despite the seeming chill of her heart.

At first she did nothing and just stood watching the waves as her hair blew in the wind. But then, ever so slowly, the young woman's fingers tightened around his. As Aleksi held her hand, he felt her chest once again warm to him. But then she turned to face him and Aleksi saw that there was a profound sadness in her eyes and a majestic glow coming from her forehead. The young woman turned away as a silent tear ran down her cheek. With his other hand, Aleksi touched her chin, gently bringing her eyes back to meet his. He reached out with his love and felt the young woman welcome it into her heart. The glow on her forehead dimmed.

Suddenly, her eyes went wide and she snatched her hand away. The young woman anxiously looked at the Zenith over Aleksi's shoulder. She did not shield her gaze and Aleksi saw that the Zenith's light was illuminating her eyes. Bringing both hands to her heart, she took a deep breath and Aleksi felt the young woman's love withdraw from him. As the feeling of her turned cold and faded in his chest, Aleksi felt as if his heart were wrenched open. His pain was mirrored on her face, and when she looked at him again there was no anger in her—only sadness.

The young woman took another deep breath and, turning, pointed out to the great ocean beyond. As Aleksi followed her gaze, his vision zoomed as if through a spyglass. Suddenly, he saw the *Illusive Diamond* sailing through the water. It was profoundly far away.

Aleksi felt her try to show him something, and his vision grew even sharper. He now saw *into* the ship itself. Into one cabin in particular— Luka's cabin. Aleksi could see that the man was seated on the floor. His feet were crossed over his knees and his hands were folded in his lap. He was meditating.

Suddenly, Aleksi's vision returned to normal and the young woman once again looked into his eyes. She was trying to tell him something— something important. By the look on her face, she was straining heavily to do so.

The young woman's mouth moved, and in the most beautiful voice Aleksi had ever heard, she said two words.

"Kill him."

Aleksi's eyes snapped open and his chest lurched with breath. He was lying on the floor of his cabin and looking at the ceiling. The room was dark, with only a silvery-blue shaft of light coming from his porthole window. There was a dismal ache in his head, but his former agony was gone. As he sat up, his body felt stiff and profoundly sore.

Aleksi put a shaky hand through his hair and it came away damp. The young woman's message had been clear, but so had the vision of his parents' murder. Aleksi wished the truth of their demise was different, but it was impossible to fabricate forced rememberings.

Not only did Rudra know who my parents were—he was the one who killed them . . . Why would he do such a thing?! Who were they and why did they deserve to die? Why would he force me to live always questioning their identity while he knew the truth all along?

Aleksi still held his father's broken pendant and his Rune seemed to be dormant. The youth stood on unsteady legs and went to his cloak. Letting out a sigh, he put the pendant back into the pocket. As he did, his hand grazed Rudra's letter.

After securing his blade at his side, Aleksi left his room. He closed his door silently and, instead of walking to the deck stairs, he stopped short. He clearly remembered which room belonged to Luka. Pausing outside the man's door, Aleksi inhaled deeply. He felt vigor flow through his body in anticipation. If the door to Luka's room was similar to his own, it would take only one swift kick of his boot heel to gain entry. After that, a slash of Aleksi's blade would end the man's life. Luka obviously was powerful, but a blade would cut every man's flesh the same if he was taken unaware.

However, as Aleksi grasped the sword's hilt and his body tensed to kick, a flicker of doubt rose up in his chest. *If Luka knows of my parents, what else can he tell me? What else does he know about my past? About Rudra? Nataraja? The pendant? My Rune? Luka was sent to assassinate me, but he stayed his hand . . .*

Suddenly, Aleksi felt the young woman of the dreams urge him on, silently begging him to strike. *But what of Domadred and the crew? If they are so keen on his proposal, what will they do when they find Luka lying in a pool of his own blood?*

The feeling of the young woman grew frantic, and Aleksi was forced to push it away. *They would surely know it was me, and then I would never make it to Vai'kel. Besides . . .* A memory of the mother from the Apothecary Guild and her hungry children rose in his mind. The memory of the woman's kind embrace warmed Aleksi's heart. *What Luka said about the people of Old City is true. The oppression of the ruling class of Guardians' Plaza is unjust and unethical.* Suddenly, the image of Aleksi's slain foes in Mindra's Haven flashed before his eyes. *And if I kill Luka like this, I will be no better than Nataraja. Is assassination seeped in anger the path of a Master? No . . . I will not do it!*

Aleksi let out a sigh and walked back to his room. *At least not yet.* As he closed the door to his chamber, the feeling of the young woman grew desperate. He tried to comfort her with his heart, but the sensation of her slipped away into an obscurity of despair. Aleksi tried to cling to her, but she quickly faded into a malaise of nothingness.

Aleksi picked up his sketchbook and left his room. As he ascended the stairs and came on deck, he was met with the strong smell of the ocean and the wind's salty spray. The soft light of the moons and the sea's glowing waters illuminated everything around him. Clutching his notebook tight, the youth tried to call out to the young woman with his heart—but sadly, she was gone.

Aleksi let out a sigh and, after tucking his notebook into his belt, climbed the mainmast's ratlines. The cool evening breeze blew over his skin. Entering into the glowing canopy of sails, Aleksi was surrounded by the rush of the wind and the creaking of the lines and tackle. There was a strong breeze and the *Diamond* cut through the water with little resistance from the waves below. This made climbing rather easy—it was his thoughts that gave Aleksi pause.

As he passed the topsail, images of his parents' murder flashed through his mind. He saw his father's bloodless body split in two and his mother's severed head steaming in the snow. Then Aleksi heard Luka's words. *You cling to a Master who has not only abandoned you but wronged you far worse than you could possibly imagine.* Bitter pain stung at Aleksi's chest. *There are others out there who can teach you, and I promise they would not abandon you like the man you search for now.*

What could my parents have possibly done to deserve such a fate? As Aleksi climbed, he felt tears well up in his eyes. *Why didn't Rudra ever tell me? Why didn't any of my teachers tell me? Why . . . ?*

Suddenly, Aleksi reached the crow's nest and was confronted with the ocean's vast majesty. Hoisting himself up onto the platform, he looked out at the water. Pulsing as if it were the heart of a great glowing creature, Terra's curving ocean was alive with rhythm and beauty for as far as his eyes could see. The immensity of it terrified Aleksi. Beautiful, yes, but also so colossal and unknown . . .

After settling himself atop the crow's nest, Aleksi took out his sketchbook and flipped through its pages. In the light of the moons, he could clearly see the many pictures he had drawn of the young woman. For well over an hour Aleksi sat atop the mast, watching the moonlight play on the glowing water and the young woman's beauty. He thought of Luka, Rudra, his parents, his past, and what he was supposed to do.

Eventually, Aleksi noticed a figure begin to emerge from below in the rigging. It was Domadred. The captain seemed to be climbing past the sails and up to the crow's nest. Soon, Domadred made it to the platform.

Seeing Aleksi, the captain smiled. "Cannot sleep?" Domadred hoisted himself over the small railing and sat next to Aleksi.

"I'm just thinking," Aleksi answered, closing his notebook.

"Well, you have come to the right place. I come up here whenever I am stuck on a dilemma. The height gives me perspective—or so I like to think."

"Are you pondering Luka's offer?"

"Yes. During their drinking I was able to gauge the crew's opinion. I told them I would give my answer on the morrow. Although they still do not fully trust Luka or Asura, the promise of vindication is very alluring. Honestly, I agree."

"So you are decided, then?"

"Oh no. If I were, then I would not be up here. There is something in my heart that says even if Asura can make good on his promises, a pact with him is not the right current to take home. But still, to be prime admiral of the Thalassocracy, that is a very tempting offer."

Aleksi remained silent and gazed out at the shimmering water. A cold wind blew across the youth's face and he clutched his notebook tight to his chest. Domadred seemed to feel it, too, as he pulled his captain's hat lower on his brow.

"The Ice Floes," Domadred said, taking a deep breath of the chill air. "I love their crisp smell! So invigorating."

Aleksi nodded and breathed deeply. The air felt fresh and frozen like newly fallen snow.

"Aleksi, remember when I told you I wanted Brayden to have a normal life? This deal with Luka would ensure it. The course to redemption I have been on has been a long one. If I stick to it, only when Brayden is grown will he see anything other than the life of a pirate and outcast. And even then, nothing is guaranteed. If I take Luka's offer, however, Brayden will grow up as I did—with honor, opportunity, and privilege."

Aleksi did not respond.

"You probably don't know this," Domadred continued, "but many years ago my father was the prime admiral of the Thalassocracy. We have had two since him, but at the time, many thought that I would be his successor. And I assure you, that is a very rare thing in the West. Sadly, my father died early and there were those that thought I was still too young for the command, so the honor went to another. My father's successor then used the might of our fleet to assist the Northern Unification Army in taking over Vai'kel. At the end of the war, however, he was assassinated and the crime was wrongfully placed at my feet."

Aleksi looked up and met Domadred's eye.

"Just recently, however, I acquired evidence which will clear my name. Despite that, I will never be able to become prime admiral without further help. These days, the friends I have are not influential in the right ways. So, not only does Asura's offer come at an opportune time, but I can also see his logic. He needs the connections I have, and in return, he will adequately repay me the political influence I lack. There is no doubt he could make me prime admiral, and it would be well worth it for both him and me personally. The question is—is it worth it for the world?"

There was a long silence before Aleksi spoke. "There must be more in it for him. What of this . . . Saiya? Didn't Luka say something about that the other night?"

"Yes, I'm sure Asura has plans within plans. But what he could possibly want with her, I do not know. However, he would never dare harm her, that much is certain."

"Who is she?"

"Never mind this talk," Domadred said, waving his hand. "Once again, I bore you with the musings of an old man. Luckily, we have made *exceptionally* good time, and in a few short days we will see land. In truth, little of our plight actually matters to you; once we dock in Vai'kel, you will be off on your own adventures, no doubt. Unless you wish to stay with us, that is."

A confused expression passed across Aleksi's face and he looked down at his sketchbook.

"You know," Domadred continued, "you never did tell me what you've been drawing these past several days. May I see? A break from these troubling thoughts will be quite a relief."

Lost in a maze of thought, Aleksi handed Domadred the sketchbook. As Domadred flipped through the pages, the captain's eyes went wide and his face lost its color. Page after page, his expression only deepened until finally he spoke.

"Aleksi, how do you know this girl?"

". . . She came to me in my dreams."

"Your dreams? How is that possible?"

"Is . . . is she Saiya?"

"What did she say to you?" Domadred demanded, his tone growing angry. "Tell me!"

"She told me to kill Luka—"

"What? Kill Luka? But why?"

"She does not trust him. Nor does she trust Asura . . ." Aleksi looked down at the sketchbook still clutched in the captain's hands. "She is the High Priestess of the West . . . dedicated to the High Arkai Aruna—"

"Never mind that! Aleksi, this is very important. Are you *sure* she wants Luka dead?"

"Yes. She is afraid of him. Afraid of what he and Asura will do to her—of what they plan to do to Terra . . ."

Aleksi's words trailed off as he remembered the raging torrent the young woman had conjured when he had given his heart to her. Next, he remembered the bitter loss that had bitten at his chest when she had pulled her hand away just an hour ago. Anger stirred in Aleksi's heart and his Rune pulsed with life. Images of his parents' murder flashed though his mind. He saw his father's hewn body and then his mother's headless corpse. Last was Rudra standing above their lifeless bodies, covered in Runes and cloaked in shining light.

"Kill Luka . . . ," Domadred said, stroking his beard.

"If you want him dead, kill Luka yourself!" Aleksi's rage swelled and he felt Runic power flood through his body. "Or accept his treaty and be the next prime admiral! I don't know what is right anymore. All I know is that I refuse to continue to be used as *everyone's* pawn—not yours, not Luka's, not Saiya's, or Rudra's! No one's."

Aleksi snatched the sketchbook from Domadred and quickly climbed down the ratlines. Fury clenched the youth's heart as he descended back to the deck. He felt anger at Saiya and anger at Luka— but most of all, Aleksi's rage burned at Rudra.

As the *Illusive Diamond* continued to glide through the glowing waters, Domadred did not follow Aleksi. Instead, the captain remained in the crow's nest, staring out into the vast glowing ocean beyond.

CHAPTER XXVI

Aleksi awoke to Zenith rays shining through his porthole. He rubbed his aching head and looked at his arm. The sharp, stinging pain had worked its way deeper into his shoulder, but other than that, nothing had changed—his Rune still seemed to be dormant.

Aleksi looked out his window. The light of Vai'kel's Zenith had now overtaken that of the Eastern Zenith, and even at such a distance, he could feel that *this* Zenith was different than the one on which he had formerly lived. Aleksi knew this light before the ship originated from the mysterious mountain island of Yad'razil located in the middle of Vai'kel.

As Aleksi got dressed, he remembered being taught that the Central Zenith was unique compared to its external brethren. Rising out of the lake of Maneir, it housed the ancient and abandoned Central Masters' Academy, strongest of all the Masters' citadels and the supposed seat of Kalki. What that was, however, was known only to the Masters, gleaned from fragmented scripts and esoteric writings. Even the island of Yad'razil, which contained the Academy's mountain, was shrouded in secret, for its surrounding waters were constantly awash in powerful storms that prevented all from approaching the island's shores.

Just more mysteries, Aleksi thought as he slid his sword into his belt. *I have enough troubles as it is; I don't need to worry about some age-old prophecy and Kalki's throne of flame.*

Aleksi left his room and went above deck. He saw the Central Zenith shining over the ship's bow. For a moment he was disoriented. Aleksi was used to the Zenith's light always being higher at the ship's back, and seeing it seemingly higher at their front was strangely disconcerting. In addition to both the Central and Eastern Zeniths' light, Aleksi also saw that not far off the starboard bow, dark storm clouds churned on the horizon.

The Ice Floes, Aleksi thought as he turned and walked up the stairs to the quarterdeck. *Just as Domadred said, they seem close.*

The air gusting off the water was fresh, and a cold wind blew back Aleksi's hair as he neared the helm. Aleksi nodded to the sailor at the wheel, but the man scowled as Aleksi passed. The youth let out a sigh as he continued on.

It's probably all for the best, Aleksi thought as he ascended the ladder to the stern deck. *I don't need any friends on this ship—soon enough I will be gone from them.*

Settling himself at the center of the stern deck, Aleksi knelt in preparation for his morning training. The hair on his arms stood on end as another cold gust blew over his body. After he took a few slow inhalations, Aleksi's hand floated to the hilt of his blade. Just as his fingers grasped the worn hilt, however, images of his parents lying dead in the snow flashed through his mind.

Exhaling violently, Aleksi took a kneeling step forward with his right foot and drew his sword in an explosion of speed and accuracy. It cut through the air with a flash as the light of the Zeniths reflected brightly on the curved blade. Aleksi swung his sword in a flowing dance and felt anger grow within him. Despite his best efforts to clear his mind, he was haunted by images of his hewn father and headless mother. Aleksi cut even faster and tried to push the thoughts away. Sadly, that did nothing but intensify the images and kindle his anger even further.

As Aleksi continued to train, he heard voices drift up from an open window in the captain's cabin below. "Thank you, Domadred. It's so very nice to receive a timely invitation after such negative previous experiences."

Luka. Aleksi sheathed his blade and moved toward the side of the deck so that he could better hear the conversation.

"Let's just focus on the future," Domadred answered. "I am still unsure if we can find common ground, considering your demands."

"Your crew does not seem to have any hesitations. In fact, they seem unanimously in favor of Asura's treaty and your new promotion."

"They also defer to my judgment, Nobleman, and I am not satisfied with your terms."

"I ask very little for what I am offering in return. Wherein lies the problem?"

"Saiya," Domadred answered. "As you well know, her rightful place is in the West. She will be needed there now more than ever."

"Indeed, you are right, Captain. And after this all plays out, she will safely be returned to her people. But if I do not bring High Priestess Saiya Vengail to Erithlen in the North, there will be no deal. How else is Asura to know that you will honor your word after you have been instated as the prime admiral?"

"Saiya will not be used as collateral, for she is not a commodity to be bargained over. I will, however, offer you a compromise."

"I am listening."

"In exchange for Lenhal, I will bring you to Saiya and you may speak with her yourself. I will even do all in my power to persuade her to your cause. But in the end, the choice to go to Erithlen will be hers, and hers alone, to make. Before any of that happens, however, you must provide me Lenhal as a sign of good faith."

"You would receive much for little in return. Do not throw away your opportunity to be the prime admiral, Domadred. All Asura is asking for is insurance that you will make good on your end of the agreement. Just provide her location and your written consent for her travel to the North, and you will once again ascend to greatness."

"Maybe I was not clear the first time." Domadred's tone darkened. "I will not give her to you for *any* price. But my current offer still stands. If you provide Lenhal, I will grant you the opportunity to speak to her for further negotiation."

"But your crew—"

"Will do as I say!" Domadred snapped. "This is your final chance, Nobleman; do you accept my offer or do you refuse?"

There was a short silence before Luka responded. When he spoke, his voice was cold and callous. "I accept. But you must divulge Saiya's location *now*. And do not lie to me—I will know."

"Even if I tell you where she is, how could you possibly know if I am telling the truth?"

"I have ways, Captain."

Domadred walks a fine line, Aleksi thought as he crouched low, still listening from the stern deck. *But Asura must want Saiya for more than simple collateral, and Domadred does not know what Luka is capable of. Should I have told the captain that Luka is a Master? But Rudra's letter . . .* "Do not unveil the truth of the noble, for the leader must seal the fate of his people untainted, lest he condemn us all to shadow."

"Fine," Domadred said, chuckling. "Although I do not think you will like the answer. But before I do, I wish you to openly swear your terms before my crew. And remember, you cannot actually *speak* to Saiya until you have provided Lenhal, regardless of how long it takes for you to procure him. That's the deal. No exceptions."

"Done."

Aleksi then heard the navigation room's doors open. He crouched low and went to the forward edge of the stern deck for a better view.

"All crew, report!" Domadred called out as he strode past the ship's helm to the quarterdeck railing. The crew quickly assembled on the main deck—Aleksi moved to stand discreetly behind them—and Domadred continued. "After a parley with our Northern ambassador, I have negotiated the first installment of our terms. While we have not yet reached a full agreement on the ship's ascension back into the Western fleet, it is my hope that this is the first step toward my rightful place of prime admiral!"

The crew let out a rowdy cheer as Luka stepped next to Domadred at the railing. When the nobleman spoke, his tone matched the grim, chill wind that blew off the water.

"Under the ardent eyes of both High Arkai Aruna and High Arkai Kaisra, I do so swear that upon the truthful divulgence of High Priestess Saiya Vengail's whereabouts, I will utilize my agents on Lenhal Veren's ship to bring his vessel to the *Illusive Diamond's* location."

"And once you have given me Lenhal," Domadred continued smugly, "I will allow you to speak with the High Priestess for further negotiations, but *no sooner!*"

"I do hereby agree to your terms, Captain."

"Wonderful!" Domadred exclaimed. "We have a deal. Men, you may go back to your duties." As the sailors dispersed, Domadred turned and spoke to Luka again. "Once we reach Vai'kel, you may send word to your men on Lenhal's vessel to make the necessary arrangements for the ambush. Sadly, this will take some time. So, until then, you are confined to your quarters as my prisoner. Oh, excuse me, I mean *guest.*" Luka's eyes narrowed as Domadred continued. "Your captivity should not be long, though. We should be able to catch Lenhal off the coast of Marikh after several weeks of preparation, and you will be able to speak to Saiya shortly thereafter."

"So I am to assume she is in Vai'kel, then?" Luka asked. "Do not forget your end of the bargain."

"No," Domadred answered with a wide smile. "She is a fair bit closer than that."

"Closer than Vai'kel . . . You can't possibly mean—"

"I am no oath breaker, Lord. You said you could tell if I was lying. Well, am I?"

Luka closed his eyes and, after a moment, slowly shook his head. "This whole time . . . If only I had known, all of this could have been avoided." Domadred looked at Luka in confusion as the nobleman continued. "Captain, despite my dislike of you, I will offer you one last chance. Allow me to take Saiya *now* and all will be forgiven. You will even have your seat as prime admiral—I swear it upon the Arkai. Just bring me to her *immediately.*"

"I'm sorry, Luka," Domadred said, as a wide smile spread across his lips. "That was not our deal. You will have to fulfill your end of the bargain before you see her. Besides, as I'm sure you have guessed, she is locked in slumber, and I have my reasons for not waking her until we reach Vai'kel."

"Captain, do not throw your life away. If you do not give Saiya to me now, you and your crew will die. I implore you to—"

"Listen up, men!" Domadred shouted, drawing the crew's attention back to the quarterdeck. "Not a moment after making a bargain, our lord Luka Norte breaks his oath and threatens your very lives!"

"I have broken no oath! I will provide Lenhal and his ship as promised. But if you do not give the girl to me now, Lenhal and his fleet will arrive to find nothing but the *Illusive Diamond* and her crew's corpses floating in the ocean. Please do not force my hand. I am trying to help you regain—"

"I grow tired of your threats, Nobleman," Domadred bellowed, drawing his sword. "Return to your cabin. But mark my words, if you threaten my life again, I will slay you where you stand!"

"When death takes you, Domadred," Luka said, shaking his head, "remember I gave you a choice."

"Enough!" Domadred raised his sword and rushed in to strike Luka. As the captain swung his blade, however, Luka easily stepped to the side of the attack. With unnatural strength, Luka then grabbed Domadred by the throat with his left hand and lifted the captain off the ground. The crew watched in disbelief as Domadred's sword clattered to the deck and their captain desperately clawed at the fingers wrapped around his neck. Aleksi's hand tightly gripped the hilt of his blade but his heart was filled with hesitation and doubt.

"And now," Luka shouted, gesturing to the crew, "I will provide Lenhal and his fleet, as promised. This is not, however, how I had wanted to give them to you!"

Still holding Domadred aloft, Luka raised his right arm, and a cluster of Runes glowed amid the lower sails of the mainmast. They danced in colors of red, magenta, and amber as they circled around the sails and rigging like glowing serpents.

Luka then gave a flourish of his wrist and molten fire erupted from the Runes. The crew gasped in horror as the sails of the mainmast instantly went up in flame. As the seamen leapt away from the blaze, some went to get buckets to douse the sails, while others drew swords and rushed toward Luka on the quarterdeck.

"Come no closer!" Luka shouted over the crackling mainsail fire. Still holding Domadred aloft, Luka extended his fist at the approaching men. "With the time remaining to you, ponder your captain's folly!" Luka then flicked his fingers open and light flashed from his palm. The approaching men suddenly doubled over and clutched their heads in agony. As the men fell to the deck, Luka tightened his grip on Domadred's throat and the captain's boots kicked weakly in midair.

Next, Luka raised his palm to the foremast. Just as Runes began to glow around the sails, Aleksi rushed at Luka from behind. Drawing his blade, Aleksi lopped off the arm that held Domadred aloft. Blood sprayed from Luka's severed limb as Domadred fell to the deck with a loud thud.

"You?!" Luka roared, turning toward Aleksi. Aleksi swung his sword again, but Luka caught the youth's blade in his remaining hand.

"Luka, please do not kill these men," Aleksi pleaded. "There must be another way!"

"I gave you the truth of your parents' murder!" Luka snarled, gripping Aleksi's blade tightly as blue light shone from his fingers. "And I even offered to save your life and become your Master! Yet you repay me with *this*?"

"It was only more manipulation," Aleksi answered, trying to wrestle his sword from Luka's grasp. "Stop this killing and tell me what *really* happened to them! Why would Rudra bring me to the Academy if he killed my parents?"

"Open your eyes, boy!" Luka growled amid the roar of the flames. "Rudra betrayed them, and you are nothing more than his pawn marching to *his* master plan! But it's not too late for you. As my Apprentice, you can free yourself from his bondage and reclaim the glory that Rudra has stolen from your bloodline!"

"If you spare the lives of the crew and tell me the truth about my father, I will join you."

Luka smiled and kicked Aleksi in the chest. The youth flew backward, tumbling over the wheel and smashing into the helmsman, who had been staring at them in frozen shock. Watching Domadred wheeze on the ground, Luka dropped Aleksi's blade to the blood-soaked deck and grasped his sodden limb's stub. Runes danced over the wound, and Luka let out a cry of pain as new growth started to sprout from his bloody forearm.

Overcoming their mental anguish, both from shock and Luka's Runic casting, the crew near the quarterdeck once again rushed forward. Several went to help Domadred, who still futilely struggled against the severed hand gripping his neck, but the majority of the men assaulted Luka head on.

Valen led the charge, but as he swung his blade, Luka stepped to the side and struck the boatswain in the throat. Valen fell to his knees and blood gurgled from his mouth. Valen's head hit the deck with a hollow thud as two more men rushed at Luka. As the mainmast's sails continued to crackle and burn overhead, Luka killed the approaching sailors just as quickly as he had their officer.

Over by the helm, Aleksi used the listing wheel to steady himself, and he rose upon shaky legs. Seeing the fallen sailors at Luka's feet and the sails continuing to burn behind them, Aleksi rushed forward once again. As Aleksi approached, Luka smiled and raised his arm to the youth. Bright Runes circled Luka's outstretched hand and Aleksi watched in horror as fire erupted from Luka's palm.

A stream of flame shot over Aleksi's head and sprayed across the sails of the mizzenmast. Feeling the heat of the fire behind him, Aleksi dove forward. In midroll, he picked up his blade from the deck and once again lunged at Luka. Closing the gap between them, Aleksi brought his blade around in an upward arc to cut off Luka's other arm.

As Aleksi swung, however, time seemed to slow and the youth watched Luka easily lean away from the blade's path. Aleksi tried to reposition his sword and use its momentum to strike downward across Luka's chest, but the nobleman moved to the side and slipped his knee behind Aleksi's legs. Time sped up again as Luka then pivoted, throwing Aleksi to the deck.

As Aleksi wheezed for breath, Luka turned toward the last remaining set of sails. Suddenly, a sharp crack cut through the air and Luka's arm was raised aloft by Fa'ell's whip. Before the nobleman could free himself, Nara grabbed Luka and put the man into a powerful headlock.

Despite his weakened state, Nara held Luka long enough for Kefta to jab a long dagger up under Luka's ribs and deep into his right lung.

Choking up blood, Luka elbowed his still regrowing left arm into Nara's gut and the large man let out a grunt as he staggered back, clutching his chest. As Kefta tried to stab again, Luka slid to the side of the blade and, freeing his arm from Fa'ell's whip, grabbed Kefta's wrist with his right hand. Using Kefta's forward momentum, Luka brought the young man around in a tight arc and then, dropping his weight and pivoting, flipped Kefta over his own blade, snapping his wrist and elbow. Kefta thudded to the deck, clutching his mangled arm, as Aleksi got back to his feet and rushed in to strike again.

As Aleksi swung his sword, Luka effortlessly caught the blade in his glowing palm. Despite the blood running down Luka's side, the man smiled. While Aleksi struggled to free himself, another deckhand rushed up behind the nobleman. The sailor tried to slash down with his sword, but Luka stepped to the side and tripped the man with his boot.

The falling sailor's blade accidentally lunged toward Aleksi's chest and the youth's eyes grew wide. Just as the man's sword was going to impale Aleksi, however, Luka knocked the blade safely away with the still re-forming flesh of his left hand. As the sailor fell to the deck, the skin of Luka's arm then finished reknitting itself and its floating Runes grew dim.

"Aleksi, after these men are dead," Luka said, wiping the blood from his mouth with his newly formed hand, "we will return to Asura and you will learn the truth of your bloodline. He will be so very pleased to welcome you home."

"No," Aleksi shouted, still struggling to free his blade from Luka's hand. "Only if you spare the crew will I go with you!"

"You just don't understand, do you, boy?" Luka laughed as the wound on his side started to heal itself. "This will be your first lesson—you do not possess the power to defy my will!"

"You are *wrong*!" Aleksi yelled, feeling the Runes embedded in his arm flood with life. Suddenly, everything slowed around him—this time, however, Aleksi knew that *he* was the one in control. Aleksi felt his hand burn beneath his bandages as a new strength suddenly surged through his body. Luka's eyes shot wide with surprise as Aleksi channeled the energy of his Rune into his sword.

The youth felt the new power flow through the metal of the blade and penetrate the defensive Runic barrier of Luka's hand. Thrusting down, Aleksi's sword now sliced through Luka's flesh with ease. As Aleksi's Rune burned with life, he continued to cut downward and his sword carved through Luka's palm and forearm. Following through with the strike, the tip of Aleksi's blade bit into Luka's chest, causing deep crimson to sprout from the nobleman's breast.

Time sped up again as the wounded Luka leaned back and smashed his pulpy forearm into Aleksi's temple. The blow caused the youth to stagger back and Luka raised his left arm, palm out. The nobleman then let out an angry snarl as vibrant Runes began to glow around his hand. Aleksi looked on in terror as Luka's palm once again erupted in flame.

Suddenly, Fa'ell's whip cracked and tethered itself around Luka's glowing wrist. Fa'ell pulled his hand up and away from Aleksi as Luka's Rune-infused palm cast its stream of flame high into the sky. Before Luka could regain his balance, however, Nara towered behind him once again. Using the last of his strength, Nara lifted Luka off his feet and dragged him to the quarterdeck's gunwale. Fa'ell then freed her whip from Luka's wrist, and Nara hurled the wounded nobleman over the side of the ship.

As Luka splashed into the water, Nara collapsed to the deck, clutching his chest and wheezing for air. Aleksi rushed to the side and tried to look into the water to see if Luka was swimming—but as the youth came to the gunwale, searing pain overtook him. Aleksi clutched his bandaged hand and felt the Runes on his wrist dig deeper into his shoulder. It felt like molten steel crawling under his skin and slithering its way into the marrow of his bones. Aleksi let out a cry of agony as he doubled over and braced himself on the deck.

Across the deck, Domadred continued to claw at the severed hand that still gripped his neck. Despite being detached, it retained much of its former strength and several sailors had to pry it off with a knife before they carried Domadred away from the burning sails.

Having failed to douse the flames on the mainmast sails, the rest of crew didn't even try to ease the blaze of the mizzen sails. Fire licked along the ratlines and fully engulfed the thick coils of line on both masts' fife rails. Those that were not aiding the wounded just watched in shock as the *Illusive Diamond*'s sternmost sails, rigging, and tackle burned in a crackling roar. The blaze rose higher and higher, casting billows of black smoke to the sky above.

"Keep that fire from the foremast, you fools!" Kairn shouted as he threw a bucket to an idle seaman. "Get up there and keep the sails wet—if we lose them, we'll be dead in the water!"

Brayden was already aloft in the foremast's rigging, trying to keep the fire from spreading forward. The flames had begun to lick across the main topsail, and Brayden used his belt knife to slash the sail's lines from the foremast. The great sheet fell from its tackle in a whoosh of flame and splayed across the deck and port gunwale. Brayden then cut another, and Aleksi heard a loud hiss as the sheet hit the water. Although now beginning to slow, the *Diamond* was still moving swiftly, and as the main topsail hit the sea, the ship momentarily trailed the half-burnt sail behind her. Aleksi then watched as the large sheet slipped over the gunwale and was lost in the ship's ashy wake.

Trying to suppress the agony of his arm, Aleksi saw men run up to the quarterdeck and drag the wounded to the front of the ship. After depositing their comrades away from the fire, the remaining crew then ran up the forward ratlines to join Brayden with buckets of water. Regaining his composure, Aleksi rushed over to Kefta. The youth had to cover his face and duck low to protect himself from the blazing heat which radiated off the crackling inferno above. After Kefta was on his feet, they both helped Fa'ell and Nara stagger to the foredeck while flaming debris and ash fell upon their heads.

As they neared the foremast, Aleksi suddenly heard a loud snapping sound. Looking back, the youth saw the stern end of the mainsail's massive boom fall to the deck with a thunderous crash. Smoke and sparks were cast into the air as the flame licked over the boom and ashy debris flowed across the deck. By now, the fire had consumed nearly all of the mainmast's sails and rigging, and the mizzenmast was not far behind. After setting Nara next to the forward chaser cannon,

Aleksi went to the gunwale to try and look past the stern of the ship. Sooty froth and bits of burning debris littered the water behind them, and Aleksi could tell that the *Illusive Diamond* was continuing to slow down. The youth did not, however, see Luka anywhere in the ship's wake.

Suddenly, Aleksi felt a hand grip his shoulder.

"Just like Beck, it seems that I, too, owe you my life." Aleksi spun and saw Domadred standing behind him. "Thank you."

"I'm sorry . . . ," Aleksi said, looking at the sails as they burned. "I'm sorry I wasn't fast enough."

"None of us could have known the bastard was a fallen Master," Nara said, still clutching his chest.

"Not fallen," Aleksi said, shaking his head. "His eyes are not black."

"But why would a *Master* do such a thing?" Fa'ell asked.

"Whatever his reasons were," Nara continued, as he struggled to his feet, "shouldn't we be getting off this boat before the whole thing goes up in flames?"

"Yalmalrah," Domadred replied as he rubbed his throat, "does not burn . . ."

"What?" Nara asked in confusion.

Domadred did not answer but looked back at the ship's wake, lost in thought.

"The ship is made of yalmalrah wood," Levain answered. "Lucky for us, it's not flammable. The sails and rigging are a different story—this fire will just have to run its course. After it's died out we can make some makeshift sails from the extra cloth and line we have below. Where is Valen? He knows our current inventory."

"He didn't make it." The voice belonged to Marlen. The doctor was kneeling over Kefta, doing his best to reset the young man's broken joints.

"How many?" Domadred asked, still looking past the ship's stern.

"By my count," Marlen answered, "we lost three from Luka directly and another four from his fire." Marlen then gestured to the handful of wounded men around him. "On top of that, we have half a dozen with bad burns."

"We were lucky." Domadred's voice was tight and harsh.

Aleksi followed Domadred's gaze to the stern of the ship. Without their sails, the masts and suspended spars looked like the branches and trunks of burning trees, charred and barren. The boom tails had fallen, but their heads, much like the spars, were still held in place by their strong metal brackets and hung limply from the masts. With only her foremast square sails and bowsprit jibs catching the wind, the *Diamond* had been stripped not only of her majesty, but also the vast majority of her speed and mobility.

We must move quickly; a Master would have survived that fall even with a knife wound, Aleksi thought darkly as he looked back towards the ship's wake. *And why was Luka so surprised by Domadred's answer about Saiya's location?*

Aleksi stepped closer to Domadred and spoke in a low tone. "The girl Saiya. What did you mean when you said she was *closer*? You didn't mean that she—"

Before Aleksi could finish, a voice called down from the foremast. "Captain!" It was Brayden and his tone was urgent. "Ten ships on the horizon!"

"Friend or foe?" Domadred called back, ignoring Aleksi's question.

"It's Lenhal's ship, the *Fury of Aruna*, with nine more beside!" Brayden answered. "And they are coming in fast!"

"Shift one," Domadred called out to the crew, "stay in the rigging with Brayden and keep those sails free of any flame! Shift two and three, clear the deck of ash and prepare to string new sails!"

"They must have seen the smoke," Kairn said, as he climbed down from the foremast's rigging.

"But how could they have followed us?" Levain asked. "No ship could keep pace with our speed."

"They didn't," Domadred answered, shaking his head. "They must have been waiting for us near Vai'kel. Luka no doubt used Runes to stay in contact with his men, keeping the ships just out of our sight. The nobleman has been hedging his bets all along, the bastard."

"Captain," Kairn said, looking at the smoldering masts, "we have only one choice. We can't engage Lenhal and his fleet like this."

"I know . . . ," Domadred said, letting out a great sigh.

Levain's eyes went wide. "You can't mean—"

"Yes," Domadred answered, rubbing his throat again. "Men, get ready to enter the *Ice Floes*."

CHAPTER XXVII

Sailors quickly descended from the forward rigging and threw buckets of water across the fire and smoldering ash on the main deck. Once the majority of the flames were doused, the crew cleared the deck and stamped out the last of the embers with their boots.

"Captain," Levain said, "if we had a full crew, it would take us days to completely retackle both masts. Even just the fore and aft booms will take hours to reline, let alone resail."

"I know," Domadred answered, still anxiously watching the ship's wake. "Take shift two and raise new tackle for the main boom while I take shift three to prep new sails. If you can get the main boom up in time, we will string a new storm trysail. If not, we will have to hope the squares and rudder will be enough to keep us in the current. We have to hurry, though; once Lenhal is on us, we will need the crew to man the guns. Besides, by then the winds will be too great to raise any new sails, let alone reline the tackle."

"Understood, Captain." Levain called out to several men still in the rigging and went down a hatch to the decks below.

"Quartermaster," Domadred said, turning back to look at Kefta, who was sitting with his back propped up against the forward chaser, "are you fit to work?"

"Yes, sir!" Kefta answered as he struggled to his feet. His left arm was tightly bound in a makeshift splint and held to his body by a sling.

Domadred looked over at Marlen and the doctor nodded. "Alright, Kefta, you and Mareth lead the men as they continue to clear the top decks. Once that is done, prep the guns to engage Lenhal's ships. Meanwhile"—Domadred then turned to the sailing master—"Kairn, once the debris is cleared and it's safe to reenter the navigation room, plot us a course through the Ice Floes and then direct Brayden as he mans the helm. Have him take us in on the eastern current. By the looks of our speed, once we turn for the storm, we should hit its outskirts very soon."

The three officers nodded and Kefta and Mareth went to assist the crew on the main deck. Kairn, however, stayed at the bow and continued to look at the brooding storm clouds before them.

"Guests," Domadred continued, now looking at Fa'ell, Nara, and Aleksi, "things are about to get rough. Help where you can, but once we hit the floes, please, for your own safety, stay belowdecks. You three already saved the ship once today—now let the *Diamond* return the favor." Domadred then shouted to several members of the crew to meet him in the storeroom and disappeared through a hatch belowdecks.

As Doc Marlen continued to tend to the wounded crew about them, Fa'ell walked up to Kairn. "What exactly are these Ice Floes?" she asked, following the sailing master's gaze to the dark clouds on the horizon. "I take it they are dangerous?"

"Yes, very," Kairn answered, still looking past the starboard bow. "The real danger of the Ice Floes, however, is caused by the cluster of storms surrounding them. When the warm waters and winds of the eastern current swirl into the cold waters of the floes, it causes powerful storms to be locked in a perpetual vortex off the coast of Vai'kel's northeastern tip. Much of the warm water is spun off back into a gyre current around Vai'kel, but enough of the stream is sucked into the floes to create a number of permanent tempests around the points of conversion."

"I've heard of the ice there," Nara said, coming to the gunwale and leaning heavily on its railing. Dark bruises were already forming where Luka had struck him, and his face was pale. "It's unnatural, if you ask me."

"Yes. It's a violent mess of hot air and warm water swirling around a lot of ice that really has no business being there in the first place. Why the Guardians created the Ice Floes is unknown, but with the *Diamond* damaged as she is, we have no choice but to try and lose Lenhal in their storms and ensuing fog."

"But if it's ice," Fa'ell said, "why is the wind blowing toward it?"

"Good question. According to the scholars, the air gets sucked into an updraft. The current's waters are much warmer than the ice, but strangely the ice does not melt when they collide. Because of this, there is a vortex of low pressure directly over the clusters as the warm air rises up and the cold air is pushed out as fog."

"My teachers said that it's kind of like the eye of a storm," Aleksi interjected. "With nowhere to go but up, the hot air from the eastern current is spun into a number of whirlwinds as it's kicked out back to the ocean, high up in the sky. This makes the actual Ice Floes them-selves free of any turbulence—the storms outside the floes, however, are another matter entirely."

"Yes," Kairn said, eyeing Aleksi keenly. "And we will use this to our advantage and ride in on the current's wind using the square sails. If we are lucky, we won't have to tack against the gusts of cold fog as they are pushed out of the vortex."

"In truth," Marlen said gruffly, without looking up as he bandaged a crew member's burnt arm, "without fore-and-aft rigged sails, tacking will be impossible. Luka saw to that."

"Indeed he did," Kairn said, looking back to the barren masts. "Let us hope that Levain and the captain can raise some storm sails, or all we will have to rely on is the mercy of Aruna and his Guardians as they blow at our back."

"Well," Fa'ell asked, "how can we help?"

"At this point, the crew knows what to do; it's just a matter of doing it before we get broadsided by Lenhal's cannons or swept over by the storm."

"Then I'll help the doctor tend to the wounded. I know a fair bit about burn treatments from back home. Besides, someone needs to keep an eye on Nara to ensure he does not further injure his broken ribs."

"I'll be fine," Nara answered. The large man was still tenderly clutching his chest, however, and his face was growing paler by the moment. "Getting belowdecks sounds like a good idea, though. Let's get the injured to safety before the storm hits."

After Fa'ell, Nara, Marlen, and the wounded sailors all left to go belowdecks, Aleksi walked up next to Kairn at the ship's bow. "Domadred mentioned something about Saiya," Aleksi said slowly as he looked out at the approaching gale swirling in the distance. "Is she on this ship? If she is, I want to see her."

Kairn broke his gaze from the storm clouds and gave Aleksi a thoughtful look. "That's a very difficult thing you are asking, son. But I have a difficult question, too—what's under those bandages on your arm?"

Aleksi took a step back and dropped his bandaged hand from the bow's gunwale.

"From where I was on deck," Kairn continued, "I could hear much of what you and Luka said to each other while you fought. In the end, I think it was because of your power that Luka was not able to kill us, and for that I am glad. But the priestess . . ." Kairn stopped himself. "Let me put it this way. With the *Diamond* damaged as she is, going into the Ice Floes is suicide. The Captain knows this, but still he pushes us onward. He does so because of one simple fact—Saiya. Because of her, this ship has a much greater chance of having High Arkai Aruna's blessing. I don't pretend to understand who you are or what business you *think* you have with Saiya. But right now, all that matters, for all our sakes, is that nothing threatens her connection with the Arkai."

Kairn paused and his blue eyes twinkled as he gazed at Aleksi. "My question about your bandage is unfair because I already know the answer—your question about Saiya is similar. What would you do if I told you that yes, she is on board? Would you go to her? Would you wake her from her slumber and break her concentration so you can selfishly speak with her? The same could be asked of me. What would I do if I saw a Rune imbued into your flesh under those bandages? Would I treat you like a runaway student, imprison you, and turn you over to the Academy's Enforcers for the grand reward? Or, rather, would I ask you about the secrets of Terra and, sating my curiosity, revel in the power of the Masters? Well, that last I very much would like to do—but right now I need to focus on plotting our course through some very dangerous waters and cannot be distracted on either account. Saiya is the same. She needs to focus on using her connection to Aruna to protect this ship. Being locked in the Dreamscape has its advantages, and we must not threaten that. More importantly, *you* must not threaten that."

Kairn let out a great sigh. "But I swear to you, if we make it out of this alive and you still ask it of me, I will introduce you to the most beautiful young woman you will ever meet. Sadly, you will not thank me for it. Son, Domadred told me about your sketchbook. You must know, if you open your heart to that young woman, that she will be the longing of your life but forever outside your reach. Despite all you do, Aleksi, you will never have her, for she belongs to the Arkai of the West and Aruna does *not* share."

There was a long silence between them as the *Diamond* continued to move toward the dark clouds before them.

Finally, Aleksi nodded. Kairn turned and grasped the youth on the shoulder. "I'm sorry. But hey, how about you help me plot our course. If our Runic ledgers are correct, no one has traversed through the Ice Floes' eddies in many an age—so, if I'm to attempt the impossible, I most certainly want company."

After the crew cleared the deck and began restringing the mainmast's boom, Aleksi and Kairn flipped through old maps in the navigation room. Methodical at first, as the waves became rougher and they did not find anything useful, they quickened their pace out of necessity and frustration.

"Nothing?" Kairn asked, as he shuffled through the maps strewn about the room's counters. "Not even in *Graff's Atlas of Vai'kel's Seas*?"

The ship suddenly hit a large wave, and several scrolls rolled from the table and fell to the floor, kicking up ash. Soot had blown in through the room's now-closed window and there was a light dusting on the floor. Luckily, no fire had entered the chamber, and the maps, books, and instruments had been unharmed by Luka's flames.

"Nothing," Aleksi answered. "All that's here are a lot of references to people who *tried* to enter the floes to chart them but never returned." Aleksi then braced himself on a bookshelf as the ship roughly descended into the wave's trough.

As Aleksi opened a new book, he heard the sound of rain patter against the deck above their heads and looked out the window. Not only had the seas become more turbulent, but the sky was dark. Suddenly, the wind gusted fiercely and threw sheets of rain against the ship.

"Wonderful . . . ," Kairn said, thumbing through another book. "I do vaguely remember seeing a diagram somewhere, but it was not with any of the standard maps. I'll have to ask the captain. You wait here and keep looking."

Just as Kairn was about to open the door, Domadred rushed in. He was dripping wet and had a stern look on his face. "We've entered the storm and Lenhal is almost within firing range. Do you have our course plotted?"

"I know our position," Kairn answered. "But other than abstract reference, we have no actual chart of the floes. I remember seeing something once, but I can't find it now."

"That's because it's not in here." Domadred rushed through the door to his chamber. After a moment of cursing, followed by the sound of scrolls falling to the floor, Domadred returned with a tightly rolled parchment. "This is it," the captain said, handing the map to Kairn. "Hurry, we do not have much time."

As Domadred turned to go back to the quarterdeck, a loud boom echoed behind the ship. Both sailors looked to the stern and braced themselves. There came only a loud splash, however, and Domadred shook his head. "It has begun." Domadred straightened his hat and, opening the navigation room's door, looked at Aleksi. "Come with me, son; you are about to experience the making of a legend."

As they emerged on deck, Aleksi was assaulted by a torrent of rain and wind. He staggered back and had to bend over and lean into the gust as he followed Domadred to the helm. The sky was filled with roiling clouds the color of mottled iron while the ocean churned frothily and the *Diamond* cut its way deeper into the storm.

Brayden was at the wheel, and when he saw Domadred and Aleksi approach, a wide smile spread across the boy's face. *He's actually enjoying this*, Aleksi thought as he clung to the dimly glowing Runic binnacle and the ship pitched high from another wave.

Suddenly, lightning cut through the sky, illuminating the newly raised main boom and trysail. A deafening clap of thunder then echoed across the turbulent sea and another explosion of cannon fire followed it. The resulting splashes landed less than a hundred meters off the *Diamond*'s port bow.

"I'm not used to having ships fire at us from astern," Domadred shouted over the wind. "Men, show some love to the stern chaser and return Lenhal's greeting!"

Aleksi staggered back to the stern deck's ladder and looked past the *Diamond*. There was a fleet of ten ships sailing abreast, each with fully rigged masts. Leading the charge was a large capital warship of the Western Thalassocracy. *That must be the* Fury *of Aruna*, Aleksi thought as he gripped the ladder tighter, bracing himself as the *Diamond* hit another wave. The rain continued to bear down around the youth as he clung to the ladder—but surprisingly, it was warm on his skin. Every so often, however, a gust of frigid air blew across the ship, fluttering the sails and chilling Aleksi to the bone.

Suddenly, there came a deep boom as a large puff of smoke and fire exploded from the *Diamond*'s stern. Near Lenhal's line of ships, a geyser of water shot up into the air, casting spray onto the *Fury*'s bow.

"Readjust, reload, and return fire!" Domadred shouted. "Let's take one of them down before we hit the storm's heavy rollers!" Aleksi shambled back to the helm as Domadred gripped Brayden's shoulder. The sky was nearly black with storm clouds, and the wind howled across the ship as the *Diamond* broke over another wave.

"That's it, son," Domadred continued. "Feel her pull and move deeper into it . . . Just a little more . . ." Brayden gracefully eased the wheel ever so slightly, and the ship slid forward and picked up speed as she surged down a large swell.

"Well done!" Domadred exclaimed. "We've almost entered the heart of this salty beast!" Brayden looked at his father, and his face beamed with pride as another salvo of cannon fire blasted over the *Diamond*'s masts.

Aleksi looked to the ship's stern and saw that the pursuing fleet had gotten closer. They were now no longer in a neat row, however, and the mighty ships bobbed on the dark horizon as the fierce waves pitched them about. The *Diamond*'s chaser then boomed again, but this time the shot was low and plummeted into the water with a violent splash.

"Cease fire until you have a clean shot," Domadred cried over the wail of the wind. "The waves are now too great for the chasers to be any good. Hold fast until we can broadside!"

The *Diamond*'s bow suddenly slammed into a twenty-meter wall of water with a hollow crash, sending a geyser of spray into the air. Aleksi clung to the binnacle as the *Diamond* crested the peak and then surfed into the trough and almost toppled. Picking up speed, the *Diamond*'s bow then dove back into the sea, plunging tip first into the wave ahead before cresting again.

After steadying himself from the impact, Aleksi looked aft and saw that one of the ships had pulled away from the group and was closing in on the *Diamond*. The vessel had unfurled more sails and was continuing to increase her speed as she approached.

Catching the wind, the pursuing ship then hit the wave immediately behind the *Diamond* with such immense force that water spouted high into the sky, nearly spraying the *Diamond* herself. Bracing against another crash, Aleksi watched as the vessel crested the wave and displayed her mighty hull to the open air with an explosion of frothy fury. The ship's bow seemed to hang suspended in the sky before she tipped forward over the peak and flew down the wave, nearly coming beside the *Diamond* as both ships surfed into a low trough.

"Prepare all cannons for port broadside!" Domadred cried.

Aleksi felt the *Diamond*'s bow surge into the wave ahead and begin to climb up to its steep crest as the gun ports below were opened. The ship beside them had built up too much speed on her descent into the trough, however, and instead of climbing up the next swell like the *Diamond*, the ship's bow plunged tip first under the wave ahead.

Domadred cast a triumphant fist into the sky as the wave directly behind the advancing ship then pushed the vessel's stern high into the air. The enemy boat shuddered and halted as her tip was forced farther into the water. Over the torrent of the storm, Aleksi heard the sharp cracking of masts as the ship pitchpoled stern over bow, capsizing in a fury of broken wood and frothing wake.

"Swallowed by the sea!" Domadred called out as he continued to grip Brayden's shoulder. "Only nine more to go!"

Another wave then thrashed against the *Diamond*'s bow, causing foamy splash to spray across the planks. Aleksi clung to the binnacle and tried to keep his boots from slipping on the wet and violently swaying deck as he looked out to the sea ahead. All about them, the ocean churned in a torrent of frothy, whitecapped breakers angrily crashing into each other. The rain and wind stung at the youth's eyes, and he was forced to wrap his arms around the binnacle so as to not be swept into the ocean as the *Diamond* plowed into the next roller.

Feeling his heart thunder in his chest, Aleksi then saw that another of Lenhal's ships had broken from the pack. Strangely, this ship seemed to be sailing diagonally across the waves instead of down them. Domadred saw it, too, and just as the *Diamond* crested another breaker, the captain cupped his hands and shouted to the crew.

"Take cover! Incoming fire on the starboard side!"

As the men ducked, the other vessel cut even sharper across the wave so that her side directly faced the *Diamond*. Aleksi saw the shots being fired before he heard the explosions. Plumes of smoke tinged with red-and-yellow flame shot out of the ship's gun ports. Aleksi heard the thunderous reverberation of explosions, the buzz of cannonballs whizzing through the air, and finally the sound of shattering wood as cannon fire bracketed the *Diamond*.

Aleksi was flung roughly to the deck, and strong hands held his head down as planks ruptured around him in a flurry of broken ship.

"Damn it, boy!" Levain shouted, pulling Aleksi back up to his feet. "Didn't you hear the captain? Next time they fire, *get down!*"

Aleksi's ears rang, but he nodded and reached for the gunwale to brace himself against another wave. Aleksi's hand, however, floundered in midair as he groped at nothingness. Looking to his right, the youth saw that where the gunwale railing had been a moment ago now was only open space, broken wood, and surging water. As another wave broke over the bow and showered the deck, Aleksi lost his balance and lurched over the side.

Levain reached out and grabbed Aleksi's wrist, pulling him back in. "Grace of the Guardians! Be careful!" the large man said, hauling Aleksi back over to the helm. "Bits of the ship are floating back there in our wake. Trust me, you do not want to join them!" Aleksi nodded with wide eyes as Levain looked over at Domadred. "Captain, shall we prepare for a return volley?"

"No," Domadred answered. "They have us on a tight angle, and we can't afford to readjust so drastically to return fire. But look!" Domadred pointed to the ship.

Instead of being bow and stern into the wave like the *Diamond*, the enemy ship had her broadside along the wave's line. As the ship crested over the next swell's top, she slid diagonally down the valley as her keel was pulled upward into the crest. This caused the ship to list on her port side, dangerously close to capsizing.

"They've cut in too tight!" Domadred bellowed. "She's going to overturn!"

As a sudden, powerful gust of cold air blew across the wave's top, the other ship's keel finally was not able to keep its edge in the water. As the wave broke, the breaker rolled the ship along her side, causing the vessel to tumble in a mess of broken wood and writhing water. Once the wave settled, the ship turtled and sank into the dark trough.

The crew of the *Illusive Diamond* gave a cheer, and Aleksi could not help but raise his own voice to their chorus.

"They will be more conservative now," Domadred shouted smugly, as the *Diamond* hit another swell. "Lenhal won't try to overtake us until we reach the ice and the waves die down. Lucky for us, we have a map of the floes and they do not. There is no way they will be able to find us in the fog. We might even be able to circle around and catch them unaware!"

Steadying himself, Aleksi tried to assess the damage of the cannon salvo. There was some superficial harm to the *Diamond*'s deck and stern, and one of the mizzenmast's spars had been shattered.

"It was only a glancing blow," Levain said. "To pierce the hull they will need a direct shot. Let's hope they don't get the chance."

Aleksi nodded and continued to hold on to the binnacle as the *Diamond* crested another swell. Behind him, the youth heard Kairn call out to Domadred.

"Captain, I have plotted our course through the ice!"

"Magnificent," Domadred shouted back. "Brayden, hold tight and keep her steady." Domadred then turned toward the navigation room and motioned for Levain to follow. As the two men pushed through the doors, Aleksi slipped inside as well.

Having a break from the wind and rain was wonderful. Aleksi let out a great sigh as he held on to one of the tables for support while the ship continued to rock tip to tail. Kairn was already leaning over a large map and motioned them over. The parchment depicted many clusters of icebergs surrounded by shaded areas that Aleksi assumed were fog banks. In addition, the icebergs commingled with weaving channels of water that snaked their way around the islands of ice. There was an odd symmetry to the multitude of groupings, and it made their organization seem more planned than organic.

"It's impossible to know if any of this is still accurate," Kairn said, still gazing at the map. "But I'm hoping that whatever causes the ice to form is a permanent installation and therefore will not have moved much in the past age."

"But remember," Domadred added, "there may be nothing to prevent a stray berg from breaking off from the main cluster and floating just below the water line."

"Indeed. One thing is for certain, though; the ice should begin right around there. Once we enter its cover, the waves will fade very quickly and we should be able to lose Lenhal in the fog."

"But with such light wind among the ice," Levain added, "it will be slow going with only the trysail and the squares."

"Exactly," Kairn said, tapping the map. "So I suggest we move in *here*." Kairn pointed to a gap between two icebergs. "And move through *like so* to take advantage of our squares." He then traced his finger through an opening in the ice islands along the Ice Floes' edge in a wide arc. Finally, his finger came out on the other side.

"But if we double back *here*," Domadred said, pointing to the map, "we could take Lenhal by surprise."

"Or get pinned down," Kairn answered, shaking his head. "No. Right now I'm more concerned with getting out of this alive than taking down his fleet."

"I'm sure you've noticed they have already lost two," Domadred said with a grin.

"Captain, the *Diamond* will be very difficult to maneuver while the wind is funneled upward over the center of the ice clusters. Even with full sails I would still *highly* advise against it."

"Alright, then direct Brayden to your plotted course. For now, we will just focus on escaping. But know this—if the opportunity presents itself, this frozen wasteland will be Lenhal's grave."

CHAPTER XXVIII

Domadred was right. As the *Illusive Diamond* approached the Ice Floes, the remainder of Lenhal's fleet lowered sail and decreased their speed to survive the rough waters. After that, the eight remaining ships stayed a safe distance behind the *Diamond* as they followed Domadred and his crew to the islands of ice. And although Lenhal's fleet still occasionally tried to fire with their chasers, none of their shots connected due to the high waves and strong winds.

With Brayden at the wheel and Kairn guiding his course, it did not take long for the *Diamond* to reach the Ice Floes. Aleksi watched from the quarterdeck in amazement as the large vessel approached what looked like a series of jagged cliffs rising out of the sea. Outside the wall, the surrounding waters were awash in turbulent waves and roaring winds, but once the ice began, the swells died down as they crashed over the frozen barricades.

As they got closer, Aleksi saw that the wind and fog were getting funneled above the icebergs in a giant cone of twirling air. As the ship came closer to the towering whirlwind, Aleksi looked ahead to the approaching icebergs and noticed a gap in the looming seawall. Kairn pointed to the opening and Brayden led the ship toward the slit in the massive icebergs.

Aleksi gripped the binnacle in anticipation as they came upon the entrance to the floes. With the strong wind at her back, the *Diamond* shot through the fissure in the icy barrier with profound force, sails flapping violently. But then, as suddenly as it came, the rush of chaotic air died down. Riding the gale's final push, the *Diamond* slowed as she passed the towering ice of the outer wall and entered into the quiet of the floes. As the *Diamond* came off the wave's dying swell, she ghosted into wispy clouds of flowing mist and small eddies that hardly hinted of the tempest's former fury.

Catching an updraft with her trysail and squares, the *Diamond* sailed through interchanging breezes of warm and cold air. The strange contrast flowed over the ship in a patchwork of moist vapor and frigid wind, causing the hair on Aleksi's arms to rise. As Kairn continued to guide Brayden's course past frozen islands, the ship became progressively more enveloped in ever-thickening patches of damp fog.

Now that they were surrounded by nothing but islands of ice and fog, an eerie silence overtook the ship. When unable to see beyond the ship, Brayden would look at the glowing instruments of the binnacle for guidance. Although Aleksi was unfamiliar with such a tool, it looked as if the binnacle's illuminated Runic readout was able to provide a rough outline and miniature map of the surrounding waters and her obstacles.

"That's *incredible*," Aleksi whispered.

"The *Diamond* has a few tricks up her sleeve," Domadred said, smiling. "And we are going to need them to outmaneuver the *Fury* and her fleet." The captain then pointed to the *Diamond*'s stern.

The first ship of Lenhal's entourage was entering the floes through the same gap the *Diamond* had used. But as the *Diamond* moved deeper into a massive cloud of mist, Aleksi's vision was obscured and the pursuing ship disappeared from sight. Looking back at the binnacle's miniature map, Aleksi could see that its Runic image was fading in and out sporadically.

"The water here is strange," Domadred continued. "For some reason it does not take kindly to our binnacle's mapping device and at times obscures its vision. This is an odd place, son—take a look for yourself."

Nodding, Aleksi went to the gunwale and looked into the depths below. The water was a deep, glowing sapphire and swirled about the hull. Upon looking closer, however, Aleksi could see that the water possessed an additional assortment of colors, all translucently flowing into each other in some kind of strange aquatic dance. Ever so faintly, blues, purples, and light greens swirled in the depths. Watching their luminescent interaction was strangely captivating but also quite unsettling. Whatever caused the water of the Ice Floes to glow, it was more than simple *algae*.

"I told you this place is not natural," Nara said, as he and Fa'ell walked up the steps to the quarterdeck.

"Whatever it is," Kefta answered, cradling his broken arm as he walked behind them, "it's going to save our lives."

No one else spoke as Brayden sailed through the weaving maze of icy, misshapen masses and thick swaths of clouds. As Aleksi watched, the binnacle's map was getting more sporadic and eventually stopped showing the icebergs around them. Due to the growing fog, and the binnacle's inability to give an accurate reading, Brayden was forced to steer the ship toward the few patches of clear air to maintain visibility of the outcroppings of ice.

Looking over at the helm, Aleksi noticed that Brayden's palms were spotted with broken blisters and blood. *From steering during the tumult of the storm*, Aleksi thought in awe, *and he is so focused he does not even seem to notice.*

A cold breeze blew over the ship, exposing the icy shelf of an iceberg looming above them. Some of them, like this one, were taller than the rest and towered high over the ship's masts. Others, however, hardly broke the water's surface and lay submerged in the unknown depths below. Interestingly, the icebergs' exteriors were also as varied as their size. Some were sharp and jagged while others were flat and smooth, possessing large swaths of open space. Each of the icy projections, however, was imbued with a faint blue glow that radiated out from its opaque core. As the *Diamond* continued on, this shine eerily cast a misty lazuline glimmer amid the grey fog and dark clouds surrounding the ship. The light was even visible below the waterline and illuminated each berg's icy foundation as it stretched down into the flow's deep obscurity. Despite the intermittent warmth of the air, the sight of so much glimmering ice chilled Aleksi to the bone.

Suddenly, a loud, hollow thump of a hull colliding with an island of ice sounded back behind the *Diamond*. It was followed by muted shouts of unknown officers and crew. All aboard the *Diamond* looked aft but could see nothing through the fog. Next, there came the screeching sound of wood and ice as a second ship scraped across a frozen formation just off the *Diamond*'s starboard bow.

"Brayden, hard port and come around," Domadred whispered. "They are following the luminescent trail of our wake and trying to cut us off!"

Brayden spun the wheel and the *Diamond* glided around a large chunk of ice. Patchy fog covered the *Diamond* and Aleksi could not see any of the approaching ships—from the sound of them, however, Aleksi knew they must not be far away. Brayden curved the *Diamond* around another iceberg, pointing the ship's bow toward where the screeching sounds had come only moments before.

"Now, angle her leeward and prepare to let fly!"

Brayden spun the wheel, and the *Diamond* cut sharply into the breeze. They suddenly emerged from the mist and Aleksi saw two of Lenhal's fleet only several ship distances away. As the *Diamond*'s cannons came in line with the enemy's hull, Domadred let out a fierce cry.

"Fire!"

The *Diamond* swayed and shuddered as the ship's guns erupted in salvo. The volley tore into the enemy's hull, causing bits of wood and shrapnel to explode into the air.

"Got her!" Domadred shouted, as the second ship turned and prepared to return fire. "Now, hard starboard!"

As the second ship's cannon barrage fired, the *Diamond* slid behind an iceberg and the enemy's salvo thunked into its ice with a deep reverberation, causing a thunderous cracking to echo across the still waters. As the *Diamond* silently ghosted away into another fog bank, Aleksi could hear gurgling bubbles and the frantic shouts of the crew as the enemy ship sank.

"Right up ahead," Kairn said, pointing to the bow and looking at his chart, "if we hug port side around this next island, we can take a path that leads through the floes to the other side."

"Brayden, keep her starboard," Domadred said, ignoring Kairn. "And men, prepare all guns for another volley!"

"Captain," Kefta urged, "we should take Kairn's suggestion and—"

"I said keep her starboard!" Domadred said harshly as the *Diamond* hooked around another floating chunk of ice.

Both officers remained silent but looked at Domadred beseechingly as Brayden brought the ship around toward their attackers.

"Prepare all guns on the starboard side," Domadred continued, eyeing the mist hungrily. The *Diamond* swiftly emerged around an iceberg and her broadside suddenly faced the stern of the second enemy ship. "Fire!"

The *Diamond*'s second salvo cut into the enemy's stern with a deafening sound of smashed wood and shattered glass. The vessel was not even able to get one shot off in retaliation before her stern started to slump in the water. As the *Diamond* glided away, Aleksi looked back and saw the enemy ship's nose arc high into the sky as she took on water and began the sluggish process of sinking.

"Now steer around that berg there," Domadred said, as the *Diamond* ghosted into another fog bank.

Suddenly, a gust of wind blew across the ship, exposing a towering island of ice directly in front of them. The berg was sharp and craggy, with a severe ledge angled at the *Diamond*'s bow, and Brayden was forced to spin the wheel furiously in hopes of avoiding the massive wall of ice.

At the last moment, the ship turned sharply and her hull scraped across the ice with a high-pitched wail. As the *Diamond* pulled away from the side of the iceberg and cleared the danger, Brayden swallowed hard and wiped his brow. The crew let out a collective sigh.

"Kairn," Domadred said, scanning the patches of mist ahead with a wary eye, "what is our location?"

"We are off course, Captain," Kairn said anxiously. "And with all this mist and no reading from the binnacle, there is no way to know our position!"

"That outcropping there," Domadred said, pointing to the map, "that means that we should be—"

Suddenly, there was a hollow crunch as the *Diamond* lurched to port, glancing off a submerged ice island. Along with the rest of the crew, Aleksi was thrown forward from the collision. The youth struggled to regain his balance as the *Diamond* skidded past the sunken ice with a painful groan.

"The hull's bound to be fractured from that," Levain said, running down the quarterdeck steps to a hatch below.

"Patch it before we take in too much water!" Domadred growled before turning back to Brayden. "Son, Lenhal must have heard that; get ready to—"

A thunderous blast of cannons erupted off the *Diamond*'s starboard quarter. Because the *Diamond* was hidden in fog, most of the salvo peppered a nearby iceberg, sending large fissures though its gossamer surface. Several of the shots, however, struck the *Diamond*'s hull and sent a flurry of wood into the air upon contact.

"About and return fire!" Domadred shouted.

As the *Diamond* slowly turned, a blast from another of Lenhal's ships came whizzing across the water behind them. This salvo took the *Diamond* directly in the stern and Aleksi felt the ship shudder as the captain's tall gallery windows shattered upon impact.

"Captain!" Brayden shouted, as the *Diamond* slowly turned and her sails once again caught the wind. "The wheel, it's hardly responding!"

"One from that volley must have hit us below the waterline and split the rudder. Just do the best you can, Son!"

"Captain!" Mareth called up from a nearby hatch. "We've been holed and are taking on water!"

Domadred rushed over to the side of the ship and leaned over. Following the captain, Aleksi looked down and saw that supplies were being swept out of a breached compartment on the starboard side. Aleksi then saw a bale of bound sailcloth flow out into the water alongside the other debris. The bale was somewhat cylindrical and about the size of a human figure. Domadred's eyes went wide.

As he saw the captain's expression, understanding flashed through Aleksi's mind. Holding his blade tight in his belt, Aleksi jumped over the side of the ship and plunged into the water's shadowy depths. Fully submerged in the dimly glowing sea, Aleksi felt his body assaulted by a mixture of warm and frigid water as he swam for the surface. The strange, swirling dichotomy between the temperatures and colors flowing over his body was shocking, and Aleksi had to kick frantically with his boots to get back to air.

The youth gasped for breath as he came above the surface, then swam hard for the bundle of cloth as he felt the strong current push him away from the ship. Aleksi kicked with all his might. Behind him, he could hear more explosions, but Aleksi paid them no thought and frantically chased the floating bundle.

Finally coming to the bale of cloth, Aleksi drew his blade. Kicking furiously to tread water, he slipped the tip of his sword under the bale's ropes and sliced its bindings. After several incisions, the cloth unraveled and Aleksi saw a hand and then a petite arm. Desperately trying to stay above the surface, Aleksi sheathed his blade. The youth then pulled back the rest of the cloth and saw the young woman's face. Although dark and dormant, the Rune of the High Arkai Aruna was clearly engraved into the flesh of her forehead.

It really is her! It's Saiya!

Aleksi pushed the rest of the binding away and, moving behind the young woman, held her in a cross-chest swimmer's carry. Making sure Saiya's head was above water, Aleksi looked around and finally noticed how far they were from the *Diamond*. The current had swept them nearly two hundred meters from the ship. Several sailors had tried to throw lines, but Aleksi was now too far away to make any use of them.

Futilely trying to swim against the current with Saiya, Aleksi saw Domadred step up onto the gunwale and give orders to the crew. The current was profoundly strong, and as the *Diamond* disappeared into a cloud bank, Aleksi realized he had no choice but to allow the water to push them toward the nearest iceberg.

"Straight ahead," Domadred said harshly to Kairn, Kefta, and Brayden as another salvo of cannon fire whizzed by the ship. "Then circle around that iceberg and meet us on the other side."

"Us?" Kefta asked in confusion.

"Yes, you should be able to lose Lenhal in the mist, but be quick about coming back and picking us up!"

Domadred then winked at his son and dove fists first over the gunwale into the swirling water below.

As Aleksi and Saiya got closer to the looming iceberg, Aleksi saw a shallow outcropping and swam for it. Its ledge seemed easily accessible, and as the current brought them alongside, Aleksi fumbled for a handhold. The cold of the ice bit into his palm but, mustering strength he did not know he had, he found a solid grip and hefted Saiya onto the berg's frozen surface.

Once the youth had hoisted his own dripping body out of the water, Aleksi felt his skin grow numb wherever it was in contact with the ice. Saiya was wearing the same white dress from his dreams and it damply clung to her now-pale skin. Breathing heavily, Aleksi sat and cradled Saiya's body on his lap so as to prevent her from touching the berg's frozen surface. As he held her, her head fell back, and Aleksi frantically brushed back her sodden hair so he could see her face. Her eyes were closed and her lips were cold and blue.

Aleksi felt for a pulse but her body was icy and still. She felt so fragile in his arms—something was wrong. Aleksi hurriedly placed his left hand behind the young woman's neck to support her head and put his right hand on her chest.

"Saiya, you have to come back!" Fear filled Aleksi's voice, and as he held her, his Rune burned beneath his bandages. "Saiya, please come back!"

A bright light shone from Aleksi's palm and searing pain flooded up his arm. He felt the power of his Rune awaken to life and flow into Saiya's cold body. The pain then surged into his shoulder as his Rune's sharp tendrils penetrated his scapula. A golden light grew around them as Runes winked into existence and danced across Saiya's pale skin. Their multicolored glow illuminated the fog around them, casting warm halos in the cool mist.

Suddenly, the Rune on Saiya's forehead erupted in piercing light, causing her back to arch and her supple chest to heave with life. Water spewed from her mouth and she took a deep, rattling inhalation. Aleksi continued to allow the power of his Rune to flow into her and her Rune, and he felt life reenter her body. As Saiya's breathing settled, Aleksi once again took her into his arms. He held her to his chest and flooded her with warmth and love as she continued to suck in air through her now-chattering teeth. The Runes floated about them both, and Aleksi felt Saiya's arms slowly, and ever so gently, wrap around his body and hold him in return.

After several moments, the light around them died down and Aleksi realized they both were dry. Her Rune was no longer blinding but instead glowed majestically. Still holding her close, Aleksi brought his hand to Saiya's face. Her cheek was both soft and warm, and she was breathing steadily. Leaning back, Saiya slowly opened her eyes and smiled. Her lips were now red and full, and her eyes shone brightly, mimicking the formations of ice that surrounded them.

"Thank you, Aleksi," Saiya said sweetly as the light of her Rune and eyes began to fade. "I . . ."

The young woman paused and looked away, causing her long blond hair to fall across her face. Aleksi brought his hand to her temple and gently brushed away her hair. She looked back up at him timidly and bit her lip. The light of her Rune and eyes were now gone. He felt her love open to him and flow into his heart. Her body seemed so small in his arms, but Aleksi could feel emotion burning strongly within her.

"Aleksi, I—"

Suddenly, a figure emerged from the water next to them and her voice stopped short. Aleksi's body tensed, and as he turned, his hand flashed to the hilt of his blade.

"Thank the Arkai!" Domadred exclaimed, hoisting himself up onto the ice with a splash. "You both are OK!"

Aleksi relaxed and once again turned his attention to Saiya. He tried to meet her eyes, but she was now looking off into the distance. Following her gaze, Aleksi heard distant cannon reports but did not see the light of their blasts.

"I'm sure you both have many questions," Domadred said, as he came over, "but we should start moving. We must reconnect with the ship and don't have much time."

Nodding, Aleksi tried to help Saiya to stand, but as she rose, her legs shook and she lowered herself back down. "I feel . . . very dizzy."

Domadred came over and knelt. "I am so very sorry, High Priestess. I know this is not how we had planned for you to wake up. But once we get to the other side of the berg, the ship will come for us. After that, we will be gone from this place and can get back to safety."

"Not the only one," Saiya said, reaching out to Aleksi.

"What?"

"Not the only one coming for us . . ." Saiya's eyes lost focus. "Aleksi, we have to hurry. He . . . will be here soon . . ."

Saiya's head rolled to the side and she fell backward—Aleksi instantly caught her. With one arm under her shoulders and the other under her knees, Aleksi gently stood. Groggily, she reached one arm around his neck and held on to him tightly.

"Thank you, Aleksi," Saiya whispered softly, resting her head on his chest. "Now please, take us away from here."

Saiya's body seemed weightless in Aleksi's arms. She felt so weak, even frail, but somewhere deep inside her, Aleksi felt a dormant power that threatened to overwhelm him.

"Once we reconnect with the *Diamond*," Domadred said, as they started walking, "Marlen can give the priestess something for the fatigue. She was not supposed to wake up like this."

Aleksi followed behind the captain and looked out across the icy expanse. The way before them was obscured in fog, however, and it was impossible to know how far the iceberg extended.

"Hurry . . . ," Saiya whispered weakly. "He is coming . . ."

"He who?" Domadred asked. "I assure you, we are the only ones—"

"No time to debate," Aleksi said, as he quickened his pace. "If she is right, we have to get away from here as fast as we can."

Together, they quickly strode across the ice and into the fog bank ahead. The sound of cannon fire was now gone, and all Aleksi could hear was the alternating gusts of warm and cold winds blowing along with the gentle rhythm of waves splashing against the ice.

As they continued on in silence, Aleksi could feel Saiya struggling to stay conscious. Her head gently rocked from side to side against his breast and her eyes periodically closed, only to flutter open again a moment later. Despite Saiya's condition, however, her grip on Aleksi's neck never faltered. The touch of her skin was wonderful—Aleksi could feel the softness of her hair and inhale the sweet smell of her skin.

She is real, she is alive, and she is in my arms.

After several minutes of walking, Aleksi saw a faint glow in the mist beyond.

"The *Diamond*'s lanterns . . . ?" Domadred's voice was doubtful.

"No," Aleksi answered. Saiya had fallen asleep and the youth very gently laid her onto the ice.

"Then what?" Domadred asked, eyeing the glow cautiously.

Aleksi didn't respond and took several steps forward, putting himself between Saiya and the light. Aleksi silently gripped his sword.

After a moment, Aleksi saw a figure approach across the ice in the distance. He was surrounded by flowing Runes and cloaked in a halo of light that radiated into the mist.

"He is here . . ." Saiya's voice was no more than a whisper. "Aleksi, you know what you must do . . ."

CHAPTER XXIX

Aleksi tightened the grip on the hilt of his sword in apprehension as shining lights swirled around the figure approaching in the mist. Aleksi saw Runes he knew, but there were also others he could only guess the meaning of.

"Hear me, Aleksi," a voice called out from across the ice. "I have underestimated your power. That, however, is not a mistake I will make again. Your Rune is not yet fully awakened, and you obviously do not know its true potential. But I can show you the secrets of Numen. I can awaken your Rune and teach you how to harness the might of Terra's creator!"

"It can't be . . . ," Domadred said, drawing his sword.

"Silence!" Luka cried as a bright light shone out from the fog. Domadred violently doubled over, clutching his head in pain. "Aleksi," Luka continued, as he emerged from the mist, "you do not need to wander Terra alone and confused. Accept me as your Master and swear fealty to Lord Asura. If you do, I will protect both you and the priestess Saiya. I swear no lasting harm will come to the girl, and by my side you will reclaim the lost honor of your house! Aleksi, your father was powerful, but as Asura's loyal vassal, you will ascend to a greatness you cannot possibly imagine!"

Unless caught unaware, Luka is powerful enough to easily kill us all. If it means saving Saiya and the crew . . .

"I will go with you," Aleksi said, eyeing Luka carefully as the man approached. "But only if you allow Saiya, Domadred, and his crew to leave this place and continue on unharmed to whatever destination they choose—"

"That I cannot do, boy. Saiya will come with me to the North with or without you. But know this—Asura has great plans for the Order of the Arkai, and once Saiya understands his vision, she will *gladly* follow his rule."

Luka paused several paces away and extended his hand to Aleksi. Runes still danced about the man's body and cast a multicolored halo across the ice. "Aleksi, do not throw your life away like the captain. Join us and live to see the dawn of a new world. You were born for this, son. It is your birthright!"

"Enough!" Domadred yelled as he struggled to his feet and stumbled forward. "You cannot have her! I don't care what power you possess or what abilities you wield. This ends now!"

"No," Aleksi shouted to Domadred. "Don't!"

Not heeding the youth's warning, Domadred rushed toward Luka and swung his blade. Luka, however, effortlessly dodged the attack and struck the captain in the chest with his fist. Upon impact, there was a flash of light and a hollow thud, followed by a deep moan of pain. Gasping for air, Domadred tried to recover and swing again, but Luka easily evaded the slash and struck out with his fist in another flash of light.

Aleksi clenched his teeth as Luka continued to toy with Domadred. Dodging the captain's attacks and countering with his own fisted strikes, Luka smiled as he struck Domadred harder and harder. Seeing the captain in pain, Aleksi felt anger swell up within his gut. The youth pushed it away and tried to clear his mind. Aleksi knew he would have only one chance to defeat Luka and he must not waste it.

"Do not suppress your power, Aleksi," Luka shouted as he hit Domadred again. "You must learn to force it to do your bidding. Shackle your rage and enslave your wrath, and its fury will be yours to control. Broken like an animal and beholden to your will, it will be at your command, ready to be unleashed to consume your enemies!" Luka then hit the captain again, and Aleksi heard the sharp crack of broken ribs. Domadred's eyes rolled up into his head and he wheezed and fell to the ice, unconscious.

Aleksi felt anger rise from his stomach to his chest. The youth desperately pushed it down and forced his mind into stillness. Taking a deep breath, he took a silent step toward Luka. *When caught unaware, all men bleed the same.* The youth knew he had to get closer; with one explosive draw of his blade, Luka could be defeated.

"You know, Aleksi," Luka said, looking down at Domadred disdainfully, "I have another way of awakening your rage—another way to awaken your *Rune*. I had not wanted to resort to this, but there are many ways of making that girl behind you suffer. Although not becoming of a Master, there are many ways to hurt her—many ways that I would greatly enjoy . . ."

Aleksi's grip tightened on the hilt of his sword as his jaw clenched in disgust. His Rune sent fiery pain up his arm as he took another careful step forward.

"What do you think, Saiya?" Luka continued with a thin smile. "Would your Arkai forgive me for breaking your vow of purity and claiming your maidenhood for myself?"

Aleksi felt a hot frenzy swell in his body as a deep growl rose in his throat.

"Now, would you give it to me willingly, Priestess?" Luka continued, watching Aleksi closely. "Or would I have to thrust myself upon you, wrenching the innocence from that sweet young body of yours by force?"

Aleksi's Rune began to spasm uncontrollably as he clung to the hilt of his blade and took another stalking step forward.

"Either way, girl, I will make you hurt! Now spread your legs!"

Channeling the power of his Rune with a throaty shout, Aleksi rushed at Luka and drew his sword. As the blade flashed out, Luka leaned back and Aleksi's blade sliced the very tip of Luka's nose. Aleksi's rage had gotten the better of him and forced him to strike too early. But as he swung his sword again and felt anger surge through his body, he no longer cared.

"Yes . . . ," Luka whispered, dodging Aleksi's attacks. "That's it. Let it flow, boy! Feel your anger *soar!*"

Aleksi pressed forward and felt his frenzy consume him. It gave him both strength and speed. There was no hesitation and no thought—just the urge to kill.

"She is sweet, is she not?" Luka said, as he continued to evade each of Aleksi's strikes. "Do not worry; after I am done, I will share her with you!" Aleksi let out a guttural cry and his blade moved even faster as it sliced through the air. "Or if you like, we can seize the innocence from her *together!*"

Molten fury flooded through him as he swung his sword with a fervor he did not know was possible. With each strike the air around his blade parted with a shimmering static discharge of light. Aleksi realized that just like the Masters of ages past, he was swinging his sword so powerfully that his Runic energy was severing the air's atomic bonds, causing electrons to shear off in the form of light.

"That's it!" Luka cried. "Channel your anger and let it flow into your Rune! Awaken it to life!"

Deep down in Aleksi's mind, a voice told him to stop, that this was not the right way—but it was too late. Aleksi suddenly saw a vision of his mother's severed head roll across the snow. The youth was filled with a scornful fury as he remembered how her loving arms had wrapped around him right before she was decapitated. Aleksi then saw the splattered blood and lifeless eyes of the man he had killed in Mindra's Haven—the nameless soldier with a sword stuck in his skull, whose erratically twitching fingers had fumbled at his cleaved face.

Aleksi swung his sword faster and faster as more memories flooded through him. They caused power to flow in the youth's veins, giving his blade speed like never before. Aleksi saw the broken students who had attacked him in his youth. He felt the easy dislocation of their joints and the pleasure of dominance as he broke them. Next, he remembered the intoxicating bliss of swinging his sword down upon the last student's head and feeling the hollow crack of the boy's broken skull. Aleksi recalled the numbness his arm had felt on impact and the secret smile that had spread across his lips.

As Aleksi saw the boy's dark blood oozed upon the floor, however, his gut churned with nausea and shame. He then remembered Kefta's battered face and his own bloody knuckles. *No, this is not the right way.*

But a memory of Nataraja's condescending smile snatched away his regret. Aleksi heard Nataraja's callous laughter and scornful reproaches as he remembered the feeling of his teacher's wooden training sword beating his young body over and over again.

Lastly, Aleksi saw Rudra, and his heart roared with an even greater rage. He saw images of his Master simultaneously abandoning him at the Academy while also standing over the slain body of his father. Rudra: the one who had supposedly rescued him as an infant—the one who was supposed to have protected and taught him.

No! Instead, Rudra has betrayed and abandoned me. Rudra was the one who butchered my parents and condemned me to this life of killing!

Fury leapt up within Aleksi's chest, and he held all of his dark memories tightly within his heart. The youth savored the sharp pain of them and felt anger surge into every facet of his being. There was power here, more than he had ever imagined!

As Aleksi and Luka danced across the ice with increasing speed and fury, they both cast shimmering halos in the mist. The rage in Aleksi's chest seeped into his arm and infused his Rune. With each swoosh of his sword, there was now a bright afterglow from the arc of the blade, and the light momentarily hovered in the air before fading in the wind. The glow splayed across both Domadred and Saiya, who continued to lie unconscious several paces away. Aleksi could feel the mist across his skin and the slick ice beneath his feet—but most of all, he could feel that his Rune had almost reached his spinal cord. His Rune had nearly *awakened*.

"Yes! It empowers you!" Luka shouted. "It engorges you with strength! Now *bind* it!"

Luka then stepped in and, using his left palm, struck Aleksi's hands with a flash of light. Luka's Runic strike caused the youth's blade to be flung from his grasp and slide across the ice with a clatter. Aleksi watched in horror as Luka reached out with his right arm with incredible speed and gripped Aleksi's throat. With his left hand, Luka grabbed Aleksi's bandaged wrist and lifted the youth's Rune-covered arm high into the air.

"Bind it to your will!"

Light and flames burst across Aleksi's arm, burning away his bandages and exposing the slithering, dark Runes etched across his skin. Aleksi felt even greater power flow into his body as Luka infused the Rune with his own wrathful energy.

In quick succession, bolts of lightning struck the iceberg around them, causing shattered ice and steam to explode into the air. Pain surged through Aleksi and he let out a scream as the Rune pulsed with new life. Domadred and Saiya continued to lie prone on the ice as clouds swirled in a thunderous vortex above, causing violent gusts of wind to blow back Aleksi's hair.

It's happening! This is it!

"Awaken!" Luka called out over the torrent. "Awaken and ascend to your rightful place as a god among men!"

Aleksi felt uncontrollable power surge within him as anguish tore through his body and into his mind. Through tears of pain, he saw the tendrils of his Rune fully slide across his arm and into his shoulder. Aleksi then felt the Rune's filaments flood up through his spine and neck into his head. Their roots dug deep inside of his skull, penetrating his brain. After grounding itself into Aleksi's mind, the Rune sent fiery pulses of energy farther down his spine.

Aleksi let out a wordless howl as the Rune completed its synchronization and fully merged with the nerves of his body. Although originating in his hand, its tendrils now lay deep within him, embedded in the fabric of his flesh and bone. Aleksi could feel the Rune pulsing with life—pulsing with *his* life. It was no longer a thing outside of him—it now *was* him. The gift of Terra had been fully given. The Rune was now truly *his*.

Suddenly, Aleksi felt Luka's grip around his neck tighten. Anguish once again assaulted the youth's mind. However, this pain was different—this was an attack.

"Now swear yourself to *me!*" Luka shouted. "Bind yourself to *my* will and I will teach you how to harness this new power. Without a Master, you will never understand your Rune; it will forever be outside your grasp and lie dormant within you, threatening to burst forth and rend you asunder at any moment. But fear not, for I will take you as my Apprentice and teach you the secrets of Numen. Swear your heart to mine and you will be a ruler of nations and command the armies of men against the darkness! Aleksi, become my Apprentice, and by Asura's side, together we will cast aside the Arkai and claim our rightful place as the *true* Guardians of Terra!"

"No!" Aleksi screamed, trying to force his body back under his own control. "I will be no man's pawn, for my will is my own!"

"After all of this?" Luka shouted incredulously. "After I told you the truth of your parents' death and even awakened your Rune, you *still* reject me?! You have been given the gift of ultimate power. Do not throw it away!"

"Although you may not be black of eye yet," Aleksi screamed through the howling wind, "yours is the path of a fallen Master and I will not succumb to the darkness!"

"Such a young fool you are," Luka shouted as he tightened his grip. "Asura *was* right about you."

Aleksi felt a new agony surge into him through Luka's palm. The energetic attack caused Aleksi's skin to feel as if it were being flayed from his flesh as his bones were set ablaze. Anger swelled in the youth's chest as his torment intensified, but that only strengthened Luka's control and deepened the man's flow of destructive power.

Aleksi urgently tried to channel his anger into his Rune and use it to lash out at Luka. Luka, however, still held Aleksi's right arm high into the sky, and all Aleksi could manage was to cause another salvo of erratic lightning bolts to shoot down against the iceberg around them. As broken bits of ice exploded into the air, Luka smiled wickedly and Aleksi's vision grew dark.

"What a waste!" Luka said, tightening his grip on Aleksi's neck. "You had such potential—but just like your father, you now will know nothing but *oblivion!*" Aleksi then felt Luka's flow of energy begin to reverse. Through his hands, Luka sucked the life out of Aleksi's body and claimed it for his own.

Aleksi's vision went black and fear took hold of his chest. For all his new power, for all his anger and rage, Aleksi was truly just afraid and alone in the darkness. And now, that darkness was going to take him into its murky embrace.

Suddenly, Aleksi felt soft arms wrap around him from behind. As Saiya's hands held him tight, Aleksi heard her sweet voice whisper in his mind.

"Aleksi, you need not give into anger, suffering, and despair. There is always another way. Let your heart guide you. Once you quell the chaos of your rage, underneath it all you will find strength greater than you could ever imagine. Trust in your heart, and you will realize your true power and potential—for power stems not from anger but from love. Love is the well source of creation, and its flow is the foundation of authentic action and all true mastery!"

Saiya squeezed him tightly and Aleksi felt her heart shine into him. It awakened something in his chest, and life flowed through him once again. Aleksi felt his chest surge with hope.

As Luka's terrible pain tore through him and the winds howled about them on the ice, Aleksi probed into the depths of his soul. Yes, Saiya was right. In that majestic place, Aleksi did feel love—but he also felt something constrict it. Something was keeping it back and tainting its flow. There was something else there in his heart, something dark and sinister, and it was powerful.

Aleksi looked past the pain of his memories, past the anger of his youth. And there, amid the torrent of lightning, ice, and agony swirling about him, he finally understood what gave his dark memories form and feeling—it was *fear*. Fear was holding his love in a tight-fisted vise of rage.

Aleksi saw it clearly now. His fear was overwhelming in its naked totality and childlike simplicity. But this fear, what was it for? Why did it have so much sway over him? Why did fear fill him with so much anger?

And then the youth understood—his fear was a warning, a powerful call to action stemming from the deepest place imaginable. Aleksi's fear was fueled by what he had already lost, and it forced him to look at the terrible threat of what might happen if he neglected what little he had left and dared dream of yearning for in the future. Sadly, however, when left unchecked, that fearful call to action came out as an angry distortion of his love. In that moment, Aleksi understood that anger was only a disordered expression of his heart to protect and preserve that which he held dear—that which he *loved*.

As Aleksi felt Luka's fingers wrap around his neck even tighter, the truth of the youth's heart laid itself bare before him. When a choice was grounded in fear and anger, its outcome would be tainted by the violent darkness that birthed it, therefore causing more suffering, pain, and destruction. Aleksi realized he had to transcend his fear and needed to make a choice grounded in nurturing the object of his love instead of clinging to it. He needed to act from a place free from that dark taint of anger—and instead, needed to let the pure power of his heart guide his hand and actions.

Yes, Saiya is right; instead of anger, there is another way. It was authentic action. A choice made on the basis of nourishing one's love—a choice that had a foundation of serenity and transcended the chaotic dissention of fear and anger.

Yes! I will fight not out of a fury-filled fear of loss, but with the desire to nurture and protect. I will channel love itself and fight not just for myself or for Saiya, but for all on Terra!

Aleksi opened his eyes as new life surged within his body. For the first time in his young life, Aleksi truly felt the winds howl around him and the deep ice moan below him. They whispered of Terra's secrets and urged him to choose with authenticity. Aleksi let love guide him, and in that moment, all of Terra was his faithful companion, responding to his willful command.

Aleksi clenched his Rune-covered hand into a fist and Luka's eyes went wide. A bolt of lightning flew down from the sky and struck Luka's shoulders with crackling power. Aleksi felt the surge of the bolt cascade through Luka's rippling flesh and then flow into his own body. To Aleksi, the lightning did not hurt, for this was the power of Terra; this was his birthright! Luka, however, let out a wordless howl as the crackling ferocity pulsed through him, sundering his flesh and bones.

Luka instantly released Aleksi from his grasp and crumpled to the ice. Aleksi staggered back and fell into Saiya's embrace. Her arms were locked tightly around his chest, and the softness of her pressed against his back. Aleksi felt Saiya's power steadily growing.

Taking a deep breath, he smelled the scent of ozone mixed with the overpoweringly smoky odor of burnt meat. Across Luka's shoulders, Aleksi saw scorched and blackened flesh and even heard the crackling hiss of smoldering bone.

Despite his injuries, the Master slowly stood. Wisps of steam and vapor rose from his body, and upon his blackened and burnt face he wore a wrathful scowl of pure hatred and rage.

"You are untrained, and your Runic castings are ineffective and unrefined," Luka said in a voice that was raspy and raw. "Even with your Rune awakened, you have no hope of defeating a Master. You are nothing more than a child, and I will now fulfill Asura's will of purging you, just like the others!"

"You are wrong!" Saiya's beautiful voice rang out across the ice with power and splendor. Her eyes blazed molten blue in the murky mists, and the Rune of High Arkai Aruna shone on her forehead with blinding light. "The Arkai protect their own and our holy father will cast you and your darkness back into the cold void beyond!"

Suddenly, Aleksi felt Saiya's strength flood into him. It was both terrifying and beautiful. It was Saiya's love for him combined with her love for her Arkai. It was a love so pure and so devout it could channel the numinous strength of a god.

Filled with Saiya's potency, Aleksi felt immeasurable energy surge into his Rune. Unimaginably empowered, he raised his arm toward Luka. Amid a whirlwind of Runes with a meaning Aleksi could not fathom, a wide shaft of molten brilliance shot out of his palm. The iceberg's fog and mist swirled around the cylinder of light as it enveloped Luka's frame in its grandeur. The beam was a torrent of shining passion and seared Luka's flesh and bone, ripping him apart on a molecular level.

Saiya has unleashed the power of an Arkai, Aleksi realized. *This is the true power of a god!*

Then, as suddenly as they appeared, the light and its corresponding Runes were gone. All that remained was an afterglow in Aleksi's eye, a deep, melted line in the ice where the shaft of brilliance had been an instant before. Standing motionless with his arm still raised, he watched in shock as tendrils of vapor rose up from the heated ice and melded back into the returning mists.

Trying to regain his senses, Aleksi lowered his hand as the clouds above lost their fury and former vehemence. The youth let out a great sigh as stillness returned to the iceberg around them. Suddenly, Aleksi felt a wave of vertigo slam into him. Saiya seemed to feel it, too, and her grip grew weak. As her hands left contact with his body, exhaustion flooded through him. He fought through the pain and spun around, catching Saiya as she fell backward.

Holding her in his arms, Aleksi saw that her eyes still shone molten blue and the Rune of High Arkai Aruna was ablaze on her forehead. Saiya's breath was coming in ragged gulps and Aleksi could feel that her heartbeat was wild and erratic. Although his fatigue was strong, Aleksi could tell that she was suffering much more deeply. He held her tight as the light in her gaze faded and her Rune's glow slowly diminished.

As her eyes returned to their natural color of sapphire, they fluttered and focused on his face.

"Are you OK?" Aleksi asked, cradling her petite body close to his.

"Yes," Saiya answered weakly. "But quickly, bring me to Domadred before the Arkai's power fully leaves."

Domadred lay wheezing several paces away, and Aleksi picked Saiya up and brought her over to the captain. Saiya lifted up Domadred's shirt and exposed a series of unnaturally dark bruises. As her Rune grew dim, Saiya placed her palms on Domadred's chest, and a soft light shone from her hands. The last of her Arkai's power flowed onto Domadred's flesh, and Aleksi saw the captain's bruises begin to heal themselves. They slowly changed from a dark, purply black to a light red. As his body rebuilt itself, Domadred's breath went from raspy, short gasps back to normal inhalations.

Once Saiya's Rune lost the last of its holy light, she put a hand on Aleksi's shoulder to steady herself as she sat back down on the ice.

"I'm so sorry . . . ," Aleksi said, gazing into her eyes. "I should have listened to you . . . I'm so sorry."

"It was as it needed to be," Saiya answered, bringing her hand to Aleksi's face, "for your Rune has now fully awakened. The will of the Arkai is mysterious and profound—"

"If it had not been for you," Aleksi continued, "Luka would have killed me. You saved me not only here on the ice, but back on the ship, too. Thank you, Saiya. Thank you for everything."

"You saved me as well," Saiya said, smiling sweetly. "Twice, in fact."

"No matter what happens, I will always—"

Saiya put her finger to Aleksi's lips. "Do not make promises you cannot keep. We have a long journey ahead, and you do not know what lies beyond. The Arkai have many plans for you—and for us . . ."

Aleksi looked at her in confusion and Saiya motioned to his hand. The youth looked down and saw a small, dormant circular Rune etched into his palm. The tendrils which had painfully scrolled all the way up his arm only moments before had now seemingly vanished into his arm.

"Where did the rest of it go?" Aleksi asked, opening and closing his fist. "I can feel it under my skin. It's embedded in the flesh of my arm, but it looks as if it has disappeared."

"It hasn't gone anywhere," Saiya answered, shaking her head. "Just like mine, your Rune now lies dormant within your nervous system. The vast majority of it remains hidden until you invoke its power—by choice or by accident."

Saiya gently touched her forehead, and the dark Rune of High Arkai Aruna once again began to glow upon her brow. Aleksi then saw luminescent tendrils grow across her face and down her neck, but a wave of exhaustion suddenly swept over her, forcing her to reach out and cling to Aleksi's shoulder to steady herself.

"Your Rune is a part of you now." Saiya took a deep breath as the light disappeared, leaving behind the dormant Rune of Aruna etched into her forehead. "It is as much a part of your body as your hand or heart. You will, however, need training from a Master to be able to use it."

"Can't you show me?"

"I would help you if I could, but our Runes are very different. Your Rune belongs to you, and its power comes from a deep place within you. My Rune, however, belongs to High Arkai Aruna, and its power comes from my devotion. It is only through my purity of heart and mind that I can empower my Rune, for I am merely a conduit for his grace in this world—a channel of his holy presence in this *realm*. Unlike me, Aleksi, you will have to find your own way to empower your Rune. I do, however, know of one who can help you. I think you know him, too. His name is *Rudra . . ."*

"Saiya, I don't care about any of that anymore," Aleksi said, taking her hands in his. "I don't care about Runes, Rudra, or even the Guardians. I just want to be with you. I'm tired of all the confusion, all the secrets, and all the manipulation. I know only one thing for sure—that I love you."

"I know," Saiya said softly as she looked into Aleksi's green eyes and gripped his hands in return. "And that's why we *cannot* be together. Not now, and maybe not ever. But my heart says . . ." She paused and smiled. "Aleksi, only time will tell."

"I . . . I don't understand."

"You won't. You can't—at least not yet. But now please wake the captain. We have already tarried here too long. I am so fatigued from my slumber and helping you defeat Luka that I can hardly stand, let alone fight Lenhal, too. So if we do not escape these Ice Floes before Lenhal's fleet finds us, my death will be swift and final. And then none of the whispers in my heart will matter, for we will never get the chance to find out what *could be . . ."*

Aleksi let out a sigh and gently leaned over and shook Domadred's shoulder. Domadred's eyes snapped open as he reached out and grabbed Aleksi's arm.

"What happened?" Domadred cried. "Priestess, are you OK?"

"Yes, Captain, for now I am safe but very fatigued."

Domadred's eyes flashed back to Aleksi "I remember you fighting Luka. What happened, son? Did you beat him?"

"Yes, but only because of Saiya." Aleksi then lifted up Domadred's shirt, exposing the captain's red bruises. "She saved us both and then healed you."

"I see," Domadred said, gently touching his ribs. "But how could Luka have survived getting knocked off the ship before we even entered the storm? How could he have—"

"There are many things he could have done," Saiya said sternly. "A Master's ability is both vast and terrifying. But what's most important now, Captain, is that we get back to your ship."

"Yes, High Priestess, of course," Domadred said, nodding slowly.

"Lenhal is somewhere in the floes," Saiya continued. "I can feel him looking for me with the Runes on his ship's altar. Now that I am awake, we do not have much time before he will be upon us. And sadly, I am too drained to protect the ship or even myself."

"Well, the *Diamond* should be just up ahead," Domadred said, slowly rising to his feet with a grimace. "Let us find her and be gone from this forsaken ice." Aleksi clutched the captain's forearm and helped him to stand, then walked across the ice to retrieve his sword.

As Saiya rose, she reached her hand out to Aleksi. "Please help me. I still feel weak and my legs are numb from the ice." Aleksi returned and gladly took her arm. As she stood, Saiya pressed her body to his and put his hand around her hip, holding him tight.

CHAPTER XXX

Aleksi heard the soft lapping of waves before he saw actual water. The fog had once again grown thick after their battle with Luka, and the edge of the ice came upon them quickly in the mist. Domadred stopped several paces from the ocean and let out two soft whistles. The small group paused in anticipation as they listened for a reply. They heard nothing.

Domadred took a deep breath and tried again, this time a little louder. Aleksi swallowed hard and heard his own heartbeat reverberate in his ears. He looked into the opaque vapor, trying to make out the outline of a ship; all he saw, however, was grey fog and lazuline ice.

Suddenly, a faint whistled reply echoed across the waves. Domadred gave a sigh of relief and smiled at Saiya. "Just a few minutes, m'lady, and we will have you back aboard the *Illusive Diamond*."

After a moment, Aleksi saw the *Diamond*'s shore boat emerge from the mist with Kefta standing at its bow. The young man's bandaged arm was still in a sling, and upon seeing Domadred, Aleksi, and Saiya, a wide smile spread across his bruised face. Kefta turned and gave three whistles back to the *Diamond*. As the small boat approached, Aleksi saw that it was manned by several crew members. One was on the oars, one on the short sail, and the last at the rudder.

Kefta threw a line to Domadred. Catching it, the captain pulled the line taut as the small craft eased against the ice.

"After you, Priestess," Domadred said.

Saiya nodded and took Kefta's hand. As she boarded, the three seamen looked at her in awe. But when Saiya smiled at them, their eyes flashed downward and they bowed their heads in reverence. As Aleksi came aboard, Kefta put a blanket around Saiya's shoulders and handed her a wineskin filled with water. After opening the skin's stopper, she drank thirstily. Domadred stepped onto the boat last and pushed the craft away from the ice. After taking a blanket for himself, the captain looked back toward the iceberg and let out a great sigh.

"Come, Aleksi," Saiya said in an officious tone. "You are also cold, no doubt, and may share my blanket." As Aleksi sat next to her, Saiya opened the blanket and draped it around the youth's shoulders. Saiya then found Aleksi's hand under the wool and slid her fingers through his. Aleksi turned his head to look at her, but she did not meet his eye. Instead, the High Priestess of the Arkai Aruna just continued to look ahead, stoic and serene.

"Kefta," Domadred said, finally breaking his gaze from the berg as the small boat made its way back into the mist, "how badly damaged is the *Diamond*?"

Kefta cleared his throat. "We have lost several crew to shrapnel and suffered heavy damages to the stern, Captain. Although the ship is no longer taking on water, she is slow to respond due to the damaged rudder and sluggish from the added weight. We have been pumping the bilge but don't have enough hands to do everything that needs doing."

"What is Levain's assessment of the rudder?" Domadred asked in a grim tone.

"He is fashioning a new one from appropriated deck planks. Until then, we can hardly turn."

"And Lenhal's fleet?"

"The *Fury of Aruna* and Lenhal's remaining fleet are using their Runic altars to stay in formation while they strafe the floes looking for us. And although Lenhal does not know our exact position, he has spread his ships out and boxed us within several islands of ice. They're moving slow, but it's only a matter of time before they tack inward and are upon us."

"I see." Domadred paused, running a hand over his short beard as the *Illusive Diamond* appeared before them. The captain then turned and addressed Saiya. "Priestess, can you destroy Lenhal's ships?"

"I wish it were that simple, Captain," Saiya answered. "I greatly taxed my body to help Aleksi defeat Luka and then to heal you. I am far too weak from my prolonged slumber in the Dreamscape to do any more. I entrust the task of escaping the Ice Floes to your capable hands, Captain Domadred. Please do not fail me—or your Arkai."

Domadred nodded his head as the shore boat neared the *Diamond's* hull. "My ship and her crew will not let you down, High Priestess. That I swear."

A rope ladder was thrown over the *Diamond's* gunwale. Domadred deftly caught it and, one by one, Saiya, Aleksi, Domadred, Kefta, and the seamen ascended the ladder.

Once all were aboard, Kefta addressed the crew. "Winch up the shore boat and unfurl the sails."

"Belay that," Domadred said. "Keep the tender in the water, and all men report on deck!" Kefta looked at Domadred in confusion as the captain then led Saiya up to the quarterdeck and scanned the faces of his men.

The ship and her sailors had been humbled by Luka's flames, the storm, and the multiple cannon barrages from Lenhal's ships. Despite this, when their captain called, the men answered. As they congregated on the main deck, however, the seamen's exhaustion and desperate circumstance were clearly visible upon their faces. Aleksi even saw Marlen and Fa'ell lead Nara and several limping injured who were forced to lean on their fellows' shoulders as they made their way on deck.

Suddenly, a series of hushed whispers spread through the group and all eyes flashed to Saiya. Men stooped down on one knee and placed their hands over their hearts in respect. As more sailors came up from below, others followed suit and soon everyone was on their knee bowing before their Arkai's High Priestess.

"Men," Domadred said, addressing them all, "while it burdened me greatly to have kept the truth from you, during the past few weeks our great ship has borne the most precious cargo of her long and illustrious life—the High Priestess of the Western Order, Saiya Vengail of the High Arkai Aruna."

More whispers went through the crew as Domadred continued. "Unbeknownst to most of you, we have been on a secret mission to fulfill the Arkai's divine will of bringing his priestess to the Resistance stronghold in Vai'kel. Men, we, and we alone, were chosen by High Arkai Aruna for this task and *must not* fail him. Without her safe arrival, the Resistance will collapse and the Western Thalassocracy will fall completely under Asura's looming shadow. I see that clearly, now more than ever."

Domadred paused and looked over his crew, meeting each man's eye. "None could have known that Luka was a Master of the Academy and would cripple us so. Nor could we have known that Lenhal would come upon us so swiftly, forcing us into the tempest of the Ice Floes. But the Arkai chose wisely, for despite all odds, we still prevailed. Sadly, our ship is now marred and maimed—and wounded as we are, each of you must know that escape from Lenhal's fleet is impossible. However, within these noble planks, the *Illusive Diamond* still has some life left. With our last remaining breath we will ensure that our mission will not fail and that Aruna's trust in us was *not* misplaced!"

Domadred placed his hands over his heart and knelt before Saiya. "High Priestess, the men of the *Illusive Diamond* are willing to give their lives to protect you. For each man by my side is dedicated to upholding the Arkai's will, even unto death!"

Saiya opened her mouth to speak, but Domadred quickly stood and spoke again.

"Crew, while the priestess safely slips away to Vai'kel on the shore boat, we will offer a diversion and ensure Saiya's survival. After the tender is set free, we will turn the *Diamond* on Lenhal and broadside the *Fury*. While destiny may have decided our dire circumstance, men, it is *we* who will decide our fate. If the *Illusive Diamond* is to perish this day, we will do so with honor in the eye of the Arkai—and not fail in our mission! If today is the day Aruna calls us to the Western Zenith to feel his final, loving embrace, we will go there with our heads held high, knowing we have earned our place in eternity!"

The entire crew let out a roar of agreement that echoed off the icebergs and reverberated through the thick mists of the floes.

"Men, go now and prepare the *Diamond* for battle and steel your hearts for holy justice! We sail forward in the name of High Arkai Aruna and cast our fate into *his* hallowed hands. May the wind forever fill our sails and the Arkai's grace stay strong in our hearts!"

As the crew went about preparing the ship for combat, Saiya stepped in front of Domadred. "Captain, you cannot kill yourself for me," she said sternly. "There must be another way!"

"Too much hangs in the balance, Priestess," Domadred said, putting a gentle hand on her shoulder. "You must make it to Vai'kel in safety and unite the Resistance against Asura. Lenhal must die, but it is Asura who is the real danger—a danger that I cannot even begin to understand."

"Captain, I—"

"M'lady," Domadred said, interrupting her, "now that you are awake, Lenhal will be able to find you with his altar's Runes. So long as he is alive and his ship is afloat, you are not safe. Sadly, this all could have played out differently. Honestly, this all *should* have played out differently. The fault, however, is mine, and now I must pay the price. I pray to the Arkai I need not pay it with my life and crew. We shall see . . ."

There was a pause as Saiya looked into Domadred's icy-blue eyes. After a moment, the captain continued. "I do, however, have one request. When you cast off, reach out to Lenhal with your mind. Let him determine your direction without knowing your exact location, and he will undoubtedly come after you—but he will also assume you are on this ship. Because of this, my men and I will lie in wait in the mist and be able to take him and his fleet by surprise. The *Diamond* will blindside the *Fury*, ram its side with our bow, board, and then slay his crew. With my dying breath, Priestess, I will ensure Lenhal falls this day and atones for his sins . . ."

Domadred's voice faltered and Aleksi saw a tear run down the captain's cheek. "And please tell her," Domadred continued, now in a rough voice, "somehow, if you can, please tell Kalisa that I did all I could. I truly did everything to bring him to justice. To avenge her . . ."

"She knows," Saiya said, taking Domadred's hand in her own. There was compassion in Saiya's young blue eyes, and her voice was both soft and regal. "I feel her watching us even now. She is proud of you, Domadred. She always was and she always will be."

Domadred cleared his throat and lowered his head. "Brayden"—the captain motioned his son over—"please fetch a bag from my cabin. It is in the chest under my bunk; you will know it when you see it. Hurry now." Brayden nodded and sprinted off through the navigation room's doors. Domadred then turned to Aleksi, his voice raw with emotion. "Aleksi, I vowed to bring you to Vai'kel, and as always, I am as good as my word. But I now must ask a favor of you. And if you agree, I trust you to not forsake your promise."

Aleksi nodded and the captain continued. "Protect the priestess with your life. She alone can unite the Resistance against Asura and therefore is the last hope of halting his looming sovereignty. And while I do not begin to understand you, or your path in this world, I do know one thing"—Domadred paused and gripped Aleksi shoulder tightly—"you are truly a young man of magnitude and will triumph over any obstacle set before you. Even not knowing what lies ahead, I know that if you and Saiya stay together, you both will be safe. If you trust in yourself, son, and trust in each other, neither of you will falter."

"Thank you, Captain," Aleksi said, nodding. "I swear it."

"There is more," Domadred continued. "The men of the *Illusive Diamond* are ready to die, knowing that they have truly lived. But Brayden, he is too young to face his death with me. He will not leave of his own will, however, and no words will convince him to abandon his home and family." Domadred shook his head. "Please promise me that you will do all in your power to protect my son and bring him with you to the Resistance stronghold. After that, if I have not rejoined you, please find him safe passage back to the East—back to General Beck Al'Beth. If I die, Brayden will have no one left in the world other than Beck and his family. Will you promise this to me, Aleksi? Will you swear it upon your honor and your life? Upon your dying breath?"

"I swear it upon my life," Aleksi said, bowing his head low.

"Thank you, Aleksi. In addition, it is my hope that the three of you will not be alone." Domadred then turned to Nara and Fa'ell. "The fates that have brought us all together are truly mysterious, but I know in my heart that your journeys are also far from over."

"Captain," Nara said, coming up behind Aleksi and placing his large hand on the youth's back, "it will be my honor to escort them in Vai'kel."

"I, too, will gladly accompany them during their travels," Fa'ell added. "Nara and I will make sure they arrive at the Resistance hideout safely. We will honor your sacrifice, Captain. Your efforts will not be in vain."

A tear welled up in Domadred's eye. "Then let us get done with it."

Brayden returned with a large satchel and Domadred put one hand on his son's cheek. "Brayden, I love you more than life itself. All that I do, I do for you. I hope that someday . . . that someday you can forgive me. Please tell Beck . . . tell him he was right, and that I am sorry."

Brayden looked up at his father in confusion as the captain balled his other hand into a fist. Domadred gazed deeply into his son's eyes for one last moment and then wound his arm back and, lunging forward, hit Brayden in the jaw. The blow took Brayden completely unaware and the boy was struck unconscious. Fa'ell rushed in and caught Brayden before he hit the deck. Nara then wrapped the boy in a blanket and hoisted Brayden over his shoulder as Fa'ell took the satchel and brought it over to the rope ladder.

"Hurry now, all of you," Domadred said, shaking out his hand. "Board the shore boat and make your way to land. Kairn will show you the current to take, and in the bag you will find all you need to reach the Resistance. Farewell . . ." Domadred then turned and strode away before anyone could respond. The captain shouted orders to his men and did not look back again.

"The Ice Floes," Kairn said, coming up and putting his hand on Aleksi's shoulder, "have currents that swirl inward and currents that swirl outward. You no doubt saw them on the map. I've established our location and if you stick to that current there"—the sailing master pointed to a visible flow of water stretching out into the fog—"and make sure you maintain Aruna's blessing and stay in its drift, you should reach the coast in just under a day. But mind the water," Kairn said, looking keenly into Aleksi's eyes. "Stay true to its flow and it will not fail you. Do you understand?"

"Yes, Kairn," Aleksi said, grasping the man's shoulder in return. "Thank you."

"Don't look so gloomy," Kairn said with a wry smile. "I don't plan on dying in these forsaken waters. And, as it seems you have already gotten your introduction, the next time we talk I expect you to make good on your end of the bargain and tell me all you know of the Masters' secrets."

"Until we meet again, then," Aleksi said, nodding.

Kefta came up next. "Aleksi, take care of Brayden. He will not understand."

"Come with us," Aleksi said, looking Kefta in the eye. "We have room on the skiff."

"Thank you for the offer. But I would not be much of a quartermaster if I abandoned my ship and her crew in their time of need. Besides, my family is here, and if we are to die this day, I will die aboard my home among my kin. But speaking of family . . ." Kefta motioned to several sailors behind him and they walked up the quarterdeck's stairs, sheepishly shuffling their feet with their blue eyes downcast. Kefta then held out his hand to Aleksi, palm up. Carefully cradled in his palm was a single green bead.

"It was their idea, and the rest of the crew voted on it when we were searching for you and Domadred." Aleksi looked over Kefta's shoulder and recognized the four men who had cursed his green eyes and shoved him his first morning aboard the *Diamond*. He also saw the two men who had taunted him during their night of drinking, and several others who had given him dark scowls during the voyage. "According to the Thalassocratic Law of the Sea, wearing a single bead in your hair marks you as a neophyte crew member aboard a ship. Usually the bead is blue, but the men wanted to give you a green one, honoring the land which gave you birth—honoring your heritage."

"We misjudged ya, son," one of the men said from behind Kefta, clearing his throat. "We'd be pleased to have ya join us as an honorary member of the *Diamond*'s crew. Fer whatever that's worth now . . ."

"And it doesn't mean you are bound to us er nothing," another of the men said, looking up. "We just want you to know how we feel. That we respect ya, is all. We just wanted ya to know before . . ." The man's voice trailed off and his eyes once again fell to the deck.

"Thank you," Aleksi said, bowing his head low. "It is a great honor, and I accept it with gratitude."

The men all returned the bow and a few patted Aleksi on the back and smiled before returning to their duties on the main deck. As they left, Kefta leaned in and deftly braided several strands of Aleksi's hair. He then slipped the bead on the braid and fastened it in place with a bit of twine. "Brayden will have to show you how it's done, but there's not much to it." Kefta paused and looked deeply into Aleksi's eyes. "When I told you about Rihat, you answered that you wished you had a brother, even a dead one. Well, I just want you to know, no matter what happens to the *Diamond*, now you do have a family. And not just Brayden, but the rest of us, too. Always remember that, Aleksi."

"Thank . . . thank you, Kefta." Aleksi's voice was raw and his eyes stung.

"And hey," Kefta continued quickly, "if the *Diamond* does make it out alive, we will come and rescue you—but if not, well, I will find out if Rihat got my letter." Kefta smiled as he extended his hand. "But no matter what happens, I know Aruna will guide your steps and lay a safe path before you. With that bead in your hair, you will never be alone."

"Likewise, Aruna will guide *your* heart and hands, Kefta," Aleksi said with conviction as he embraced the young man. "The Arkai will not forget you in your time of need—we *will* meet again."

"I hope to be worthy of his blessing," Kefta answered with a grin. "Farewell, brother."

"Farewell."

Suddenly, Levain patted Aleksi on the back, knocking the youth slightly forward. "Be safe out there," he said. "Vai'kel was dangerous before the occupation, and now it's even worse. But if you travel disguised as refugees, you should get overlooked in the crowd. So keep that sword handy, but not too handy, eh?"

Aleksi nodded.

"Oh, and another thing . . ." Levain pulled an envelope out of his pocket and held it out to Aleksi. "When you were out swimming, I found this in a storeroom below. I think it is meant for you." Aleksi looked at the letter in confusion. Upon the envelope's front, Aleksi's name was written in flowing script. "Go on, take it."

Aleksi timidly reached out and grasped the envelope. Flipping it over, he saw that its back was sealed with a wax-stamped emblem of an *R.*

"While looking for supplies to fix the rudder, I found it in a sealed box of goods for the Resistance. Odd, yes. But stranger things have happened aboard this ship—even just in the past day."

Nodding again, Aleksi put the letter in his pocket. "Thank you, Levain."

"Don't thank me yet," Levain answered with a smile. "You don't know what it says." Before Aleksi could respond, Levain winked and walked away.

After the others had said their good-byes, Nara brought Brayden down the ladder to the shore boat and was soon followed by Fa'ell and Saiya. Aleksi came last. As the youth stepped down onto the small skiff, he noticed that the crew had already stocked the boat with provisions. There were several bags of food, water, and other spare provisions aboard. Opening one of the bags, Aleksi saw his sleeveless cloak and sketchbook. He reached down and picked up his cloak. After sliding his arms through the shoulders, Aleksi patted its pocket and felt the familiar shape of his father's broken pendant.

Inhaling deeply, Aleksi untied the shore boat's mooring line and looked up at the *Diamond*. Her hull and railing were badly disfigured from the cannon fire, and her masts looked naked without full sails. Despite all her damage, however, the vessel still maintained an air of majestic splendor. Aleksi raised his hand and fingered the single green bead in his hair. The *Illusive Diamond* was a beautiful ship with a noble crew.

As Aleksi pushed the skiff away from the *Diamond*'s hull, Kairn and Kefta looked down at them and waved. Aleksi waved back. The two officers then turned and went back to their duty of preparing the ship for battle. Aleksi let out a deep sigh as Fa'ell raised the skiff's sail and steered their small craft into the Ice Floes' outward-moving current.

Aleksi looked down at Brayden sleeping in his blanket. The boy looked so serene and peaceful huddled up against the boat's low bulkhead. So young, so innocent. Suddenly, Saiya reached out and took Aleksi's hand. Aleksi met her eyes. They shone brighter than the clear blue ice and sapphire waters about them. The young woman smiled. Her face was filled with compassion and knowing—her heart was filled with love.

Aleksi sat down next to Saiya on the hard wooden planks and looked over at Fa'ell and Nara. Despite his sickly pale face, Nara glanced at Saiya and gave Aleksi a knowing smile. Next to Nara, Fa'ell was bracing herself on the ship's edge as she used the rudder to set their course. Gently, Fa'ell then put her free hand on Nara's shoulder. The Lionman looked over at her and his smile deepened as the small group silently sailed off into the mist.

As the shore boat surfed across the Ice Floes' strong current, Aleksi grazed his fingers across Rudra's old letter in his cloak pocket. The youth then reached into his other pocket and let out a sigh as he felt the unbroken wax seal of the new letter.

Suddenly, Aleksi heard the first boom of the cannons echo out across the water. The guns' dull light cast a menacing halo in the dark fog behind them. Instead of looking back, however, Aleksi turned his face forward and looked out into the grey mist beyond the bow.

Holding Saiya tightly with one hand, and breaking the wax seal of Rudra's new letter with his other, Aleksi felt his Rune pulse with numinous power as he cast his gaze to the journey that lay ahead.

ACKNOWLEDGMENTS

I have heard it said "Creation is like the silence between the words, the space between the letters; always present within looking, but never directly observed."

Creation never occurs in isolation and there are several whose presence is deeply felt within these pages but not directly seen. I would like to acknowledge their contributions to this work and humbly thank them for walking with me upon this long road: Becca Bainbridge, Michael Stone, Terri Benton, NickyStone90, Buzz and Sandy Bainbridge, Patricia and Bill Roberts, Jen Stone, Paula Kosior, Stuart Lord, Peter Parcell, Dana Kingsbury, Adam Gomolin, Jeremy Thomas, Angela Melamud, Emily Zach, Clete Smith, M.S. Corley, Kirsten Colton, Geoffrey Shugen Arnold, Benjamin Pincus, and Andrew Watt.

Lastly, I would like to thank Forrest Landry—for what is an Apprentice without a Master?

ABOUT THE AUTHOR

© Heather Gray 2015

Jamison Stone was born in Massachusetts and raised throughout New England on a healthy diet of magic, martial arts, and meditation. He lives with a loving wife and wolf, but expects to have their pack grow soon. When he is not getting distracted by video games, Jamison is the director of Apotheosis Studios. *Rune of the Apprentice* is his first novel; however, there are more on the way. Jamison is also the coauthor of *Heart Warrior*, an emotive memoir coming in 2018. To learn more about Jamison and his various projects, visit www.stonejamison.com.

LIST OF PATRONS

This book was made possible in part by the following grand patrons who preordered the book on inkshares.com. Thank you.

Adam Gomolin
Alex Benton
Alex Estin
Becca Bainbridge
Bill Roberts
Buzz Bainbridge
Calvin Hobbes
Casey Ottinger
Chris Cole
Daniela Ladner
Dave Barrett
David Stone
Devon Rinicella
Emmett Potemet
Forrest Landry
Jennifer Stone
Jh Lee
John Robin
Joseph Parenteau
Karen Collins
Laleh Azarshin Tobin
Leanne Phillips

Lisa Hall
Mary Wagner
Michael A. Stone
Michael Stone
Nicholas Stone
Norman Stone
Patricia Roberts
Peter Michael
Peter Parcell
Raoul Graf
Ray Vanagas
Robert Cherry
Samantha Taylor
Sandy Rinicella
Scott "Chili" Michaels
Sergio Acosta
Steven Stone
Stuart Lord
Terri Jo Messina
Tim Stone
Troy Paolantonio
W. Clement Stone

INKSHARES

Inkshares is a crowdfunded book publisher. We democratize publishing by having readers select the books we publish—we edit, design, print, distribute, and market any book that meets a preorder threshold.

Interested in making a book idea come to life? Visit inkshares.com to find new book projects or start your own.